THIS IS YOUR SONG, LOLA ROSE

Donna Hay

WINDSOR
PARAGON

THIS IS YOUR SONG,
LOLA ROSE

First published 2008
by Orion Books
This Large Print edition published 2009
by BBC Audiobooks Ltd
by arrangement with
Orion Books

Hardcover ISBN: 978 1 408 41449 1
Softcover   ISBN: 978 1 408 41450 7

British Library Cataloguing in Publication Data available

Printed and bound in Great Britain by
CPI Antony Rowe, Chippenham, Wiltshire

To my sister, Jane, who helped me dream up the story on a road trip up the west coast of Canada. If they ever make the movie, you can definitely be Executive Producer.

PROLOGUE

Madison Square Garden, New York City, 1986. A hot, sweaty night, bright lights strobing across the darkness, illuminating the expectant faces of the fans. Excitement throbbed across the huge arena like a giant heartbeat. Everything went black, until out of the darkness came the thunder of drums, joined a moment later by the wail of a guitar that sent a roar of appreciation up from the crowd.

Suddenly, a shard of light pierced the darkness and there he was, centre stage, filling the vast auditorium with his trademark throat-tearing vocals.

He snatched up the mike stand and strutted with it across the stage, full of arrogance, his mane of curls already sticking to the gleaming sweat on his face. He looked like a god, bathed in the golden glow from the stage lights. Every woman in that place wanted him.

The whole time he was on that stage he was scanning the sea of faces, choosing the one he wanted. He could take his pick, and he knew it. It was written all over that arrogant face as his gaze swept over the crowd. The girls would be screaming for him, trying to catch his attention. All of them begging for their moment with the Wild Man.

Afterwards they'd wait at the stage door with the others, holding their breath, dizzy with anticipation. If they were lucky, the roadies would invite them backstage to 'meet the band'. Being whisked past the other clamouring, disappointed fans was like winning the golden ticket to paradise.

Except it wasn't really paradise backstage. But who noticed the grubby dressing rooms when they got to hang out and party with Poleaxe? The air would be thick with sweat and sex and cigarette smoke. There would be plenty of booze, and drugs, too. Uppers, downers, you only had to ask.

But who needed drugs when you had the rush of being with the great Rick Wild? Sitting on his knee or squashed up on the sofa beside him, feeling his arm around you, fingers idly caressing your neck. Hearing him whisper in that oh-so-sexy voice of his asking whether you wanted to go somewhere more private . . .

As if anyone would refuse the Wild Man.

But it was over as soon as it was over. There would be no second chance, no long goodbye. If she insisted on giving him her number he'd throw it away, or maybe pass it on to one of the crew guys just in case they were ever in town again. She'd be left with memories; he'd forget her as soon as she walked out of the door.

Too many girls. Too many shattered dreams and broken hearts. And Rick Wild would go back to his wife and never feel a shred of guilt about what he'd done.

The Devoted Fan picked up the remote control and froze the DVD picture. Rick Wild filled the screen, golden curls rippling, bare chest gleaming with sweat under the lights, brandishing the microphone, arrogant, sexy, king of all he surveyed.

Bastard. He didn't care who he hurt. He didn't care that he played with people's lives. He just picked them up and then dropped them without a care.

Well, he'd learn to care.

Filled with a sudden surge of hatred, the Devoted Fan picked up the pen and began to write.

CHAPTER ONE

'And so, we gather together today to give thanks for the life of Edward Derek Lambert. Loving husband, devoted father, loyal friend . . .'

Lola Rose Lambert glanced around the crematorium. Her father would have been proud of the turn-out, she thought. The rows were filled with his workmates from the factory and his friends from the White Lion, looking uncomfortable in their best suits and too-tight collars. They'd all come to pay their respects. to their old mate Eddie Lambert, firm but fair factory inspector, stalwart of the pub darts team, and all-round good bloke.

Lola had come to say goodbye to the man who had made her life hell.

As the vicar droned on, she fixed her gaze on the coffin sitting on its polished wood dais, surrounded by purple Dralon curtains. Soon those curtains would close and he'd be gone.

She'd never imagined it would happen. He seemed so strong and powerful, she thought he would be a looming presence in her life for ever. It had shocked her and everyone else when he was felled by a heart attack at the age of just fifty-one.

In the front row, her father's two sisters were snuffling into hankies and comforting each other. Lola stayed defiantly dry-eyed. She wasn't allowed to cry when her mother died, so why should she waste her tears now?

They knelt to pray. The vicar talked, in his well-practised monotone, about heaven and the

1

afterlife, and their hopes for an eternal future in a better place. Lola closed her eyes and prayed, too. She prayed that wherever Eddie Lambert ended up, it wouldn't be the same place as Mum. She deserved some peace after everything she'd had to put up with in life.

The prayers ended. The mourners rose to their feet, as piped music began to play 'Nearer My God To Thee'.

Her best friend Sam gently touched her arm. 'You don't have to stay,' she whispered.

'I want to.' She'd been running away from him for too long. She had to know he was gone.

Sam nodded understandingly. She knew better than anyone what was going through Lola's mind. They'd known each other since they were eleven, and it was to Sam's family that Lola had fled at the age of sixteen after her mother died.

As the music played, the curtains glided silently around the coffin.

Goodbye, Dad. Lola watched unflinchingly as it disappeared from sight, her fingers curled tightly around her hymn book. All she felt was relief.

When they came out of the crematorium, the rain of that April morning had given way to watery sunshine. Lola squinted up at the pale rays forcing their way through cracks in the cloud. How symbolic is that? she thought.

The other mourners came out, dabbing their eyes, and filed slowly past the bank of flowers that had been arranged outside.

'Look at them,' Sam said with disgust. 'They wouldn't be so upset if they knew what he was really like.'

'He was their friend.' Lola didn't blame them.

2

She knew only too well that the face Eddie Lambert presented to the rest of the world was very different from the one she knew.

'Home?' Sam said, as they crunched down the gravel path towards the car park.

Lola shook her head. 'I'm going back to the house. There are some photos and things I want to pick up.' She'd hidden a box in a corner of the attic years ago. She only hoped it was still there.

Sam frowned. 'Do you want me to come with you?'

'I'll be fine. I will,' she insisted, as Sam looked uncertain. 'I'll just collect the box and come straight back to the flat.'

'Brendan's supposed to be taking me out tonight,' Sam said. 'But I can cancel if you'd rather I stayed in with you?'

'Definitely not,' Lola said. Knowing how besotted Sam was with her new boyfriend, she'd probably be devastated. She'd also spend the whole night texting him anyway.

Almir Close was a row of 1960s semis just off the Armley Road, south-west of Leeds city centre. The houses, with their double-glazed porches and neat front gardens, had pretensions to middle class but were let down by their scruffy neighbours: the Creighton estate on one side and the local secondary school on the other.

It was the end of the day at Pickley Park Comp, and Lola had to slow her car to avoid the teenagers surging out of the gates and into the road ahead of her, laughing, shouting and fighting.

She reached number 14 and felt a jolt when she saw her father's old Vauxhall Astra parked in the drive. For a moment she sat paralysed, her hands

3

clammy on the steering wheel.

Then she gave herself a mental shake. 'Pull yourself together,' she muttered. 'He's gone.'

But it still took all her courage to make herself get out of the car, walk up the front path and put her key in the door.

As soon as she stepped inside, it all came flooding back. It smelt so frighteningly familiar; furniture polish mingled with stale cooking and her father's Benson and Hedges. Everything was just the same as it had always been: the red swirly hall carpet; the striped wallpaper; the ornate gold mirror where Eddie Lambert always stood to knot his tie and smooth down his hair in the morning before he set off for work. Fastidious about his appearance, he never liked to leave the house without his shoes shone to perfection and his suit brushed.

There was the clothes brush on the hallstand where he always kept it. Once, when her mother had forgotten to pick up his favourite jacket from the dry cleaners, he'd used it to smash her knuckles so hard that she couldn't move her fingers for a week.

Lola rocked back on her heels as a wave of nausea swept over her.

This is ridiculous, she thought then as she sat down on the stairs, feeling shaky. You're nearly thirty years old. You're a police officer. You've chased burglars and faced down drunken thugs outside nightclubs in the early hours of the morning. So why was she still so afraid of a dead man?

Eddie Lambert might be gone, but some habits took longer to die. Lola hadn't lived with him since

4

she was sixteen, but even now the sound of a key turning in a lock could make her heart race with panic.

She was just six years old when she first saw her father hit her mother. Before that, for as long as she could remember, she'd been aware that her parents weren't like other mummies and daddies. There was no laughter, no fun or affection. Only tense, anxious silences.

She found out why when she came downstairs to the kitchen for a drink of water late one night and found her mother curled up in a whimpering ball by the fridge while her father aimed a savage kick in her ribs.

As she stared in confusion, trying to take in what she was seeing, her father had calmly pushed past her and walked out of the room. Even more bizarrely, her mother had stayed on the floor, her arms wrapped around her body, and smiled up at Lola.

'Be a good girl and go back to bed, sweetheart,' was all she'd said. As if it were the most natural thing in the world to be cowering in the corner, nursing a cracked rib.

Nothing was ever said about that night.

Her mother might have been able to stay silent, but Lola couldn't. Fearful as she was of her father, she had a feisty streak that just wouldn't allow her to put up with his bullying.

He'd only hit her once, when she was thirteen. It was during yet another strained mealtime. As usual, Lola tried to stay quiet while her father picked fault with everything. But in the end, as she watched her mother shrinking under his onslaught of criticism, she couldn't stand it any more.

5

'Why don't you leave her alone?' she'd said. The next thing she knew, her father had lashed out with a sudden blow to her head that caught her off-guard and knocked her sideways.

She was more shocked than hurt. But what shocked her more was her mother's reaction. She'd snatched up her knife and brandished it at her husband's face.

'Touch her again and so help me, I'll murder you,' she threatened in a low voice that Lola barely recognised.

It must have taken Eddie Lambert by surprise, too. It was a full ten seconds before he managed to get any words out. 'You wouldn't dare,' he'd said. But Lola caught the uncertain look in his eyes as he stared at the blade hovering inches from his face.

'Try me.'

Amazingly, he'd backed down, and, for a brief moment, Lola thought the tables had turned. But then, when she got up the following morning, her mother had more black bruises on her arms, and Lola knew nothing had changed.

At the age of thirty-eight, her mother finally lost the fight for good. The doctors reckoned she must have lived with the brain aneurysm for years, like a ticking time bomb inside her head. One day it finally exploded, and she was gone.

From that moment on, it was as if she'd never existed. Her father cleared all trace of her from the house. He sold her beloved piano, gave her clothes to charity and threw all her other possessions on a skip, apart from a box of photos that Lola had managed to save and hide away in the attic.

But her belongings weren't the only thing he'd

thrown out. Three months after her mother died, Lola had come home from school to find two suitcases lined up in the hall.

'Who do they belong to?' she'd asked.

'They're yours. I want you out of this house. Your mother's dead and you're not my problem any more.'

She didn't beg to stay. She knew there would be no point, and anyway, she hated being in the house with him now her mother was no longer there. Instead she'd dragged her bags round the corner to Sam's house. They'd taken her in and become her surrogate family. Three years later, she and Sam had found a flat and moved in together, and they'd been sharing ever since.

She went upstairs now, found a torch in the airing cupboard, opened up the loft hatch and pulled down the ladder tucked inside. Holding the torch in one hand, she carefully climbed the steps up into the attic.

The air was cool and musty. As she swung her torch around, the beam picked out random shapes of old furniture and boxes stacked around the sloping walls.

Good thing I'm not scared of the dark, she thought as she climbed up through the hatch. Perhaps her father had been; from the thick layer of dust on everything, it was clear he hadn't ventured up there for a very long time. Which meant he wouldn't have found the box she'd stashed all those years ago.

It didn't take her long to find it, tucked away under the eaves, covered by an old picnic blanket. As she pulled the blanket off, a disgruntled spider scuttled into the shadows. Lola watched it run,

7

then her eye caught something else tucked in the corner.

Her mother's old violin.

She blew the dust away and examined it in the dim torchlight. She was amazed it had escaped her father's purge.

Lola had never heard her play it. Sometimes she'd play the piano, if Lola's father wasn't around. But he hated her music, and banned it from the house.

'I can't stand that classical crap,' he always complained.

Claire Lambert was a gifted musician. She'd studied at the Royal College of Music, and had a promising career ahead of her. Then, for reasons Lola could never get her to explain, she'd given it all up and moved back to Leeds to marry Eddie.

'Sometimes life just doesn't turn out the way you'd expect,' was all she'd say.

Lola could never work out how they'd ended up together. They couldn't be more different. Her mother was gentle, artistic, well-educated. Eddie was what people kindly called 'rough and ready'. He was from working-class Creighton, had left school at sixteen and drifted into all kinds of trouble before buckling down to an apprenticeship at the ball-bearing factory. He'd gradually worked his way up to supervisor, but he hadn't lost any of his rough edges.

Lola was backing down the ladder from the attic, carefully balancing the box of photos on one arm, when she heard the key in the front door.

She froze, panic surging through her. Even though her head told her she had nothing to fear, somehow the message didn't get through to her

8

pounding heart. Somehow she got to the bottom, carefully pushed the ladder back into place and replaced the loft hatch. Then she made her way downstairs, clutching the box.

She could hear them in the kitchen. Two women, bickering over the contents of the fridge.

'It doesn't seem right to me,' one was saying. 'Maybe we should just chuck it all out.'

'Are you mad? Some of that stuff hasn't reached its sell-by. Besides, Eddie wouldn't have wanted to see good food going to waste. Stick it in the carrier bag; that ham'll do for the kids' tea.'

Lola let out the breath she'd been holding all the way down the stairs. Her father's sisters, Auntie Wendy and Auntie Lorraine. Lola had been named after Lorraine, until she started shortening it. No prizes for guessing why they were here. Half an hour after their beloved brother's funeral, they'd come to pick over his belongings like a pair of vultures. She thought about sneaking out and leaving them to it. But as she made a move, the floorboard creaked. Auntie Wendy swung round.

'Oh, it's you.' Her face fell. 'What are you doing here?'

'I just came to pick up a few things. Same as you.'

'We've got a right to be here,' Auntie Wendy snapped defensively. 'This is all ours now.'

'Eddie left us this house,' Auntie Lorraine chimed in. 'We've been to see the solicitor and it's all official.'

Why doesn't that surprise me? Lola thought. Her father had probably barely hit the ground from his heart attack before they were hammering on the lawyer's door, laying claim to what was rightfully theirs.

'I'm so pleased for you,' she said.

Auntie Lorraine's eyes narrowed, sensing sarcasm. 'He didn't want to leave it to you. He told us you weren't to get a penny.'

'He said he'd given you enough during his life,' Auntie Wendy added.

And what would that be? Lola wondered. The nightmares? The dark memories? The need to keep every man she met at arm's length?

'He was generous to a fault, all right,' she said.

The irony was lost on her aunts. While Auntie Lorraine went back to scooping the contents of the fridge into Asda bags, Auntie Wendy spied the box Lola was holding. 'What have you got there?' she demanded.

'Just old photo albums. I wanted some pictures of Mum.'

'Let's have a look. You could be sneaking anything out of here.'

'Believe me, there's nothing else I want.'

Lola winced as Auntie Wendy pawed through the box, carelessly tossing aside handfuls of photos. She would have asked her to be careful, but she guessed that would only make her tear a few out of spite. Wendy was Eddie Lambert's sister, after all.

Finally, she said, 'I don't know if we should let you take these. They're part of our brother's estate.'

There was a vindictive gleam in her eye. Lola could feel her hackles rising, and fought for control.

'Fine,' she said. 'If you won't give them to me I'll just have to consult my own solicitor about getting them. And while I'm at it, I might ask about getting

10

my share of the rest of the estate, too,' she added sweetly.

Her aunts exchanged looks. 'Just take the bloody things,' Auntie Lorraine grunted, checking the date on a ready meal.

But Auntie Wendy wasn't one to give up without a fight. She was as tenacious as a bull terrier. She looked a bit like one, too.

'You wouldn't be entitled to anything anyway,' she stated firmly.

'Are you sure about that? I think I could claim something, as his only child.'

'That's just it. You're not.'

Her mouth snapped shut like a trap, but it was too late. The words were already out there. The silence that followed them was like a vacuum, sucking everything in. Even Auntie Lorraine stopped rustling her carrier bags.

'What did you say?' Lola said.

Her aunts looked at each other again. Then Lorraine said in a low voice, 'Wendy, we promised.'

'We promised we wouldn't say anything while he was alive. But what difference does it make now he's dead? Anyway, it's about time she knew the truth. She's been looking down her nose at us for too long, acting like she's so bloody superior. Just like that mother of hers. As if *she* had anything to be uppity about!'

Lola looked from one to the other. Surprised at her own calmness, she said, 'What are you talking about?'

'Haven't you worked it out yet?' Auntie Wendy turned on her. 'You're not our brother's kid. Your oh-so-perfect mother went and got herself pregnant by another man. But of course, he didn't want to know her once he'd had his fun, so poor Eddie took her on and married her.'

Blood sang in Lola's ears. 'You're lying.'

'Suit yourself. It doesn't bother me if you believe it or not. But it's the truth.'

She went back to packing her carrier bags. Lola watched her, dumbstruck. She had to be lying. There was no way her father would have kept something like that a secret. Not if it meant missing out on the chance to be spiteful and vindictive.

Auntie Wendy seemed to guess her thoughts. 'He had his pride,' she said. 'Which is more than anyone can say about your mother.'

'Leave my mother out of this!'

She laughed scornfully. 'You think she was so wonderful, don't you, with her posh voice and her fiddle-playing. But let me tell you something. She was no better than those whores up on Canning Road. I'll tell you something else, too. If it hadn't been for my brother you would have both ended up on the streets. And if you ask me, that's where you belonged!'

CHAPTER TWO

Sam was in her bedroom posing in front of the wardrobe mirror in a purple bra and white jeans when Lola got back to the flat. Her bed was hidden under a pile of discarded clothes, a sure sign she was having another pre-date fashion crisis.

'Can I get away with these, do you think? Or do

they make me look fat?' She pinched a roll of flab above her waistband. 'Bloody low-rise jeans would give Kate Moss love handles. I don't know why I even bought them.'

'Because you're a complete fashion victim?' Lola suggested.

'I think it was because they were a size twelve and I was so thrilled to get into them I had to have them.' Sam turned sideways and pulled a face at her reflection. 'Be honest, they make my thighs look huge, don't they?'

'Well . . .'

'I knew it. Maybe I'd better wear a skirt instead. Brendan prefers skirts.'

'Yes, but do they suit him?' Lola carried the box of photos into the sitting room and set it down on the coffee table.

Sam followed her, pulling on a T-shirt. 'Did you get everything you wanted from your dad's place?'

'I got more than I expected, that's for sure. My aunts were there.'

'Oh, God, not the Ugly Sisters? What did they want?'

'Just about everything, I think. Dad left the house to them.'

'No!' Sam's mouth fell open. 'That's not fair.'

'It was his house. Anyway, I didn't really expect him to leave me anything. We weren't exactly close.'

'Only because he was so vile to you and your mum.' Sam's face was the picture of outrage. 'You deserve something for what you had to put up with.'

Lola went into the kitchen and poured herself a glass of wine from the fridge. She was still dazed with shock.

Sam eyed her with concern when she came back to the sitting room. 'This has really upset you, hasn't it?'

'Not the house. It's just something my aunts said to me.'

'Oh, take no notice of them,' Sam was dismissive. 'They were probably just trying to get at you. What did they say?'

'That I wasn't really their brother's daughter.'

'*What?*'

As she explained what she'd been told, Sam's eyes went round with shock, then she laughed. 'If that was true, don't you think you would have found out before now? You know what your dad was like. He would have thrown that back in your face a long time ago.'

'That's what I thought.'

But if it *was* true, it explained a lot. Like why he hated her so much.

'If I were you I'd just forget all about it,' Sam advised. 'They were probably just saying that to make sure you didn't try to take the house from them.'

The doorbell rang. 'That's Brendan.' Sam shot off to answer it.

Lola heard Brendan's voice and steeled herself. She tried hard to like him for Sam's sake, but there was something about him that set her teeth on edge.

He was a car salesman, and he'd chatted Sam up while offering her easy terms on a Renault Clio six months ago. But his gift of the gab didn't work on Lola.

He didn't seem to like her much, either. Sam

had finally admitted Lola made him nervous because he thought she was a lesbian.

'It's because you don't have a boyfriend and you wear flat shoes for work,' she'd told her.

'I'm a police officer. I can't chase criminals in high heels, can I?'

'That's another thing. Brendan says all policewomen are lesbians. That's why they want to do a man's job.'

Lola heard them whispering in the hall now and guessed they were talking about her when she heard the words 'funeral' and 'try to be nice to her, please'.

'Can't I come and watch you getting changed instead?' Brendan asked. A second later he was catapulted into the sitting room and the door closed behind him.

He shifted from one foot to the other, hands thrust into the pockets of his chinos.

'All right?' he asked finally.

'Yes, thanks. You?'

'So-so. You know.'

And that was it. Their full conversational repertoire exhausted. Lola didn't know why Sam was so determined to make them like each other. It was never going to happen.

Brendan sat down on the sofa, crossed his legs and examined an imaginary scuff on his loafers. He wasn't bad-looking in a shifty-eyed, over-confident, too-much-hair-gel kind of way.

His eyebrows were going up and down, a sure sign he was working up to another conversational show-stopper.

'So . . . um . . . your dad's dead?'

'Yep.'

15

'Bummer.'

'It is for him.'

He regarded her warily. That was another thing about her that confused him, according to Sam. Men made jokes; women just laughed.

But at least he'd made an effort. Now it was her turn. 'Sold any good cars lately?' she ventured.

'It's funny you should ask that . . .' He launched into a complicated story about splitting the commission on a top-of-the-range Merc. Lola was still struggling to concentrate when Sam came back.

'I'm ready.' She did a little twirl for Brendan's approval. She was wearing a denim mini-skirt, pink vest top and perilously high strappy sandals.

'You look amazing.' He gave her thigh an appreciative stroke. Sam giggled.

Blimey, Lola thought, looking down at her jeans and trainers. No wonder he thinks I'm a lesbian.

'Now, are you sure you'll be all right on your own?' Sam asked anxiously as they headed for the door.

'I'll be fine.'

'You could always come with us, if you like? We're only going out for a drink.'

'No,' Lola and Brendan said together.

As the door closed, she heard him hissing, 'What did you say that for?'

*   *   *

On her own in the flat, Lola had a bath, blitzed herself a ready meal, poured another glass of wine and set about sorting through the box she'd brought home.

It wasn't much to show for someone's life. A battered box of old photographs, the years all jumbled together, baby pictures mixed up with school portraits and holiday snapshots.

Lola gulped her wine and flicked through them a handful at a time. It was painful to look at them. Not just because she missed her mum so badly, although seeing her face again brought back an ache of loneliness. It was because they made her think of how bad those days had been. Those tense Christmases when her father lost his temper and left her mother in tears in the kitchen. Those miserable holidays when they'd shivered on Bridlington beach and tried to pretend they were having a good time. That school photo of the little girl with her hair in plaits, smiling for the camera and dreading the time when she had to go home.

But there was one that made her smile. A strip of black-and-white prints of her and her mum in a passport photo booth. She was about eight years old. The photos weren't exactly flattering—their faces were squashed together, distorted by the fish-eye lens—but they were laughing, really laughing, not just the stiff smiles they put on for her father's camera.

It reminded Lola of the times when they were alone, just her and her mum. Then they'd fool around, her mother would sing and teach her to play little duets on the piano, and they'd eat biscuits and watch *Blue Peter* without being scared of getting crumbs on the carpet.

And then they'd hear her father's key in the door.

Lola had never understood their relationship, or why her mother stayed with him. As she got older, she would beg her to leave.

'I can't,' her mother would say. 'If you knew the full story you'd understand.' But she would never tell her. 'Maybe when you're older,' she promised.

But by the time Lola was old enough to hear it, her mother was gone.

She finished her wine and was just about to pack the photos away again when she spotted two more, right at the bottom of the box, wedged under the flap.

She barely recognised her mother in the first photo. She was scarcely more than a teenager and looked like a hippie in her flowing cheesecloth dress and embroidered shawl, her straight fair hair pinned on top of her head. She was sitting on a sofa, arm in arm with a dark-haired girl. They were both clutching their violins and grinning at the camera. Sprawled on the far end of the sofa was a young man with rippling golden hair, kohl-rimmed eyes and a moody expression.

Lola turned it over and looked at the back. 'Me, Sarah and Rick' was scrawled in pencil.

She looked at the photo again. Of course. Auntie Sarah, her mother's friend from music college. She often used to come up from London to visit. Lola enjoyed seeing her. She was exotic and arty-looking, and she made her mother laugh. But Eddie Lambert didn't like her and made her visits so awkward that, in the end, she stopped coming. The last time Lola saw her was at her mother's funeral.

She picked up the last photo. It must have been taken at the same time. This time it was a close-up, just her mum and the young man. He had a cigarette in one hand and the other draped

18

languidly around her shoulders. On the back she read 'Me and Rick, 1977'.

The year before she was born.

Suddenly she heard her Auntie Wendy's voice, crowing in her ear.

'Your oh-so-perfect mother went and got herself pregnant by another man . . .'

She looked again at the photo, and felt a sudden, awful jolt of recognition.

That tawny hair, those green eyes, that full, turned-down mouth. It was the same face she saw when she looked in the mirror.

CHAPTER THREE

Anyone who believed sexism in the police force was dead had obviously never visited Carlyle Street nick. While her male colleagues fought organised crime and chased speeding cars up and down the M62, PC Lola Lambert was stuck in community liaison, filing lost dog reports and giving talks to the local Neighbourhood Watch.

But in spite of her workplace being as enlightened as the local branch of Spearmint Rhino, Lola still had high hopes. There was a job coming up in CID and she'd applied for it. She had all the qualifications and experience, her record was excellent and, more importantly, there was very little competition.

'If there's any justice in the world, that job should be yours,' her friend Will said as they ate lunch in the canteen. 'They took *me* on, and I'm not nearly as well qualified as you!'

Thanks for reminding me, Lola thought, plunging her fork into her egg and chips. It still rankled that Will had made the jump to CID six months earlier. But he was her friend, and she tried not to hold his success against him. Anyway, he gave her lots of good gossip about what went on 'upstairs'. At the moment, he was working on the case of a gang trafficking girls into the country for prostitution.

'We know who's behind it,' he said now, helping himself to a chip from her plate. 'All we've got to do is piece together a case. But we can't do that without witnesses.'

'Won't the girls come forward?' Lola asked.

'And get deported? No chance. Besides, they're too scared of this gang. Most of them are just kids; they barely speak English. Have you finished with the rest of those chips?'

'No wonder they're terrified.' Lola pushed the plate towards him. 'What about the gang's associates? Can't you lean on them?'

'Not while they're making easy money out of it.'

'Then don't make it easy for them. Find out where they're channelling the money and turn up the heat. Surely you could—'

'Hang on!' Will laughed. 'Who's the detective here, you or me?'

'You are. For now.' She stirred her teaspoon around in her mug. 'I can't wait to get out of this uniform.'

'I don't know. I find it quite a turn-on.'

'Will!' She flicked her spoon at him. She wasn't sure if he was serious or not, but preferred to think he wasn't. It was less complicated that way.

'What are you doing later?' he asked as they

walked back from the canteen.

'Preparing a talk on antisocial behaviour for Pickley Park Comp. As if they need to be told anything about it. They could probably give me some tips.'

'No, I mean after work. Some of the rugby club are going out for an Indian after training tonight, if you want to join us?'

Lola pulled a face. 'Go out for a curry with you and your rugger bugger mates? No thanks.'

'We can be quite civilised when we want to be.'

'I'll take your word for it.'

'So will you come?'

She shook her head. 'Thanks, but I'm busy tonight. I've got some detective work of my own to do.'

'Yeah? What's that?'

'I'm looking up an old friend of my mum's. All I know so far is her name's Sarah Doyle, she's a musician and she lives in London.'

'That narrows it down.'

'Lucky I'm such a good detective, isn't it?' She grinned at him.

*   *   *

In spite of her confidence, it took her several hours and a lot of pointless trawling on the Internet, including a time-wasting detour to eBay to browse the shoes, before she finally tracked down her mother's friend via a website of musicians offering lessons. She lived in West Hampstead, wherever that was.

Lola picked up the phone, then put it down again. What would she say after all this time?

Maybe it was better to write her a letter. Or better still, go to see her.

Sam wasn't so sure. 'You're going to travel two hundred miles to London to meet some woman you haven't seen for fifteen years?' she said the following morning as she watched Lola throwing clothes in an overnight bag 'Wouldn't it just be easier to call her?'

'I wouldn't know what to say.'

'So what are you going to do when you get there? Ring the doorbell and run away?'

'I'm hoping I will have worked it out by the time I get there.' She zipped up her bag. Luckily for her, she'd been rostered off for the following day.

'Well, I think you're mad. And extremely selfish. If you'd waited until Saturday I could have come with you.'

'Thanks, but I don't need moral support.'

'Who said anything about moral support? I was thinking about the shopping.'

Lola smiled and hitched her bag on to her shoulder. 'Look on the bright side. At least you and Brendan will have the flat to yourselves tonight.'

*   *   *

Apart from a couple of school trips and a hen weekend, Lola had seldom been to London. By the time she'd negotiated the Thameslink from King's Cross to West Hampstead, she was beginning to lose some of her confidence. Maybe she should have phoned first, after all. What if she'd come all this way and Sarah wasn't even there?

It was early afternoon and raining steadily when

22

she stepped out of the station. Raindrops dripped off her hair and splashed the pages of her *A–Z* as she stood in the middle of the street, trying to work out which way to go.

It was the kind of area estate agents described as 'cosmopolitan' or 'up and coming'. The shops offering cheap clothes and plastic fancy goods were slowly being squeezed out by chic coffee shops, bars and smart little galleries, all freshly painted with neatly trimmed bay trees outside. Boarded-up buildings were busily being converted into desirable flats.

A couple of builders stopped to give Lola a quick appraising glance as she hurried past, then went back to work without a word. She knew she wasn't exactly looking her best in her rain-soaked denim jacket, cargo trousers and squelching Converses, her carefully straightened hair a frizzed-up mess.

Sarah Doyle lived on the top floor of an imposing redbrick Victorian house in a tree-lined street. All kinds of thoughts raged in Lola's head as she climbed the steps to the front door. By the time she rang the bell she'd convinced herself that Sarah wouldn't be there, or if she was she wouldn't remember her.

For a few minutes no one came. Lola had begun to give up hope when suddenly the door was flung open and a woman stood there. Tall and big-boned under flowing hippie clothes, she seemed to be in her early fifties. Her dark hair was heavily laced with grey and pinned in an untidy top-knot.

Lola opened her mouth but it was a few more seconds before she could force any sound out.

'Hello,' she managed. 'You might not remember

me. I'm—'

'Lola Rose,' the woman cut in. 'I've been expecting you for the last fifteen years.'

* * *

Sarah regarded her with frank grey eyes. 'I wondered when he'd tell you.'

'It's true, then?'

She nodded. 'You'd better come in.'

Inside the flat was blissfully warm compared to the wet April weather outside.

'You're soaked,' Sarah said. 'Take those wet things off and go through. I'll bring you a towel.'

Lola peeled off her damp jacket and shoes and went into the sitting room. The flat was built into the eaves of the house, all sloping walls and interesting angles. Rain pattered on to the skylights. It was cosy, arty and Bohemian, a rich mixture of Persian rugs, Indian silk cushions and vintage shawls draped over the big squashy sofas. The walls were crammed with bookshelves, paintings, photos and framed concert posters. A grand piano dominated the room, piled high with sheet music.

Lola was studying the photos when Sarah returned with an armful of towels.

'If you're looking for your mother, she's over there.' She nodded towards an array of photos on the piano.

Lola examined one of them. It was a posed portrait of an orchestra, an arc of middle-aged men and women in evening dress. In the middle of them were two young women, one blonde, one dark, dressed in stiff white shirts and long black

24

skirts, clutching violins and staring at the camera with rabbit-in-the-headlights expressions.

'Our first professional appearance,' Sarah said, looking over her shoulder. 'We were terrified.' She handed her the towel. 'Do you play?'

'Mum tried to teach me the piano, but my . . . he didn't like it, so we had to stop.'

'That figures. Eddie Lambert hated anything to do with Claire's past, anything he couldn't control.' She stopped herself. 'I'm sorry, I probably shouldn't say too much. But it made me so angry, the way he treated her. That was why I had to stop coming in the end. I couldn't bear to watch him slowly crushing the life out of her.'

'She let him do it.'

'I suppose she felt she had no choice.' Sarah took the damp towels back. 'Have you eaten? I was just about to make myself a sandwich. Can I get one for you?'

Lola followed her into the kitchen. Like the rest of the flat, every wall and surface was crammed with interesting, arty bric-à-brac. Sarah put the kettle on, then took a wholemeal loaf from the bread bin and began to slice it.

'So you think she should have left him?' Lola said.

'As I said, she didn't think she had a choice.' Sarah sawed away at the bread. 'I begged her to move back down to London. She was so talented, she could have played professionally, taught music, anything she wanted. But she always said no. She said she owed him something after everything he'd done for her.' She put down the knife. 'I think he made her feel so guilty she felt she deserved to be treated badly.'

She threw open the fridge and surveyed the shelves. 'What can I get you? Ham? Cheese? I think I've got some salami somewhere . . .'

'Whatever you're having will be fine.'

Sarah gathered together cheese and salad, then nudged the door closed with her foot. 'How is he, anyway? Does he know you're here?'

'He died last week.'

'Ah.' She paused. 'Well, I can't say I'm sorry because that would be hypocritical.' She pulled another knife out of the drawer and started to butter the bread. 'When did he tell you he wasn't your father?'

'He didn't. His sisters filled me in on that bit.'

Sarah clicked her tongue. 'Why doesn't that surprise me? They always were a pair of venomous bitches. It must run in the family.'

'Why didn't my mother tell me herself ?'

'He wouldn't let her. He didn't want any gossip, anyone laughing at him, thinking he was less of a man for bringing up someone else's child.'

'So why did he do it?'

'He was desperate to marry her.' Sarah nodded to the kettle. 'Do you want to make some coffee? The pot's over there and the mugs are in the cupboard.'

Lola busied herself spooning coffee into the pot. 'What do you mean by desperate?'

'She was the one he couldn't have.' Sarah paused. 'Claire told me they'd met in school. She didn't think much of him. I suppose he wasn't that different in those days, always swaggering around, so full of himself. He had a crush on her, apparently. More like an obsession, I reckon. He wouldn't take no for an answer. Claire didn't manage to shake him off until she got a place at college and moved to London.'

'And that's where she met Rick?'

Sarah's eyebrows shot up. 'How did you know about *him*? I wasn't aware your father knew who he was.'

'I saw this photo.' Lola took it out of her bag and showed it to her. 'I guessed he was the one.'

'That's him all right.' Sarah smiled. 'You look so alike.' She handed the photo back to her. 'She'd left college by the time they met. They were both struggling musicians, and he was just starting to make it with his band. They were together for about six months, but things didn't work out and then he wanted to go back to his wife, so—'

'Wait a minute. He was *married*?'

'They were living separate lives. He was on the road all the time, and she stayed at home. Their marriage was on the rocks long before your mother came along,' she said defensively.

Lola was silent as she poured the coffee. It had never occurred to her that her mother might have had an affair with a married man.

'Anyway, it ended, they went their separate ways, and then Claire found out she was pregnant. By then Rick was trying to make a go of his marriage, so she didn't feel she could go back to him. It wouldn't have worked, anyway. They'd moved too far apart.'

She sliced up a tomato and arranged it on top of the cheese. 'She just didn't know what to do. I tried to talk her into staying in London but she wasn't sure she could cope. You've got to remember it wasn't like it is now. Being a single mum was a big deal in those days.'

27

'So she went home?'

'She said she was going up to Leeds to tell her parents, but I found out afterwards she went up there to die.' Sarah's hand shook as she cut the sandwich. 'She felt so ashamed and couldn't face telling her family. She thought it would be the easy way out. She stood on a bridge over a railway line and was going to jump when Eddie came along. He asked what she was doing and Claire ended up spilling out all her troubles.

'He persuaded her there was another way. He offered to marry her and bring you up as his own. No one would ever find out, he said. I can understand why she did it. There she was, a pregnant single girl, and he offered her security, a solution to her troubles.'

'So he saved her life?' Lola remembered what her mother had said to her: *If you knew the full story you'd understand.* No wonder she felt she couldn't leave him.

'More like took it away from her, slowly but surely. Maybe he was punishing her for rejecting him. Or he felt that controlling her was the only way to keep her. I don't know. Either way, she put up with it.'

'I bet there were times when she wished I'd never been born.'

'She *never* felt like that!' Sarah insisted. 'She told me once that you were the light of her life, the only thing that kept her going. Whatever else she regretted in her life, she never regretted having you.'

Lola turned away so Sarah wouldn't see the tears pricking her eyes. 'I wonder what happened to him,' she said, changing the subject.

28

'Who?'

'Rick. I expect he's a bank manager or something by now.' She looked at Sarah, who was staring at her. 'What?'

'You mean you don't know? I thought you said you'd worked it out?'

'Worked out what?'

Sarah put down her coffee mug. 'Lola, your father is Rick Wild.'

CHAPTER FOUR

It took a full minute before she could take in what Sarah was saying. Then, slowly, she realised.

'Rick Wild? *The* Rick Wild? As in Poleaxe?'

'You've heard of him, then?'

'Who hasn't?' She wasn't a heavy metal fan, but even she knew that Poleaxe was one of the biggest rock bands on the planet. Rick Wild was the lead singer, all teased hair and tight leather trousers.

And he was her father.

She laughed. It was too mad for her to do anything else.

'I thought you said you'd worked it out?' Sarah repeated.

'I knew his first name, and I thought he must be a musician. But I never realised it was *him*.' She hadn't even recognised him from the photo.

'He wasn't so famous back in the seventies. The band was just starting out then, making their first album. Claire played violin on a couple of tracks and they liked the sound, so they asked us to go on tour with them.'

'It must have been exciting, going on the road with a rock band.'

'It was certainly different.' Sarah smiled. 'We'd been used to chamber orchestras and string quartets, lots of middle-aged men playing Mozart. Suddenly we were travelling around Europe in a beaten-up tour bus, living on dope and Jack Daniels. Not your mum, of course,' she added quickly.

Lola wasn't sure if she believed her. 'And that's when she and Rick got together?'

'They were inseparable,' Sarah remembered. 'I don't know how Rick felt about her, but I know Claire was absolutely in love with him. She was convinced they'd be together for ever.'

'Even though he was married?'

'I told you, he and his wife had separate lives.' Sarah pulled the crust off her sandwich and nibbled on it. 'But that's what it's like on the road. Every night you pack up, move on to the next town and the next girl. And then, when it's all over, you go home to your family and act like nothing's happened. Claire didn't understand the rules. But when the tour ended, so did their relationship. Over, just like that.'

'And she never heard from him again?'

'Not as far as I know. But she never forgot him. How could she, when she had you?'

Was that a good or a bad thing? Lola wondered. She wasn't sure she'd want to live with a constant reminder of how she'd been let down in love.

She wasn't sure how her father could have lived with it, either. No wonder Eddie Lambert found it so hard to accept her. For a moment she almost felt sorry for him.

'What are you going to do now?' Sarah asked as she cleared away their plates.

'I don't know.' Lola was completely at a loss.

'Are you going to get in touch with him?'

'Do you think I should?'

Sarah's face said it all. 'That's your call,' she replied carefully. 'But I'd consider the consequences if I were you.'

Lola had planned to find a cheap hotel and stay over in London, but after all the shocks of that day she decided to go home instead.

'You're welcome to sleep on my sofa,' Sarah offered.

'Thanks, but right now I need my own bed.'

As she left, Sarah hugged her. 'Keep in touch,' she said. 'Let me know what you decide to do.'

It was nearly ten when she got back to the flat. The place was in darkness. Sam and Brendan must have gone out clubbing.

She went into her bedroom to dump her bag, and noticed her wardrobe door was open.

Lola sighed. No need to check what was missing. There was only one thing in her closet Sam was ever interested in borrowing.

She stomped into the hall. 'Sam! Get out here now!'

There was a muffled scuffling from the other side of the door. 'Can it wait?' Sam called out.

'Now, Sam. Otherwise I'm coming in to get you.'

A moment later her bedroom door opened a fraction and Sam inched out, clutching Lola's truncheon. She was wearing high heels, black stockings, a thong, Lola's uniform jacket and cap, and a very guilty expression.

'I thought you weren't coming home until

31

tomorrow.'

'Obviously.' Lola glanced through the crack in the door. Brendan was spreadeagled on the bed, his wrists fastened to the wrought-iron bedhead with her handcuffs. 'Taking down his particulars, are you?'

'It was only a bit of fun.'

Lola could see her black push-up bra under the open jacket. 'You do realise I could arrest you for impersonating a police officer?'

'Sorry.' Sam swung the truncheon limply. 'Why are you back so early anyway? Didn't you find the mysterious Sarah?'

'Oh, I found her all right.'

'And?'

'And you'll never believe what she told me.'

Sam's eyes grew huge when Lola told her the whole story. 'Bloody hell, Lola, you're joking? Your dad's a real live rock star?'

'It seems like it.' It still felt totally unreal that she even had another father, let alone one so famous.

'Babe?' Brendan called from the bedroom.

'Just a minute.' Sam closed the door on him. 'I don't know about you, but I need a drink,' she said to Lola.

They went into the kitchen, cracked open a couple of beers, and Sam made her tell the whole story all over again.

'I still can't believe it,' she said. 'You're rock royalty. That makes you like Jade Jagger, or Kelly Osbourne. God, you might even be in *Heat* magazine one day.'

'Hardly!' Lola laughed.

'Why not? I can just see you looking really

dodgy in the Sack the Stylist section. And they'll probably want to do an interview with you once word gets out.'

'*If* it gets out.'

'What?' Sam slammed down her bottle so hard her cap slid over her eyes. 'What do you mean? You're going to get in touch with him, right?'

'Why should I?'

'Because . . . because he's famous! And rich! And he's your father,' she added as an afterthought.

'We've never met, he doesn't even know I exist, and he probably wouldn't want anything to do with me if he did.'

'You don't know that until you try.'

'Yeah, right. You can just see him jumping on the first plane to meet me, can't you? I mean, we'd have so much in common. He could tell me all about his fabulous celebrity lifestyle in LA, and I could take him to Ali's kebab shop in the precinct—'

'All right, you've made your point.' Sam looked irritable.

Lola had thought about it all the way back to Leeds on the train. One minute she was intrigued by the idea of having a brand-new family. The next she was thinking there was no way they'd ever want to meet her.

She kept remembering Sarah's warning to consider the consequences. What if she contacted him and he didn't want to know? She wasn't sure she could stand being rejected by another father.

'Babe?' Brendan's voice croaked faintly from Sam's bedroom. 'I need the toilet.'

'Bloody hell, I forgot about him.' Sam adjusted

her police cap and stood up. 'For what it's worth, I think you're making a big mistake,' she said.

'We'll never know, will we?' Lola replied.

*   *   *

Her decision not to contact her father didn't stop Lola Googling his name on her office computer two days later. It was a boring Saturday afternoon, most of her male colleagues had been sent off to do crowd control at the local football match, and she was left to man the desk and catch up on her paperwork.

She typed in 'Rick Wild' and clicked on the 'Go' button. A photo of the band appeared, taken at last year's Reading Festival. Underneath was a headline, 'BAND BANNED', and a report about how Poleaxe had been barred from an entire hotel chain after drummer Jonno Jones had been found with a large quantity of cocaine, two sheep and a donkey in his suite. There was a photo of Rick on stage, bare-chested, sweat gleaming on his muscled torso under the spotlights, his head thrown back, golden hair rippling, as he screamed into the mike.

There were hundreds of stories about him. Lola read one about his marriage to a Swedish supermodel, and another revealing that he had been found in bed with two backing singers. An even more recent one, with the headline 'wild man's battle with the booze', announced he was going into rehab after admitting to alcohol, drug and sex addiction.

Lola quickly tried another website, and found herself looking at an early band shot, probably taken around the time her mother knew Rick.

Four young men stared moodily into the camera, all long hair, leather and attitude.

Lola could see why her mother had fallen for Rick. He was easily the most beautiful member of the band. The drummer was stocky, bearded and mad-looking, the bassist pale, thin and vacant. The fourth was tall, dark and rake-thin with a brooding intensity in his eyes that she found faintly disturbing.

'What are you looking at?'

Lola jumped as Will came up behind her. She made a move to close down the page, but wasn't quick enough.

He looked over her shoulder. 'Rick Wild, eh? I didn't know you had a thing for rockers.'

'I don't.'

Will nodded towards the screen. 'He's old enough to be your dad.'

'Funny you should say that,' Lola muttered.

'Sorry?'

'Nothing.' She closed down the computer and swivelled her chair round to face him. 'Was there something you wanted?'

'I just wondered if you fancied a night out? There's a gang of us going into town and I thought you might like to come along.'

He made it sound oh-so-casual, but Lola wasn't fooled. She knew when she was being asked out. Will had tried it often enough.

'Sorry, I'm busy tonight,' she lied. 'Maybe some other time?'

Will looked deflated. 'That's what you always say. I'm beginning to get a complex.'

'I just don't want it to get complicated, that's all.'

'Lola, I'm asking you out for a few drinks. I don't want to get engaged!'

'As I said, maybe—'

'Some other time. Yeah, I get it. I won't hold my breath.'

As she drove home later, Lola wondered whether she should have accepted Will's offer. After all, it wasn't as if she had anything better planned than watching *Casualty*.

She really had to do something about her social life, she decided. As in getting one.

She also had to stop thinking all men were like Eddie Lambert. Otherwise she'd never find herself a boyfriend.

She considered the idea of going out with Will. He was a bit chunky from all the rugby playing, and in the wrong light his hair looked slightly too ginger. But maybe, as Sam always said, she was just being too choosy.

'You'll never find a man if you keep finding fault with everyone,' she said. But maybe that was why she did it. Because then she wouldn't run the risk of ending up with someone like Eddie Lambert.

But Will was nothing like Eddie. He was kind and caring and . . . OK, she didn't remotely fancy him. But surely she could get over that?

She was still pondering the question as she pulled up in the car park of her block of flats. She got out of the car and was digging around in the depths of her bag for her key when someone called out her name. She looked up and flinched, as a flashbulb exploded in her face.

CHAPTER FIVE

'What the—'

Before she could react, a man sprang out in front of her and shoved a dictaphone under her nose.

'How do you feel about having such a famous father, Lola?' he leered. 'Must have been a big shock for you. Any plans to meet up with your dad?'

She sidestepped him and fell headlong over the photographer, who was crouching in front of her.

'Give us a smile, sweetheart!'

'Leave me alone!'

She ran across the car park, the camera still snapping behind her.

'Better get used to this, love,' one of the men called after her. 'We'll be watching you from now on.'

*   *   *

Sam came out of the kitchen, a tub of cottage cheese in one hand, a KitKat in the other. 'Can you believe chocolate has less calories than a whole tub of cottage cheese? It's no contest as far as I'm concerned.' She stopped when she saw Lola, pressed against the front door, panting for breath. 'What's the matter with you? You look like you're having an asthma attack.'

The entryphone rang.

'Don't answer it!' Lola snatched it out of Sam's hand as she went to pick it up. 'It might be *them.*'

Sam frowned. 'Who?'

Lola pointed to the window. 'Take a look.'

Sam pulled back the curtain and peered down to the car park. 'Who are those two men?'

'They're not Jehovah's Witnesses, that's for sure.'

'They're looking up here . . . now they're waving. What's that he's got? Ooh, it's a camera. He's pointing it this way and . . .' She dropped the curtain and spun round. 'Oh my God, they're *paparazzi*!' She jumped up and down. 'Can you believe it? This is so exciting!'

'You're not the one they chased across the car park.'

Lola looked down at her hands. They'd only just stopped shaking. She snatched the KitKat out of Sam's hands, unwrapped it and shoved a whole finger of it into her mouth.

'How did they find you?' Sam asked.

'Good question,' Lola replied through a mouth full of chocolate. She stared meaningfully at Sam.

'I didn't tell anyone, if that's what you're thinking.'

'Are you sure?'

'Swear to God. Except Brendan, of course.'

'Sam!'

'I had to. I was going to burst if I didn't tell someone. Anyway, he's my boyfriend,' she added piously. 'We have no secrets from each other.'

'Neither do I, apparently.'

'He wouldn't tell anyone. He promised.'

'Sam, he's a second-hand car salesman. They're hardly known for their integrity.'

Lola ate another finger of KitKat and edged the curtain aside to peep down into the car park. The men were still there, pacing around the front entrance directly below.

'What are we going to do?' Sam asked.

'Sit here until they get bored and go away, I suppose.'

They had a glass of wine and watched *Dirty Dancing* on DVD. At least, Lola tried to watch it. Sam fidgeted, checked her texts and went to the window every few minutes.

'I hate this,' she complained. 'It's Saturday night and I'm trapped indoors. This must be what Britney Spears feels like. A prisoner in her own home.'

'You've only been here an hour.'

Sam sent her a sulky look. 'It's all right for you; you're used to having no social life.'

'Why don't you invite Brendan round?' Lola wouldn't have minded having a chat with him herself.

'He's away on a course. I've already texted him a million times. Now my phone's out of credit.' She looked down into the street. 'And I'm hungry,' she wailed.

'Isn't there anything in the fridge?'

Sam shook her head. 'I didn't buy any food because I wanted to lose half a stone before Brendan came home.' She turned to Lola. 'Can't we ring the police?'

'No one's committed a crime.'

'Can't you get one of your police mates to come round and scare them anyway?' She brightened up. 'What about your friend Will? I bet he'd be round here like a shot if you rang him.'

I bet he would, Lola thought. 'Then I'd have to explain what all this was about. I don't want anyone to know.'

'The whole world will know anyway, if this gets into the papers.' Sam prowled around the flat for a few more minutes, then announced, 'Stuff this, I'm going out for a pizza.'

'Why are you wearing sunglasses?' Lola asked as she watched her get ready.

'It's a disguise.' Sam pulled her cap down low over her auburn curls.

'You do realise it's not you they're after?'

'You don't know that. They might want me to sell my story.' She adjusted her sunglasses and turned to face Lola. 'How do I look?'

'A bit ridiculous, frankly.'

Her disguise certainly fooled the waiting reporters. It fooled them into thinking Sam was Lola, trying to make her escape. Lola watched from the window as Sam sprinted across the car park, chased by the two men. They must have realised their mistake when she got into the wrong car because they didn't try to follow when she drove off.

Half an hour later she was back, clutching a pizza box. By now the men had made the connection between her and Lola. They blocked her way to the front entrance, firing questions at her and taking photos. Sam was pinned against the front door, scrabbling for her key. Then she dropped her bag, scattering its contents over the front step. The men closed in on her.

Without thinking, Lola reached for the first thing to hand, which happened to be the half-empty wine bottle, and dropped it out of the window. She'd only meant to scare the men, but by sheer fluke the bottle scored a direct hit between the photographer's shoulders as he looked down to adjust his lens. He dropped to the ground.

There was a brief, shocked silence. Even Sam stopped gathering up her belongings and looked up.

Then, to Lola's relief, the photographer groaned and stirred. Sam grabbed her chance and escaped.

She collapsed through the front door two minutes later, laughing. 'Oh my God, Lola, you should have seen your face!'

'I thought I'd killed him.' She was still trembling.

'So did he.' Sam rushed to the window. 'It's scared them off, anyway. They're getting into their car.'

'Probably going straight to the police.' Lola groaned.

Her job in CID suddenly looked a long way away.

*   *   *

The police didn't arrive, but that didn't stop Lola having a sleepless night. Luckily, she was working the six o'clock shift the following morning, so she didn't have too long to toss and turn.

The Creighton estate slumbered in the crisp, early-morning sunshine. The teenagers had gone home to sleep off their hangovers after a night of antisocial rampaging, and their kid brothers hadn't surfaced to start the day shift. Takeaway cartons and discarded beer cans littered the front gardens, and a burnt-out car smouldered on the patch of wasteland beside the railway line. The community

41

centre had had two of its windows smashed.

All in all, it had been a quiet night.

The shops in the precinct were still hidden behind steel shutters, except for the convenience store on the corner which never seemed to close. Its windows were covered in posters advertising cut-price canned goods and the latest DVD rentals.

'I'm just nipping in for a packet of fags,' her partner Gordon said. 'Can I get you anything?'

'No thanks.'

'Sure I can't tempt you to a Sunday morning gossip rag?'

'What makes you ask that?' She turned on him sharply.

'OK, calm down.' Gordon held up his hands. 'What's got into you today? You're not usually this jumpy.'

Lola was saved from answering as her radio crackled into life. A badly beaten-up girl had been found by a dog-walker beside the railway line.

The woman and her dog were still with the girl when Lola and Gordon arrived.

'I just found her lying here,' the woman stammered. She was very shaken, and it wasn't hard to see why. The girl was in a terrible state, her mouth and eyes battered and swollen with purple bruises.

While Gordon radioed for an ambulance, Lola knelt down beside her. 'Can you tell me what happened, love?'

The girl flinched and gasped in pain, her arms wrapped protectively around her. Lola guessed her body was as bruised as her face.

They busied themselves taking a statement from

the dog-walker until the ambulance arrived.

'I don't know why we're bothering,' Gordon said dismissively as they followed it to the hospital. 'It's obvious what's happened. She's a tom. Probably got beaten up by a punter.'

'She was terrified, poor kid.'

'Serves her right for going out on the streets.'

'So just because she's a prostitute it's OK for some bloke to use her as a punchbag, is it?'

He shrugged. 'Occupational hazard, I reckon.'

Lola shot him a disgusted look. 'You're all heart.'

'Fine. If you want to waste your time trying to get a statement out of her, go ahead.'

As it turned out, he was right to be sceptical. The girl refused to speak to Lola. She just sat shivering in the hospital's cubicle, wide-eyed and fearful. No amount of coaxing would get her to open her mouth.

Fortunately, A&E wasn't too busy; just a couple of fight injuries and a few random drunks left over from Saturday night.

'She's got a cracked rib and she'll need a couple of stitches in that eye,' the doctor told them.

'Might as well leave them to it,' Gordon said. 'We're not going to get any sense out of her.'

Lola looked back at the girl. 'I want to stay with her.'

'But she's not talking.'

'I don't care. Look at her; she's scared. I don't even think she speaks English. I can't leave her by herself.'

Gordon sighed. 'Ten minutes,' he said firmly. 'I'll be in the coffee shop if you need me.'

Lola stayed with the girl, holding her hand,

while the nurse patched her up. Slowly, it seemed some of her mistrust and fear started to leave her.

'Thank you,' she said haltingly. 'You very kind. No one kind to me since I come to England.' Then she burst into tears.

'How long have you been here?' Lola asked, putting her arms around her.

'Two weeks. But I hate life,' she said. 'It not like they said. Man said it would be good job, good money. But is very bad.'

'Which man?' Lola asked. 'Who brought you here?'

The girl shook her head, her fear returning. 'I must not say.'

'If you tell us, maybe we can help you.'

She looked at her hopefully. 'You get me home?'

'Yes, we can get you home. Just tell me who—'

The curtain swished aside and a man stood there. Short, stocky, with cropped hair and a long scar on one side of his face, he looked as if he'd stepped straight out of a Bond movie. Lola felt the girl flinch with shock and fear.

'Hello, Ruta,' he said. But his eyes were fixed on Lola. 'I hear you had an accident.'

'Who are you?' Lola asked.

'I'm her boyfriend. I've come to take her home.' He held out his hand, but Ruta shrank back.

'It doesn't look like she wants to go,' Lola said.

The man's smile didn't waver. 'She's confused, poor girl. This has all been a bit of a trauma for her. Isn't that right, Ruta?'

Before she could answer, the nurse appeared. 'Could you come, officer?' she said to Lola. 'One of the drunks is causing a disturbance in

44

reception.'

'Can't my colleague deal with it?'

'I can't find him. And I mustn't leave the desk for long.'

Reluctantly she stood up. 'Stay here,' she told the girl. 'I won't be long.'

It took her a while to calm the drunk and persuade him to go. By the time she got back to the cubicle, Ruta and the man had disappeared.

*   *   *

'She'll be back on the street by tomorrow,' Gordon predicted as they headed back into the office after their shift. 'It's the only life these foreign girls know.'

'All the same, I shouldn't have left her on her own. I might have known—oh my God!'

She stopped dead and stared at the photo plastered on the wall ahead of her. A blurry, photocopied image of her getting out of her car, hair all over the place and a look of bug-eyed panic on her face.

She looked around at her sniggering colleagues. 'Where did it come from?'

'You're all over the *Sunday News*,' one of them told her.

'Not your best angle, though,' another remarked.

'Why didn't you tell us your dad was a rock star?'

Lola waved her hand at the photos. 'Why do you think? Anyway, it's a long story and right now I don't feel like telling it, OK?'

She turned her back on them and sat down at

45

her desk. There was another photo Blu-Tacked to her computer screen, and a stack of them where the printer paper should have been.

'Very funny,' she said. 'Am I going to be finding these all day?'

'Put it this way,' said Steve the desk sergeant. 'I wouldn't go into the canteen if you're easily offended.'

Lola decided to ignore them. But it wasn't easy trying to write up her statements while the others whistled their way through Poleaxe's greatest hits.

Will was just as bad. 'Why didn't you tell me?' he demanded when he came in later.

'I didn't know myself until a few days ago.' She hesitated. 'I suppose you've read the article?'

'Haven't you?'

'I didn't dare. Is it really awful?'

He pulled a copy of the *Sunday News* out of his bag. 'See for yourself.'

She went to take it, then snatched her hand away. 'I can't.'

'It's not that bad.' He picked up the paper and started flicking through it. 'Just a whole load of stuff about how you're Rick Wild's long-lost love child, and how you're desperate to find your father.'

'Oh God.' Lola buried her face in her hands.

'As I said, it's not that bad. Apart from the photo, which is pretty dire.' He went on leafing his way through the paper.

Lola tried to change the subject. 'Gordon and I picked up a prostitute this morning.'

'Yeah? Did you get your money's worth?'

She ignored him. 'She didn't speak very good English, but I worked out she was from somewhere in Eastern Europe. She could be one of the girls your gang smuggled over.'

Will looked up. 'Did she tell you that?'

'Not exactly. I think she was going to, then some guy turned up and took her away. But I found out her name. She's desperate to go home. Maybe if you tracked her down, she'd be willing to talk.'

'You want me to trawl around the red light area, looking for a prostitute who may or may not be connected to this case?'

Why not? You're supposed to be a detective. Lola bit her lip. 'I just thought it might be a useful lead.'

'Right little Miss Marple, aren't you?' Will smiled indulgently. 'Make a note of the name and I'll look into it.' He offered her the newspaper. 'Are you sure you don't want to read this?'

'No thanks.' She shuddered. 'I'm just hoping everyone will have forgotten about it by tomorrow.'

'I doubt it,' Will said. 'You're not going to be allowed to forget this in a hurry. Especially if your father sees it.'

'Oh my God, do you think he will?' The thought hadn't occurred to her.

Will grinned. 'You'll soon find out, won't you?'

CHAPTER SIX

'Would someone mind telling me what the hell is going on?'

Dinah Abraham slapped the newspaper down on her ex-husband's back as he sprawled on his sun-lounger.

She wasn't happy. She'd been up half the night arguing about ticket sales with some tightwad New Jersey promoter. Then, just as she'd solved that problem, the record company PR in England had emailed her this story, and Dinah had caught the first plane from New York to Rick's beach house in the Bahamas. She was tired, wound up and in no mood to be messed around.

Frankly, she needed this like she needed a one-night stand with Hannibal Lecter.

'Well?' she demanded. 'What do you know about this kid?'

As Rick rolled over slowly to look up at her, Dinah couldn't help checking out his lean, tanned torso. In his early fifties, he was still in terrific shape. Not that she was interested any more. She'd got over all that once she'd realised what a royal pain in the backside he could be.

He flipped back his trademark mane of golden hair. 'Relax, will you? You're stressing me out.'

'I'm stressing *you* out? Sorry, are you the one who hasn't slept in the last thirty-three hours?'

'Now you mention it, I didn't get a lot of sleep last night.' Rick smiled lazily at the long-limbed blonde sunning herself beside him. Britt Petersen-Wild, ex-supermodel, and Rick's third wife.

'Oh, please.' Dinah curled her lip. 'Way too much information.'

'Rick shouldn't get stressed,' Britt put in, her husky Scandinavian accent tinged with a touch of transatlantic. 'It interferes with his creativity.'

So does hanging around with a leech like you. Dinah looked down at them, lying side by side on their loungers. Both tall, golden and beautiful, and not a brain cell between them.

48

If they ever had a baby, the poor brat would look like an angel and have the IQ of an amoeba.

She picked up the newspaper that had slipped off Rick's back on to the decking. 'Do you know this girl?'

'Never met her before in my life.'

'What about her mother? According to this, you certainly met *her*.'

'I don't know.'

'What do you mean, you don't know?'

'Look, it was a long time ago. The whole of the seventies is kinda fuzzy, y'know?' He turned to Britt. 'Baby, I need another drink.'

'Iced tea?'

'Perfect.'

'Coming up.' Britt slithered off the lounger and headed for the house. She was wearing the briefest pink bikini Dinah had ever seen. Dental floss was more substantial.

She hadn't had time to think about dressing for the hot Bahamian sun, and sweltered inside her fitted black suit. Her ankles had swollen up on the plane. She could feel them spilling over her Louboutin courts like expanding bread dough.

That swimming pool looked so cool and refreshing, the sun sparkling on the turquoise water. She longed to dive in, but was due back on the next flight to New York in less than two hours, and then on to Illinois to interview a potential tour manager.

Not that Rick would be interested in her schedule. Like most spoilt rock stars, he assumed everything around him just happened, as if by magic.

And Dinah had spent the last thirty years

49

making it happen.

Britt returned with two long, frosted glasses. Typically, she didn't offer one to Dinah.

'We'd have to have a DNA test,' she said, slipping back on to the lounger beside Rick.

Hell, why didn't I think of that? Didn't she think she knew her job by now? Dinah had been clearing up Rick's messes while Britt was still in her bedroom listening to Abba records.

'The lawyers are already on to it,' she said.

'Cool.' Rick rolled back on to his stomach, a signal that the interview was over.

'The question is, what do you want to do about it?'

'What do you expect me to do?'

'Rick, there's a kid here who says you're her father. You can't just ignore it.'

'Why not?'

'Because she's your daughter. Your own flesh and blood.'

'Not until the DNA—' Britt started to say.

Dinah turned on her. 'Don't you have shoes to buy, or something?'

Britt narrowed her ice-blue eyes. 'I'm just saying, she could be making the whole thing up.'

'Wow. Do you know, that never occurred to me?'

'Then you should wait until you know for sure before you start bothering Rick,' Britt said, not noticing the sarcasm. She'd obviously had an irony by-pass at the same time as her last lipo session. 'He's got a lot to think about at the moment, with the album to finish and the tour coming up.'

'You think I don't know that? Who do you think has all the sleepless nights schmoozing the record

50

companies and sealing the deals?'

'That's what you're paid for,' Britt said haughtily.

'Ladies, please,' Rick cut in as they squared up to each other. 'Britt's right,' he told Dinah. 'I am pretty exhausted right now.'

'You look it,' she said.

'He's allowed some down-time.' Britt picked up the bottle of sun lotion. 'Would you like me to do your back, baby?' she purred.

'Sure.'

Dinah watched as she moved to his lounger, swinging her long leg over to sit astride him. Rick growled with pleasure as she massaged lazy arcs on his back. It was like having a walk-on part in a porn movie.

'So I'm guessing you want me to make this go away?' she sighed.

Rick waved his hand dismissively. 'Yeah, make it go away.'

'Whatever it takes?'

'Whatever.'

He'd already lost interest as he twisted round to take Britt in his arms. Dinah watched the bottle of sun lotion roll across the wooden decking.

'There's something else you should know,' she said. 'We've had another letter from You-Know-Who.'

'The Devoted Fan?' Rick sat up, nearly tipping Britt on to the deck. 'When?'

'Two days ago.'

'What did it say?'

'Same as last time. Nasty, threatening. Saying if the tour went ahead you'd be a dead man.'

'Great.' Rick tried to smile but he'd turned pale

under his tan. 'He must have heard our new material.'

'This isn't funny, Rick!' Britt turned on him. 'You've got to cancel this tour.'

'We can't, baby. We've spent money, signed contracts. If we pull out we stand to lose millions.'

'And if you go ahead you could lose your life.'

Rick looked at Dinah. 'What do you think?'

She didn't want to tell him what was really going through her mind. 'It's nothing to worry about,' she said. 'Just some crazy fan looking for attention.'

'So was the guy who shot John Lennon,' Britt said ominously.

CHAPTER SEVEN

I must be mad, Lola thought.

She was sitting at a window table in the greasy spoon café, a mug of stone-cold tea in front of her, her gaze fixed on the shop across the street.

It was nearly lunchtime. Outside it was a chilly grey day, but inside the café was bright, warm and crowded with workmen, laughing and shouting as they crammed around the Formica-topped tables. A smell of frying bacon and chips hung in the air.

It was her day off. But instead of catching up with her ironing and watching Jeremy Kyle like a normal person, she'd decided to take a trip to the seediest part of town and stake out a massage parlour.

She couldn't help it. It nagged at her that Will hadn't followed up her lead about Ruta. She was sure that if they spoke to the girl, managed to win her trust, she would tell them everything they needed to know about the gang who'd brought her to England.

And if Will didn't want to do it, she would.

She'd spent the previous night trawling the red light area, looking for Ruta. None of the girls knew anything about her, but one had pointed her in the direction of the massage parlour. 'That's where most of the foreign girls work,' she'd said.

'Finished with that?'

Lola looked up. A large woman stood over her, pointing to her mug.

'Not yet.' She picked it up and took a defiant sip. The woman glared at her and stomped off. No wonder, Lola thought. She'd been nursing that same mug of tea for two hours.

She cleaned a patch in the steamed-up windows with her sleeve and peered out. Apart from a couple of shifty-looking men, no one had been in or out of the massage parlour in all that time.

Then, just as she was beginning to think she was wasting her time, the door opened and Ruta came out. She looked so young, huddled in a fleece, her hands thrust deep into the pockets. She stood outside for a moment, blinking in the daylight, then turned and hurried off down the street.

Lola found her at the bus stop, carefully counting change into her hand.

'Hi. Remember me?'

Ruta looked up and started with fear when she saw Lola. She made a move to run, but Lola caught her arm.

'Don't go. I only want to talk to you.'

'No.' Her thin arm trembled under Lola's grasp. There were still faint yellow and black bruises under her heavy mask of make-up. 'You bad. You put me in prison.'

'No one's going to put you in prison, Ruta. Trust me. It's your boss we want.'

Ruta said nothing. Her body was still tense, ready to run. She was just a kid, Lola thought. Barely eighteen, if that. No wonder she was terrified.

'We can make all this stop, Ruta,' she said calmly. 'We can send you home to your family. All you have to do is talk to us.'

Just then a silver Mercedes pulled up alongside them. Two men got out, one middle-aged, one younger, dressed in suits and carrying briefcases.

'Miss Lambert?' the older one said.

As she turned to face them, Ruta broke free of her grasp and tore off down the street. Lola started to run after her but she'd soon disappeared into the warren of a high-rise estate.

When Lola returned, the two men were still waiting for her. She confronted them angrily.

'Now look what you've done. I was just about to get that girl to talk to me. Who the hell are you, anyway?'

The older man handed her a card. 'We represent the firm of Witchell and Pearce. We're here on behalf of our client, Mr Rick Wild.'

Suddenly she forgot all about Ruta and her failed stakeout. 'Rick Wild sent you to see me?'

'That's correct.' The man cleared his throat. 'We understand you've been making certain allegations regarding your relationship with Mr Wild?'

'You mean the story in the paper?'

The man nodded. 'As you can imagine, our client was understandably concerned to find out about these allegations. He's requested that we deal with the situation.'

'Right. OK.'

She could hardly take in what they were saying, her mind was racing too fast. All she could think was that Rick Wild knew she existed.

And he'd sent his lawyers to see her. That must mean he wanted something. To meet her, maybe? She tried to put a lid on her excitement and tell herself she mustn't expect too much, but all the time she couldn't help thinking . . .

'. . . and with that in mind, our client has authorised us to make an offer of remuneration on condition that there be no more claims on your part, now or at any future time.'

It took a second to register what he was saying. When she did, it was like having a bucket of cold water emptied over her. 'Let me get this straight,' Lola said. 'You're offering me money to go away?'

The lawyers looked at each other. 'Our client appreciates that this situation may have caused you considerable distress and embarrassment. He would just like to compensate you in some way. Of course, this in no way constitutes any acceptance of blame, liability or—'

'How much are we talking about?' Lola interrupted him.

'Excuse me?'

'How much cash does he want to give me?'

The older man looked uncomfortable. 'The sum in question is negotiable, depending on what we feel to be necessary and appropriate at the time.'

Lola was silent, taking it in. So he was willing to pay as much as it took for her to stay out of his life.

'Of course, any offer is subject to a DNA test

55

being carried out to establish the validity of your claim,' the lawyer went on.

'Forget it,' Lola said.

The lawyers exchanged an anxious look. 'You do realise that without a test you'll have no claim on our client?'

'Tell your client I don't want his test and I certainly don't want his money.'

She started to walk away. She felt like crying, she was so angry and humiliated.

'Wait.'

She glanced over her shoulder. A woman had stepped out of the back of the silver car. She was shorter than Lola, even in her shiny killer heels, her black designer suit packed with powerful curves.

Lola stood her ground and eyed her with suspicion as she approached. 'Who are you?'

'I'm Dinah Abraham, Rick's manager.' Her accent was no-nonsense New York. Her face was more striking than beautiful, strong-featured, her pale skin contrasting with her sharp black bob, crimson lips and shrewd dark eyes.

Those eyes were fixed on her now, assessing her. 'So you're Rick's daughter,' she said.

'Not unless the DNA test says so, apparently.'

'Oh, I don't think we need one of those. I only have to look at you.' She scanned the street. 'Is there someplace around here we could talk?'

'I don't think we've got anything to say to each other.'

'Maybe not. But I'm dying for some coffee, and I hoped maybe you'd keep me company. If you've nothing better to do?'

Lola looked back towards the high-rise estate.

56

There wasn't much chance of Ruta coming back. 'It doesn't look like it,' she said.

They went back to the greasy spoon. Dinah's designer suit looked out of place among the workmen's scruffy clothes, to say the least.

'Well, this is . . . unusual,' she said, polishing a spot of dried egg off the table.

The large woman scowled when she saw Lola. 'Another tea?' she said.

'And a bacon sandwich.'

Dinah smiled hopefully. 'I don't suppose you do soya latte?' The woman's brows lowered threateningly. 'I guess not. I'll just have a straight coffee. Black, no sugar.'

Lola forced herself not to smile. She had no reason to be friendly to Dinah. She guessed she was only trying to win her over because the lawyers hadn't managed to scare her off.

'I suppose you've been sent to make the problem go away?' she said.

'Pretty much.' Her frankness took Lola aback. 'To be honest, I've been making Rick's problems go away for ever. But every time I get rid of one, another comes along.'

Lola itched to ask about him, but wouldn't let herself.

The woman brought their drinks over. Lola stirred three sugars into her tea. 'Have you worked for him long?' she asked finally.

'Twenty-five years. If I'd killed somebody I'd be out of jail in less time.'

Lola glanced at Dinah's hands, perfectly manicured and heavy with rings. She wondered if those duck egg diamonds were real. 'It must be quite a glamorous job.'

'Oh, sure. Like when you're stuck in Tokyo at midnight and they've screwed up your hotel reservation and you've got to find rooms for a hundred people and you don't speak a word of Japanese. And those are the good days.' She smiled. 'I'm kidding. It's not that bad. Easier than being married to him, anyway.'

Lola looked up sharply. 'You and Rick were married?'

'For eight years. I was wife number two.'

Lola took in the information. So she must have come along after Rick split with her mother. 'Any children?'

'One daughter. Tiffany. She's twenty-three.'

Of course. Lola wanted to knock her head against the table. Why hadn't she made that connection before? Tiffany Wild was one of the LA brat pack, a real party girl who spent her life shopping and clubbing. A total waste of space, in other words.

Dinah sipped her coffee and grimaced. 'Ugh, instant. When will you guys learn to make decent coffee?'

'When you learn to make decent tea?'

Dinah peered at the mahogany brew in Lola's mug. 'You call that decent?'

'Maybe not.' Lola fought the urge to smile again. She picked the rind off her bacon. 'How did you two meet?'

'I was working for their record company in New York. I was given the job of going with Poleaxe on their first US tour, to keep them out of trouble. Some hope!' She smiled at the memory. 'They were just hitting the big-time, but I found out they weren't making a bean thanks to their shitty manager Brian Reed. I realised I could do better, and told them so.'

'And they took you on?'

'They couldn't afford not to. My family had been in showbiz management for years, so it was in my blood. By the time I was fifteen, I could read the small print on a contract like most other teenagers read fan mags. Brian Reed was strictly small-time; he didn't have the balls to stand up to the record company or the tour promoters. I did.'

Lola regarded her across the table. She could imagine Dinah steamrollering her way into the band's lives, flattening anyone who stood in her way. She had so much drive and confidence.

But Lola wasn't about to be steamrollered. No way.

'Why did you and Rick split up?'

'The usual story. Rick can't stay faithful for more than five minutes. It was OK at first because I was on the road with him the whole time. But after Tiffany was born I had to take some time off, and he went back to his old tricks. I decided I didn't want to be humiliated any more, so I called it a day.'

'But you stayed on as his manager?'

'Why not?' She shrugged. 'Rick Wild might be a lousy husband and human being, but he's one hell of a rock star.' She pointed her spoon at Lola. 'OK, we've had the twenty questions about me. Now it's your turn.'

'There's nothing to tell.'

'I bet there is. You seemed pretty determined you didn't want that DNA test. Why?'

Lola's chin lifted. 'I don't have to prove anything.'

'You do if you want to get your hands on Rick's cash.'

'Who says I want his cash?'

'Then what do you want?'

Lola took a bite of her bacon sandwich. That was a good question. She didn't think she wanted anything. But she'd been startled by her own reaction when those lawyers turned up. For a split second she'd had this crazy idea . . .

She pushed the thought away. 'I don't want anything,' she said flatly.

'So why did you go to the papers?'

'I didn't.'

'Someone did.'

'I didn't ask them to do it. I didn't,' she insisted, seeing Dinah's sceptical face. 'The first I knew about it was when a pair of reporters turned up on my doorstep, pointing a camera in my face.'

Dinah's mouth twisted. 'You're seriously expecting me to believe that you didn't hope to make something out of this? Come on! I bet you thought you'd won the lottery when you found out. Your dad, one of the richest men in rock? And you, stuck here in some deadbeat neighbourhood, scratching out a living as a cop . . .'

Lola threw down her sandwich. 'I may not be dripping in diamonds, but at least I'm doing something worthwhile. It's better than babysitting a bunch of overpaid, egotistical rock stars. How dare you look down your nose at me for what I do, when your daughter spends her whole life shopping and falling out of nightclubs?'

Dinah's eyes flashed. 'Now you listen to me—'

'No, you listen to me. This may come as a shock to you, but I don't want anything to do with Rick

Wild, or his money. I've got no intention of bothering him—or you.' She stood up, pushing her chair back. 'So you can go and tell him I won't be expecting any Christmas or birthday presents from him. Ever.'

The cold air hit her after the steamy fug of the café. She heard Dinah's high heels tapping on the street behind her, but she didn't look back.

'So you don't want to meet him, then?' Dinah called after her.

'That's not going to happen, is it? You've already made that very clear.'

'I've changed my mind.'

Lola stopped in her tracks and looked back at her cautiously, sensing a trick. 'I don't get it.'

'I think it would be good if you met your father. I certainly think it would do him good to meet you. So what do you say? He's had to go back to the Bahamas to remix one of the album tracks. I could fly you out there next week, if you like?'

Lola's heart started to race with panic. 'I'm not sure. It's a big step. I don't think I'm ready—'

'Think about it.' Dinah handed her a card. 'Here's my number. Call me if you decide you want to go.'

*   *   *

'So how much did you have to pay her?' Dinah's assistant Carlos asked slyly when she got back into the car.

'I didn't.' She closed the car door. 'But I need you to book me a ticket to Nassau for next week. First class. On second thoughts, better make that two.' She was bound to want to bring a friend with

61

her for moral support.

Carlos looked excited. 'Are we going to the Bahamas?'

'Uh-uh. *We're* going back to New York. This is for Rick's daughter.'

'I don't get it,' Carlos frowned. 'I thought you were supposed to get rid of her?'

'I was.' She'd had every intention of making the problem go away with a big fat cheque. But that was before she'd met Lola.

'Rick won't like it.'

'He can damn well put up with it.'

She watched Lola, still standing on the pavement, staring down at the business card she'd given her. She was quite a girl. Feisty, proud, unspoilt. She also had the nerve to stand up to Dinah, and not many people could do that.

It *would* do Rick good to meet her, she decided. Maybe she could teach him a couple of things about real life.

Carlos tapped a note into his BlackBerry. 'Shall I call her with the details when I've booked the flights?'

'Wait until she calls us. She hasn't actually agreed to go yet.'

'You think she'll change her mind?'

'I'm sure of it.'

Lola Rose Lambert might insist she wanted nothing, but Dinah knew that wasn't true. She didn't want money, but she wanted a father.

Dinah only hoped she wouldn't be too disappointed.

CHAPTER EIGHT

'This is great, isn't it?' Sam reclined in her leather seat and sipped her champagne. 'I've never flown first class before. I could get used to it.'

'I'm glad you're enjoying it.' Lola stared out of the tiny window. Bright sunshine pierced the clouds, flooding the cabin with light.

She felt sick to her stomach. She hadn't been able to face any of the free champagne, and barely managed the complimentary pretzels.

Sam looked sideways at her. 'Are you all right? You've gone a bit green.'

'I'm just wondering what I'm doing here.' She wished she'd never let Sam talk her into it. But she'd been so excited by the idea of a free holiday in the Bahamas that Lola didn't have the heart to say no.

'We don't have to do this,' Sam said.

Lola smiled faintly. 'It's a bit late now, isn't it?'

'Don't you want to meet your dad?'

That was the million-dollar question. Part of her desperately wanted to meet him. But the other part was utterly terrified.

'What if he doesn't want to meet me?' she said.

'Why would he fly us all the way to the Bahamas if he didn't want to get to know you?'

'Hmm.' Deep down she couldn't help thinking it was all too good to be true.

Lola's stomach was in so many knots she could hardly take in the spectacular view as the plane banked over the stretch of jade and sapphire sea with its fringe of white beach, on its way to land.

There was no one waiting for them at the airport. They searched the crowds in vain for a sign with their name.

'You'd think they would have sent someone,' Sam complained, as they struggled to push their wayward luggage trolley through the arrivals hall.

Lola let out the breath she'd been holding ever since they passed through customs. She didn't know whether to be relieved or disappointed. Had she really expected Rick Wild to be standing there, holding up a sign with her name on it?

'Maybe they forgot.'

'Oh yeah. You'd really forget something like that, wouldn't you?'

The Bahamian heat hit them as soon as they stepped out of the air-conditioned airport. Lola peeled off her cardigan. Her linen dress was already sticking to her.

'Perhaps we should just find a hotel?' she suggested.

'No way. Call them and find out what's going on.'

'But I don't have the number.'

'Then call his manager.'

She tried Dinah's number but there was no reply. 'She must have her phone switched off,' she said, giving up.

'Then we'll take a cab.'

Lola was dismayed. 'Can't we just book into a hotel and sort this out tomorrow?' she pleaded. 'We can't just turn up on their doorstep.'

'We're not just turning up. They're expecting us, remember?'

Then why hadn't anyone come to meet them? It didn't look good, as far as Lola was concerned.

*   *   *

'There's something I've been meaning to ask you,' Sam said, as the cab crawled through the crowded streets of downtown Nassau. The palm-tree-lined streets seemed alive with people and colour, the sun sparkling on the pastel colonial buildings. A horse-drawn taxi clattered past, ferrying tourists. 'How do you feel about Brendan moving in? It wouldn't be for long,' she rushed on, before Lola could speak. 'We're saving up for a place of our own and it would really help if we could cut down on some rent. And it would be cheaper for you, too, if we split the bills three ways.'

Lola looked out of the window. A policeman was directing traffic at the side of the road, looking smart in a trim white jacket and pith helmet.

'Don't you think it might be a bit crowded?' she said.

'Honestly, you won't even know he's there.'

Apart from when I catch you at it on the sofa, Lola thought. She'd got used to reversing into every room, just in case.

But Sam looked so hopeful she didn't like to disappoint her. 'I suppose we could give it a try,' she agreed reluctantly. 'But I'm warning you, if I catch him using my home waxing kit on his back again, that's it.'

The cab headed south, hugging the coastline. The beachfront houses were brilliant against the clear blue sky, a paintbox of orange, yellow, purple and pink.

Sam wound the window down so the sea breeze ruffled her hair. 'Isn't this amazing?' she said

65

happily.

Lola smiled back. It was just a shame she felt too sick with apprehension to enjoy it.

They stopped on a lonely stretch of beach road. 'Can't go any further.' The driver pointed ahead of him. 'Private property.'

'What do we do now?' Lola asked, as they stood in the middle of the deserted road. On one side, the ocean crashed against the shore. On the other were flat, scrubby fields. The salt-tinged air felt warm against her face.

'Start walking, I suppose.' Sam picked up her suitcase. 'It can't be very far.'

Five minutes later they were still walking.

'They like their privacy, don't they?' Sam said.

'This is a joke. I don't even think there is a house. Why don't we just go back into town and try again tomorrow?' Lola pleaded.

'I don't know if you'd noticed, but we're in the middle of nowhere. We might as well keep walking.' She peered into the distance. 'I think I see a gate up ahead.'

'A gate? Terrific. Maybe there'll be a nice long drive on the other side of it.'

'Stop moaning.'

Sam was right. There was a pair of tall, white, wrought-iron gates ahead, with a towering wall on either side. CCTV stared down at them from high above.

Lola peered through the gates. On the other side were lush lawns and bushes of vivid purple, hot pink and scarlet. In the distance, she could hear the tinkle of a fountain.

Sam pressed the button on the complicated-looking intercom, and they stood expectantly facing the video screen, fussing with their hair. Nothing happened. She pressed it again.

'Doesn't look like anyone's home,' she said. 'Bit strange, isn't it?'

'It's bloody rude!' Lola was suddenly filled with anger.

'Lola—'

'But it is. We've come all this way and now this.' Not to mention getting herself all worked up over nothing.

Furious, she kicked out at the gates. They swung open a fraction.

Sam grinned at her. 'What do you know? They were open all the time.' She pushed the gate open.

Lola backed away. 'You're not going in?'

'Have you got any better ideas?'

Before she could reply Sam was already heading up the path. Lola had no choice but to follow.

They came to a low, beachfront house, its pale turquoise stuccoed walls blending perfectly with the ocean that stretched out beyond it. One wall was made of glass, and led out on to a terrace. Beyond that was a swimming pool surrounded by loungers.

'Wow,' Sam breathed. 'Talk about how the other half lives.'

They started towards the house, but the sound of frenzied barking stopped them in their tracks. A second later a huge hound came tearing around the side of the house, bearing down on them, all fangs and glowing eyes.

Sam started to run but Lola grabbed her. 'Stay still,' she hissed.

The dog stopped a few yards away, hackles raised, a warning growl low in its throat. Maybe,

Lola thought, standing still wasn't such a good idea.

'I want to pee,' Sam whimpered.

'Brutus!'

A dumpy, dark-haired woman in a white apron came out of the house on to the terrace, and glared at Lola and Sam.

'Who are you?' She grabbed the snarling hound by its collar, hauling it away. 'What do you want?' Her accent was thickly Mediterranean.

'I'm looking for Rick.'

'He's not here.'

Lola eyed the dog, which was straining against the woman's grasp. 'Do you know when he'll be back?'

'I know nothing. Now you go.'

'But you don't understand. I'm Lola Lambert. They're expecting me.'

The woman shook her head. 'We not expecting anyone. You trespass.'

'You've got it all wrong,' Sam put in. 'We were invited—'

'You trespass!'

Lola and Sam jumped, as the woman pulled a gun out of her overall pocket and aimed it at them. 'You go now, or I shoot.'

Lola eyed the gun nervously. 'I think she means it.'

'Tell her again who you are.'

'I don't think she really cares.'

'You go.' The woman waved her gun at them.

At that moment the straining dog sprang forward. As the woman struggled to hold him, the gun went off.

'Bloody hell!' Sam ducked.

'Now can we go?' Lola said, dragging her away.

'Couldn't we just ask if we can ring for a taxi?'

'*Now*, Sam. Before she blows our heads off.'

Lola started back down the path, Sam hurrying after her.

'This is crazy,' she said.

'You're telling me.' Lola didn't look back. She kept her eyes determinedly forward as she marched towards the gates. All she wanted was to keep walking and never turn back. She felt exhausted, terrified and utterly humiliated.

'We'll sort this out.' Sam jogged to keep up with her. 'We'll check in to a hotel and then try to call again.'

'No,' Lola said firmly. 'We'll go straight back to the airport and find out the time of the next flight back to England.'

'But you can't come all this way and not meet your father.'

'He's not my father!' Lola swung round to face her. 'And he obviously doesn't want to meet me. Why else would he leave that deranged woman and the Hound of the Baskervilles to greet us?'

'It was probably just a mistake.'

'The only mistake was me getting on that plane.'

She couldn't explain to Sam why she wanted to get away so badly. She didn't want to tell her that while they were arguing with the housekeeper from hell she was sure she'd seen a woman standing at the window, watching them.

* * *

The next flight back to England wasn't until the following morning, so they booked into a hotel in

69

downtown Nassau. They showered, changed and found a fish restaurant overlooking the harbour for dinner.

'This has been quite an experience, hasn't it?' Sam said, as they sat on the terrace and admired the cruise ships.

'Sorry to drag you all this way for nothing.'

'I wouldn't have missed it for the world. Although it might have been nice to meet a famous rock star.'

I'm not so sure about *that*, Lola thought. At that moment, Rick Wild was the last person she wanted to meet.

Even so, she half expected there to be a message waiting for them at the hotel when they got back. But there wasn't. Nor was anyone waiting for them at the airport the following morning.

'Are you sure you don't want to go back to the house and try again?' Sam said as they headed for the check-in desk.

'No way.'

She felt bitter and rejected. She'd put herself out there, made herself vulnerable, and had it thrown back in her face.

She wouldn't make that mistake again.

CHAPTER NINE

'Let me get this straight,' Dinah said. 'Your long-lost daughter came all the way from England to see you for the first time in her life, and you didn't show up?'

Another day, another country, another

70

argument. This time, they were in the Royal Suite at Claridges hotel in London. Poleaxe were doing a few days of press interviews and TV appearances before the launch of their album the following week.

Rick squirmed defensively. 'It wasn't my fault, OK? I got held up at the recording studio.'

'And *I* had to take Bjorn to the therapist,' Britt put in.

Dinah stared at her. 'You take your dog to a *shrink*?'

'Past life regression therapist,' Britt corrected her. 'We're working through Bjorn's trust issues.' She hugged the tiny scrap of white fur closer to her.

A kick up his canine ass would soon sort those out, Dinah thought, eyeing the tiny snapping teeth with dislike. Britt was unbelievable. Why couldn't she have a proper dog, instead of a rat with attitude?

'So you left your housekeeper to chase Rick's daughter off the premises at gunpoint?'

'Can I help it if Conchita's paranoid? Especially with this crazy Devoted Fan around at the moment.' She gave Dinah a meaningful look. 'Anyway, I told her this girl was coming. I guess her English isn't so good.'

'Says the Swedish meatball,' Dinah muttered.

She wouldn't have put it past Britt to tell Conchita to send Lola away. It wasn't just the maid who was paranoid; Britt couldn't stand any other woman within ten miles of her man. She only tolerated Dinah because she made them so much money, and knew too many secrets to be sacked.

She should have known that left to his own

devices Rick would make a mess of it. She'd wanted to be there herself but a last-minute meeting in LA had stopped her.

'Look, it's cool. What's the problem?' Rick lay on the sofa, flicking channels restlessly. 'We'll just make it some other time.'

'That's just it. She doesn't want to now.'

Dinah had been on the phone for two hours, apologizing her backside off on Rick's behalf. But still Lola refused to see him. Dinah didn't really blame her.

'There you go. Problem solved. How do you work this thing?' Rick punched a few more buttons on the remote, then threw it down in frustration. It bounced off the sofa and on to the floor.

'Allow me.' Dinah picked it up with a sigh, pointed it at the plasma screen and switched it on. 'There you go.' She offered him back the remote.

Rick folded his arms. 'Find me the football,' he said sulkily.

'Find it yourself.' Dinah dropped the remote on to the sofa beside him. 'And while you're at it, you can sort out this mess, too. I already have enough to deal with.'

The US tour was turning out to be a nightmare. The set was nowhere near finished, the promoters were squeezing them over ticket sales, the band were under-rehearsed, and her new tour manager had gone back into rehab before he'd even started the job.

Right now, Dinah felt like joining him.

'There's nothing to sort out.' Britt shrugged. 'If this girl doesn't want to see him, what can he do?'

Dinah ignored her and turned to Rick. 'You could go to see her.'

Rick dragged his eyes away from the TV screen. 'Are you serious? Do you know how busy I am? I've got all this press stuff to do, and rehearsals for the tour—'

'Don't bullshit me, Rick. I know your schedule better than you do. I also know you're flying out to LA to get your highlights done on Thursday.'

'That's different.'

'You're damn right. That's a complete waste of time, and this is a necessity.'

'Why are you so keen for him to meet this girl anyway?' Britt asked.

Dinah hesitated. The truth was, she felt responsible. She was the one who'd set this trip up, and she was the one who'd let Lola down. She was a nice kid and didn't deserve that.

'I just think it would be a PR disaster if you don't,' she said eventually. 'Think about it. What if Lola went to the press and told them what had happened. How do you think that would make you look?'

Rick frowned hard, a sure sign he was thinking. He punched a few more buttons on the remote control. 'Are you sure this thing's not broken?' he said finally.

Dinah rolled her eyes. His attention span would make a goldfish look like Stephen Hawking.

'I've cancelled your trip to LA,' she said. 'I've organised for the limo to take you up to Leeds instead.'

Rick shot her a mutinous look. 'Forget it. I'm not going.'

Dinah smiled sweetly. 'Then you can find yourself another manager, can't you?'

'What a dickhead.' Will was outraged when Lola told him about her wasted trip. 'I reckon you had a lucky escape. Who needs a father like that?'

'That's what I thought,' Lola agreed. But she couldn't help feeling sad, too.

'It's really got to you, hasn't it?' Will guessed.

'I just feel a bit of an idiot, that's all. I wish I'd never got on that plane.'

'Poor Lola. I hate to see you upset.'

He put his hand on her shoulder. Lola let it rest there awkwardly for a moment, then moved away on the pretext of putting some papers in the filing cabinet.

'Did you ever follow up that lead I gave you?' she asked, to distract him.

'What lead?'

'That girl I told you about. Ruta, the prostitute?'

'Oh, that. I haven't had time.'

Lola watched him flicking through the football results in the newspaper. 'But it might have been important.'

'And it might have been a dead end. We don't have the manpower to follow up everything.' He looked up. 'What's that noise?'

'Just kids playing around outside, I think.' She closed the filing cabinet drawer. 'Talking of manpower, have you heard anything about that CID job?'

'Hmm?'

'Do you know when they might be doing the interviews? I put my application in ages ago; I thought I might have heard something by now.'

Will went over to the window and craned his

74

neck to look down the street. 'What the hell's going on out there? It sounds like a riot.'

Lola knew when she was being distracted, and she wasn't about to fall for it. 'I know I shouldn't go on to you about it, but I just really want that job. You will let me know if you hear anything, won't you? Will?'

He didn't reply for a moment. Then he said, 'Lola, about your father—'

'Oh, him. He's not worth worrying about. I just want to forget he ever existed.'

'That might not be so easy.'

'Why not?'

'Because—' Will pointed out of the window '—a bloody great limo just pulled up outside.'

CHAPTER TEN

Lola watched Rick Wild step out of the limo, followed by a bulky, shaven-headed man. He was tall, long-legged and every inch the rock star in his jeans, suede jacket and mirrored shades, his tawny golden curls rippling.

A small crowd had gathered as the car pulled up. Limos weren't known in that part of Leeds unless they were bright pink with a drunken hen party falling out of them. The crowd went mad when he got out, shouting his name, mobile phones held up to snap a photo.

Rick acknowledged them all with a careless wave.

Panic surged through her. 'I don't want to see him.'

'It's a bit late now,' Will said. 'They're coming across the street.'

Lola thought fast. 'I've got an idea. Who's on the front desk?'

'Steve, I think.'

'Get him in here, will you? I need a big favour.'

*   *   *

Police stations always made Rick Wild nervous. They reminded him of Poleaxe's early days when the band was always getting busted. Sometimes he'd wondered why they wasted money on hotels when they so often spent the night in a cell.

He stayed outside for as long as he could, mindlessly signing autographs, stalling for time. He wasn't looking forward to this. Emotional scenes always made him edgy. And, after all these years, the kid was bound to hold a grudge. He wished he'd never let Dinah talk him into it. He was sure she was only doing it to piss him off.

He switched on his best rock star smile to pose with a girl while her friend took their photo.

She was bound to want to talk about her mum, too. Probably wanted to hear it was the romance of the century, or something. Rick wished he could tell her what she wanted, but he'd been racking his brain and still couldn't remember a thing about her.

At least he had his back-up plan. He felt in his pocket for the Tiffany box. A tiny diamond on a chain, not too showy but enough to make her feel like he cared.

A girl pushed her way to the front. 'Can I have your autograph?' she asked.

'Sure. What do you want me to sign?'

'These.' The girl yanked up her T-shirt, revealing an enormous pair of silicone-enhanced boobs.

Rick took a moment to admire them while he uncapped his pen. 'Not bad.'

Anyway, he thought as he scrawled his name, he'd give her the present, spend half an hour listening to her troubles, then he'd be gone. The kid would be happy, Dinah would be happy, and they could all get on with their lives.

No problemo.

The girl pulled down her top and gave him a big French kiss. Then she handed him a piece of paper with her phone number scribbled on it.

Rick waited until she'd gone, then passed it to Gus, his minder. 'One for you,' he said.

'Not your type?'

He shook his head. 'Too cheap.' He stared up at the grim, 1970s police station. 'Let's get this over with,' he said.

It took a long time for anyone to come to the front desk. Rick stood with his hand pressed on the buzzer for a full five minutes before the guy came out of the back room.

'Can I help you?'

'I'm here to see Lola Rose Lambert.'

'Is she expecting you?'

Rick smirked at Gus. 'I doubt it.'

'And who shall I say is calling?'

Rick stared at him. Was he serious? 'My name,' he said slowly, giving it time to sink in, 'is Rick Wild.'

He waited for the flicker of recognition, the embarrassed laugh, the apology. But the guy just scribbled it down on a piece of paper, said, 'I won't be a moment,' and disappeared into the back room.

A few minutes later, he returned. 'I'm afraid PC Lambert's been called out to deal with an emergency. Perhaps you'd like to wait for her?'

Rick could feel himself hovering on the brink of a major tantrum. The pressure was building up inside his head, making his ears buzz. He thought about walking out, then remembered the hard time Dinah would give him.

'Sure,' he said, through gritted teeth. 'Why not?'

He went to sit on one of the benches but the policeman said, 'Maybe you'd be more comfortable waiting somewhere private? People come through here all the time and we wouldn't want you being pestered.'

Rick smiled. So the guy *did* recognise him. He could feel his bad mood ebbing away. 'That would be great,' he said.

The policeman opened a side door to let him through, but barred the way to Gus. 'Sorry, you'll have to wait outside.'

Gus squared up to him. 'I go where Mr Wild goes. It's my job to protect him.'

'This is a police station, pal. He's hardly going to need protecting in here, is he?'

'Man's got a point,' Rick drawled. 'Why don't you wait outside?'

'But Dinah said—' Gus started to argue, then gave up. 'I'll be in the car,' he said.

'Go and grab something to eat. I'll call you when I'm ready to leave.'

The policeman led the way down a corridor with doors on either side.

Rick laughed uneasily. 'Where are you taking me? The cells?'

'Not quite.' He opened a door marked 'Interview Room 3'.

Inside, it was small, dingy and windowless, the air thick with the stale smell of sweat. The only pieces of furniture were a couple of hard chairs, a table and a tape recorder. A fluorescent tube light flickered and buzzed overhead.

Rick took a step backwards. 'Maybe I'd be better waiting out front after all?'

'You'll be more comfortable in here.'

'I seriously doubt that.'

The policeman didn't crack a smile. 'I'll tell PC Lambert you're here the minute she gets in,' he said. Then he left, the door clanging ominously behind him.

Rick sat down on the hard chair, put his feet up on the table, and waited.

And waited. And waited. Fifteen minutes, then half an hour.

OK, that's it, he thought. He'd done his best. Even Dinah couldn't give him a hard time over this. Rick stood up and went to leave. The door was locked.

'Hey!' He banged on it with his fist. 'What's going on?'

No reply. He put his ear to the door. Nothing. It sounded as if everyone had packed up and gone home.

'A joke's a joke. Now let me out of here.'

Still no response. This was beginning to get scary.

He took out his mobile phone to call Gus. Or Dinah. Or anyone who could get him out of this hell hole.

No signal.

Damn. He paced the room, trying to think. Mainly about who he could sue when he got out.

Meanwhile, the minutes kept ticking by. Forty, fifty, an hour . . .

This was crazy. They couldn't keep him here for ever. Sooner or later someone would come looking for him.

He picked up a chair and threw it at the door. 'Open up! This is a violation of my human rights. If you don't let me out right now, I am going to personally make sure you all—'

He didn't get to finish his threat because a moment later the door opened and she walked in.

The first thing that struck him was the physical resemblance. Dinah was right; he didn't need a DNA test. It was right there, in the golden hair and those green eyes.

But she was different, too. He couldn't work out why. Maybe it was just the uniform.

'Hello,' she said. 'I'm Lola Lambert.'

She shook his hand. Her handshake was firm, no nonsense.

He struggled for something to say. 'You kept me waiting quite a while,' he managed at last.

'Did I? Sorry.' She bent down and picked up the chair he'd just thrown across the room. 'At least I turned up in the end. It would have been terrible for you to come all this way for nothing, wouldn't it?'

Suddenly he got it. This was payback time. Yeah, well, he'd let her have that one.

'I guess it would,' he agreed.

There was a silence. Rick was no expert, but he

sensed he was expected to say something.

'Too bad we didn't manage to hook up in the Bahamas,' he said. 'I got called back to the studio to deal with a problem on the album.' She was silent. 'I hear you got a lousy welcome from our housekeeper, too. We've been having some trouble with fans turning up, and I guess the staff are a bit paranoid.'

'That's putting it mildly.'

'Anyhow, by the time I'd got back from the studio you were already gone.'

'So why didn't you try to find me?'

That took him aback. 'How could I? The Bahamas is a pretty big place.'

'You could have called the local hotels. Or checked what time the next flight to England left, and found out if I was booked on it.'

'I didn't think of that. Hey, you're the police lady, not me.'

'You don't have to be a police officer to have common sense.'

'I'm a rock singer, baby. I pay people to think for me.'

It was a joke, but she didn't laugh. She just went on staring at him with that direct gaze of hers.

He got the feeling she was distinctly unimpressed by him. Well, it was mutual, he thought defiantly. She had way too much attitude for his liking. Women weren't supposed to answer him back. Except for Dinah, and that was only because he paid her to give it to him straight. But obviously no one had told Lola that.

She faced him now, her arms folded across her chest. 'Well?' she said.

'Well what?'

'What did you want to see me for?'

'I thought you wanted to see me.'

'No, I didn't. I made that clear to your manager.'

A weird sensation crept up his neck and into his face. To his horror he realised he was blushing. 'I . . . um . . . thought it might be cool to talk.'

'What about?'

'I don't know. Anything you like.' Damn, this was excruciating. He was beginning to think he preferred being locked in on his own. 'Do you want to ask about your mum?'

'Do you remember her?'

'Not really.'

'Not much point in me asking then, is there?'

He opened his mouth and closed it again, completely wrong-footed. 'I guess not.'

Another silence. He could feel the sweat breaking out on his brow.

He tried again. 'I guess it must have been a real shock for you, finding out your father was a rock star?'

'You could say that.'

'Kind of neat, though, huh?'

'You think so?' There it was again, that shrewd look that cut him down to size.

'Are you a fan of Poleaxe?'

'I don't know much about them.'

'You mean you've never heard "Love in a Parking Lot"? "Bang Me Up, Baby"?'

She shook her head. 'I'm more of a Celine Dion girl myself.'

He stared at her. Was she joking? It was hard to tell what was going on behind that enigmatic expression of hers.

'Are you sure you're really my kid?' he frowned.

'You tell me.'

He fiddled with his lighter. He was desperate to smoke, but he'd left his cigarettes in the car.

'Look,' Lola said finally, 'let's be honest, shall we? You don't really want to be here, do you?'

'That's not true!'

'So this wasn't all Dinah's idea?'

'I . . . she might have suggested it.'

She nodded. 'I thought so. So now you've done your bit, you've been here, we've met. Now we never have to see each other again.'

She went to the door and held it open. Rick looked at it, then back at her. 'So that's it?'

'I think we can live without each other, don't you?'

She shook his hand again, said goodbye, and a few minutes later he was back out in the street.

Gus closed in on him straight away. 'I was getting worried. What happened, boss?'

'I don't really know.'

He stared back at the police station. He had the bad feeling he'd been sent packing.

Damn nerve! No one gave Rick Wild the kiss-off. He was the one who always left them wanting more, not the other way around.

He stuffed his hand in his pocket. The Tiffany box was still there. He thought about going back inside to give it to her, then changed his mind.

'C'mon,' he said. 'Let's get out of here.'

*   *   *

'How did it go?' Dinah asked when she called the hotel later.

'She kept me waiting a goddamn hour before

she'd even talk to me. I've a good mind to sue her for wasting my time.' Now he'd had time to think about it, he was even angrier. 'I never, ever want to see her again.'

Dinah chuckled on the other end of the line. 'She's quite something, isn't she?'

'She's a nightmare. It's like my DNA has been mixed with the Terminator. And d'you know what? She doesn't even like my music!'

'Wow. You're right, she *is* a nightmare.'

Rick frowned. He was never sure if Dinah was making fun of him or not. 'So I was thinking, maybe you should invite her along to the album launch,' he said.

'I thought you didn't want to see her again?'

'I don't. But no kid of mine is going to be a Celine Dion fan.'

CHAPTER ELEVEN

A week later, Sam and Lola were in London.

'I can't believe we're really here,' Sam squealed as they got out of the cab in Leicester Square. It was nine o'clock in the evening and the neon-lit square was buzzing.

'Neither can I,' Lola said. She still couldn't work out how it had happened. When Rick left the police station that day, she was absolutely certain it was the last they were going to see of each other. Then Dinah had phoned to invite her to the launch of Poleaxe's new album, *Bleeding Heart*.

'Rick's very keen to see you again,' she'd said.

Lola seriously doubted that. They'd made a

pretty bad impression on each other at their first meeting. She half regretted giving him such a hard time, but then she decided he'd deserved it. She'd never met anyone so full of himself.

In the end it was Sam who convinced her to go to London.

'Lola Rose Lambert,' she'd said sternly. 'Until this moment my only brush with fame was when my dad got me the Chuckle Brothers' autograph. If you don't let me have this chance to rub shoulders with the rich and famous, I swear I'll never speak to you again.'

And so here they were.

It took them a while to find the Magnum nightclub among gaudy bars, casinos and cinemas. They circled the square twice before they finally spotted the line of people snaking towards a discreet, darkened doorway.

Sam nearly hyperventilated with excitement as they swept past and headed for the front of the queue. The doorman checked their names on the guest list then lowered the red velvet rope and ushered them through.

'Ooh, I feel like Kate Moss,' she said as they handed their coats to the disdainful-looking cloakroom girl. Lola was too busy staring at everyone else. The women all seemed to be wearing chic black, while the men just looked plain scruffy. She felt as if she stood out for all the wrong reasons in her blue New Look prom dress.

Sam, as ever, had really gone for it in a sassy red mini-dress, fishnets and shiny high heels.

'We look like a couple of tarts,' Lola hissed.

'Perfect,' Sam said, fluffing up her hair.

The club was heaving. Record company and

media types jawed, while Z-list celebrities did their best to look bored. Rock music pumped like a heartbeat, rising up through Lola's feet and shaking her fillings.

A scantily-clad waitress skimmed by with a tray of blood-red cocktails. Lola took one; Sam had two.

Lola eyed hers suspiciously. 'What's in it, do you think?'

'Only one way to find out.' Sam tipped her head back and downed it in one. She paused for a moment, waiting for it to take effect, then shrugged. 'Whatever it is, it's nothing two Leeds lasses can't handle.' She held up her other glass. 'Cheers.'

Lola grinned, and downed hers, too. 'I don't see the band,' she said afterwards.

'If they're here, they'll be in the VIP area.' Sam craned her neck to look. 'Nope, no sign. But I do see the winner of last year's *Big Brother*.'

'There was no sign of Dinah, either. Lola was disappointed. She'd started to like her. Straight-talking and no nonsense, she was just like Lola.

For the next half an hour, they almost forgot why they'd come. They drank more cocktails, danced, and flirted with a couple of children's TV presenters.

Then, suddenly, the music went down, the lights went up, and the band walked in to a round of applause, followed closely by their entourage of wives, girlfriends and assorted hangers-on.

As they headed for the VIP area, Sam whispered a quick commentary in Lola's ear. 'The one in front is Jonno Jones, the drummer. Absolutely mental, apparently,' she hissed, as a stocky man with manic eyes and a bushy black beard lumbered past them. He was followed by a slight, sandy-haired man with a vacant expression. 'That's their bassist, Simon Monroe. And the dark-haired one's Kyle Stern, their lead guitarist.'

'He looks a lot younger than the others,' Lola commented. He didn't seem much older than her.

'He's only been with the band a few years. Ooh, and there's Rick.' She nudged her.

The applause grew louder as Rick Wild loped across the room. He was dressed all in black, from his tight leather trousers and T-shirt to his cowboy hat. Lola hated to admit it, but he had more charisma than all the rest of the band put together.

'I'm really sorry, Lola, but I think I fancy your dad,' Sam whispered. 'How wrong is *that*?'

She wasn't the only one, Lola thought. Every woman in the room seemed to have their eyes fixed on Rick. Including, she noticed, the tall, frosty-looking blonde behind him. She was the same height as Rick, long-legged and slender in a chic cream trouser suit.

'That's Britt Petersen-Wild,' Sam said. 'Your stepmother,' she added mischievously.

'The wicked variety, by the look of her.'

'She's a supermodel. Or she was, until she married Rick. Now I suppose she just shops all day.' Sam sighed with envy.

Britt scanned the room, and caught Lola's eye. They locked stares for a moment, then she looked away.

It was the woman she'd seen at the villa in the Bahamas. Lola watched her sashaying through the crowd after Rick. Why had she allowed the housekeeper to turn her away?

Sam grabbed Lola's arm. 'Let's go and say hello.'

'We can't go in the VIP area.'

'You're Rick Wild's daughter. You can go wherever you like.'

She was already elbowing her way through the crowd. Lola followed reluctantly, convinced they wouldn't be allowed inside. But Rick's minder, the bulky man she'd seen with him in Leeds, let them straight through.

'You see?' Sam smiled. 'What did I tell you?'

The VIP area was all subdued lighting, black leather padded walls and red velvet seats. Sam headed straight for Rick, Lola trailing behind. He was in the corner with Britt, clutching a can of Coke and looking hacked off. They seemed to be having a row.

Sam called his name and he turned. He looked blankly at Lola and, for a moment, she was afraid he'd forgotten who she was.

Then he grinned. 'Well, look who it is. I thought you'd decided we weren't going to see each other again?' His voice was as she remembered: flat Estuary English mingled with a twangy American drawl.

'My friend wanted to come,' Lola said defensively.

'Yeah, right. That's a hundred dollars Dinah owes me.' He looked around. 'Where is she, anyway?'

'She's on her way. She called to say her meeting was running late,' Britt said.

Lola frowned. 'You had a bet with Dinah?'

'A hundred bucks that you wouldn't come. Man, she's going to be spitting. She hates losing more than I do.'

He looked so pleased with himself that it dawned on Lola his grin was more to do with him getting one over on his manager than seeing her again.

'And who's this?' He turned his attention to Sam.

'This is my friend, Sam Evans.'

Sam looked as if she was just about ready to burst with excitement. 'Can I have your autograph?' she blurted out.

'Babe, you can have whatever you want.'

She giggled like a schoolgirl. Lola cringed. Oh God, he's hitting on my best friend, she thought.

She turned to Britt, who was glaring at Sam as if she wanted to smash her glass in her face.

'And is this your wife?' she asked, to distract him.

'Oh, yeah. This is Britt.' Rick waved his hand carelessly in her direction, his hungry gaze still fixed on Sam's cleavage.

It was as if a light had gone on behind Britt's eyes. Suddenly she was all smiles. 'I'm so pleased to meet you at last,' she purred in a seductive Swedish accent. That's not how it seemed in Nassau, Lola thought. Close to, Britt was ethereally beautiful, her pale blonde hair drawn back to reveal an amazing, luminous face, a wide, sexy mouth and cheekbones to die for. But there was no warmth in those ice-blue eyes.

'Haven't we met before?' she asked, testing her.

Britt's smile didn't waver. 'I doubt it. Perhaps you remember me from my modelling days? Although I don't know if you read fashion magazines . . .' Her gaze flicked dismissively over

Lola's dress.

'I'm sure it was more recently than that.' Lola pretended to ponder. 'For some reason I keep thinking of Nassau. But of course, you weren't there, were you?'

'No, I wasn't,' Britt said firmly.

Before Lola could say any more they were interrupted by a middle-aged man. He looked like all the other media types in his Gap casuals and scruffy leather jacket.

He went straight up to Rick and held out his hand. 'Hello, Rick. Remember me?'

Rick was already clasping his hand when he looked into his face. 'Sorry, have we met?' he asked blankly.

'John Henderson. I used to be on *NME*, back in the seventies. I was the one who gave you your big break, remember?'

Rick's smile froze. 'John?'

'Just thought I'd drop by to see how you're getting on. Catch up on old times.' His voice was quiet, friendly even. But something about him sent warning prickles up Lola's spine. She looked around for Rick's minder but there was no one standing at the entrance to the VIP area.

'You've done all right for yourself, haven't you?' He looked around. 'Really made the big time. Hard to believe you and Terry used to practise in that garage back in Borehamwood all those years ago. I wished I'd kept some of those tapes you sent me. I bet they'd be worth a fortune now.'

Even in the semi-darkness, she could see Rick turn pale. 'What do you want?'

'Like I said, just to catch up on old times, and congratulate you on your success. It's just a pity

Terry's not here to enjoy the fame and fortune too. But I guess it didn't work out, did it? He just got left behind.'

'I—'

'Do you ever miss him, Rick?'

Lola caught the look of panic in Rick's eyes. Without thinking, she stepped forward. 'Sorry to break up the reunion, Rick, but you promised to pose for some photos with Sam and me?' she said.

He stared at her, dazed. 'Huh?'

'Those photos you promised us?' she prompted him. 'Can we do them now? Only Sam and I are leaving in a minute.'

'Are we?' Now it was Sam's turn to look dazed.

John Henderson smiled nastily. 'Mustn't keep your adoring public waiting, must we?'

Lola took Rick's arm and propelled him away from the man towards a door leading off from the VIP area. As they went she heard the man call out, 'We must keep in touch, Rick. It's been way too long.'

As he turned to go, she spotted Rick's minder ambling back through the crowd towards the VIP area. Lola left Rick with Britt and Sam, and went over to him.

'See that guy over there?' She pointed at the man's departing back. 'Can you make sure he leaves?'

The minder peered. 'Who is he?'

'I don't know. But I don't think Rick wants him around.'

His thick brows drew together. 'Leave it to me,' he grunted, and shouldered his way back into the throng.

Lola went back to find Rick. He was in the small

room next to the VIP area. It was lushly furnished in boudoir style, with a black velvet chaise longue and an ornate gold and marble dressing table. Rick was sprawled on the chaise longue, looking sullen, while Britt tried to comfort him.

Sam came over to Lola. 'What was that all about?'

'God knows.' She nodded towards Rick. 'Has he said anything?'

'Only swear words. I don't think he's in a very good mood.' Sam looked around. 'You do realise we're in the VIP room of the VIP room? I wonder what goes on in here?'

'I dread to think.'

Rick looked over and noticed Lola. 'You got rid of him?'

She nodded.

Britt looked from one to the other, clearly annoyed at being left out. 'Would someone mind telling me what's going on? Who was that man, Rick?'

'Just some nobody from way back.' But the look in his eyes told a different story. Whoever the mystery man was, he'd left Rick Wild very shaken.

The next second he was all bluster and bravado. 'How did he get in, anyway? Why didn't anyone check the guest list? Where was my security? Where's that bloody useless PR girl?'

Unfortunately for her, the very same PR girl chose that moment to stick her head around the door.

'Sorry to bother you, but I just wanted to remind you it's time for your speech,' she said.

Rick looked up. 'Speech? What speech?' he snapped.

The girl faltered in the face of his anger. 'You're due to say a couple of words with the head of Charisma Records.'

'Here's a couple of words for you: piss off.' He held up his can of Coke. 'Someone take this away and get me a real drink.'

Sam went to reach for it, but Britt waved her away. 'Baby, you promised,' she said in a low voice. 'You said you'd really try this time.'

'I don't feel like trying. And I don't feel like giving a speech, either.' He turned on the PR girl, snarling, 'You should be doing something useful, like checking the guest list instead of hassling me.'

'But it's in the schedule—'

'I don't care if it was written on tablets of stone. I'm not doing it.'

The girl bit her lip, near to tears. 'I don't understand—'

'He just needs a moment to get his head together,' Lola told her calmly. 'He'll be out in five minutes.'

'No, I won't. I told you, I'm not going anywhere. NOW WHERE'S MY DRINK?' he shouted.

There was an awkward silence while everyone quaked. The PR girl ran off. Sam went to get another cocktail. Britt fawned over Rick anxiously.

Only Lola stood over him, arms folded, distinctly unimpressed.

He looked up at her. 'What are you staring at?'

'You,' Lola said. 'I've never seen a grown man have a tantrum before.'

He opened his mouth to reply, but Britt got in first. 'Rick's been under a lot of strain lately,' she said, stroking his hair. 'You don't know what it's been like for him.'

'Oh yeah, I can imagine. Sunning yourself in the Bahamas and being taken to parties in limos must be sheer hell. I don't know how you cope.'

He chewed broodingly on his thumbnail and said nothing.

'Why did that man upset you so much?'

'I don't know what you're talking about. I'm not upset.'

'In that case, why won't you go and make that speech?'

'I told you, I don't feel like it. What does it matter to you, anyway?'

'Because I was brought up to believe that it was wrong to let people down.' She planted her hands on her hips. 'These people from your record company have all worked really hard for you. They're looking forward to seeing you. And that poor PR girl might lose her job if you don't show up.'

'Serves her right,' Rick growled.

'Five minutes,' Lola said. 'That's all they want from you. And I reckon they deserve it. Bloody hell, they pay you enough—'

'All right!' Rick stood up, nearly tipping Britt off the chaise longue. 'I'm going, OK? I'll make the damn speech, if it'll shut you up.' He jabbed his finger at her. 'But I don't want to hear another word out of you for the rest of the night. Understood?'

'You won't know I'm here,' Lola promised him solemnly.

He strode off, muttering, 'Bloody women, always getting on my case.' Britt followed him, leaving Lola alone in the room.

Or so she thought. She sat down on the chaise

94

longue to gather her thoughts, then heard a voice from the doorway.

'Very impressive.'

She looked up. Dinah stood watching her. She looked as if she'd come straight from the office in her trademark black suit, an oversized Hermès bag slung over her shoulder.

'How long have you been there?'

'Long enough. You did a great job handling Rick just then. I couldn't have done better myself. And believe me, I've had a lot of practice.'

She sat down at the dressing table and delved in her bag for her make-up. Lola watched her applying crimson lipstick.

'I pity you,' she said. 'It's like dealing with a five-year-old.'

'Oh, I don't know. It can be fun, too.' She caught Lola's eye in the mirror. 'Why don't you come on tour and find out?'

'What?'

'I'm looking for a tour manager. Would you like the job?'

'But I don't know anything about managing a tour.'

'It's basically what you've just done. Making sure the band are at the right place, at the right time. Sorting out problems, soothing ruffled feathers, massaging egos, kicking asses when necessary—the usual stuff.'

Lola watched her dusting powder on to her nose. 'I thought that was your job?'

'Most of the time. But I can't be on tour with them for three months. I've got other acts to look after. I need someone I can trust to look after the day-to-day stuff, make sure the crew gets paid,

95

organise the transport and the accommodation, check the venues and bank the money. You'd have someone to help you, of course. My accounts guy Hamish is a whiz with figures.' She snapped her compact shut and shoved it back into her bag. 'What do you think?'

Lola considered it for a full three seconds. 'I don't really fancy the idea of babysitting a band for three months.'

'Are you sure? It'd be a chance for you to get to know your father.'

That's what I'm afraid of, Lola thought. She'd already seen enough of Rick to know he was a big spoilt kid. He reminded her of a toddler who'd been allowed to gorge out on E-numbers and never heard the word no.

'Thanks, but no thanks,' she said. 'Anyway, I've already got a job. I'm expecting a promotion to CID soon.' She'd finally heard that her interview was in two days' time.

Dinah shrugged. 'Hey, I had to ask. I think you'd be perfect for the job.'

As they went to rejoin the party, Lola said, 'By the way, who's Terry?'

Dinah stopped dead. 'Why do you ask?'

'Some bloke burst in earlier. A journalist. He seemed to know Rick and Terry from way back. Rick got pretty upset.'

'I'm not surprised.' Dinah looked grim.

'So who is he?' Lola asked again.

Dinah sent her a steady look. 'Terry MacIntyre,' she said, 'is someone we never, ever mention.'

CHAPTER TWELVE

Two weeks on, and the reality of living with Brendan was beginning to sink in. It was bad enough that he'd cleared the bathroom shelves to make way for his vast array of cleansers, exfoliants and shaving balms, and left his toenail clippings scattered around the sitting-room floor. But when he re-set the DVD to record the Champions' League instead of the final episode of *Desperate Housewives*, Lola finally flipped.

'Maybe it's time I found a place of my own,' she said to Sam.

'You can't!' Sam was horrified. 'This is your home.'

Not since you two started practising for the sex Olympics next door, she thought.

'You two need your space.' Preferably soundproofed, with a reinforced mattress. 'Besides, if I get my own flat you'll have somewhere to take refuge when Brendan's hogging the remote control.'

But finding her own place was more difficult than she thought. After three days of scouring the 'To Rent' section of the local paper and trawling around potential flatshares, Lola was just about ready to give up.

'They're all either miles out of town, or a dump, or the person I'd be sharing with has serious mental health issues,' she sighed when she got into work after yet another wasted journey.

'I know somewhere you could try,' Will said. 'It's clean, modern and ten minutes' walk from here.'

'You're joking?' Lola looked up at him hopefully. 'Please tell me the current occupant isn't about to be sectioned?'

'I don't think so,' Will laughed. 'It's me.'

'You?'

'I've got a spare room you could have. It's pretty small, and I'd need to clear my junk out, but you're welcome to it.'

'Er . . .'

'I promise I wouldn't use your waxing kit. Not without asking you, anyway.'

'Don't you think it might be difficult, living and working together?'

He shrugged. 'We get on OK, don't we? Besides, it doesn't have to be for ever. Don't look so nervous. It's not like I'm asking you to marry me!' he guffawed, a little too loudly.

Lola was doubtful. Was it such a good idea? He was already persistent enough; if they were living together she might find it even more difficult to keep him at arm's length.

But then again, it had to be better than sitting on the sofa watching Sam and Brendan's Saturday night snogathon.

*   *   *

Sam was in tears as she watched Lola pack.

'I can't believe you're going,' she sniffed. 'It won't be the same without you.'

'At least you won't have such a long queue for the bathroom in the morning.' Although she didn't fancy Sam's chances against Brendan. He'd taken personal grooming to a tantric level. 'And you'll have Brendan to keep you company.'

'He's no fun,' Sam wailed. 'He doesn't have any clothes I can nick. And he hates *Deal or No Deal*. And he sulks when I lust after hot children's TV presenters. In fact, why am I even doing this?'

'Because you're in lurve?' Lola grinned.

Sam smiled shyly. 'Maybe.'

'Anyway, it's not like I'm going to the other side of the world,' Lola went on as she sorted through her CDs.

'I s'pose not.' Sam blew her nose. 'And it's nice that you're moving in with Will. Perhaps you two will finally get together now?'

'Oh no.' Lola piled her CDs into a box. 'Forget it. That's not going to happen.'

'Why not? He's nice.'

'I agree. But he's not my type.'

'Your type doesn't exist.'

'Maybe not.'

'You should learn to be less picky,' Sam advised. 'Then you might get someone like my Brendan.'

There was a pause while they both thought about what she'd said.

'That didn't come out right, did it?' Sam said.

No, Lola thought. But it was true all the same.

'Anyway, it's about time you found yourself a boyfriend,' Sam went on. 'I can't remember the last time you had one.'

'That's because I don't want one.'

She definitely wouldn't miss Sam's constant attempts to match-make.

'Will and I are just good friends,' she said primly.

Sam smiled. 'For now,' she said.

*   *   *

99

Obviously no one had told Will about being just good friends. When she took her stuff round to his flat that night, he was in the middle of cooking dinner.

'Sorry, are you expecting someone?' she asked.

'Only you.' He took the box from her. 'Here, let me carry that.'

She followed him into the flat, sniffing. 'It smells really good. What is it?'

'Pan-fried sea bass with lemon and garlic, dauphinoise potatoes and chocolate cheesecake to follow. Nothing special.'

Lola wondered if she should break it to him that she'd just shared a farewell pizza with Sam.

'You shouldn't have gone to so much trouble,' she said.

'Only the best for you.' Will dumped the box then headed for the kitchen. He was wearing a new shirt. She could tell by the fold creases down the chest. She felt scruffy in her house-moving outfit of jeans, sneakers and a faded Miss Piggy T-shirt.

'Make yourself comfortable. I'll bring you a glass of wine,' Will called out from the kitchen.

'Shouldn't I get the rest of my stuff in first?'

'We can do that later.' Will came out of the kitchen with the wine. 'Just relax,' he said.

It was easier said than done. Lola perched on the sofa and looked around the sitting room. It was bright, modern and unnaturally neat for a guy living on his own. Every surface was uncluttered, the cushions were plumped, and there was a smell of Jif and furniture polish in the air. Either Will was gay, or he was out to impress.

'Are you always this tidy?' she asked nervously.

'Pretty much.'

'That's bad news. I'm the world's worst slob.'

He stuck his head around the door, a pan in his hands. 'I'll just have to house-train you, won't I?'

'Good luck with that. It's taken Sam ten years to get me to pile the dirty dishes in the sink and not under my bed.'

Will went back to his cooking, leaving her to browse. What she saw made her feel nervous. A selection of smoochy soul CDs were piled up beside the hi-fi and there were candles on the coffee table, waiting to be lit. She had a bad feeling that if she went into Will's bedroom she would find a bottle of massage oil and a copy of the *Kama Sutra*.

She thought about texting Sam, asking her to call and say there was an emergency back at the flat.

'I see your family's in the headlines again,' Will called out over the sound of frying. 'Have you seen today's paper?'

She found it folded carefully in the magazine rack. She and Sam didn't even own a magazine rack.

She flicked through to the celeb gossip pages. Splashed right across the centre was a paparazzi snap of a skinny blonde, her mini-skirt around her hips, being hoisted into the back of a car by a pair of frowning minders.

Underneath the headline, 'rock princess back in rehab', Lola read:

LA party girl Tiffany Wild was admitted to the Sands rehab centre last night after her latest drunken binge resulted in two people being taken to hospital. The incident, which took place at the Whiplash nightclub, is understood to have involved Tiffany's on-off boyfriend, club owner Tony Sciotta, and her pal, actress Ashley Anderson. Starlet Tiffany, daughter of rock legend Rick Wild, was recently fired as the face of Go Girl cosmetics after allegedly turning up intoxicated to a photo shoot. Her publicist says she is 'suffering from nervous exhaustion'.

Lola closed the newspaper just as Will came in.

'Dinner's ready.' He nodded towards the paper. 'Sounds a real headcase, doesn't she?'

'I feel a bit sorry for her, actually,' Lola said as she followed him to the kitchen. 'It can't be much fun having every mistake you make splashed all over the tabloids.'

Her own brush with the press had been bad enough. She wouldn't be able to take the pressure of the paparazzi following her constantly.

'If you ask me, she loves the attention.' Will put the serving dishes in the middle of the table. 'Just think, if you'd taken that tour manager's job you would have been surrounded by nutters like that all the time. You've had a lucky escape, I reckon.'

Lola watched him light the candles and said nothing.

He topped up their wine, then sat down and held up his glass. 'I think we should have a toast, don't you?'

'To what?'

'How about . . . to us?'

He smiled at her in the flickering candlelight.

Help, Lola thought.

In LA, Dinah Abraham was having a hard time, too. Jonno, Poleaxe's drummer, had broken his finger throwing a bidet out of a hotel window. Bassist Simon had failed his life insurance medical because of all the Class A drugs in his system. And yet another potential tour manager had quit, this time over rumours that Rick had tried to bed his wife.

'Why?' she demanded when she confronted Rick. They were in the playroom of his mansion on Doheny Drive, a vast room full of boys' toys. Rick was practising his snooker trick shots. Britt, as usual, wasn't too far away, sunning herself on the terrace with Bjorn the dog. 'Why did it have to be *his* wife, of all people? You could find a woman anywhere. Where am I going to get a new tour manager?'

'Relax, it'll be cool.' He potted the black ball. 'Did you see that? Right off the red. Am I good, or what?'

'You're an idiot. You do realise this tour starts in a week?'

'Exactly. A whole week. That's seven days for you to get it all sorted.' He gave her a winning smile. 'You can do it, babe. You always do.'

Britt wandered in from the terrace, fastening a sarong over her narrow hips. 'I've consulted my psychic,' she announced. 'She said you should cancel the tour.'

'Oh well, that's it then.' Dinah said. 'I'll get right on the phone to the promoters, shall I? Tell them to cancel the venues and send all the ticket money back because your psychic reckons it's a bad idea.'

'I'm only telling you what she said,' Britt pouted. 'She says if you go ahead with this tour bad things will happen.'

'I've got news for her,' Dinah muttered. 'They already have.'

On the way back to her downtown office, Dinah called the Sands to check on Tiffany.

'She's proving slightly . . . resistant at the moment.' The therapist sounded harassed.

'In what way?'

'She set off the sprinklers during group therapy, and then we caught her trying to escape through a window.'

Dinah sighed. 'Take away her shoes. It's the only way you'll stop her.'

She hung up. She didn't need this. Why did Tiff have to choose now of all times to pull a stunt like this? If she wasn't working her ass off trying to organise the tour, she was tearing her hair out over her wayward daughter.

She checked her watch, then hit the speed-dial button on her phone.

Lola answered on the third ring. 'Hello?'

'Hey, how's it going?' Dinah did her best to sound bright and breezy and not at all desperate.

'OK, thanks. How are you?'

'Pretty cool.' She paused. 'I was wondering if you'd thought any more about the tour manager's job?'

'I'm sorry, the answer's still no.'

Shit. 'Are you sure? It would be an experience for you. And I'd double whatever you're getting now.'

'That's not the point—'

'Treble. How about that?'

Lola laughed. 'Are you desperate?'

'No, not at all. OK, I am. What do you say? Will you help me out? Please?'

'I can't. I'm sorry.'

But Dinah thought she heard a waver in her voice. She decided to go for it. 'Here's the deal. I'm buying you an airline ticket to Cincinnati. One way, leaving Friday. Just in case you change your mind.'

'I won't be there.'

'See you Friday,' Dinah said, and ended the call.

CHAPTER THIRTEEN

The thought of the airline ticket haunted Lola all through the following week. It haunted her even more on the Friday morning when she did her usual tour of the grey, overcast Creighton estate, rounding up the teenage truants making nuisances of themselves in the shopping precinct.

I don't have to do this, she reminded herself as she herded them towards the local comp. This time tomorrow I could be on tour with a rock band. She couldn't imagine what it would be like, but it had to be more glamorous than listening to abuse from a bunch of kids in hoodies.

It certainly had to be more glamorous than dealing with old Mr Finch. He was Creighton's local eccentric, an old man who filled his dilapidated council house with rubbish filched from bins. He could often be seen tramping the streets, pushing a shopping trolley full of his latest spoils. No one had ever seen inside his house, but the neighbours were constantly complaining about the smell, the marauding rats and other examples of Mr Finch's antisocial behaviour.

This morning Lola had received a call from the council. They were going to make yet another attempt to get into Mr Finch's property, and, from past experience, knew they would need back-up.

They were waiting for her in his overgrown front garden. The tangled patch of weeds was littered with a couple of broken bikes, an old pram with no wheels and a rusting lawnmower. The local kids had enthusiastically added takeaway cartons and empty beer cans to Mr Finch's rubbish collection

'We've been knocking for ten minutes, but we're not getting any answer,' the man from the council told her.

Lola picked her way up the path and peered through the letterbox. She nearly gagged on the smell of rotting rubbish. Piles of stinking carrier bags blocked the narrow hallway.

'Mr Finch? Mr Finch, it's PC Lambert. Can you open the door?'

'Go away,' came a muffled voice from deep inside.

'I can't, Mr Finch. Not until I've talked to you.' She glanced over her shoulder. They'd attracted quite a crowd of interested neighbours.

'Hang on,' one of the council men said. 'I think I see him at the upstairs window.'

Lola took a step back and looked up. One of the upstairs windows opened and Mr Finch stuck his grizzled head out.

'You're Nazis, the lot of you.'

'We just want to help you, Mr Finch. Please be reasonable.'

What am I saying? she thought. The man collects dog poo and old chip wrappers.

'Why don't you come downstairs and we'll—'

She didn't manage to say any more, as a torrent of cold, greasy water hit her full in the face, knocking her flat. A washing-up bowl hit the ground beside her, narrowly missing her ear. Then the window slammed shut.

Lola lay on her back among the rusting rubbish, dazed. She could hear the neighbours laughing behind her.

'You should be glad it was only washing-up water,' one of the council officials said. 'I've seen him throw much worse than that.'

She limped back to the station, wet and bedraggled. Luckily, Steve the desk sergeant was busy with a caller so she could sidle in without him making any jokes.

She headed for the locker rooms. As she passed the CID incident room, she heard laughter and loud voices.

She turned the corner and bumped into Will.

'Blimey, what happened to you? And what's that smell?' He sniffed the air.

'Don't ask.' She nodded towards the CID incident room. 'What's going on in there? It sounds like they're having a party.'

'They've finally made a breakthrough on the trafficking case.'

'No!' She forgot all about being soaked. 'What happened?'

Before Will could reply, Detective Inspector Marsh sauntered down the corridor towards them.

'Not joining the celebrations, Will?' He slapped him on the back. 'You should be in there, making the most of your big moment.'

'Big moment?' Lola said.

'We've got our man, thanks to Will here. If he hadn't found that prostitute and got her to talk, we would never have nailed him.'

'Is that right?' Lola stared at Will.

Will stared at his shoes. 'Well, um—'

'He's just being modest. Big Will here's our man of the match.'

'How did you find the girl?' Lola asked.

'I—'

'Good detective work,' the DI answered. 'That's what it's all about in this game. Will's got a good copper's instincts.' He frowned at Lola then, as if noticing her for the first time. 'You're wet.'

Nothing gets past you, does it? Lola thought. Must be those good copper's instincts.

'Better get yourself cleaned up,' he went on. 'And make sure you sort out that puddle on the floor before someone breaks their neck.' He turned back to Will. 'Coming in?'

Will eyed Lola nervously. 'In a minute, sir.'

'Don't let me keep you,' she muttered.

As she walked off, the DI called after her, 'And make sure you come back with that mop.'

Will caught up with her in the locker room. 'I'm sorry,' he said. 'I tried to tell them it was you who put me on to her.'

'Oh yeah?' Lola wrenched the door of her locker open. 'It looked like you were trying really hard.'

Will squared his shoulders defensively. 'I don't know why you're so moody about it. You only gave me the lead; I followed it up.'

'Only because I nagged you into it. You kept

telling me it was a waste of time, remember? So much for your good copper's instincts.'

'You're right. I'm sorry.' He looked downcast. 'I just got carried away. It's my first big case and I wanted to make a good impression.'

Lola sighed. There was no point in being furious with him. 'Just remember, you owe me one, OK?' she said. 'I expect you to pay me back when I join CID.'

Will stared down at his shoes again. 'I've been meaning to talk to you about that,' he mumbled.

Realisation hit her like a punch in the stomach. 'I haven't got the job, have I?'

'They gave it to a guy from Doyle Road nick. I'm really sorry, Lola, I did my best to put in a good word for you,' he gabbled.

'Like you tried to tell them it wasn't you who found that prostitute?' She looked at him shrewdly.

'That's not fair.'

'I don't suppose you know why I didn't get it? On second thoughts, I think I know. It's because I'm not a man, isn't it?'

Will's blushing face was the only answer she needed. 'You could apply for the next vacancy,' he said.

'I'd be wasting my time, wouldn't I?' She knew that now. No matter how hard she worked, or how many exams she passed, she would never get her transfer.

'I'm really sorry,' Will said.

'Forget it. At least I know where I stand now.'

'You're still a really good police officer.'

Good for what? Lola thought. For finding lost dogs and helping old ladies who'd locked themselves out? Good for getting filthy water dumped on her by mad old men? It might be worthwhile work, but it wasn't what she'd signed up for. She'd wanted to stretch herself, to do something really different.

And she'd never find that at Carlyle Street nick. If she really wanted to change her life, she would have to look further afield to do it.

Two seconds later, she'd made up her mind. 'I've decided I'm going to move out of the flat,' she told Will.

His mouth fell open. 'This job business wasn't my fault.'

'I know, and I'm not blaming you. But it's time for me to move on.'

And not just because of the job, either. In the last few days, Will had made it clear he had high hopes they'd get together. He wanted something she wasn't prepared to give.

'Where will you go?' Will asked.

She looked at her watch. 'Cincinnati,' she said. 'In about four hours' time.'

CHAPTER FOURTEEN

One day later, she found herself in the empty stands of a giant auditorium, watching the Poleaxe set take shape on stage.

High above her the riggers were working hard, pulling up lighting trusses, sound cabinets and giant video screens to the grids overhead. Below them, stagehands were shifting road cases of equipment, while others were running cables to the lighting, sound and pyrotechnics from the front-of-house console.

She still couldn't believe it was all real. The past twenty-four hours had been a blur. Throwing her stuff together, racing to the airport, being met by a limo and taken to a hotel . . . it wasn't the kind of thing that happened to a nice girl from Leeds.

She still couldn't believe she'd walked out of her job without working her notice, but at the time she'd been too angry to care. If they made any trouble, she'd take them to court for sex discrimination.

Sam would love this, Lola thought as she pulled out her phone to take a photo. It was about four o'clock in England. She could just imagine her sitting at her desk, looking at the clock, wondering if another Snickers bar would make the afternoon go faster. Then her mobile would beep and she'd get the shock of her life . . .

'No pictures!' a voice barked out. Lola looked up to see a man striding towards her. He was about thirty years old with unruly dark hair, and was wearing faded Levis, a Poleaxe T-shirt and a hacked-off expression.

'Sorry.' She slipped her phone back into her pocket. 'I didn't realise.'

'If you're looking for a tourist attraction, try the zoo.' He glanced at the laminated backstage pass around her neck. 'Who are you, anyway?'

She held out her hand. 'I'm Lola Lambert. The new—'

'Yeah, yeah, I've heard of you.' He had an English accent, but he wasn't exactly being friendly towards a fellow countryman. 'So you're the one who's going to be in charge of all this?'

Lola looked around the cavernous auditorium and took a deep breath to quell the quake of fear. 'It looks like it.'

'What kind of tours have you managed before?'

'Um, well, I haven't exactly—'

He frowned. 'You've toured with a band, right?' She shook her head, suddenly feeling very small. 'Do you know *anything* about the music business?'

'I've watched *The X-Factor*, if that helps?'

He didn't laugh. 'So how exactly are you qualified for this job? Oh no, don't tell me. You're Rick Wild's daughter. Silly question.'

Lola felt herself blushing. 'Maybe you shouldn't put me down until you've found out what I can do,' she said.

'I thought I'd get my criticism in first, before the rush starts.'

Lola sized him up quickly. So he was a bully. Well, she'd met a few of those during her time in the police; she wasn't going to let this one get the better of her.

'And who are *you*? Apart, obviously, from a world expert on everything.'

'I'm a backline tech.' He paused for a moment, then sneered. 'You don't know what that is, do you?'

'No, but I'm sure you'd love to put me straight.'

'I would, but I haven't got time. Some of us have a job to do.'

'Make the most of it,' Lola muttered. 'With an attitude like that you might not have one for long.'

His eyebrows rose. 'You're planning to fire me? Now that really would be funny.'

'Why? Do you think you're that indispensable?'

'Put it this way: I think they'd get rid of you

before me.' He glanced at his watch. 'Got to go,' he said.

You said it, Lola thought. As he walked away, she called after him, 'It was nice to meet you. Thank you so much for your encouragement and advice.'

'Here's some more: stay out of my way.'

'With pleasure.'

Lola watched him head towards the backstage area. Whatever a backline tech was, she hoped their paths wouldn't cross too often.

'I see you've met Jay.' Dinah came up behind her.

Lola glared in the direction of his retreating back. 'Are they all as friendly as him?'

'I'm afraid he does have a chip on his shoulder.'

'He's a nightmare.'

'He's also your brother.'

'*What*?' Lola's mouth fell open.

'His mother was Rick's first wife, Annie. His teenage sweetheart.' She smiled cynically. 'Until Rick made the big time, and then he dumped her. Jay was about four or five when they split up.'

'And he gave *me* a hard time for using family connections,' Lola murmured.

'I wouldn't say he and Rick are particularly connected.'

'Don't they get on?'

Dinah looked enigmatic. 'You'll find out. Now, why don't we talk about your job?' She reached into her briefcase and pulled out a stack of paperwork. 'As you can see, we're pretty much set up here. Hamish has already sorted out the PDs for today, so you won't have to worry about that.'

'Hamish? PDs?'

113

'Hamish is your assistant. He's also our accounts guy, computer whiz and all round general genius. You'll like him, he's English like you. Well Scottish, really, but it's kind of all the same, isn't it? Per diems are the daily allowance the band and crew get. You mess those up at your peril,' she breezed on, not waiting for a reply. 'Hamish can also sort out any day-to-day stuff here, like transport. All you need to do is make sure everything's set up for the next few gigs . . . Maybe you should be writing this down?'

Lola sat down on one of the empty seats, balanced the stack of papers on her knee and took a notebook out of her bag. 'Ready,' she said.

'You'll have to advance the show,' Dinah explained. 'That means calling the promoters and making sure all the riders are in place. You know what a rider is, don't you?'

'I've heard of them.' She remembered reading a piece in Sam's *Heat* magazine. 'They're all the weird things bands have written into their contract, aren't they? No blue M&Ms, white rose petals strewn around the dressing room, that kind of thing?'

'Dream on,' Dinah smiled. 'I think some artists go for that egotistical rubbish, but we usually stick to the basic stuff. Just make sure there are clean towels in the bathroom, plenty of vodka and Jack Daniel's, and somewhere for Jonno to snort his coke, and you'll be fine.' She grinned at Lola's shocked expression. 'And you'll have to sort out the technical rider, too. That means making sure they've got enough power at the venue to cope with our lighting and sound, checking the site catering and local crews are in place, that kind of thing.'

'Light and sound . . . catering . . .' Lola scribbled furiously. 'Anything else?'

'It wouldn't hurt to double-check on the hotels. The promoters are meant to do it, but sometimes they get it wrong. You really don't want to get there and find you've got nowhere to stay. And they can't just be any old rooms, either. Simon can't have a mirror at the bottom of the bed—bad *feng shui* apparently—Britt won't have anything but white flowers in their suite, and Jonno has to have a room as close to the ground floor as possible.'

'*Feng shui*?' Lola queried.

'He has a tendency to jump. Do you think you've got all that?'

'I hope so.' There was so much to take in; her head was already spinning.

'Fine. I'll let you get on with it, then. I'll be around today and most of tomorrow, then I have to head off for a meeting in London. But you can ask Hamish if you get stuck with anything.' She started to walk off, then turned back. 'Oh, I nearly forgot. Jonno's left his lucky sticks behind. You're going to have to track them down and get them sent over for tonight. He says he can't play without them.'

Lola scribbled another note. 'Where did he leave them?'

'Japan.'

She stopped, her pen poised, and stared at Dinah, who smiled back.

'Welcome to the wonderful world of rock 'n' roll, kid,' she said.

*　　*　　*

With a name like Hamish McTavish, she'd expected someone flame-haired with a fiery temper to match, perhaps wearing a kilt, with a caber under his desk. But Hamish turned out to be a lanky Clark Kent lookalike in a suit with an impeccable accent. Like Miss Jean Brodie, only more butch.

'You must be Lola,' he greeted her when she staggered into the production office, her arms full of paperwork. 'Welcome to your humble domain. Here, let me take that lot for you.'

As he lifted the paperwork out of her arms, Lola looked around. It *was* pretty humble. Not much more than a glorified trailer, with a desk at either end, and an assortment of laptops, phones, printers, fax machines and photocopiers. There were a couple of tatty vinyl easy chairs lined up against one of the walls, a small portable TV and a kettle. It looked like an upmarket minicab office.

Hamish reached for the kettle. 'I'll brew up and then I'll take you through the basics, shall I?'

'The basics' turned out to be a two-hour introduction to the world of tour management, from sorting out the daily accounts and checking arrangements, to dealing with deliveries and organizing transport. Lola's head was reeling by the time he'd finished, but at least she felt she could handle the job. Even if she couldn't handle it quite as well as Hamish, who, she found out, had a Masters in business administration and was terrifyingly competent.

'How did you end up working here?' she asked, as he cleared away their mugs. 'You should be running an international conglomerate somewhere.'

He shrugged. 'Just lucky, I guess.' He looked at his watch. 'It's time for the sound-check. Shall we go and take a look?'

The production trailer was in the backstage area behind the auditorium. It was crammed with the Poleaxe circus of tour buses and tractor-trailers. Roadies, riggers and stagehands wandered around, making last-minute changes.

They picked their way between the tons of road cases and miles of thick cabling to the front of house, where the support act was just coming off stage after their sound-check.

In the middle of the empty stalls, a man wearing headphones was sitting at a console, concentrating hard as he made adjustments via a laptop computer.

'That's where they control all the sound,' Hamish explained. 'There's a separate console over there for the lighting and pyrotechnics. All the cues are done by computer now.'

But Lola wasn't listening. She was watching Jay, standing in the shadows to one side of the stage, laughing and joking with Kyle the lead guitarist. Just seeing him riled her all over again.

'What exactly is a backline tech?' she asked Hamish.

'The techs are in charge of the instruments, amps, stands and cables,' he explained. 'They pack up the instruments, maintain them, tune them, guard them with their lives—some of those babies are worth a small fortune. They have to make sure everything's set up just how the guys like it. All the musicians have their own personal techs; they build up a relationship of trust. Jay's been with Kyle for at least five years, maybe more.'

Lola couldn't imagine anyone putting up with Jay for more than five minutes. 'He must be good at his job.'

'He's also a pretty talented musician himself. Most of the techs are, or they wouldn't be able to get the sound right.'

Lola looked at him. 'You really do know a lot, don't you?'

He blushed. 'OK, you've guessed my dirty secret. I'm a metalhead.'

'You?' Lola laughed. He looked so straight, it was hard to imagine him throwing himself around in a mosh pit.

Hamish looked offended. 'Don't let this suit fool you. I might have the body of a bank manager, but I have the heart of a headbanger. To tell the truth, I've been obsessed with Poleaxe for years. This is my dream job.' He nudged her. 'Here they are.'

'I'm surprised they didn't offer you my job,' Lola said, as Simon and Jonno took to the stage.

'Oh, they did. I turned it down.'

'Why?'

He kept his eyes fixed on the stage. 'Let me see. The last tour manager got pitched out of a hotel window. The one before that got dumped on the roadside in the middle of the Arizona desert for a joke. The one before that's in rehab and—'

'Thanks, I get the picture,' Lola interrupted.

'This band gets through tour managers like Kyle gets through guitar picks. Although I'm sure you'll be all right,' he added as a comforting afterthought.

But Lola was already beginning to feel an

118

ominous churning in the pit of her stomach. Had she stepped out of a spitting frying pan into a great big inferno?

On stage, Simon was playing a few experimental riffs while his tech watched him closely. Kyle and Jay were still messing about off-stage, Jonno was in deep discussion with his tech, while Rick prowled around bad-temperedly.

'Can we get started?' he snapped finally. 'Some of us haven't got all day.'

Jonno's tech peered down at them from the lip of the stage. 'Any news on Jonno's lucky sticks?' he pleaded.

'Tell him we're working on it,' Lola lied.

They started to play. Short blasts of music, followed by lots of discussion, as the roadies checked cables and the lighting director on the front desk twiddled and tweaked furiously.

They finally started to play their first song. But a minute in, Rick suddenly stopped. 'Your guitar's off,' he complained to Kyle.

'Sounds OK to me.'

'Believe me, it's way off.' Rick glared at Jay.

Kyle handed it over to him with an apologetic shrug. Jay tuned it again, while Rick stomped around muttering under his breath about 'morons' who 'couldn't do their job properly'.

Lola glanced at Jay. His head was bent over the guitar, but she knew he'd heard. She was surprised he didn't respond. He'd been quick enough to attack her.

'Why is he picking on him?' she wondered aloud.

'They have a complicated relationship,' Hamish whispered. 'Rick may be a genius but he's not that

119

great a human being.' Then, remembering who he was talking to, he added, 'No offence.'

'None taken.'

She actually started to feel sorry for Jay, until she remembered the hard time he'd given her earlier.

The sound-check finished and they headed back to the office. Lola was so intent on staying out of Jay's way that she collided with Rick on his way out.

It was the first time they'd met since the album launch party. Lola was hesitant about approaching him. She had the bad feeling he never quite remembered who she was, and that if he did, he didn't much care.

'Hi,' she said, trying to be casual. 'Remember me?' Then, just in case he didn't, she added, 'I'm Lola, your . . .' She tried to say 'daughter' but the word wouldn't come out. '. . . Your new tour manager,' she managed instead.

'Yeah, right. Of course. Dinah said you were joining us.' His face cleared. 'As a matter of fact, I was hoping I'd get to see you.'

'Really?' Her heart gave a little bump of hope. Maybe he did care, after all.

'There's a problem with my hotel suite. I don't like the colour of the curtains.'

Lola stared at him, deflated. 'Your curtains?'

'They're brown. I hate that. I want them a different colour.'

'Anything in particular?'

He considered it for a moment. 'Blue would be OK. Or green. Green would be cool.'

'I'll see what I can do,' she heard herself say faintly.

She watched him saunter away. No 'how are you?' or 'what have you been up to?'. Not even a 'we must catch up sometime'. She hadn't expected him to embrace her like a long-lost child, but she'd expected more than a complaint about his curtains.

Hamish sidled up to her. 'See what I mean?' he whispered. 'Not that great a human being.'

CHAPTER FIFTEEN

Lola had never been to a real gig before, unless hanging around the stage door of a Bros concert when she was fifteen counted. She'd seen a few local bands in pubs, but she'd certainly never been to anything as huge as Poleaxe's opening night at the Riverbend Music Center in Cincinnati, Ohio.

The sun had all but disappeared above the open-air arena, leaving its last purple and magenta streaks in the darkening sky. A slight breeze blew in off the Ohio River, which gave the venue its name.

The Riverbend consisted of a vast rectangular canopy over the seating area for around six thousand people, with room for at least twice that number on the lawns that stretched beyond it. The rows were already full when Lola went to take a quick walk around.

She was careful to slip her laminate inside her T-shirt as she mingled with the crowds, just as Dinah had told her.

'They'll rip it right off your neck, and your head with it, if you're not careful,' she'd warned. 'Those passes are like gold dust.'

The concession stands were busy, selling Poleaxe T-shirts, posters, CDs and souvenir programmes. Further along, crowds queued for burgers and beer. It wasn't until the wafting aroma of pizza and fries hit her that Lola realised she hadn't stopped to eat all day. She bought a slice of pepperoni pizza and a Diet Coke, then slipped past security and headed backstage.

The warren of narrow, dark corridors was littered with generators, smoke machines, snaking electrical cables and other random stage equipment. Beyond that was the area where the techs stood guard over the artists' spare instruments, ready for a quick change at a moment's notice. Lola noticed Jay there, making some last-minute adjustments to Kyle's favourite Les Paul.

At the far end of the corridor was the band's dressing room. As she headed towards it, Lola saw a man coming out, furtively stuffing cash in his top pocket. He caught her watching and smiled brazenly as he brushed past. She didn't need her police officer's instincts to tell her he was a dealer.

She was just about to challenge him when she spotted Dinah. She'd changed her trademark black suit for a sizzling scarlet Roland Mouret dress than clung to her spectacular curves. Her dark hair was slicked back in a smooth knot and fastened with an exotic hibiscus flower that made her look like a Spanish señorita.

'There you are,' she greeted her. 'You're just in time. The band's due on in a minute.' She cocked her head. 'Do you hear that?'

There was a hum in the air, like distant thunder. Lola could almost feel the rising excitement of the

122

crowd, whooshing like adrenaline through her veins.

'Great, isn't it?' Dinah smiled. 'The gig's a sell-out.'

Lola pointed down the corridor. 'Did you see that guy go past?'

'What guy? Oh, you mean Eric?'

'I think he's a dealer.'

'Of course he's a dealer. One of the best in the business.'

Lola's mouth dropped in shock. 'Should I call the police?'

'Why? Eric's practically on the payroll.' Dinah gave her an almost pitying smile. 'Honey, this is a rock band, not a bunch of cheerleaders. Drugs are part of the game. You've got to accept that. All you can do is keep an eye on the situation, make sure it doesn't get in the way of the tour. As long as the band keeps playing, that's all you need to worry about.' She adjusted the flower in the hair. 'Are you coming to the after-show party?'

'I'm not sure . . .'

'You've got to come. It'll be a new experience for you.'

Lola glanced back down the corridor in the direction Eric had disappeared. 'I think I've already had enough of those for one day.'

Just then Jonno's drum tech Mo rushed up, looking worried.

'Any sign of Jonno's lucky sticks?' he pleaded. 'He's going mental in there. Says he's not going on without them.'

'Thanks for reminding me.' Lola reached into her bag and brought out a long thin package wrapped in brown paper. 'They arrived ten minutes ago.'

Mo pulled the sticks out of their wrapping and stared at them reverently. 'How did you manage that?' he asked.

Lola glanced at Dinah. Straight-faced, she said, 'Special megasonic jet.'

'Wow.' Mo ran his fingers along the length of the sticks. 'They haven't been, like, damaged or anything?'

'They came first class,' Lola said. 'They even had their own seat.'

As Mo ran to deliver the sticks to his boss, Dinah turned to Lola. 'Megasonic jet?' she queried, one eyebrow rising.

'OK, so I got them from a music shop in the mall.' Lola shrugged.

Dinah looked impressed. 'You're learning fast.'

Britt emerged from the band's dressing room, looking tall and leggy and catwalk fabulous as ever in jeans, heels and an Armani jacket. She didn't smile or look at either of them as she swept past.

Lola watched her go. 'There's someone I haven't learned to handle yet,' she said.

'Oh, just ignore her,' Dinah advised. 'It's · nothing personal. She's jealous as hell of any woman who comes within a hundred miles of Rick. It's just insecurity.'

'What's she got to be insecure about? She's stunning.'

'She's also married to the biggest horndog in rock,' Dinah said. 'Believe me, that's enough to make anyone insecure.' She looked up, distracted. 'The house lights are going down. That means the band's about to go on.'

They moved around to the VIP patio area on

the other side of the stage to get a better view. An eerie silence fell as a solitary spotlight swooped across the crowd. From somewhere on the darkened stage came a beat, slow and steady as a heartbeat, pulsing through the auditorium. It was so loud Lola could feel it all the way through her body.

Then, suddenly, came an explosion of sound and light with all the force of a volcano erupting, the crowd went mad and there were the band, on stage. Lola could feel her eardrums being pushed outwards like sails full of wind. She held her breath as the spotlight picked out the bassist, Simon, and the lead guitarist Kyle. Simon stood rooted to the spot, laying down a steady bass riff while Kyle tore around the stage, aiming his guitar like a bayonet into the crowd, whipping them into a frenzy.

The noise cajunked and beefed outwards, filling the night sky. The spotlight picked out Jonno, going crazy on the drums.

And then there was Rick, stepping out of a billowing cloud of dry ice smoke, arms outstretched, outlined in blinding white light.

Lola felt a pain in her chest and realised she hadn't breathed out for a full two minutes.

She watched, transfixed, as he rushed to the front of the stage, grabbed the mike, put it to his mouth, and screamed loud and long, the opening bars of 'Bite Me'. The crowd went berserk, roaring their approval.

His voice rose and rasped, writhed and twisted, like an angry rattlesnake on the end of a stick.

'He's quite something, isn't he?' Dinah said.

Lola nodded, speechless. Suddenly she understood what all the fuss was about, why everyone treated Rick Wild like some kind of god. It was because on stage he *was* one. A glittering demigod in black leather, strutting around the stage, dominating it with the sheer force of his voice and his personality.

*   *   *

If there was one thing in the world Rick Wild loved, it was being on stage. Just standing up there, feeling the intense heat of the lights on his face, the music pulsing through his veins, in front of thousands of people, all screaming for him, adoring him . . . It was better than sex, better than the highest high drugs could offer.

That was how he felt as he looked out over the ten thousand people fanned out in front of him in the auditorium. The stage lights dipped and swooped over thousands of faces, hands, bodies, in the stands and on the lawn beyond, as far as he could see.

Rick stalked above them, brandishing his microphone and screaming out the music that sent them crazy. He played with them, teased them, darting to the edge of the stage until they could almost reach out and touch him, then springing away at the last minute, laughing as the seething swell was pushed back by the grim wall of security guards.

Behind him, Jonno was playing a stampede of drums and sharp, slashed cymbals with his usual trademark frenzy. His face and black hair were drenched. To his right, Simon hugged the shadows, his sandy hair flopping into his eyes as he played bass with his usual quiet intensity.

On the other side of the stage Kyle was slamming chords, scrubbing the strings of his guitar until they blurred, his mass of dark curls flopped forwards, hiding his face. Then suddenly he swung round and looked up, and Rick reeled back in shock as he found himself staring at the gaunt, white, grinning face of Terry Mac.

The next second there was a flash of blinding light and an explosion that came out of nowhere, knocking him off his feet. He hit the ground and everything went black.

*   *   *

Lola didn't see what had happened but suddenly everyone was screaming, the music stopped and there was a mad rush to the stage.

She managed to push her way past everyone just in time to see Rick being hauled down the narrow corridor that led from the stage between two burly roadies. Britt was hanging on to him, tears streaming down her face, holding the sleeve of her Armani jacket to his head, trying to stem the blood that oozed from his temple.

'Someone help him!' she screamed. 'He's dying!'

With everyone else around her talking at once and going into a flat panic, Lola decided to take charge. 'Take him to the dressing room,' she ordered the roadies.

They all crowded into the dressing room—Lola, Rick, Britt, Dinah, various assorted roadies and the rest of the band, who'd come off stage.

The roadies helped Rick on to the sofa where he lay, white-faced and shaking.

'Did you see him?' He looked around at them

wildly. 'Did anyone see him?'

'See who?' Lola asked.

'He's delirious,' Britt said.

'You only get delirious with a fever. But he could have concussion.'

She knelt down in front of Rick and peered into his face, checking his pupils. He stared groggily back at her.

'What happened?' he croaked.

'One of the pyros exploded at the wrong time and knocked you off your feet,' a roadie explained.

'It could have killed you,' Britt put in.

Rick looked at Lola. 'That's all that happened? Nothing else?'

'You nearly died. Isn't that enough?' Britt shrieked.

Dinah reached for the bottle of Jack Daniel's and poured out a large measure.

'Don't give him that,' Britt snapped. 'He's on the twelve-step programme.'

'Who says it's for him?' Dinah downed it in one. 'Oh God, our insurance premiums will go through the roof after this.'

'*Rick* nearly went through the roof,' Jonno said. 'Sorry, bad joke,' he mumbled, as everyone turned to glare at him.

They all looked anxiously at Rick.

'Does he need an ambulance?' Britt asked.

'I'm not sure.' Lola peered into his eyes again. 'His pupils don't seem dilated.'

'You don't have to talk about me as if I'm retarded,' Rick growled.

'How many fingers am I holding up?'

'Three. But you also have a parrot on your head.'.

Lola smiled. 'He seems OK to me.'

'What do you know about it? He could be dead by tomorrow.' Britt fumbled in her bag for her mobile. 'We've got to call the police.'

'No,' Dinah said. 'No police. We agreed, remember?'

'That was before he nearly got killed.'

'It was an accident.'

'You really believe that?'

Lola looked from Britt to Dinah and back again, as they confronted each other across the dressing room. 'Will someone tell me what's going on?'

No one spoke. They all just looked at each other nervously.

'Why do I get the feeling there's something no one's telling me?' Lola said.

'It's nothing,' Rick muttered. 'It's not important.'

'Not important?' Britt's voice was shrill. 'Someone's trying to kill you and you say it's not important?'

Lola stared at Rick. 'Someone's trying to kill you?'

'No.' Rick didn't meet her eye.

'He's been getting threatening letters from a fan,' Dinah put in.

'It's just some crazy guy, nothing to worry about,' Rick said.

'Crazy enough to want you dead,' Britt reminded him.

'C'mon, everyone gets this kind of mail. It means nothing.' He reached for Britt's hand, but she pulled away, her expression frosty.

'He's right,' Jonno agreed. 'I'm always getting letters from nutters.'

'That's because they recognise a kindred spirit,' Dinah said. 'Rick's right, it's probably nothing,' she told Lola.

'How long has it been going on?'

'A few months. Ever since Poleaxe announced their tour. This person says he's going to kill Rick on stage. It looks like he almost did it tonight.' Britt's mouth thinned into an angry line. 'Now maybe he'll see sense and cancel this tour.'

'And you haven't gone to the police?' Lola asked.

Dinah shook her head. 'We're handling it ourselves. I've stepped up personal security for the whole band.'

'If anyone wants to get to me they'll have to get through big Gus first. Isn't that right, Gus?' Rick looked up at the man mountain standing like a huge lump of granite beside the door.

'He wasn't there tonight, was he?' Britt said quietly.

Rick took away the cloth that he'd held clamped to his head and inspected the wound gingerly with his fingers. 'It's stopped bleeding.'

'Next time you might not be so lucky,' Britt muttered.

Rick ignored her and staggered to his feet.

'Where are you going?' Lola asked.

'Back on stage, where do you think?' He nodded towards the door.

'You can't!' Britt, Lola and Dinah chorused together. Even the band looked uneasy.

'Are you sure about this, man?' Kyle asked.

'Listen to that lot.' Rick cocked his head. In the distance, like the rumble of thunder, they could hear the crowd stamping and clapping a slow, steady beat of expectation. 'Do you think they'll just go away quietly? No, they came to see Poleaxe, and that's what we're going to give them.'

Simon looked uneasy. 'But if there's really some maniac out there trying to kill you—'

'The only maniac in that theatre is Jonno.' Rick summoned up a stretched grin. 'Now come on, before they start ripping up the seats.'

The band filed out, followed by the roadies, closing the door behind them. Lola, Britt, and Dinah stood in frozen silence until they heard the crowd erupt into wild cheering. Moments later, the music started up again, as wild and powerful as before.

'You've got to admit, he is pretty brave,' Dinah commented.

'You think so?' Britt turned on her, bitter and angry. 'I think he's a vain, arrogant fool. The limelight means more to him than his own life.'

CHAPTER SIXTEEN

By the after-show party, Rick had managed to shrug off any ill-effects. He partied as hard as everyone else, with apparently not a care in the world. But the evening had already lost its magic for Lola.

It was hardly the kind of bring-a-bottle party she was used to back in Leeds. The place was heaving with musicians, roadies and record executives, plus a whole load of gorgeous girls who seemed to have come from nowhere.

'Do you know any of them?' she asked Dinah.

131

Dinah smiled. 'Honey, they couldn't care less about me. They're here for *them*.' She nodded towards the band, laughing and drinking with their entourage at the other end of the room.

'Groupies?'

She nodded. 'Some of them are regulars; they follow the band to every gig. Some are probably local, fishing for what they can catch. You see the same faces over and over again.'

'Who invited them? I didn't see them on the guest list.'

Dinah sent her an amused, pitying look. 'They don't need a guest list. They wait around the stage door, and the roadies come and pick out the ones they want. Sometimes there could be maybe a hundred of them, all clamouring to come backstage. You should have a look sometime. It's a real cattle market.'

'I'm not sure I'd want to.' Lola watched them. They were laughing and drinking like everyone else, but all the time they were watching the band, waiting for the nod, the eye contact, anything that told them they'd got lucky.

'Why do they do it?' she wondered aloud.

'Why do you think?' Dinah said. 'Mostly it's just a competition, like scalp-hunting. They'd sleep with anyone famous. Some just love the band and want to get near them. They'll do it with a roadie, if they can't get one of the guys. And then there are the ones you really have to watch out for.' She nodded towards a beautiful, exotic, dark-haired woman in a skimpy orange dress. 'They're the real predators. They're thinking long-term relationships, not one-night stands.'

Lola caught the woman's eye. They stared at

132

each other for a moment, then she looked away dismissively.

No wonder Britt didn't move from Rick's side. Those girls were like circling sharks, waiting to attack. As soon as Britt went to the loo, they closed in. Lola fought her way through them and found Rick enthusiastically signing a girl's thigh.

'Can I talk to you for a moment?' she asked.

'Sure.'

'In private?'

Rick shrugged at the girl, who shot Lola a sour look then stomped back to her friends. Rick watched her go, a longing expression on his face.

'About what happened tonight . . .' Lola said.

'It was an accident.' Rick cut her off.

'I wasn't talking about that. When you came off stage you kept asking if anyone had seen him.'

'Seen who?'

'That's what I wanted to know.'

Rick frowned. 'I don't remember saying that. Are you sure you heard right?'

'I'm sure. You looked pretty scared.'

'I'd just been blown up on stage. How else was I supposed to look?'

'So you don't remember anything?'

He shook his head. 'Nope. Not a thing. One minute I was halfway through the opening number, the next I was flat on my back.'

He was lying, Lola knew it. He was smiling, but he couldn't meet her eye.

'Do you think this fan of yours means to kill you?' she asked.

'No!' This time his smile was genuine. 'Like I keep saying, he's just some crazy guy. Probably locked up somewhere.'

133

'Britt seems to think you should cancel the tour.'

'Are you serious? That would cost us thousands. Then Dinah really would kill me, and, believe me, I'm way more scared of her than I am of some mad stranger.' He looked around. 'Can I go back to the party now?' he said impatiently.

'What's the rush?' Lola started to say. Then, across the room, she saw the woman in the orange dress watching them fixedly.

'Britt won't be happy,' Lola worried.

'Britt's not here.' He gave her a roguish smile, and disappeared into the crowd.

The party soon started to descend into debauchery. The vodka, beer and Jack Daniel's flowed, the music got louder and the groupies began to writhe on the dance floor, showing off their sexiest moves for the band. One or two had already managed to snag an invitation to join the real party in the VIP area; as Lola passed it, she saw Kyle stretched out on the chaise longue, a girl on either side of him, like some potentate in a harem.

When she went to the loo and bumped into Jonno coming out of a cubicle with a frighteningly young blonde, she knew it was time to call it a night. She slipped away and caught a cab back to the hotel. It was already three in the morning, and she was shattered. She also had to be up first thing to make sure everyone made it on to the bus to Pennsylvania. And by the way the crew were getting stuck into the booze when she'd left the party, she didn't think that would be an easy job.

She was making her way to the hotel lifts when she spotted a solitary figure sitting at the bar. It was Jay. He was still dressed in his jeans and a

134

faded purple Iron Maiden T-shirt, nursing a drink and ignoring the pointed looks the barman was giving him.

Lola hesitated. Should she go and speak to him? Probably not, she decided. But they had to work together for the next three months and it would be a lot easier if there was no bad feeling between them. Even though her body was screaming to go to bed, she dragged herself to the bar.

'So you didn't fancy it, either?'

He flinched when she touched his shoulder. 'What?'

'The party.'

He picked up his glass. 'I'm not the sociable type.'

'I'd worked that out for myself.'

'In that case, you won't mind if I finish my drink alone.'

He turned away from her. But Lola refused to let his rudeness put her off. 'The tour certainly got off with a bang, didn't it?' she remarked. He stared at her blankly. 'The explosion?'

'Oh, that.'

Lola frowned at him. 'Rick could have been badly hurt. You don't seem too concerned.' Come to think about it, she couldn't remember seeing him in the dressing room after the accident, either.

'He survived, didn't he? Worse luck,' he added under his breath.

'You don't mean that.'

'Don't I? That's all right, then.' He drained his glass and pushed it across the bar for a refill. 'Anyway, there was never any chance of that happening. There's not enough explosive in those flash pans.'

'You seem to know a lot about it,' Lola said.

He sent her an amused sidelong look. 'Does that make me your chief suspect?'

'Sorry?'

'That's what this is about, isn't it? You don't think that explosion was an accident. You're trying to find out Who Nearly Killed Rick Wild, and now I've just put myself right at the top of your list.'

She might have known he'd be shrewd enough to guess what was going on in her mind. He might be the rudest man on the planet but he was also very smart.

'*Do* you think it was an accident?' she said.

'Who cares? I suppose someone could have mixed in more gunpowder to make a bigger bang if they'd wanted to.' He caught her questioning look. 'Sorry to disappoint you, but most of the crew knows how to put basic pyrotechnics together. And some of them hate him nearly as much as me.'

'Do you really hate him?'

The shadow of a smile touched his lips. 'Haven't you worked that out yet?' The barman handed him another drink and he took a big gulp. 'My father and I don't exactly see eye to eye.'

'Since when?'

'Since the day he walked out on my mother.'

'That must have been very hard for you, losing your father,' Lola said carefully.

'Hard?' Jay fixed her with his intense, dark green stare. 'No, it wasn't *hard*. He was never around anyway. I'll tell you what was hard, shall I? Watching my mother's face every time he appeared on television, flaunting another new woman. Hearing her cry and knowing I couldn't do anything to make it better for her. *That* was hard.'

136

His hand was trembling as he reached for his drink. 'She adored him and he just threw her aside like a useless old rag when he'd finished with her. Like he does with everyone in the end.'

He tipped his head back and emptied his drink down his throat.

Lola watched him. 'Why do you hang around if you hate him that much?'

'I have no choice.' He shrugged. 'I was working for Kyle long before he joined the band. It was just my bad luck he ended up with Poleaxe.'

'You could always find another job.'

'Why should I? I like working with Kyle. And if me being around makes Rick uncomfortable, then that's just tough. Besides, maybe he needs to get his conscience pricked. If he has one.' He turned to her. 'So why are you here? Do you want to bond with your new daddy?'

His cynical expression annoyed her. 'Would it be so bad if I did?'

'That's up to you. But I'm warning you, you're wasting your time. Rick isn't interested in playing happy families with you or anyone else. You'll find that out soon enough. If you stay around.'

'What makes you think I'm not going to stay around?'

He smiled nastily. 'This is only the first night. It gets a lot tougher from here on, tougher than you could ever imagine. I don't know if you'll be able to hack it. Might be best all round if you just quit now while you're still ahead.'

'If you're trying to put me off then you're wasting *your* time.'

He sent her an enigmatic look. 'We'll see,' he said.

CHAPTER SEVENTEEN

With resignation, Lola stared at the dog poo on her pillow.

Her bunk on the crew bus had been trashed. Again. This time a disgusting pool of what looked like tomato ketchup, washing-up liquid and, she hoped, Marmite was sinking into her sheets, with the plastic poo the *pièce de résistance*.

Playing practical jokes on her had become a popular pastime for the crew in the two weeks since the tour began. The first time it happened, when she'd crawled up to her hotel room after a long, frustrating day and found all her furniture in the corridor, she'd been so exhausted she'd cried.

Since then she'd learned that it was a rite of passage for all tour managers, and stopped taking it so personally. Now she half expected to go to her room and find her bed upside down or her underwear strung like a line of bunting out of the window.

Once, in Milwaukee, she'd managed to get her own back by pretending she'd had to swap rooms at the last minute with a visiting executive from the record company. Seeing the panic on the crew's faces had made her laugh for days.

Sighing, she dragged the bedding off the bunk. From the back lounge of the bus came the sound of sniggering, as the riggers and lighting guys crowded around the doorway to watch.

'Nice try, boys,' she said. 'But after ten years in the police it'll take more than a plastic dog poo to scare me off.'

'We'll have to try harder next time, won't we?' Jay said.

They eyeballed each other. He wasn't laughing like the others. While for the rest of the crew it was just good-natured teasing, Lola sensed Jay was more malicious. He really didn't want her around, and he meant to do his damnedest to get rid of her.

'Bring it on,' she mouthed.

He could do what he liked because she wasn't going anywhere. She was having way too much fun for that.

She would never have imagined in a million years that she would love being on the road with a rock band so much. She even enjoyed the bits everyone else hated, like the constant travelling and living out of a suitcase. After spending all her life in Leeds, she loved waking up in a different city nearly every day. And after a lifetime of caravan holidays and dreary B&Bs, she got very excited by the hotels, with their king-sized beds, plasma TVs and designer toiletries. Her room might not have been as luxurious as the mega-suites the rest of the band stayed in, but she was easily impressed.

The work was fun, too. Every day was different and incredibly busy. She had to sort out accommodation for the hundred-plus tour crew, checking and confirming rooms for everyone, and sweet-talking nervous hotel managers who'd suddenly heard of the band's reputation and were wondering what they'd let themselves in for. Once they arrived at a venue, she had to make sure it was set up according to the band's contract, or riders. This meant everything from the type of lights supplied to the bottles of Jack Daniel's waiting in the dressing rooms. Most venues in the States had their own local crews of stagehands, and it was part of Lola's job to liaise between them and the band's own road crew, making sure everyone did their job, and acting as referee when arguments got out of hand.

On top of that, she also had to get the daily allowances, or per diems, distributed to the crew, organise transport to and from the hotel for the band, pay the bus driver—and make sure he cleaned the bus regularly—and hand out the vital all-access passes that only the crew and very special guests were allowed to have.

And then there were the really fun bits, like tracking down obscure bits of equipment that had somehow got left behind, fielding calls from tearful wives and girlfriends, and making sure the groupies were well out of the way when they came to visit.

The only thing Lola refused to get involved in was drugs. Something she made very clear when Simon the bass player asked her to send a car to pick up a package from Eric.

'I didn't realise I'd gone on tour with *The Sound of Music*,' he grumbled when Lola sent him on his way.

She liked the people, too. Hamish was great fun to work with, and the rest of the crew were OK, too, despite their stupid practical jokes. Even the band were all right, although with their habit of losing things, forgetting arrangements, ignoring instructions and generally doing whatever they liked whenever they felt like it, it was sometimes like being in charge of a group of pre-schoolers on an outing.

The only one she couldn't get on with was Jay. She'd tried hard enough, but he rebuffed all her attempts to be friendly. In the end Lola decided she couldn't be bothered. If he didn't like her, then it was just tough on both of them.

She was still stripping her bunk when Dinah turned up. She'd been with them on and off since the tour began in Ohio two weeks before. Lola wondered if she was checking up on her.

She eyed the bundle of sheets on the floor. 'Had an accident?'

'Yes,' Lola replied. 'And there might be another one soon, if certain people don't watch their step.' She shot a warning look over her shoulder at Neil the rigger, who quickly ducked inside the back lounge and closed the door. She licked a sticky smear experimentally off one of her fingers. Actually, it didn't taste bad, apart from the washing-up liquid. 'What can I do for you?'

'I need a favour.'

'OK.'

She waited for Dinah to tell her she needed an extra hotel room booked, or comp tickets for a record company bigwig, so she was taken aback when she said, 'I want you to drive to Long Island and pick something up for me.'

She wiped her hands down her jeans. 'What am I picking up?'

'My daughter.'

Lola stopped. 'Tiffany?'

'She gets out of rehab tomorrow morning. I thought you could drive up there tonight, stay over, then collect her, drive back and meet us in New Jersey.'

'But what about the tour?'

141

'Hamish can cover for you while you're away. You won't be gone long.'

Lola hesitated. 'Wouldn't it be better if you collected her? You are her mother, after all. I expect she'll be looking forward to seeing you.'

'You think?' Dinah quirked one perfectly plucked dark brow. 'You obviously don't know my daughter.'

'All the same, it might be nice if—'

'Look, you're right,' Dinah interrupted her. 'It would be just great if I could drive ninety miles to collect her. But right now I don't have enough time in my schedule to go to the bathroom. So would you mind doing it for me?'

'Go to the bathroom?'

Dinah smiled. 'God, you're funny. You and Tiffany are going to get along just brilliantly.'

*   *   *

The Sands was one of the East Coast's most discreet and exclusive rehab clinics. Originally built for a wealthy industrialist at the turn of the century, the elegant country mansion occupied a prime spot on Long Island's fabulously wealthy Gold Coast. It was surrounded by a hundred acres of formal landscaped gardens, ornamental lakes, tennis courts and golf driving ranges.

A wide, tree-lined drive led from the gates to the house, its porticoed entrance guarded by a pair of stone lions. Ironically, very few of its rich and famous guests ever used those elegant front doors. Most of them came and went from the nondescript servants' entrance at the back of the building.

It was from here that Tiffany Wild stepped into

the pleasantly warm May sunshine. She was free at last. No more therapy sessions, no more group hugs, no more creative journaling or denial management. Never again would she have to practise tai chi, pat horses or sit cross-legged on the floor banging a drum and pretending it was helping to sort out all her problems.

Rehab or jail: that was the stark choice the judge had given her. At the time it seemed like a no-brainer. But after a month spent watching a bunch of wealthy, bored losers getting in touch with their inner child, she was beginning to wonder if a couple of weeks in a cell wouldn't have been easier. At least she wouldn't have had to share her room with an obsessive compulsive who kept her up half the night straightening the coat hangers.

And all because she'd socked Ashley Anderson.

Tiffany smiled. It had been worth it. That cow had it coming to her, pretending to be her best friend and all the while secretly sleeping with her man. Seeing them sneaking out of the toilets together at the Whiplash that night she'd just lost it completely. She didn't know who was more surprised, Ashley, Tony or the owner of the bottle of vintage Cristal she'd used to smack them.

She peered over her shades and looked around. There should have been a car waiting for her. Mom had promised she wouldn't forget this time. Tiffany hoped she might even come herself, as the band was only down the coast in New Jersey. Maybe even her dad would find the time to drop by . . .

She hiked her holdall over her shoulder and walked around to the front of the building. She passed a group of people, some of them in dressing gowns, sitting on the terrace and grinning inanely up at the sky.

She shuddered. Smile therapy. That was the worst.

A silver Merc was parked around the front of the building. A woman leaned against it, waiting. Tiffany gave her an instant, critical once-over, taking in every detail. Scuffed green Converses, faded jeans and a pink T-shirt, none of it designer. Medium height, medium build, way too chunky for LA. Dark gold hair cut in a messy bob, although whether that was deliberate or just because she'd forgotten her hairbrush Tiffany couldn't tell. Her face was heart-shaped, attractive more than pretty . . . and oddly familiar.

With a jolt Tiffany suddenly realised who she was, seconds before the woman said, 'Hi, you must be Tiffany. I'm Lola, your new half-sister.'

Tiffany bristled. Lola was smiling, coming towards her. She backed away, worried she might try to hug her or something. But all she said was, 'Can I take your bag for you?'

Tiffany gripped the handles. 'Where are Mom and Dad?'

'Dinah suggested I should come instead. She thought it would be a chance for us to get to know each other.'

Yeah, right. More likely she'd just looked around and picked the first person she found. Last time Tiffany needed rehab, Mom had sent the housekeeper to the family therapy session.

'Shall we go?' Lola said.

Tiffany considered her options for a moment, but they were limited. She needed to get out of there, and Lola had a car.

144

'Take me to the airport,' she commanded, sliding into the back seat. 'And make it quick. I want to catch the first flight to LA.' The sooner she got away from this dump, the better.

Lola looked as if she might try to make conversation, so Tiffany pulled out her mobile phone and started calling up all her old friends in LA to catch up on the gossip. Among all the 'Ohmygods' and the 'Jeez, I can't believe you did thats', she found out that everyone agreed Ashley Anderson was a scheming little slut, that most of the kids in West Hollywood had taken to sporting either 'Team Tiffany' or 'Team Ashley' T-shirts (and she was winning by a mile), and that Tony was single again.

Her finger hovered over his number on speed-dial, wondering if she should call him. It wasn't all his fault, she reasoned, in spite of what she'd said when she aimed the champagne bottle at his head. He was just a guy, after all. What chance did he have against a man-eater like Ashley?

Then something caught her eye and distracted her. She glanced out of the window. They were on a stretch of highway, heading out of the city. The green road sign that flashed by announced that the New Jersey Turnpike was ahead.

'This isn't the way to the airport,' she said, putting down her phone and lifting her sunglasses.

'We're going to New Jersey.'

'But I don't want to go to New Jersey. I told you, I want to go to LA.'

'Your mother told me to bring you. I guess she wants to see you.'

'Wants to keep her eye on me, you mean.' There was only one reason why her mother would want her around—to make sure she didn't end up in any more trouble.

'Don't you want to see your family?' Lola asked.

'They're not exactly busting a gut to see me, are they?' She stared moodily out of the window at the strip malls and fast-food chain restaurants that lined the highway. 'No one came to see me in rehab,' she blurted out, then wished she hadn't when she caught the sympathetic look Lola gave her in the rear-view mirror. The last thing she needed was a complete stranger going all mushy and caring on her. She'd had enough of that at the Sands.

Too late. Lola was already trying to talk to her again, asking questions about rehab. Tiffany pulled her iPod out of her bag, clamped on her headphones, and turned up Metallica full blast. After a while, Lola gave up trying to make conversation and concentrated on her driving.

She leaned back and closed her eyes while she thought about what to do next. Much as she wanted to ignore Lola, her instincts told her she needed a different approach. Underneath all that dumb touchy-feely stuff, she suspected Lola was a lot tougher and smarter than she seemed. She wasn't going to be rattled by tantrums or the silent treatment.

If she was going to get her own way she was going to have to go for the charm offensive.

Tiffany took off her headphones. 'So how do you like life on the road?' she asked sweetly.

Her question caught Lola off-guard. She'd been humming along to some grotty ballad on the radio.

'I'm getting used to it.' She leaned forward and turned the volume down. 'It was a bit like being thrown into the deep end, having to manage the tour. But so far I don't think I've made any real howlers.'

But Tiffany wasn't listening. 'You're the tour manager?' she said.

Lola smiled. 'Didn't you know?'

'No, I didn't.' Tiffany took a moment to digest the information. She wouldn't be allowed to scrape the chewing gum off the dressing-room floor, let alone manage the whole tour. 'I guess Mom must really like you,' she said in a small voice.

'I don't think she had much choice,' Lola replied frankly. 'I was the best of a pretty bad bunch.'

So modest, Tiffany thought bitterly. And all the while she was worming her way into the family. But it wasn't as if she was taking Tiffany's place, because she didn't even have a place. No one wanted her around. They couldn't even be bothered to collect her from rehab.

She chewed at what was left of her nails. The first thing she had to do when she got back to LA was to get a decent manicure.

After she'd got drunk and stoned, of course.

But in order to do any of those things she had to go on being nice to Lola. She asked about her life back in England, her job, her friends, her family.

She knew she'd hit a sore point when Lola said, 'I don't have any family. There's just me.'

So you decided to come over and steal mine, Tiffany thought. 'You've got Rick now,' she said.

'I suppose so.' Lola caught her eye and grinned. 'But let's face it, he's not exactly your typical father figure, is he? Although it might be different for you, growing up with him around.'

When he *was* around. Tiffany's earliest

memories were of her parents walking out of the door, embarking on yet another tour, while she was left behind with the latest nanny or housekeeper.

She gazed out of the window, choosing her moment. When she saw a gas station looming on the horizon, she said, 'Could we pull over? I need to use the bathroom.'

Lola frowned uncertainly. 'Well . . .'

'I really am desperate,' Tiffany said. 'Maybe we could get some coffee, too. They wouldn't allow it in rehab.' That was true, at least. Caffeine was banned, along with everything else that made life worth living.

Lola relented. 'I suppose it wouldn't hurt,' she said. 'And I do need to top up the petrol.' She caught Tiffany's eye. 'You're not going to try anything, are you?'

'As if!' Tiffany beamed back winningly.

CHAPTER EIGHTEEN

Lola drew up at the pumps and started to fill the car, while Tiffany scooted off in the direction of the bathroom. She hid around the back of the low building, pulled out her mobile phone and found the number she wanted on speed-dial.

'American Airlines? I need a ticket from New York to LA, first class, leaving tonight.'

She bobbed up and down, twitching with nerves, as the operator took forever to punch in the details. She kept sneaking looks around the edge of the building, but there was no sign of Lola.

Finally it was done and the operator asked for

her credit card number. Tiffany reached into her bag, then broke out in a cold sweat as she realised her wallet was gone.

She scrabbled around in the depths of her bag, growing increasingly desperate, until she heard a voice say, 'Is this what you're looking for?'

She looked up sharply. Lola was standing there, holding up her pink leather wallet.

'I'll call you back,' she snapped into her phone, and switched it off. 'Where did you get that?' she demanded.

'I took it out of your bag. I had a feeling you'd try to pull a stunt like this.' She didn't sound angry, just resigned and kind of disappointed.

Tiffany went to snatch the wallet from her hand, but Lola was too quick for her.

'Give me that,' Tiffany demanded.

'No.' Lola stuffed it into her own bag, then said, 'I'm going to get the coffees. I assume you still want one, or were you lying about that, too?'

She turned and headed back around the corner. Tiffany followed her, outraged and embarrassed that her masterplan hadn't worked. The fact that Lola was so annoyingly calm about the whole thing just made her hate her even more.

By the time they'd got into the gas station mini-mart, she'd worked herself up into a frenzy of fuming indignation.

'This is a violation of my human rights,' she shouted, as Lola calmly filled two paper cups with coffee from the machine.

'Milk and sugar?' Lola asked.

Tiffany swung round to face the other customers browsing among the magazines and confectionary shelves.

'Help, I'm being kidnapped!' she screamed at the top of her voice. No one looked at her. 'This person has taken my cash and credit cards and is holding me prisoner.'

Still no one reacted. The man beside her picked up a pastrami sandwich from the chiller cabinet and headed for the cash desk.

'I think you'll find they don't want to get involved,' Lola pointed out helpfully. 'I also think they've worked out that if you were really a prisoner you'd be bound and gagged in the boot of the car, not standing here watching me buy you a coffee. Would you like anything to eat, by the way?'

'No.' Tiffany stared around sulkily. What was happening to the world? She could strip off and streak through the store and none of these morons would even blink.

'You should eat something. You're too thin.'

'And you're too fat.'

'Maybe.' Lola shrugged.

She picked up the coffees, a BLT sandwich and a tube of Pringles, and headed for the cash desk. Tiffany stomped outside and leaned against the doorway, her arms folded across her chest, trying to figure out what to do next.

Lola came out and made for the car. She got halfway across the forecourt, then looked back at Tiffany. 'Are you coming?'

'Not unless you give me my wallet and take me back to the airport.'

Lola smiled wryly. 'You're hardly in a great bargaining position, are you?'

Tiffany plonked herself down on the kerb. 'Then I'm not going anywhere.'

She braced herself, waiting for the wheedling and pleading to start. But to her astonishment, Lola just said, 'Suit yourself.'

Tiffany watched her stroll towards the car. She was too surprised to react until she drove off.

She'll be back, she thought. Her mother would kick Lola's ass if she came back without her.

She leaned against the wall and assumed a suitably insouciant expression, waiting for Lola's return.

Ten minutes later she still hadn't come back. Tiffany's confidence was beginning to crumble into panic. She looked around, taking in her surroundings. A gas station on an anonymous stretch of highway, miles from the nearest city. She had no idea where she might be. She pulled out her mobile phone, ready to call someone for help. The red 'low battery' sign flashed at her, then it went dead.

Ever resourceful, Tiffany went to find the payphone she'd spotted around the back of the bathroom block earlier. It was wrecked.

Oh, man. She rested her head against the rough stucco wall and forced herself to think.

'Are you OK, miss?'

She turned. A burly trucker was watching her, frowning with concern. Usually Tiffany would have told him to take a hike but right now she decided she needed help more than she needed to be rude to a random stranger.

'I'm stuck,' she said. 'My . . . er . . . friend's driven off and left me here.'

'Some friend,' the trucker commented. 'Where were you headed?'

'New York. I have to catch a flight.'

'JFK or LaGuardia?'

'JFK.'

'Then it's your lucky day.' He smiled broadly. 'I'm going back to New York myself. I could drop you off on the way.'

Hope fluttered inside her, then died again. 'My friend also took all my cash and credit cards. And my phone has no battery.'

'Wow, that must have been some fight you guys had.' The trucker shook his head. 'No problem, I guess I could lend you my phone to call up your bank and set up some credit.'

'Really?' Hope surged again. Take that, Lola Wiseass, she thought defiantly.

'Sure, no problem. I've left my phone in the truck. Come with me.' He strode off towards the truck stop. Tiffany scrambled to her feet and started to follow him. Then something made her stop.

'Why are you helping me like this?' she asked.

'I hate to see a lady in distress. Especially one as pretty as you.'

His smile was warm, but there was something about the look in his eyes that set alarm bells ringing.

'Hey, come on,' he said. 'We'd better hit the road if you want to catch that flight. The traffic's starting to build up.'

Tiffany hesitated. 'I've changed my mind,' she started to say. 'I think I'll just wait here and—' She grasped in shock as his hand flashed out and grabbed her arm. 'Ow! Stop it, you're hurting me. Let me go!'

She tried to twist out of his grip, but the harder she pulled, the tighter his fingers bit into her flesh.

152

Then, behind them, came a voice.

'You heard her. She's changed her mind.'

Lola was standing behind them. Tiffany had never been so pleased to see anyone in her whole life.

She and the trucker squared up to each other for a moment. She was about half his size, but she had fixed him with a real 'don't mess with me' stare.

He let go of Tiffany's arm. 'I was only trying to help,' he mumbled.

'Thanks, but I'll take it from here.' Lola was still smiling, but that look would have killed a man at twenty paces. Tiffany was so impressed she almost forgot she was supposed to be annoyed.

As the trucker hurried back to his vehicle, Lola turned to her and said, 'Hasn't anyone ever told you about accepting lifts from strangers?'

'Hasn't anyone ever told you about dumping people in the middle of nowhere?' Tiffany screamed, her anger returning.

'I didn't dump you. You decided to stay.'

'I could have ended up dead.' She suddenly felt weak, trembly and near to tears.

'I came back, didn't I?' Lola handed her a paper cup. 'Your coffee's getting cold.'

'Can I have my wallet back?' Tiffany asked as she followed her to the car.

'Of course. When we get to New Jersey.'

Tiffany stared at her back with loathing. 'Bitch.'

Lola smiled over her shoulder. 'Takes one to know one,' she said.

*   *   *

They finally got back to New Jersey late in the afternoon, by which time Lola was shaking with exhaustion from the sheer effort of not strangling Tiffany. At least she didn't have to talk to her, since Tiffany gave her the silent treatment all the way.

The only time she spoke was when they pulled up at the waterfront overlooking the Delaware River. The Philadelphia skyline stretched in a magnificent panorama against the pale blue sky.

'Why are we here?' Tiffany asked sulkily as she climbed out of the car. 'Why haven't you dropped me at the hotel?'

'Don't you want to say hello to your mum and dad?'

'You mean you're scared to leave me alone in case I get into trouble?'

'Did I say that?' Although she'd certainly been thinking it.

'Can I have my wallet back now? You promised,' she insisted, as Lola hesitated.

She reached into her bag, pulled out the wallet and gave it to her. 'Just don't run off, OK?' she warned.

Tiffany rolled her eyes like a teenager. It was hard to believe she was twenty-three. She even looked like a kid, small and skinny in tight black jeans and a vest top that exposed the deep hollows of her collarbone and her waiflike arms. Lola could almost count the bones in her shoulders under her skin.

She headed for the production office, Tiffany trailing behind. Hamish was on the phone, organizing some local stagehands for the next stop in Connecticut later that week. He hung up as they

154

walked in.

'Hello, you must be Tiffany.' He held out his hand.

Tiffany looked at it as if he'd offered her a dead rat. 'No shit, Sherlock.' She threw herself down in Lola's chair and spun it around a few times.

Lola glanced at Hamish and shook her head. 'Do you have any idea where Tiffany's parents might be?' she said sweetly.

'Rick's doing a sound-check. Dinah's in Canada.'

Tiffany stopped spinning.

'Canada?' Lola repeated.

'There was some problem with the album distribution. It was important, apparently.'

And seeing her daughter isn't, Lola thought.

'Hey, don't stress about it.' Tiffany seemed to guess what was going through her mind. 'She wouldn't have been there at the birth if she could help it.'

She kicked away from the desk and started spinning again, her head lolled back, staring up at the ceiling. She reminded Lola of the prickly, defensive teenagers she used to meet on the Creighton estate. The ones who pretended they didn't care that their mums and dads ignored them, and hung out all night in the bus shelter.

Just then, Jay burst in. 'Have those picks I ordered come yet?' he demanded.

'Let me see . . . picks, picks . . .' Lola checked the paperwork on her desk. She had a vague feeling she'd forgotten all about them.

Jay's eyes narrowed. 'You did remember to send the order, didn't you?'

'I—'

'We did it yesterday,' Hamish cut in. 'I'll call them and check. If they haven't sent them already I'll get someone to collect them.'

'Thanks. I'm glad at least one person's efficient around here.' Jay glared at Lola.

She glared back. 'If you were that efficient you wouldn't need to order extra picks halfway through the tour, would you? Anyway, for your information, I've just come back from a two-hundred-mile round trip to pick up your sister.'

'My—' Jay spotted Tiffany lolling in Lola's chair in the corner. 'Oh, it's you.'

'Thrilled to see you too, asshole,' she snapped back.

'Ah, family reunions. Makes you feel all warm and fuzzy inside, doesn't it?' Hamish whispered to Lola.

'Let me know when those picks get here,' Jay said, then left.

Lola followed him outside. 'What was all that about?' she demanded.

'Sorry?' Jay looked blank.

'Are you that unpleasant to everyone, or just close family?'

'I haven't got any family,' Jay glowered. 'If you're talking about that waste of space in there, she's nothing to do with me. Thank God.'

'I realise you have issues, but at least you could give Tiffany a break. She's been through a tough time.'

He laughed. 'Oh yeah, really tough. Spending a month in a country club for rich boozehounds? Must have been hell.'

Lola frowned at him. 'Do you have any pity for anyone else, or do you save it all for yourself?'

156

'Oh, I've got compassion all right. For people with genuine problems. Not for spoilt, self-indulgent little brats like Tiffany.'

'How do you know she hasn't got a genuine problem? Just because she acts the way she does doesn't mean she can't be hurt just like other people.'

'Wow, you must have had a real girlie bonding session on the way back from rehab.'

'As a matter of fact, it was a nightmare,' Lola admitted frankly. 'But that doesn't stop me feeling sorry for her. She deserves the chance to turn her life around.'

'You really think she *wants* to turn her life around?'

'Yes, I do.'

'In that case, why have I just seen her heading for your car?'

'What?' Lola turned round, but it was too late. Her silver Merc was already speeding towards the security gate.

'Probably off to get wasted again,' Jay added wisely.

'Bloody hell!' Lola chewed her lip. 'Why didn't you tell me?'

'And miss seeing the look on your face?' He smirked. 'Anyway, it's not my problem. You're the one who wants to rescue everyone, not me. I couldn't care less.'

CHAPTER NINETEEN

Fortunately, Tiffany returned from her two-day bender hitting the bars and clubs by the time the show was ready to roll on to North Carolina. The lorries carrying all the dismantled rigging and stage equipment had set off straight after the show in the early hours. The buses followed. Some of the crew were trying to snatch some precious sleep before the whole process started again. Others were still running on adrenaline, playing cards, watching DVDs and generally hanging out.

Lola squashed into her narrow bunk and tried to sleep, but it wasn't easy with all the laughter and loud voices around her. Jay's seemed to be the loudest of all; Lola wondered if he was doing it deliberately, or if exhaustion had just made her paranoid.

It was mid-morning by the time they reached their hotel, by which time all Lola could think about was falling into bed. Just her luck that she ended up in the lift with Jay.

'Didn't you get much rest?' he asked with mock sympathy, as she failed to stifle a yawn with the back of her hand.

Lola ignored him. She was frazzled from lack of sleep, and knew that if she opened her mouth she would let loose a stream of abuse.

She held her breath and her temper until they reached the eighth floor. The lift doors opened, and they both got out. Jay followed her all the way down the corridor to her room.

'Looks like we're neighbours.' He smiled

unpleasantly as he let himself in next door.

She dragged herself and her bags into her room, and threw herself down on the bed. Straight away she felt herself drifting off, her head sinking into the deliciously soft pillows . . .

A crash of heavy metal music from next door shocked her awake almost before her eyes had closed. Lola groaned. Jay had his hi-fi turned upto the max.

She rolled over and pulled the pillow over her head, but she couldn't block out the noise of smashing drums and twanging, insistent guitar licks. Ignore it, she told herself. He's only doing it to wind you up.

But the more she ignored it, the worse it seemed to get. After twenty minutes she couldn't stand it any longer.

Jay came to the door dressed in nothing but a towel draped around his narrow hips, his dark hair dripping.

'Yes?' he said, his voice barely audible over the clashing music in the background. 'What can I do for you?'

'You can stop being so bloody childish, for a start.'

'I'm sorry, I don't get you.'

'Your music. It's very loud.'

'Is it? I hadn't noticed.'

Forcing herself to stay icily polite, she said, 'Can you turn it down?'

He thought for a moment. 'Probably not.'

She dug her nails into her palms to stop herself punching him. 'Do you have any idea how pathetic you're being?'

He shrugged. 'I like music in the bath. Hey,' he

stepped back as she shouldered past him, 'what are you doing?'

'Watch me.' Lola disconnected the music system and yanked the plug from the wall. Then she picked it up, carried it to the bathroom and dropped it into the tub. Water splashed everywhere, sloshing over the floor and her shoes.

She turned to face him. 'You like music in the bath? There it is.'

He looked from the bath to her and back again. 'Have you gone mad?'

'Ask me again when I've had some sleep.'

As she squelched past him and headed for the door he called after her, 'Is it all getting a bit too much for you? Maybe you're just not cut out for life on the road.'

She swung round to face him. She didn't have the energy to retaliate any more. 'Why do you hate me so much?'

Her question shocked him briefly, she could see it in his eyes. Then he recovered. 'I couldn't care less about you.'

'That's not true. You really hate me. I just wish I knew what I'd done to upset you so badly.'

His eyes narrowed. Then he said, 'You really want to know? It's because every time I look at you I remember what my father did to my mother.' He took a step closer. 'How old are you, Lola?'

'Nearly thirty.'

'So I must have been two years old when he was screwing around with your mother. They were having a great time while my mum was at home with me, breaking her heart.'

'He broke my mother's heart, too,' Lola said quietly.

160

'So what? She deserved it. She knew what she was doing when she got involved with a married man.' He thrust his face closer to hers. 'Did she ever think of his wife and what she was going through? I don't think so. All she cared about was shagging a rock star. She probably got herself pregnant hoping he'd leave us—'

The resounding slap that Lola gave him shocked them both. Jay stopped in mid-rant, his hand to his cheek.

'Get over yourself, will you?' Lola said quietly. 'You're not the only one in the world who's had problems to deal with. The difference is we're not all drowning in self-pity like you.'

*   *   *

She was still seething about it when she went to work early the following morning. The production office was always the first thing to be set up, mainly because the crew wanted to make sure their expenses were sorted out.

Hamish was already in the office when she got there, organizing transport to take the band to a TV appearance at lunchtime.

'With any luck they'll still be sober by then.' His smile disappeared when he saw her grim face. 'What's wrong with you? Don't tell me the crew have been posting your mobile number on those naughty websites again?'

'I could handle that,' Lola said, throwing her bag down on the desk. 'It's Jay and his attitude problem I can't deal with.'

'I don't get it,' Hamish said. 'He's always OK with me. Not exactly the life and soul of the party,

161

but not too bad.'

'That's because you're not related to him.' She heaved a sigh and ran her fingers through her hair. 'God, why didn't someone tell me this family was going to be such a bloody nightmare? They make the Borgias look like the Waltons. What with him and Britt and Tiffany—'

'Someone say my name?' She sloped in, looking absurdly young in cut-off denim shorts, pink Skechers and a midriff-skimming yellow T-shirt. She also looked deeply hungover.

Lola peered at the dark shadows under her eyes. 'What happened to you?' she asked. 'We've hardly seen you.'

'So?'

'So you could have called. I was worried about you'

Tiffany sent her a scathing look. 'Who are you, my mother?'

No, thank God, Lola thought. 'What do you want?'

'A favour.' Tiffany lay down on Lola's desk and stretched her arms above her head, showing off a lot of tanned, flat stomach. On the other side of the office Hamish dropped a ream of paper he'd been trying to stuff the wrong way into the photocopier. 'I need some backstage passes for my friends.'

'Which friends?'

'Does it matter?' Tiffany frowned, irritated at being questioned. 'Just some guys I met last night. You don't know them.'

'I'm going to need some names.'

'Wow, you're such a Nazi. Can't you just give me the damn passes?'

162

'Of course. When you give me the names. It's for security reasons,' she explained, when Tiffany looked as if she was going to explode into another of her famous tantrums.

'For crying out loud! Who do you think I'm going to give them to? The Al-Qaeda social club?'

Hamish, still gathering up the scattered copier paper, made a sound somewhere between a laugh and a cough. Tiffany glared at him.

'That's not the point,' Lola began to explain. 'It's because—'

They were interrupted by a woman strutting into the office. Over six feet tall in spiked heels, with red hair, and wearing way more make-up than clothing, she strutted up to Lola's desk and said, 'I was told to come to you about the guest list.'

'What about it?'

'I want my name on it.' She leaned across the desk, ignoring Tiffany, who was still stretched across it.

Lola struggled to be businesslike. 'And your name is?'

'Tawnee Wallis. I'm a friend of the band.'

I bet you are. Lola looked her up and down as she reached for the message book where all the requests were noted.

She flicked through the pages of the book. 'I'm sorry, there's no mention of you in here.'

'I only got into town this morning. But last time I spoke to the guys, they definitely said they wanted to hook up next time I was around. Call them and check if you don't believe me.'

Lola was just about to reach for the phone when she caught Hamish giving her the finger-drawn-across-the-throat gesture from the other end of the

163

office. 'Actually, I've just remembered, the band has left for the TV studio,' she lied. 'If you could leave me your name and a contact number, I'll certainly ask them to call you . . .'

'Just forget it.' Tawnee jabbed a terrifying, scarlet-tipped nail a few inches from Lola's nose. 'But let me tell you, you've made a big mistake here. When the band finds out about this, you're going to be in some serious trouble.'

She stormed out, slamming the door behind her. It was as if a hurricane had just blown through the office.

'Who was *she*?' Lola asked.

'Bad news,' Hamish said. 'Tawnee Wallis is a real scalp-hunter. She and Rick had a thing a couple of years ago. Sorry.' He glanced at Tiffany.

She shrugged. 'My dad screwing around is hardly big news.'

'This time it got quite heavy,' Hamish went on. 'He and Britt were going through a rough patch and for a while Tawnee looked like a serious threat.'

Tiffany's lip curled. '*That* was nearly my stepmom? Gross.'

'Luckily they sorted out their problems and Tawnee was history. But now she's banned from coming anywhere near Rick. Thank God you didn't give her a pass. Britt would have gone through the roof.'

'Talking of which,' Tiffany interrupted, sitting up. 'Can I have my passes now?'

'I told you, I'm going to need more details.'

The phone rang. Tiffany heaved a dramatic sigh as Lola answered it.

'Hello? . . . Oh, OK, I'll come and fetch it.

164

Thanks for letting me know. Bye.' She hung up. 'A package has just arrived at the gate,' she said to Hamish.

'I'll go,' he said. 'I've got to leave something down there for collection anyway.'

'Can you tell the runner he'll need to go to the airport later? Britt's astrologer is coming in for a personal consultation.'

'Er . . . hello? I'm still here.' Tiffany gave them a little wave. 'Passes?'

Lola sighed. 'Look, just take them.' She knew Tiffany wasn't going to give up, and she was too busy to argue.

Tiffany grabbed them, her face lighting up.

'I'm still going to need names,' Lola called after her. But she'd already gone. 'I hope I did the right thing,' she said to Hamish, chewing her lip.

'I don't think you had much choice. I'm going to fetch that package.'

While Hamish was gone, Lola tried to catch up with putting receipts on to the accounts system. Every incidental the crew spent had to be accounted for. It was another of the little jobs Hamish did brilliantly; she sucked at it.

She was still tapping figures into the computer when Hamish returned a few minutes later.

Not looking up, she said, 'Sorry, I still don't get this. Is it the figure and then enter, or enter and then the figure? Hamish?' She glanced at him. He was standing in the doorway, clutching what looked like a shoe box. His face was as white as his shirt.

Lola stood up. 'Hamish, what is it? What's wrong?'

He moved forward slowly and put the box down

165

on her desk.

'I think you'd better take a look at this,' he said.

CHAPTER TWENTY

She looked warily at the box in front of her. 'What is it?'

'Open it and take a look.'

She reached out and gingerly flipped the lid, then jumped back as a sickly, metallic smell hit her. Clamping her hand over her mouth, she peered cautiously at the congealing red lump inside the box.

'Is that . . . what I think it is?'

'If you're thinking it's a heart, then yes, it is.'

Her stomach flipped queasily. 'Is it human?'

'How should I know?' Hamish took a step away from it. 'What's that taped inside the lid?'

'It looks like a note.' Lola eyed the blue envelope. Rick's name was scrawled on the front. 'Maybe we'd better not touch it. We don't want to get our prints on it.'

'How will we know what it says?'

'Perhaps it's better we don't know.' Lola shivered. She and Hamish stood staring at the box for another ten seconds, then her curiosity got the better of her. 'Maybe it will be all right, as long as we're careful,' she said.

She picked off the tape with the tips of her fingers and extracted the note, as if she were defusing a bomb. Hamish watched her from a safe distance.

'Well?' he said.

'Hang on.' She unfolded it carefully, then read it through. 'Well, it's not exactly a fan letter.' She sat down, her legs suddenly shaky. ' "A pig's heart for a pig," ' she read out. ' "Give up the tour, or the next bleeding heart could be yours. From Your Devoted Fan." '

'Well, it least we know it's not human,' Hamish said bracingly.

Lola put the letter carefully back into the envelope, her mind made up. 'We've got to show this to the police,' she said.

'But Rick said he doesn't want them involved.'

'Never mind what he wants. This is getting way too serious.'

'All the same, maybe you'd better talk to him first?' Hamish suggested.

It took a long time for Rick to answer the phone in his suite. He sounded groggy and half asleep, even though it was mid-morning.

'Do you know what time it is?' he demanded.

'Do you?'

'No,' he admitted. 'But it feels too early. What do you want, anyway?'

'I thought you'd like to know we've got a parcel for you. A gift from a fan.'

'So?'

'Not just any fan. *The* fan.'

There was a long silence. She could sense Rick rousing himself to wakefulness on the other end of the line. 'What is it?' he asked finally.

'A heart. In a box.'

'A real heart? Not, like, a heart balloon or anything?'

'Definitely not a balloon.'

She heard him exhale long and loud. 'Oh, shit.'

167

'I'm calling the police.'

'No, don't do that.'

'Rick, this isn't just a few batty letters any more. This is practically a death threat. We've got to tell someone.'

Another long silence. 'Can't you deal with it?' Rick asked.

'What?'

'You're a cop, aren't you?'

'Yes, but—'

'So do some detective work. Find out who's behind it.'

'I can't do that. It's way out of my league.'

'Just do what you've got to do. Except tell the police. Or Britt,' he added, and rang off.

'What did he say?' Hamish asked, as she sat staring at the phone. He'd retreated to his end of the office, as far away from the offending box as possible.

'He wants me to find out who sent it.'

'Really? How thrilling. Can I help? I've always fancied being a detective.'

'This isn't an episode of *Murder, She Wrote*,' Lola snapped. 'You can't solve this kind of thing without expert help. You need fingerprints, forensics, handwriting experts, DNA samples—'

'We could make a list of all the possible suspects,' Hamish said brightly, pulling a sheet of paper from his drawer.

'Wow, yes, that would help.' Lola was too edgy to hide her sarcasm. 'Then we could get them all in a room together and unmask the culprit.'

'Good idea.' Hamish went on scribbling.

'And maybe you could wear a funny moustache and speak in a French accent.'

He looked up, hurt. 'If you're referring to Hercule Poirot, I think you'll find he's Belgian.'

'I was thinking more of Inspector Clouseau.' She carefully moved the box from her desk to the floor. Just the sight of it made her feel sick.

'Very constructive, I'm sure,' Hamish said. 'While you've been bitching, I've come up with a definitive list of suspects.'

'Let's hear it, then. Who have you got so far?'

He looked down the list. 'Pretty much everyone, I'm afraid. Including you.'

'Me?'

'He dumped your mum, didn't he? That's a pretty good motive.'

'I suppose so,' she agreed. 'But it wasn't me,' she added hastily.

'I'd already ruled you out, actually.'

Lola reached for a biscuit, remembered the heart at her feet, and put it back. 'So who have we got?'

Hamish consulted his list again. 'It could be any of his wives. He's humiliated and cheated on them all at some time. But I don't think it can be Dinah or Britt, because they could just help themselves to his money if they really wanted to hurt him.'

'True.'

'Then I thought it might be one of his kids.'

'Tiffany's been away in rehab,' Lola said.

'I suppose that rules her out, then.' Hamish drew a line through her name. 'That leaves Jay. We all know he hates Rick.'

'Yes, but why would he want him to cancel the tour? I don't see the point.' Lola read the note again. 'That's all this is about. Whoever sent this is just trying to frighten him.'

169

'Can't be any of the crew, then. They wouldn't want to put themselves out of a job.' Hamish scratched out a few more names.

'Maybe it really is a fan,' Lola mused.

'Or someone who used to be.'

She frowned. 'Meaning?'

'There are some people who think Poleaxe hasn't been the same without Terry Mac.'

Lola's ears pricked. Now where had she heard that name before? Then she remembered: it was the journalist at the album launch, John Henderson. And Rick hadn't been too pleased about it, as she recalled.

'Who's Terry Mac?' she asked.

Hamish looked around furtively. 'Rick doesn't like anyone talking about him. He thinks it's bad luck.'

'Why? What did he do that was so wrong?'

'Nothing. Terry MacIntyre was a genius,' Hamish said stoutly. 'He's responsible for some of the finest songs in the Poleaxe back catalogue. Or so some of the older fans reckon, anyway. He and Rick started the band together while they were still at school.'

'What happened to him?'

'The usual story. He might have been a genius, but he was a tortured one. When Poleaxe hit the big time, he got heavily into drink and drugs. And I mean *really* into them. Sometimes it got so bad they had to carry him on stage. In the end, Rick and the other guys decided he was a liability and dumped him. That's the official story, anyway.'

'And the unofficial one?'

Hamish leaned forward confidingly. 'There are a few people who reckon Rick got him kicked out because he was getting too much attention. Terry may have been a bit wild and unpredictable, but the girls loved that. He was the one with the natural charisma. And Rick couldn't stand the competition. Dinah had just taken over as manager, so it must have been an easy job to get him kicked out of the band.'

Lola thought about it for a moment. What was it John Henderson had said? Then it came to her: *A pity Terry's not here to enjoy the fame and fortune, too.* 'Do you think it might be a Terry Mac fan sending these letters?' Then another thought struck her. 'Or maybe it's Terry himself ? Maybe he's an embittered has-been, trying to wreak his revenge?'

'I doubt it.' Hamish's brown eyes were solemn behind his spectacles. 'Terry was killed in a house fire three months after he got kicked out of the band.'

*   *   *

Lola mulled it over for the rest of the day. At the gig that night she watched the band from the backstage area and scanned the crowd, although she had no idea what she was looking for.

She still wanted to go to the police, but Rick had been adamant about it when she talked to him again before the show.

'You're getting this all wrong,' he said. 'It was probably meant as a kind of tribute.'

'What kind of person sends a heart as a token of their appreciation?'

'Ever heard of a Valentine?'

'Valentines don't bleed over people's desks.'

171

She couldn't work out whether he was ridiculously brave, or too dim to realise a genuine threat when he saw one. Or perhaps he thought he was so godlike nothing could hurt him.

But at least Lola noticed that he'd upped his personal security. His minder Gus was never far from his side, except when he was on stage.

That night after the show there was the usual backstage get-together, as the band, their entourages and various invited guests crowded into the dressing room to party while the crew struck out the set and loaded it on to the lorries.

Lola was too shattered to face another late-night session. It had been a long, scary day and all she wanted to do was climb into her bed.

She was making her way back down the corridor that led away from the stage when she heard a commotion coming from the backstage area.

She turned the corner and slammed into a ring of roadies, all cheering and cat-calling. She pushed her way through to the front—ducking under waving arms, and sidling between the solid mass of sweaty bodies—and found what they were watching.

Two women were fighting. Lola caught sight of two heads—one blonde, one flaming red. Britt and Tawnee. They were locked into each other, kicking, biting and grabbing handfuls of hair.

The roadies, meanwhile, were cheering them on, loving every second.

'Damn! Why is there never any mud around when you need it?' one of them shouted, as the women fell to the ground, writhing, spitting and punching.

Lola looked around. 'Where's Rick?'

'Hiding, if he's got any sense. C'mon, Britt! Give her another slap!'

Lola had broken up enough Saturday night bitch fights to know what to do. She pitched in, hauling one off the other, forcing them apart while the roadies booed and jeered.

She held the women at arm's length where they stood, breathing hard and eyeballing each other fiercely.

'I've told you to stay away from my husband,' Britt warned.

'Maybe you'd better tell your husband to stay away from *me*.' Tawnee looked her up and down insultingly. 'I can't help it if he'd rather have a real woman than a toothpick in a designer dress, can I?'

'Whore!' Britt screamed, and launched herself at Tawnee, hands clawing, aiming for her eyes.

Lola forced herself between them again. 'How did you get in here?' she asked Tawnee.

'How do you think?' She proudly displayed the laminated pass bouncing on her inflated breasts. 'Access all areas,' she said. 'And I mean *all*.'

The roadies laughed and cheered. Tawnee looked around, smiling, delighted to have an audience.

'I didn't give you that,' Lola said. 'How did you—'

Then Rick appeared. 'Hey guys, what's the big deal?' He stopped when he saw Tawnee. 'What are you doing here?'

'*She* let her in.' Britt pointed an accusing finger at Lola. A trickle of blood oozed from her lip.

Rick looked back at Tawnee. For a split second Lola thought she saw a smile pass between them. But by the time he turned to Gus his frown was

173

firmly back in place.

'Get rid of her,' he said gruffly. 'She's bothering my wife.'

As Gus handled Tawnee out, Rick put his arm around Britt, who quickly transformed from bitch-slapping Amazon to weepy, helpless little wife.

The crew, disappointed that the show was over, started to drift back to work.

Lola was left there, feeling awkward. 'I'm sorry,' she began. 'I don't know how it happened.'

'What do you mean, you don't know?' Britt turned on her from the protection of Rick's arm, her blue eyes flashing. 'You're supposed to check the guest list.'

'Yes, but—' Just then Lola caught sight of Tiffany smirking in the corner of her vision. Suddenly she understood. 'Maybe I didn't check it properly,' she said.

'Maybe you just don't know how to do your job!' Britt raged. 'Thanks to you, I've been totally humiliated. This is all your fault.'

'Now hang on—'

Rick held up his hand, silencing her. 'That's enough. Have you any idea how much trouble you've caused?'

'I didn't—' she began to protest.

But Rick wasn't listening. He squeezed his arm tighter around Britt's shoulders. 'Come on, let's go home.' As they swept past Lola, he muttered ominously, 'I'll deal with you later.'

CHAPTER TWENTY-ONE

As it turned out, Rick's way of dealing with her was to give her the silent treatment all the way to Tennessee.

Lola was used to him ignoring her, but this was a different kind of silence. If she tried to speak to him, he pretended he hadn't heard her. If they happened to be in the same room together, he acted as if she wasn't there. Lola was embarrassed, but she was also furious. How could a grown man be so childish?

But then, Rick wasn't exactly known for his maturity.

'It's not fair,' she complained to Hamish, as they set up the office at the new venue the following day. 'I didn't do anything wrong.'

'Don't take it personally,' he advised. 'I've seen this before. It's all part of the game.'

'Game?'

He nodded. 'He doesn't want to upset Britt in case she gives him a hard time. And Britt hates you at the moment, so he's got to hate you, too.'

'Terrific,' Lola muttered.

'It'll be OK soon. Once you've apologised.'

'Me, apologise?'

'And grovelled a bit,' Hamish said. 'Grovelling never does any harm.'

'They can forget about that.' Lola scrambled under the table to plug in the printer cable. 'If anyone's going to apologise, it should be him. Pass me that adaptor, would you?'

Hamish smiled as he handed it over. 'I know it's

turned a bit chilly, but I don't think hell's ready to freeze over yet.'

'We'll just have to see, won't we?' She certainly wasn't about to grovel to anyone. Especially when it wasn't her fault.

'I wonder how Tawnee got hold of that pass?' Hamish mused as he mulled over *The Times* crossword. The newspapers were sent over from England every day, and he always made sure he got to *The Times* first. Not that there was much competition; the rest of the crew preferred to fight over *The Sun*.

'Haven't you worked it out yet? I thought you liked playing detective.' She watched him scratch his head, trying to catch up. 'Who was in here at the same time as Tawnee? And who left with a handful of passes?'

It dawned on him. 'Tiffany?'

Lola nodded. 'She must have caught up with her outside. I bet Tawnee thought all her birthdays had come at once.'

'But why would she do that?'

'To stir things up, I suppose.' Lola couldn't think of any other reason. 'Some people just like making trouble.'

And Tiffany had it in for her just as much as Jay did. It was quite tiring, being hated by so many people.

'Are you going to tell Rick?'

'What's the point?' There was enough bad feeling around, she didn't need to create any more. Tiffany might enjoy making trouble, but she didn't.

She worked all morning, arranging transport, sorting out the guest list and handing out the PDs. Then, just as she thought she'd got it all sorted, the

176

promoter from Salt Lake City called to say there was a problem with the hotel booking. Apparently the hotel management had got wind of Jonno's reputation for trashing places and decided they didn't want the band in their establishment after all. Which meant frantically ringing around, trying to find accommodation for everyone.

And of course, it couldn't be just anywhere. The band insisted on a top hotel, city centre, and the best suites available.

To complicate matters still further, there was an international window manufacturers' conference going on in the city at the same time, which meant every hotel was booked solid.

It took two hours of pleading and wheedling before she'd finally dealt with the problem. By which time it was mid-afternoon and her stomach was protesting loudly.

She went to the catering trailer for a late lunch. Some of the crew were hanging around outside, taking a coffee break and playing cards. Jay was with them. He was the only one who didn't look up and greet her as she approached.

She stepped up to the catering trailer and surveyed the remnants of lunch laid out on the buffet table. There wasn't a lot after the hungry crew had devoured their share. Just a couple of stringy chicken legs, a few hardened bread rolls and whole lot of salad. Lola stifled a sigh. Why was there only ever salad left over? She glanced back at the squared, beefy shoulders of the crew as they crammed around the small plastic table. Because that lot couldn't stand the stuff any more than she could.

She helped herself to a piece of chicken and

grudgingly filled up her plate with lettuce. Balancing it and a bottle of water on her tray, she headed for an empty table.

'What are you sitting over there for? There's room over here,' Neil the rigger shouted across to her.

Lola caught Jay's forbidding eye. 'Thanks, but I'm OK here.'

'Don't be unsociable. Come and sit with us.' The others budged round to make room for her.

'I'm leaving now. You can have my space.' Jay stood abruptly and picked up his tray.

The others stared at him. 'But we're in the middle of a game!'

'I've got to re-string Kyle's Fender.'

'Liar, I saw you do that this morning,' Mo the drum tech jeered. 'He just doesn't want to give us a chance to win back some of that cash,' he said to the others.

With obvious reluctance, Jay sat back down, Lola opposite him. She could hardly eat for the poisonous looks he kept shooting her.

Finally she gave up and pushed her plate away, her appetite shrunk to nothing. Neil immediately fell on her leftovers like a ravenous wolf.

'How can you still be hungry?' Lola said.

'I can't help it, I'm a growing boy.'

'Are we playing or not?' Jay said irritably, holding up the cards.

'Sure.' Neil turned to Lola. 'Do you play poker?'

She opened her mouth to tell them, then saw the way they were smirking at each other. 'A little,' she said.

'Shall we deal you in?'

She caught Jay's eye across the table. 'Why not?'

They played a couple of hands, and Jay won both times. He was obviously the crew's champion player, and Lola wasn't surprised. It was impossible to tell what was going on behind those green eyes.

She smiled to herself. It was time to show her own hand.

*   *   *

'I thought you said you weren't any good at this game?' Mo said crossly, as Lola scooped in the dollar bills from the centre of the table for the third time.

'I said I'd only played a little. I didn't say I wasn't any good.'

'You'll beat Jay at this rate,' Neil said.

'Nah,' Mo shook his head. 'No one can beat Jay.'

Lola smiled. 'I like a challenge.'

Jay said nothing. All his concentration was fixed on Neil as he dealt out the cards.

He was taking this far too seriously, Lola thought. Maybe it was time to show him what she could really do?

The deal went her way from the start. Two kings and a ten. She pushed a handful of dollars into the middle of the table. The others matched it.

Neil dealt the flop. Three cards in the centre of the table, eight of clubs, seven of diamonds—and another king. He dropped his cards on the table face down. 'I'm out.'

'Me too,' Mo said.

Neil dealt another card into the centre of the table. A six of clubs this time. The other two riggers folded, leaving just her and Jay.

179

Lola looked at him. His eyes gave nothing away, but a muscle was pounding in his cheek. It was just possible he had the right cards to make a straight, which would beat her three kings. But if he didn't . . .

She took a deep breath and pushed the remainder of her dollars into the centre of the table. 'I'm all in,' she said.

She caught the flash of dismay in his eyes. Either he'd have to match her bet, or he'd have to fold and admit he'd lost. From the way he hesitated, there was no way he had that straight in his hand.

But there was no way he was going to admit defeat, either.

Looking her straight in the eye, he pushed all his money into the centre of the table.

Mo drew in a sharp breath. 'A fight to the death,' he said. 'That's what I like to see.'

Neil dealt the final card into the centre of the table. Lola glanced at it, and had to bite her lip to stop herself yelping.

The fourth king. Now she had four of a kind, she was unbeatable. She knew it, and so did Jay. She could see it in his face.

Everyone else knew it, too. The others were already laughing, teasing Jay about losing his crown. If she beat him, he'd hate her even more. And she wasn't sure she could face that.

She laid her cards face down. 'I fold.'

There was a gasp of amazement around the table.

'What?' Neil was outraged. 'What did you have?'

'I'm not telling you.' She shoved her cards quickly back into the pile and shuffled them before

180

he had a chance to look. 'But it wasn't good enough.'

Neil shook his head. 'You must be good at bluffing, because you certainly had me fooled.'

'Aren't I just?' She glanced across at Jay. 'Aren't you going to collect your money? You won it fair and square.'

'Did I?' he scowled.

They stared at each other for a moment. They both knew she'd let him win. From the pained look on his face, that hurt more than if she'd beaten him hands down.

'I've got to get back to work.' He stuffed the notes in his pocket and stood up.

What happened next took place so quickly that Lola couldn't be sure if it was an accident or deliberate. As Jay reached across the table for his mobile phone, his elbow shot out and upended the cold remains of a cup of coffee straight into her bag.

'Jesus, Jay!' Neil stood up, brushing down his spattered jeans.

'It was an accident.' He didn't even bother to sound convincing, but Lola was too busy emptying her bag to take any notice.

'Is there much damage?' Jay asked.

Like you care, she thought.

'All pretty much ruined, thanks.' Lola pulled out her phone, her purse, her sopping address book.

Then she remembered something else and dived back into her bag. Oh no, please don't let that be ruined, too, she prayed.

But it was.

'What's that?' Neil asked.

'It *was* a photo.' Not just any photo. The dog-eared strip of her and her mother, laughing together in the passport booth. Her most treasured possession. Except now it was just a soggy strip of nothing, the images blurred out of recognition. She held it between her two fingers and watched the coffee drip on to the table. Hot tears stung the backs of her eyes and she knew it wouldn't be long before they spilled out.

She gathered up her wrecked belongings, stuffed them back in her bag and fled. There was no way she would give Jay the satisfaction of seeing her cry.

Back in her hotel room, she did her best to salvage the photos. She carefully mopped the coffee up with clean water, then tried to dry the strip with a hairdryer, but it was no good. She could hardly make out her mother's face any more.

Suddenly it was all too much for her. Jay's cruelty, Rick's pathetic childishness, Britt's cold indifference, Tiffany's tantrums and all the other stupid stuff she had to put up with—everything seemed to overwhelm her in a great crashing wave of despair. She curled up on the bed and cried.

Half an hour of solid sobbing later, she felt her head clear. This is ridiculous, she told herself. You don't need all this. She'd already spent too much of her life having to deal with other people's nonsense. She didn't have to do it any more. She was free to walk away whenever she liked.

And that was exactly what she was going to do.

Twenty minutes later she'd washed her face, reapplied her mascara and was feeling much more optimistic when there was a knock on her door. Thinking it would be Hamish with yet another problem, and preparing herself to tell him he'd have to deal with it, she answered the door.

The last person she expected to see was Jay.

'Can I come in?' he said.

'If you must.' She stood aside.

'I just wanted to say . . .' He was halfway across the room when he spotted the open suitcase on the bed. 'What's all this?'

'You got what you wanted. I'm leaving.' She managed a sarcastic smile. 'It's OK, you don't have to pretend to look so devastated.'

He stared at the case, then back at her. 'Why?'

'Why do you think?'

'Is it because of me?'

She lifted her eyebrow. 'It always has to be about you, doesn't it? But you're wrong. This time it's about *me*. I can't deal with all this any more. You were right; I can't hack it. I should never have tried.'

He regarded her steadily. He'd never looked her in the eye for so long before. 'I didn't have you down as a quitter.'

'Life's full of surprises, isn't it?' She folded up a pair of jeans and laid them in her suitcase. 'It's like poker. You've got to know when to fold your cards.'

'You gave up on that too quickly as well.'

'Maybe,' she agreed. 'Or maybe I just got tired of trying to join a game where no one wanted me.'

He was silent for a long time. Lola went on packing. There wasn't much to do; they moved on so quickly from place to place she scarcely bothered to take her stuff out of her suitcase these days. But as she emptied drawers and shelves she was aware of Jay watching her every move.

'I haven't made things very easy for you, have I?'

he said finally.

'That's an understatement.'

'I'm sorry. What you said the other day was right. I do sometimes forget other people have problems, too.'

He picked up the photo, which she'd left under her bedside lamp to dry. 'It really was an accident, you know.'

'It doesn't matter.'

'It mattered to you; I could see it in your face.' He studied the photo. 'This is your mum, right?'

'It was.' She took the photo from him.

'I'm sorry. I know how I would have felt if it had been my mum's photo.'

'At least you still have her.' She didn't mean to sound so self-pitying, but she couldn't help it.

'Were you very close?' Jay asked.

Lola nodded. 'Until she died when I was sixteen. Then I was on my own.'

'You had your dad, didn't you?'

'Oh yes, I had my dad.' She smiled bitterly.

He read her expression. 'You didn't get on?'

'Most of the time he just pretended I wasn't around. But at least that was better than what he did to my mum.'

Realisation dawned and he looked genuinely shocked. 'I had no idea.'

'No one did. You never know what goes on behind closed doors, do you?'

She smiled down at the blurry outline of her mother's face, crammed close to her own in the narrow frame of the photo booth. 'I remember when this was taken. It was a Saturday afternoon and we were supposed to be shopping for new school shoes in the precinct. I must have been about eight years old. We finished our shopping extra quick, then Mum took me to the new McDonald's that had just opened in the town centre. I can even remember what we ate. Mum had a coffee; I had a cheeseburger and a chocolate shake.' She smiled at the memory. 'It was the first time I'd ever had anything like it. Dad didn't approve, you see. We never ate out anywhere; he always said it was a waste of money.'

Why am I telling him all this? she wondered. He was the last person she should have been baring her soul to. And yet, somehow, she still wanted to. She needed him to understand.

'Anyway, we were terrified that he'd find out where we'd been. We tried to keep it a secret, but it was pointless trying to hide anything from him. When we got home he went through Mum's purse, checked what was left of her housekeeping money against the receipt for the shoes, and worked out what she'd spent.'

'What happened?' Jay asked.

'The usual.' She tried to sound matter-of-fact, but she couldn't keep the tremor of emotion out of her voice as she remembered how she'd sat in her bedroom, listening to her father ranting downstairs. Then it all went ominously silent and she knew the worst had happened. 'She tried to hide the bruises, pretend it was all OK. But I knew. I always knew.'

'I'm so sorry,' Jay said.

'Like I said, you weren't to know.' Lola was brisk, realizing she'd said too much. Even her best friend Sam hardly knew the full story. Anyway, it didn't matter now. It wasn't as if their paths were ever going to cross again. She put down the photo and pulled herself together. 'I'd better get a move on. The airline said they'd hold a ticket for me if I could pick it up by five.'

'You're really going?'

'It looks like it.'

'Are you sure it's not because of me. Because if it is—'

'I told you, it's everything. I just don't fit in here. I'm too—'

'Normal?' he finished for her. The shadow of a curve touched his lips. Not quite a smile, but the closest he'd ever given her. 'Maybe that's why we need you around. To help make sense of our hideously dysfunctional lives.'

Lola found herself smiling back reluctantly. 'It would take Sigmund Freud a lifetime to do that.'

'True,' he admitted. 'But you could give it a go.'

She thought for a moment, going over what he'd just said. 'Hang on a minute,' she said. 'Did I just hear you say you needed me around?'

He blushed. 'I'll admit, you haven't made quite as big a hash of this job as I thought you would.'

'High praise indeed.'

'It's the best you're going to get.' He looked at her consideringly. 'So will you stay?'

She hesitated. She was tempted. Knowing that Jay was on her side would certainly make life a little easier. But it wasn't just him she had to win over. 'What about Rick?' she said. 'I don't think he wants me around.'

'Take no notice of him.' Jay shrugged dismissively. 'Anyway, he'll get over it soon. He may be a jerk, but he has the memory of a goldfish.'

CHAPTER TWENTY-TWO

But Rick didn't forget. He was still sulking when they reached Montana four days later.

Dinah suspected he might have got over it if Britt hadn't kept needling him. She was still smarting over the Tawnee incident. But rather than tackle Rick, she'd decided to blame Lola instead. And if grudge-bearing had been an Olympic event, Britt Petersen-Wild would have definitely gone home with the gold.

Meanwhile, Lola was feeling increasingly confused and hurt. Dinah didn't like to see her so upset. She was also worried that she might have to start looking for yet another new tour manager.

So she went to see Rick in his hotel suite. Britt answered the door, wrapped in a silk bathrobe.

'Where's Rick?' Dinah stalked straight past her without waiting for an invitation.

'He's taking a bath . . . Wait! You can't go in there,' Britt yelped, as Dinah headed for the bathroom.

'Keep your hair on. I've seen it all before.'

Rick was stretched out in the sunken tub, reading *Metal Edge*. He flicked his eyes to Dinah, then back to his magazine. 'Can't a guy get any peace around here?' he sighed.

'What are you going to do about your daughter?' Dinah demanded.

'Which one?'

'The one you've been ignoring for the past four days.'

He turned the page. 'Is she still here?'

'No thanks to you. Why are you giving her such a hard time? She doesn't deserve it.'

'Rick's still very upset about what happened in North Carolina,' Britt put in clutching Bjorn, the hideous rat dog, to her chest.

You mean *you* are, Dinah thought. And you're not going to let anyone forget it.

'Don't you think you're being a bit tough on her?' she asked Rick. 'The kid's doing her best. How can she be expected to keep track of all your groupies when you can't remember them yourself?'

She saw Britt's jaw tighten. So what? she thought. It was the truth, and they all knew it. No matter how much Britt tried to kid herself that Rick was a loving, faithful husband, the whole world knew he screwed around whenever he felt like it.

Rick dropped his magazine and disappeared under the water for a few seconds. Dinah waited for him to resurface.

'So what are you going to do?' she said, when his face came out of the water, golden hair slicked in a dripping tail down his back.

'About what?'

Dinah stifled a sigh. 'Lola.'

'Maybe he won't have to do anything,' Britt said. 'Maybe she'll give up and go home when she realises she's not wanted.'

Dinah glared at her. You'd love that, wouldn't you? she thought. One less female to fight.

She turned back to Rick. 'And how will you cope if your tour manager leaves? Because *I'm* not going to find you another one.'

'If she's not doing her job properly—' Britt started to say.

Dinah turned on her. 'I'd like to see *you* do better.'

'Ladies, please.' Rick looked pained. 'I'm trying to relax here.'

'Maybe it's best if you leave?' Britt said to Dinah.

'Not until Rick promises to talk to Lola.'

He gave a martyred sigh. 'I'll think about it, OK?'

*   *   *

He did think about it. He thought until his head hurt. In the end he realised he couldn't win. If he started talking to Lola again, Britt would give him a hard time. But if he didn't, he'd get it in the neck from Dinah. He didn't know which was worse.

But in the end he realised Dinah was right. It wasn't completely Lola's fault. Everyone screwed up sometimes. And besides, if she walked out, the band would be in a real mess. How would they get their own taxis, and stuff like that?

He discussed it with Britt while they were in bed later that afternoon. As usual, she didn't see it Dinah's way.

'You can't back down. Not after what she did.'

'It wasn't that bad.'

'Not bad? She let that . . . whore backstage, and you say it wasn't that bad?' Britt sat up in bed and pulled the sheet around her. 'She made me look a fool. I feel sick when I think about it. And she humiliated you, too.'

Rick frowned. He couldn't really see how, but he let it pass. 'So you don't think I should talk to her?' he ventured.

189

'Absolutely not.' Britt let the sheet drop and snuggled up against him, stroking his chest. 'If anyone makes the first move, it should be her,' she said.

'You think she will?'

'Definitely. She'll come crawling back soon, you wait and see.'

She slipped her hand under the covers, her fingers moving lower. Rick closed his eyes, groaned with pleasure, and forgot all about Lola.

*　　　*　　　*

He managed to forget her all the way to Idaho. But by the time they'd reached the salt flats of Utah the following Saturday, he was beginning to feel restless.

Lola wasn't going to apologise, that much was obvious. She was stubborn, like every other woman in his life. He decided the best approach was just to start talking to her again, pretend nothing had happened. Britt wouldn't be too thrilled about it, but he couldn't go on ignoring Lola for ever. It was bloody inconvenient, apart from anything else.

And Dinah was right; she *was* a pretty good tour manager. Things certainly seemed to go a lot more smoothly when she was around.

He caught up with her on the crew bus the night before the show. She was in the back lounge playing poker with Jonno's drum tech and a couple of the riggers. The sound and lighting guys were in their bunks, watching DVDs.

Everyone turned to look at Rick when he walked in. Everyone except Lola, who calmly went on dealing cards.

'Mind if I join you?' He pulled up a chair.

Lola didn't respond.

He tried again. 'Quite a bit of cash you've got there. How much have you taken from these guys?'

Again, no reply. Everyone was looking from one to the other, like spectators at a tennis match.

Then, just as he was starting to feel panicky, she looked up. 'Sorry, were you speaking to me?' she asked.

He smiled around at everyone. 'Sure,' he said.

'And that's it?'

'Sorry?'

'After a fortnight of giving me the silent treatment you suddenly decide to start talking to me again? No please, no thank you, no sorry I've been behaving like an utter jerk for the past week?'

'Er . . .' He felt a prickle of sweat on his upper lip. What was going on? He'd decided to make everything OK again. Why wasn't it OK?

'What do you expect?'

'An apology might be nice.'

'An apology?' He could barely get the words out. 'But it was all your fault. If you hadn't handed out passes like they were candy—'

'I made a mistake. I admitted it and I apologised for that. But you've been behaving like a toddler with an attitude problem.'

One of the riggers started to laugh, then turned it into a cough when Rick whipped round to look at him.

'Do you know what?' Lola went on. 'I think I preferred it when you weren't speaking to me. Then at least I didn't have to put up with your diva strops.'

Rick stared at her, speechless with shock. This

191

wasn't going as he'd planned. He'd set out to forgive her, and she'd wrong-footed him. She'd made him look dumb, not magnanimous. He looked around for someone to blame, but there was no one.

'If you don't like it, you know what you can do.' He turned to Neil the rigger beside him. 'Collect her laminate. She's off the tour.'

There was a long pause. The crew looked at each other. Then Neil said, 'If she's off the tour, then so am I.'

He unhooked the backstage pass from around his neck and laid it on the table. Then, one by one, the rest of the crew did the same.

Rick stared at the pile in front of him. He could feel the panic rising, blood burning his ears.

'Fine,' he snapped. 'You're all fired.'

*   *   *

He forgot all about it for the rest of the night, as he partied with the rest of the band. He knew they didn't really mean it. But the following morning he was rudely awakened by a phone call from Dinah.

'Would you mind telling me what's going on?' she screamed. 'No one's showed up for work. Apparently you fired them all last night.'

Rick rolled over and squinted at the clock. It was just before eight. 'Relax, it was just a joke. They'll be there.'

'I don't think so. I've just called Neil's room and he reckons they're all going sightseeing later on.'

'They're just kidding.'

'It didn't sound like it to me. I don't think we're going to have a show tonight.'

Rick stared up at the ceiling, suddenly fully awake. This wasn't good. In fact, it was very, very bad. So he did what he always did when things got tough. He blamed someone else.

'This is all your fault,' he accused Dinah. 'You were the one who told me to talk to Lola.'

'I didn't tell you to start World War Three,' she snapped back.

'Just sort it out, will you?'

'Uh-uh. This is your mess. *You* sort it out.'

'What am I supposed to do?'

'Eat some humble pie. Unless you want to get your backside down here and start putting up some rigging?'

Britt stirred beside him as he put the phone down. 'What's going on?' she murmured sleepily.

He told her. Britt was suitably outraged on his behalf. 'I can't believe they're being so disloyal,' she said. 'Who pays their wages?'

'I guess they must really like Lola.' He couldn't imagine them standing up for him like that, no matter how much he paid them.

'I knew that girl would be trouble. What Dinah was thinking, bringing her along? She's caused nothing but problems.'

'That's not exactly true, babe.'

'No? She humiliated me with that groupie, and now she's turned the whole crew against you. She's a nightmare, Rick. The sooner you send her packing the better.'

Rick's mind worked overtime, trying to believe what Britt was telling him, that he was right and everyone else was wrong.

But deep down he realised it wasn't true. He'd screwed up, and it was up to him to put it all right.

He only had himself to blame. It was a weird feeling.

CHAPTER TWENTY-THREE

Meanwhile, Lola was wondering if she'd made the wrong move, too. In spite of her begging the crew to go back to work, they'd defiantly insisted on taking a sightseeing tour to the old pioneer village just outside Salt Lake City.

'This is great, isn't it?' Neil grumbled as they got off. 'We spend half our lives on a bus. Then what do we do as soon as we get a day off ? Get on another one.'

It was a fiercely hot June day, and Lola's T-shirt and shorts stuck to her as they wandered around the village. It had been reconstructed as it would have been when the first pioneers settled there, and at any other time she would have been charmed by the old-fashioned shops, house and log cabins against the dramatic backdrop of the Wasatch mountains. But her mind was wandering too much to take anything in.

She knew everyone else felt the same. They tried to pretend they were having a good time, taking photos of each other and peering through the windows of the houses, but she kept catching them glancing at their watches, and knew they were counting the hours until show-time.

As they got back on the bus, she said, 'OK, a joke's a joke. Maybe you should all go back to work now.'

'No way,' Neil said firmly.

'Not until Rick apologises,' Mo agreed.

'But you'll never set up the show on time if you don't start soon. You've got to load all the stuff in. Then there's the rigging, sound and lighting—'

'It'll be Rick's fault if we don't,' Neil said.

'It won't be Rick who suffers, will it? It will be all those fans who paid their money to come and see the band. You don't want to let them down, do you?'

They looked at each other. 'She's got a point,' Mo said.

She left them heading to the theatre and caught a cab back to the hotel. She'd made up her mind to clear the air with Rick, even if it meant apologizing to him herself.

He wasn't in his suite, but Tiffany was. She lounged on the sofa, watching MTV.

'Daddy's not here.' She didn't take her eyes from the screen.

'Do you know where he is?'

Tiffany lifted her shoulders in a careless shrug. She looked like a teenager, in her Scooby Doo T-shirt and cut-off denim shorts, her hair in a pony-tail. 'He won't want to see you anyway. He's real mad with you. Mom's furious, too. You've ruined everything.' She twisted to look at Lola over the back of the sofa. 'I guess the best thing you could do right now is catch the first plane back to England.'

'Thanks for the encouragement,' Lola said.

'I'm just telling it like it is. Don't blame me if you screwed up.'

'Tell Rick I'm looking for him, would you?' She turned to leave, and slammed straight into him as he came in through the door.

'Oh,' he said. 'I've been looking for you.' He glanced at Tiffany, who was watching them over the back of the sofa. She looked like a ringsider at a boxing match, avidly waiting for blood to spatter and teeth to fly. 'Could you give us a moment in private?'

Tiffany pulled a face. 'You can't throw me out. I was here first.'

'Tiffany—'

'I mean it. I'm not going anyway.' She folded her arms and turned back to the television.

Rick looked at Lola. 'Let's walk,' he said.

The midday heat hit them like a blast furnace as they left the air-conditioned cool of the hotel and crossed South Main Street.

'Where to?' Rick asked.

'There's a coffee shop on the corner. We could go there.'

South Main was a broad, tidy thoroughfare of turn-of-the-century brick buildings, modern office blocks and shops selling the usual touristy Native American pottery and wood carvings, jewellery, T-shirts and prints of the Wasatch mountains.

The coffee shop was packed with tourists and officer workers on their lunch breaks. Rick pulled his hat down low over his eyes as he took a corner table, leaving Lola to order and pay for their drinks.

'You've caused a riot among the crew,' he said when she returned with two cups of coffee and a blueberry muffin for herself.

'You helped.'

'They've never walked off the job before. I guess they must like you a lot. Or they hate me!' He laughed.

196

Lola was silent. She didn't want to tell him that when she'd left the bus they'd been swapping their most outrageous Rick Wild stories.

He sent her a nervous, sideways look. 'They don't really hate me, do they?'

'They might get a bit . . . exasperated.' Lola chose her words carefully. 'They know you're the boss and the star of the show, but sometimes you can be a bit—'

'Demanding?'

'Unreasonable,' Lola said. 'And childish. And arrogant. And—'

'OK, I get the picture,' Rick interrupted. 'I'm trying to apologise here.'

She stared at him in surprise. 'Are you?'

'Hadn't you noticed?'

'I thought you were never wrong.'

'I didn't say I was wrong, did I? I just said I was apologizing.'

Lola couldn't help smiling. 'Wow, that really came from the heart.'

'I got you a gift, too.'

'Let me guess. Jewellery?'

He looked irritable. 'Don't you want it?'

'Give it to Britt. She'll appreciate it more than me.'

He frowned. 'You're the only woman I know who turns down expensive jewellery.'

'Maybe you're just mixing with the wrong women.'

'Maybe.' He eyed her bag, which she'd left on the chair beside them. 'What's that book?'

She showed it to him. He peered at the small print on the back. 'Why do you need a guide book to Salt Lake City?'

'I like to do some sightseeing wherever we go.'

'Why?'

'Because that's what you do when you've lived all your life in a semi in Leeds.'

He put the book back on the table. 'Everywhere seems the same when you've been on the road a while.'

'That's because you never look around.'

'I don't need to look. I go to the hotel, then to the show, then back to the hotel. That's all I need to know.'

'You don't know what you're missing.'

He leaned back in his chair. 'Go on, then. What's so special about this place?'

'Well . . .' She picked up the guidebook and flipped through it. 'This city is the centre of the Mormon church. They used to practise polygamy.'

'No kidding.' He looked impressed, then said, 'What is that, exactly?'

'Having more than one wife.'

'Yeah?' He grinned. 'I can relate to that.'

'At the same time.'

His smile dropped. 'Are they crazy?'

Lola laughed. It suddenly occurred to her that, apart from the day they'd met, this was the first time she and Rick had been alone together. She was surprised at how human he was when he wasn't surrounded by his fawning minions.

Then a couple of long-haired teenagers in board shorts and Poleaxe T-shirts sidled up to their table. Rick immediately switched into Rock Star mode, signing their paper napkins and smiling broadly as they told him over and over again how much they worshipped the band, how they had all their albums and how much they were looking forward to the show that night.

It must be weird, she thought, having people adore you so much. No wonder he had an ego the size of Texas.

The boys left, ecstatically clutching their autographed napkins like they were holy relics.

'Did you hear that?' Rick said when they were gone. 'They said they're looking forward to the show tonight. I didn't want to tell them there might not be one.'

'There'll be a show,' Lola said. 'The crew are already setting up.'

'What?' He looked outraged. 'You mean I went through all this apology for nothing?'

'You feel better for it, don't you?'

'Absolutely not,' he said sulkily.

As they finished their coffee, Lola said, 'There's something else I wanted to talk to you about.'

'Yeah? What's that?'

'Terry Mac.'

Panic flared in his eyes. 'What about him?'

'Why doesn't anyone ever talk about him?'

'There's nothing to talk about. Terry's dead.'

'But he was your friend. Surely—' He pushed his coffee cup away and stood up. 'I haven't finished,' Lola said.

'I have.'

As he started to make his way between the crowded tables, Lola called after him, 'Is it true you were jealous of him?'

He ignored her and left the coffee shop, letting the door slam behind him. Lola grabbed her bag and followed him. She couldn't see him on the street at first. Then she spotted him heading up South Main Street, away from the hotel.

She caught up with him as he reached the corner. 'Where are you going?'

'Just walking.'

He strode across the road, cars screeching to a halt in front of him. Lola dodged and darted behind him.

'I heard you got him kicked out of the band, because you didn't like him getting all the attention. Is that why you don't like to talk about him? Because you feel guilty?'

He stopped suddenly and turned to face her. 'You know all about it, don't you? You and everyone else, you've all got your little theories about what happened. You don't know what he was really like.'

'So why don't you tell me?'

He hesitated for a moment. Then he muttered, 'As I said, it's over. Forgotten.'

'*You* haven't forgotten. You can't even bear to hear his name.'

Rick turned away and started to walk again.

'Fine,' Lola called after him. 'But secrets have a habit of eating away at you.'

She didn't go back to the hotel. Following the map in her guidebook, she headed for Temple Square. She sat on a bench in the lushly landscaped gardens and gazed up at the Gothic Mormon temple, its dazzling white granite spires thrusting towards the sky.

She was so lost in her own thoughts that, she didn't realise she wasn't alone until a shadow fell over her.

'I saw him,' Rick said.

She wasn't surprised he'd come after her. He looked like a man with a lot on his mind.

She looked up, squinting into the sun. 'Who?'

'Terry. That night I got blown up on stage. I was in the middle of the song, I looked across and there he was. Just like in the old days.'

Lola moved up the bench. After a moment's hesitation, Rick sat down beside her, his long legs stretched out in front of him. She couldn't see his face because of the hat pulled down low over his eyes.

'It shook me up,' he said. 'I saw his face, then there was this huge bang, and . . .'

'What?' Lola prompted.

'I thought he'd come back for me.' Rick looked embarrassed. 'Sounds pathetic, doesn't it? Being haunted by a ghost.'

'Why would he want to come back for you? I thought he was your friend.'

'We weren't exactly close by the time he died.'

'Because you threw him out of the band?'

'Because he wasn't Terry any more.' He tipped back his head to look up at the temple, his eyes narrowing against the sun. 'Everyone thinks I wanted him out of the band because I was jealous. That's the story the press picked up on, and I let them run with it. I didn't want anyone to know the truth.'

'And what's that?'

He turned to look at her. 'I was scared of him.'

He got up and started to walk again, this time slow enough for her to keep up. For a while they were silent. But just as she began to think he wasn't going to tell her any more, he suddenly said, 'Terry and I were best mates at school. God knows why. He was way cooler than I ever was. There was just something about him. You couldn't miss him

201

when he walked into a room. He had . . . what's the word?'

'Charisma?' Lola suggested.

'That's it. Charisma. And he was a brilliant guitarist, too. If it hadn't been for his talent we would never have got picked up by the record label. He had so much star quality, they couldn't get enough of him. But then it all started to go wrong.'

'Drugs?'

He shook his head. 'We all did our fair share of them. And booze, too. Maybe Terry went over the edge. But he could still handle it. He was my mate; I took care of him.'

He stopped in front of the Seagull Monument, took out a pack of cigarettes and shook one out.

'It was his other friends,' he said at last. 'After we started to make it big, he began to hang out with some really strange people. Staying away from us, spending all his time with them. They got him into some seriously weird shit.' His hand shook as he held the lighter to the end of his cigarette. 'I mean, we all messed about with the occult thing. It was our image, skulls and blood and pretend sacrifices, that kind of stuff. The fans loved it. But Terry took it too far. He started to scare me. He even told me the only reason the band was a success was because he'd made a pact with Satan.'

Lola shivered in spite of the heat of the day.

'That's why I wanted him out,' Rick said. 'It was like he'd gone into this dark place and wanted us to follow him. I couldn't let that happen.'

'So you kicked him out of the band?'

'I wanted to get help for him. I thought it might shock him into going into therapy, or something.

202

But it turned out the band was the only thing keeping him half-sane. When he lost that, he lost everything. It wasn't my fault,' he insisted. 'I didn't know he'd end up dead.'

He took a long drag on his cigarette. His fingers were shaking. 'He called me, the night before it happened. The band was going to France the next day. It was our first tour without him. He was totally out of it, kept ranting on and on about how they were out to get him. He said it had all gone wrong, that they had turned against him. He sounded terrified.'

'Who were they?'

'God knows. The drugs had made him so deluded and paranoid. It could have been anyone or no one.' He exhaled a long plume of smoke. 'I just hung up on him. I didn't need the hassle, not just before we went on tour. Then the next morning we found out about the fire. An accident, so they said. Some electrical fault.'

'You sound as if you don't believe it.'

'I don't know what to believe. Maybe it was some kind of freak accident. Or maybe he did it deliberately. Or maybe . . .' He stopped.

'You think someone killed him?'

'Someone. Or something.'

Lola stared at him for a moment. 'You really believe all that supernatural stuff?'

'I don't know what to believe. I told you, he was way out of his depth. He freaked me out.'

'Did you tell the police about the phone call?'

He shook his head. 'I've never told anyone. I don't want them to blame me even more.'

'No one blames you.'

'Don't they? They all think Terry went downhill

because I got jealous and threw him out of the band. And maybe they're right. Maybe if I'd been more of a friend he'd still be alive today.' His eyes were troubled. 'I've had to live with that for nearly thirty years. You don't know how many times I've wished I could turn back the clock and not put that phone down.'

'You weren't to know what was going to happen.'

'I was supposed to be his mate. We promised to look out for each other. And when he needed me, I turned my back on him.' He looked at his watch. 'It's getting late,' he said with a sigh. 'We'd better be heading back.'

As they walked down South Main again, he said, 'You won't tell anyone else about this, will you?'

'Not if you don't want me to.'

They didn't say another word until they reached the hotel. Rick crossed the lobby and summoned the lift.

'Coming up?' he asked.

Lola shook her head. 'I'd better get over to the auditorium. Everyone will be wondering where their per diem is.'

He smiled. 'I'll see you there.'

The lift arrived and he stepped in. As the doors began to close, he said, 'Do you know, the weirdest thing of all was . . .'

'What?'

'They never found Terry's body.'

CHAPTER TWENTY-FOUR

'That'll be four thousand, three hundred and sixty-two dollars, please.'

'Put it on my father's account.' Tiffany pushed the credit card across the counter.

The salesgirl smiled. She was about the same age as Tiffany, dark-haired and pretty. 'You're lucky to have such a generous dad.'

'He doesn't know it yet.'

'Are you kidding? My dad would go ape if I maxed out his card.'

'Mine won't even notice.'

Tiffany watched her carefully folding up the clothes and slipping them into glossy Neiman Marcus black and white bags. She couldn't even remember what she'd bought, she'd grabbed stuff off the rails so fast. It was just a way of releasing some of the pressure inside her head.

Now she felt ashamed, like she did when she binged on chocolate and potato chips and had to make herself throw up afterwards.

The salesgirl paused, her hand ready over the chip and pin machine to collect the receipt. Nothing happened. She punched in the numbers again. There was a loud beep.

Her smile froze. 'I'm sorry, the transaction has been refused.'

'It can't be. Try it again.'

She punched in a few more numbers. Another loud beep.

'Still refused,' the salesgirl said. 'If you'd like to call your bank—'

'Forget it. I didn't really want this crap anyway.' Tiffany snatched the card back and stormed off, leaving her shopping behind. As she went, she heard the salesgirl say to her colleague, 'Not such a daddy's girl now, is she?'

Tiffany tried to call her mother as she headed back to the parking lot. But her vile camp sidekick Carlos said she was in a meeting and couldn't be disturbed.

'Do you know why my credit card's been stopped?' Tiffany demanded.

'No idea. Sorry.' But he didn't sound sorry at all. He sounded as if he was laughing.

By the time she got to her Audi TT, she was burning with anger and humiliation. How dare they do this to her, she fumed as she swung left on to University Boulevard, barely heeding the oncoming traffic that screeched to a halt amid a clamour of beeping horns. She made the three-mile drive down to the Coors Amphitheatre in five minutes flat, jumping red lights and ignoring speed limits in her blind rage.

The theatre was a vast, open-air place, with seating fanning out from the stage, which was set into a long, high-banked wall with the mountains beyond. On one side of the backstage area were the buses and trailers belonging to Poleaxe and their support bands. Tiffany abandoned her car among them and headed for the stage.

The security guards took one look at her storming towards them, hands balled into fists by her sides, and stepped aside.

Her father and the rest of the band were already on stage for their sound-check. Tiffany stopped for a moment and listened to them, her anger abating.

It made her so proud to see him there on stage. Sometimes she imagined he was singing just to her. She moved forward to sit down so she could listen some more, then spotted Lola in the front row.

Tiffany stared at the back of her head. What was so bloody special about her, anyway? She was so ordinary, with her chainstore clothes and home highlights. And yet, everyone seemed to adore her. Even Jay didn't seem to scowl as much these days, except when Tiffany was around.

Tiffany really thought she'd managed to drive a wedge between Lola and her dad with the Tawnee Wallis stunt. He'd been so mad, she was convinced it would only be a matter of time before Lola was finally sent packing. But somehow it had all gone wrong and now they were closer than ever.

It wasn't fair. At least *her* parents had been married; Rick couldn't even remember Lola's mother. She was the result of a backstage fling. Yet there she was, sitting in the front row, while Tiffany skulked at the back.

The song finished. While Kyle and Simon consulted their techs for more tuning, and the sound guy feverishly adjusted knobs on his front-of-house console, Rick came over to the edge of the stage. Tiffany watched, sick with jealousy, as he stooped down to talk to Lola. She said something back, and they both laughed.

Tiffany shouldered her way back past the security guards and headed for the production trailer.

It was empty. Lola's desk, at one end of the trailer, was littered with paperwork, empty coffee cups and chocolate wrappers. The other desk, at the opposite end, was super neat. Tiffany's lip curled. She obviously couldn't even do her job properly.

Tiffany wandered over and idly flicked through some of the papers on Lola's desk. Printed emails, receipts and scribbled notes, nothing exciting. Tiffany thought about dumping them all in the trash and leaving Lola to sort it out.

Then something caught her eye. One of Lola's scribbled notes, headed 'To Do'. Top of the list was 'Confirm hotel booking for Wyoming' and a date.

Tiffany screwed it up and stuffed it in her pocket. Maybe Lola would forget all about it and they'd have nowhere to stay. That would get her dad really mad. Then another thought occurred to her. What if she emailed the hotel and cancelled the booking completely? Even if Lola did remember, it would be too late.

She sat down at the desk and switched on her laptop. Lucky she knew how to get into Lola's email account. Her fingers were trembling with excitement as she typed in the password and . . . nothing.

Tiffany stared in frustration at the red letters on the screen: 'Password not accepted.' Why the hell not? She typed it in again, quicker this time, as if that would somehow make a difference. It didn't.

'We changed the password yesterday.'

She looked up sharply. Lola's geeky assistant Hamish was standing in the doorway, watching her over his mad professor specs.

She quickly decided attack was the best form of defence. 'Do you always go around creeping up on people?'

'Do you always go around trying to hack into

other people's emails?' He stepped into the trailer. He had to stoop under the low doorway. 'What were you planning to do, anyway? Delete everything? Send an obscene message to the bank manager?'

Tiffany slammed the laptop shut and stood up. 'I have to go.'

She'd reached the door when Hamish said, 'I don't know why you want to make trouble for Lola. If it hadn't been for her, you would have been on your way back to LA by now.'

'Oh yeah? How do you figure that?'

'We all know who gave that pass to Tawnee Wallis. But Lola covered for you.'

'I didn't ask her to!'

'Why don't you give her a break? She's just trying to find her feet.'

'She's found them, all right. I've just seen her getting real cosy with my dad!'

He sent her a considering look. 'Are you jealous?'

'No!' she lied.

'You should be angry with Rick, not Lola. He's the one who's ignoring you.'

'We were fine before she turned up.'

'Are you sure about that? From what I recall, you weren't flavour of the month then, either.'

Tiffany felt her face flaming. 'Are you a psychiatrist or something?'

'No, I'm an accountant.'

Something about the quiet, measured way he spoke made her want to spit. The calmer he was, the more mad she wanted to get.

'In that case, you can tell me why my credit card's been stopped.'

He shrugged. 'Nothing to do with me. Sorry.'

He sat down at his desk and opened up his laptop. Tiffany watched him tapping at the keys, her fury boiling over.

'I want you to sort it out,' she said. 'Call whoever it is and tell them I want my credit card.'

'No can do.'

'Then give me some cash.'

'I don't think so.'

'What am I supposed to do for money?'

He looked up at her, his dark eyes serious behind his thick-rimmed glasses. 'You could be like the rest of the world and get a job.'

Tiffany screamed. She couldn't help herself, she was so angry and frustrated it just burst out of her. Hamish watched her calmly, his head tilted to one side.

'How dare you talk to me like that! Who the hell do you think you are? Some jumped-up number-cruncher in a bad suit, that's all you are. YOU MAKE ME SICK!'

He smiled. Actually *smiled*. She wanted to launch herself across the desk, grab his glasses and smash them. She raged and spat until she couldn't do it any more. She flopped down on Lola's desk, exhausted and light-headed.

'Finished?' Hamish said mildly.

She nodded. Her throat was sore from yelling.

'So you don't think much of my job suggestion?'

'Screw you.' Tiffany stared at the ground. 'Who'd want to employ me?'

'Why not?'

'In case you hadn't noticed, most people think I'm a dumb, drunk party girl.'

'That's unfair. You're not always drunk.'

It took her a moment to register the insult. 'Screw you,' she said again, but this time she had to struggle to stop herself smiling.

He leaned back in his seat and regarded her thoughtfully. 'Actually, you seem pretty bright to me.'

She glanced up. 'Do I?'

'You're bright enough to dream up ways to make Lola's life a misery. I bet if you turned your criminal genius to good you could rule the world.'

Tiffany frowned. She couldn't decide whether he was still making fun of her or not. 'You're nuts,' she said.

'You're right,' Hamish agreed amiably. 'It's part of the job description.'

CHAPTER TWENTY-FIVE

Cheyenne, Wyoming began life as a small town of drinking and gambling establishments built along the line of the Pacific Union railroad as it pushed its way west over the great plains. Once the playground of transient cowboys, ranch hands and soldiers from the nearby fort, it was transformed by cattle barons into one of the richest cities in the west.

But it never forgot its western roots, and every year the city still hosted the biggest outdoor rodeo in America. Thousands came from all over the States for the Frontier Days event in July, ten days of bronc- and bull-riding, steer-wrestling and wild horse races. In the evening a carnival and concerts took place in the giant outdoor arena.

It was Poleaxe's last gig before they took a few days' break, so everyone was in high spirits as they struck down the set in the early hours of the morning. It was a warm, still evening, and the smell of frying onions and cotton candy still hung in the air from the now-darkened fairground.

'Shame it's all closed down,' Mo said as he unbolted Jonno's kit from the ground. 'I wouldn't have minded a ride on a Ferris wheel.'

'Sod that,' Neil said. 'I want some breakfast.'

It was nearly three when they got back to the hotel. Usually they would have headed straight out on the road to get to the next city, but tonight there was no hurry. While the band and the rest of the city slept, the Poleaxe crew crowded into Neil's room and ordered breakfast from room service. Bacon, eggs, hash browns, pancakes and French toast dripping with syrup were all wheeled in, along with gallons of fresh coffee and orange juice.

Lola blanched at the sight of all the food, already thinking about the added extras on the bill the next day.

'It's a tradition,' Neil explained as he dolloped ketchup over his hash browns. 'Anyway, don't worry about it. I'm sure the band aren't losing any sleep over it, tucked up in their suites the size of aircraft hangars.'

Lola had to admit he had a point.

'Someone put some music on,' Mo said.

Neil reached over the bed and rifled through his CD collection. 'Any requests?'

'Anything but bloody Poleaxe!' one of the sound guys grumbled.

'You really think I have Poleaxe CDs? How sad do you think I am?' Neil selected one and pulled it out. 'Here's one I think you'll like. A very talented, up-and-coming young artist.'

He slipped the CD into the player and switched it on. A moment later the sound of an acoustic guitar filled the room. Someone laughed. A couple of people groaned.

Jay scowled. 'Turn it off.' He reached for the knob on the CD player, but Lola stopped him.

'Leave it, it's beautiful.' She listened as a low, soulful voice joined in, weaving in and out of the melody. It was a love song, heartfelt and haunting. 'Who is it?' she asked.

All eyes turned to Jay, who'd turned a deep shade of crimson. 'It's not finished,' he mumbled.

Lola could hardly believe it. 'Is it really you?'

Neil smirked. 'Like I said, a very talented, up-and-coming young artist.'

Jay turned it off. 'It still needs a lot of work,' he said.

'I think it's great. You should be on stage, not working behind the scenes.'

'That's what we all keep telling him,' Mo said.

Lola turned back to Jay. 'Has Rick heard it?'

'No. Why should he?' He was instantly defensive.

Lola looked around at the rest of the crew. None of them met her eye. 'I just thought maybe he'd be able to help.'

'I don't need his help,' Jay said shortly. He pulled the CD out of the player and snapped it back in its case. 'Anyway, it's rubbish.'

'But . . .' Lola thought about arguing, but Jay's forbidding look told her to shut up.

Dawn was just breaking when Lola finally crawled back to her hotel room. She was so spaced

213

out with exhaustion she barely registered the blinking red message light on her phone. No doubt it was Simon, complaining that his bed was facing in the wrong direction, or Jonno needing instructions on how to close his curtains. Whatever it was, it could wait until morning, she thought as she flopped into bed.

By the following morning the set and equipment had been stowed away and the crew had dispersed to catch up with their loved ones back home. The band headed off, too, back to New York and California. Tiffany trailed after her mother to LA, while Hamish flew to Boston to meet up with some old friends.

The only ones left behind, ironically enough, were Lola and Jay.

She wasn't looking forward to spending time with him. Even though they now got on well enough when they were with the others, it was the first time they'd be on their own, and she wasn't sure how awkward it would be in each other's company.

She did her best to stay out of his way, and headed off to explore the Frontier Days showground. But as she sat in the rodeo stands, clutching her box of popcorn, who should she see coming up the steps towards her but Jay.

She tried to pretend she hadn't noticed him, but then she accidentally caught his eye so had to wave. He waved back, but from the expression on his face he was as uncertain about the encounter as she was.

But of course, by then it had all become way too awkward for him to walk away, so he had to come and sit next to her.

'Fancy seeing you here,' she joked weakly.

Jay pointed to the empty seat. 'Mind if I join you?'

'Be my guest.' She moved her bag to let him sit down.

Once they'd exhausted the usual pleasantries about the weather, they retreated into polite silence. Lola watched the men in their chaps and stetsons pacing around the dusty arena, and willed something to happen.

'Do you, um, know anything about rodeo?' she asked.

'This is my first time.'

She nodded, as if he'd said the wisest thing she'd ever heard in her life. Then she studied the list of events in her programme, trying to commit it to memory.

The silence between them stretched so far Lola could almost feel it twanging. Then Jay suddenly said, 'I can sit somewhere else, if you like?'

Lola, who'd been willing him to do just that ever since he'd arrived, looked up in surprise. 'Why?'

'No reason. I just get the feeling you'd be happier if I wasn't here.'

'I was just thinking the same thing,' she admitted.

He frowned. 'That you'd be happier if I wasn't here?'

'No, that you would.'

He was quiet for a moment, taking it in. 'Well, we're both here, so we might as well live with it,' he said.

'Popcorn?' She offered him the box.

'Thanks.'

The first bronc was lining up. Lola watched him

tossing his head and jerking in the chute as the cowboy tried to mount him.

'Looks like a lively one,' she commented.

Then the chute opened and the bronc shot out, rearing and bucking while the rider clung on grimly. A second later he was flung through the air and ended up lying face down in the dust.

'That didn't last long,' Jay said.

'He was disqualified anyway.' Lola point to the flag. 'He touched the saddle with his free hand. That's against the rules.'

Jay sent her a sideways look. 'You understand the rules?'

'I wanted to be a cowboy when I was a kid.'

'I thought all little girls wanted to be ballet dancers?'

'Not me.' She reached for another handful of popcorn. 'Here's another contestant. Let's see if this one manages the full eight seconds.'

He barely made it out of the chute before the judge's flag went down again. 'What is it this time?' Jay asked, reaching absent-mindedly into her popcorn box.

'I don't think he was in the right position. His heels should be above the horse's shoulder on the first jump out of the chute.'

Jay looked impressed. 'You really are an expert, aren't you?'

'I told you, I wanted to be a cowboy.'

'So how did you end up being a police officer?'

She shrugged. 'There weren't that many vacancies for cattle-wranglers in Leeds. And my friend Sam's dad was in the police, so I decided I'd join too. I certainly didn't want to be like my father,' she said.

'Me neither,' said Jay, his eyes fixed on the next horse, a bay, plunging and rearing in the arena.

Lola glanced at him. 'So how come you ended up in this business?'

'I couldn't help it. I hated my father, but I loved music. When I was a kid, all I wanted was to play guitar and write songs.'

'Did Rick encourage you?'

'Hardly. I barely saw him from the day he left Mum. I got cards and presents for birthdays and Christmas, but I think they were from Dinah, not him.' He winced as yet another rider went flying through the air. 'But someone must have told him something, because, when I was thirteen, he suddenly sent me a vintage Stratocaster.' His lip curled. 'Typically over the top. Must have cost an absolute fortune.'

'Do you still have it?'

He shook his head. 'I sold it and used the money to buy my mum a present. She deserved it after all the crap she'd put up with from him.' His face darkened. 'I saved up and bought my own guitar. I didn't want anything from Rick.'

The last bronc rider came out of the chute, and bit the dust—literally.

Lola turned back to Jay. 'He might have been able to help you, put in a word . . .'

'He would never have done that. I didn't want him to, anyway. I wanted to make it on my own, or not at all. That's why I never told anyone who I was.'

'Didn't they find out?'

'Sometimes. I remember I joined a band just after I left school. We did really well, nearly got ourselves a record contract and everything. Then the local press got wind of who I was, and did a big feature on us. I quit the next day.'

'Why?'

'Because I didn't want to live in *his* shadow.' His expression was grim. 'If I succeeded, everyone would just think it was because I was his son. And if I failed everyone would know about it. I wanted to do something for myself, to make it on my own merits. Except I didn't.' He smiled wryly. 'So I gave up the idea of being on stage and started working in the crew instead. That's how I met Kyle, when I was working as a backline tech in his last band. Then he joined Poleaxe.' He shook his head. 'It was just about my worst nightmare come true. My only consolation was that Rick was pretty unhappy about it, too.'

Lola gazed at him wonderingly. 'You really don't get on, do you?'

Jay's eyes glazed over. 'I can't ever forgive him for the way he treated my mum.'

Lola wondered if all the resentment was for his mum, or if he felt just as hurt for himself. It couldn't have been easy to watch his father walk away and start again with another family.

The bronc-riding was over, and the ranchhands were organizing the arena for the next event.

Jay put down his programme. 'I think I'll get something to eat.' Then, to Lola's surprise, he added, 'Would you like to come with me? You don't have to,' he said quickly, not meeting her eye. 'I mean, if you want to stay here and watch the rest of the show—'

'I'd love to,' she interrupted before he could talk himself out of asking her.

Outside the rodeo arena, the showground was

busy. They queued up at a fast-food stall where a man in a cowboy hat was flipping burgers.

'I feel like everyone's gone home for the holidays, and we're the only kids stuck at boarding school,' Lola said as she squirted mustard on to her burger.

'I know what you mean,' Jay agreed. He gave her a shy look. 'You don't have to stick with me if you don't want to.'

'Why wouldn't I want to?'

He shrugged. 'I know I'm not exactly the person you'd choose to spend time with.'

'I'd rather spend it with you than with Britt.'

'That's not saying much.'

She tugged his sleeve. 'Come on, let's go for a ride on the Ferris wheel.'

They wandered around the sideshows and tried their hand at the shooting gallery. Lola beat Jay easily and won a giant stuffed raccoon.

'That's not fair,' he protested. 'You're a cop. You get more practice than me.'

'We don't carry guns in England,' Lola reminded him. 'We're not even allowed to fire insults. Although we get enough of them on the Creighton estate.'

'So what's it like?' Jay asked. 'Is it tough?'

She told him about life on the estate, the kind of problems she had to deal with, even her frustration about not getting the promotion she wanted so badly. She also told him about Sam and how close they'd been until Brendan came on the scene.

'Don't you have anyone special back in England?' Jay asked.

She smiled. 'If you're asking if I have a boyfriend, the answer's no.'

'Why not? You're not that bad.'

'Gee, thanks.'

He stopped at a coconut shy and handed a five-dollar bill to the man behind the stall.

'I mean it.' He took six balls and handed her three. 'So why haven't you got a boyfriend?'

'You sound just like Sam!' She aimed a ball at the coconuts and missed. 'What about you? Have you got a girlfriend back home?'

'No one special.'

'You haven't met Miss Right, is that it?'

'The truth is, I'm too scared to look.'

She looked at him sharply and missed another coconut. That was exactly how she felt.

Jay bowled a ball straight at a coconut, sending it flying. 'Look at that,' he grinned. 'I guess that makes us even.'

'You think so?' Lola hugged her raccoon. 'I'd like to see you cuddling up to a coconut at night.'

They wandered around the stalls. Lola had stopped to admire some Native American turquoise jewellery when she realised Jay had gone.

A moment later he returned, holding something behind his back. 'I've got you a present,' he said, producing it with a flourish.

'A real cowboy hat! That's brilliant.' She reached out, but he held on to it.

'Let me,' he said. He placed it on her head, carefully angling it low over her eyes. 'Perfect,' he said.

Their eyes met and held under the brim of the hat for a second. Then they both looked away at the same time.

'We'd better head back to the hotel,' she said,

feeling suddenly shy.

All the way back, she sensed Jay had something on his mind. It wasn't until they were getting into the lift that he suddenly blurted out, 'Say no if you want to, but . . . would you like to have dinner with me tonight?'

'Yes, please.'

'I mean, you don't have to. I just thought as there's only the two of us around, it might . . .' He paused. 'Did you say yes?'

She nodded. 'I'd like that very much,' she said. And to her surprise, she actually meant it.

Back in her room, the red message light on her phone was still blinking away furiously. Lola instantly felt guilty about ignoring it the previous night.

She picked up the phone, pressed the button and listened.

At first all she heard were muffled sounds. Then she realised someone was sobbing.

'Lola?' a voice croaked. 'Are you there? Pick up, will you?'

'Sam?' she said, forgetting for a moment it was a recording.

'Please be there. I need you.' She sounded small, choked and very far away. 'Call me back when you get this message.' Then the line went dead.

Lola dialled straight back. Sam picked up on the first ring.

'Brendan?' Her voice was full of hope.

'It's me, Lola.'

'Oh, Lola.' She started crying again. Lola listened to her heart-wrenching sobs on the other end of the line and wished she was there to comfort her. 'I'm sorry, I shouldn't have called

221

you. I just didn't know who else to turn to.'

'Tell me what's happened.' But deep down she already knew.

'It's Brendan,' Sam wept. 'He's d-dumped me.'

Lola's hand tightened on the receiver. 'When?'

'Last night. He packed his bags and moved out. He was seeing someone else.' She sounded shaky. 'God, Lola, I've been such an idiot.'

'He's the idiot, not you. He doesn't deserve you.' Lola was just about to launch into a comforting spiel about what a low-life he was, and how Sam was far too good for him anyway, but her friend cut her off.

'I know all that,' she said. 'But you see, the thing is . . . I think I might be pregnant.'

CHAPTER TWENTY-SIX

Lola put the key into the lock of her old flat, terrified of what she might find inside. Sam had sounded so distraught on the phone, anything could have happened.

She dumped her bags in the hall and went into the living room, picking her way through empty wine glasses and chocolate wrappers. It looked as if Sam had been working her way through her heartache in the usual time-honoured fashion.

'Sam?' she called out. There was no reply. Then she heard a muffled sound in the bathroom.

She tapped on the door. 'Sam, are you in there?'

'Lola?' Sam sniffed. 'Is that you?'

'Yes, it's me.' There was another long pause. 'Sam, are you OK?'

'I . . . I can't come out,' Sam sobbed. 'I've done something really stupid.'

Lola's heart shot into her throat. Fighting to keep the panic out of her voice, she said, 'Open the door, Sam.'

'I c-can't.'

'It's OK,' she soothed. 'We can sort this out.'

'You . . . can't,' Sam sobbed. 'No one can help me. It's t-too . . . late.'

Her voice faded. Lola forgot all about staying calm and rattled the doorknob frantically. 'Hang on, Sam. I'm going to call an ambulance.'

She was halfway down the hall when the bathroom door opened a crack and Sam peeped out. 'What do I need an ambulance for?'

Lola nearly fainted with relief. 'Thank God you're all right!'

'You call *this* all right?' Sam flung open the door and Lola saw the reason for her tears. Her hair was sticking up in frizzled orange clumps all over her head. She looked as if she'd been Tangoed.

'What happened?' Lola whispered.

'I wanted a m-makeover,' Sam's voice was shaky. 'It was supposed to be b-blonde. N-natural honey, it said on the pack.'

Lola stared. Whatever was on Sam's head certainly wasn't natural. 'Are you sure you followed the instructions?'

'Of course I followed the instructions!' Sam said. Then she caught another glimpse of herself in the bathroom mirror and started to cry again. 'It's solved my problem, anyway. At least I won't have to worry about my love life any more. No m-man's ever going to look at me again.'

Then, suddenly, another thought struck her. She

223

looked through her fingers at Lola. 'What are you doing here, anyway?'

'I came to see you. You sounded so upset on the phone, I wanted to make sure you were OK.'

'So you came all the way back from America?'

'Of course. You're my best mate.'

'Oh, Lola, that's so nice.' Sam started to cry again, her mouth folded down like a sad clown, nose streaming, and tears running down her swollen, blotchy face. With her mop of orange hair, she looked like Ronald McDonald's depressive twin. 'I'm in such a mess,' she wept.

'Shh, it's OK. I'm here now.' She'd been preparing her speech on the plane. 'We can sort this out, I promise. I'll be with you all the way. And so will Brendan.' She'd make damn sure of that. 'Now have you taken a test?'

Sam looked at her blankly. 'A test? What for?'

Lola sighed. She was jet-lagged and not feeling very patient. 'A pregnancy test?'

'Oh, that.' Sam beamed. 'Yes, I did one last night. It was negative.'

Lola's shoulders slumped. She didn't know whether to laugh or cry. 'And you didn't think to let me know?'

'I tried calling your hotel, but there was no reply.' Sam stared at her, realisation dawning. 'You mean you came all this way thinking I was . . . oh, blimey!' She clamped her hand over her mouth.

'Well, I didn't come because you were having a bad hair day, did I?'

'Sorry.' Sam looked contrite.

'It doesn't matter. It's probably a good thing I came anyway.' Lola peered at her head. 'From the look of your hair, it was worth a mercy dash.'

She made an emergency trip to Tesco's for another bottle of wine, some groceries—Sam had apparently been living on cigarettes and Ferrero Rochers since Brendan cleared out—and another pack of hair dye.

'You'll have to forget about going blonde for a while,' she said as she helped Sam comb the rich red-brown colourant through her matted locks. 'You might not look like Gwen Stefani, but at least you won't look like a Belisha beacon.'

Later, after she'd cooked pasta and cleared their plates away, they curled up on the sofa and Sam told her the whole sorry story. How Brendan seemed to cool off within weeks of moving in.

'I think the novelty wore off,' she said sadly. 'He liked the idea of having his meals cooked and sex on tap, but he wasn't so keen on not going out with his mates and picking up girls. Then he went on a stag weekend to Newcastle, which was when it really started to go downhill.'

She plunged her hand into the bag of Doritos propped between them. 'I thought he seemed different when he came back, kind of distant. He was always on the Internet, too. Sometimes he'd be on there all night. He told me he was booking us a holiday in Tenerife.'

All night? Lola said nothing.

'Then a few days ago, when he was in the shower, I happened to be going through his mobile phone and I found these texts—'

'Hang on a second,' Lola interrupted. 'You happened to be going through his phone?'

'You know what I mean,' Sam said impatiently. 'Anyway, I found all these messages from a girl called Mandy. And pictures, too.'

'What kind of pictures?'

Sam sent her a look. 'Not the kind you'd want in your passport.'

'Ah. Go on.'

'Anyway, I talked to Brendan about it, expecting him to deny it or pretend it was just a joke from his mates or something. I wanted him to say it wasn't true. Whatever he'd told me, I would have believed him. But he didn't. He said he'd met this girl in Newcastle and they'd been texting and talking on the Internet ever since. He said he'd wanted me to find out and that was why he hadn't deleted the messages on his phone.'

'Why didn't he just tell you?'

'I don't know, do I?' Sam plunged her hand into the Doritos again, maudlin with misery. 'Maybe he didn't want to hurt me.'

Or maybe he's just a cowardly little creep, Lola thought.

Sam scarfed down another handful of nachos. 'What am I going to do?' she whined.

Lola hugged her. 'The first thing we're going to do,' she said, 'is get very drunk.'

'I've already tried that. It's all part of the grief stage.'

'Sorry?'

'I bought a book about it. *Every Woman's Guide to Relationships*, it's called. It says there are four stages to the end of a relationship. First is grief, then it's denial, then anger and finally resolution.'

'Where does compulsive eating come into all this?' Lola asked, looking at the near-empty bag of Doritos.

'It's part of the process,' Sam said, helping herself to another fistful. 'I'm literally swallowing

226

my unhappiness.'

You'll look like you've swallowed a duvet soon, Lola thought.

'Anyway,' Sam said. 'I've had enough wallowing in misery for a while. Now I want to hear all about you.' She tucked her feet up underneath her and hugged her knees, waiting for the story.

'There's nothing to tell, really,' Lola shrugged. 'Except what I've already said in my emails.'

'What?' Sam's eyes widened in horror. 'You mean to tell me you spend your entire working day surrounded by rock stars and you still haven't managed to meet anyone decent?'

'Rock stars aren't all they're cracked up to be, you know.'

'I bet they're a lot more interesting than the creeps I meet,' Sam said. 'Come on, surely someone must have caught your eye?'

Lola must have hesitated a fraction too long before she shook her head.

Sam pounced. 'I knew it! There *is* someone, isn't there? Go on, you can tell me. Who is it?'

'There really isn't anyone,' Lola insisted apologetically.

Sam glared at her, outraged. 'You're lying,' she accused. 'That's not fair. If I'm doomed to be single and celibate, then I should be allowed to enjoy someone else's love life.'

'Mine's just as boring as yours, I'm afraid.' She could tell from the look Sam gave her that she didn't believe her. 'Anyway,' she changed the subject, 'shall we check on your hair? You don't want to overdo it again.'

Thankfully just the thought of that was enough to send Sam scuttling to the bathroom, Lola's love life forgotten.

She had nothing to tell, anyway. Certainly nothing that she wanted to put into words.

By the time they'd rinsed it out, conditioned it three times and blow-dried it, Sam's hair was almost restored to its former glory.

Sam sighed with relief as she admired her reflection in the bathroom mirror. 'I'll be able to go out in public again.' She turned to Lola. 'Thanks so much. I think I would have gone mad if you hadn't been here.'

'That's what friends are for.' Lola grinned.

Sam smiled back sadly. In a quiet voice, she said, 'I wish you were still living here.'

I don't. Lola was shocked at herself for even thinking it. But it was true. Her life had changed so much in the past few weeks. And even though it had been an emotional rollercoaster, she wouldn't have missed the ride for the world. She couldn't even remember when she'd stopped missing her old life. Living with Sam and patrolling the Creighton estate seemed such a long time ago now.

But that wasn't the response Sam was hoping for. Lola could see that from the way she was watching her, her eyes round and sad.

'I'll stay for a few days,' she promised. 'It'll be just like old times.'

*   *   *

It was lucky she did stay, because Sam's mood changed abruptly over the next twenty-four hours, as she moved from Grief into Denial. One minute she was leaving a trail of soggy tissues and standing at the fridge eating ham straight out of the packet.

228

The next she was sending sneaky texts to Brendan.

'I need to talk to him,' she complained, when Lola took her phone away. 'There's still some stuff he needs to pick up.'

'He'll call if he needs it,' Lola said firmly.

'What if he's too afraid to call because he thinks I'll be angry with him?'

Lola kept her thoughts to herself, although she suspected Brendan was having too good a time to worry what Sam was feeling at that moment. But it was no use telling Sam that. She was grimly determined to see the best in her ex, come what may.

'I think he has a serious problem with commitment,' she said as she watched Lola cook supper. She'd moved on from *Every Woman's Guide to Relationships* and was now getting stuck into *Loving a Bastard: Men Who Won't Say Yes*. 'It's not his fault. He has issues stemming from his childhood, you see. His parents divorced when he was two, and he's afraid of allowing anyone too close in case he has to go through the same pain he witnessed in them.'

'When he was *two*?' Lola said, but Sam wasn't listening.

'It's a good sign, really, that he can't commit to me,' she said. 'Because it means he loves me too much.'

Lola tensed her shoulders and stirred the chilli she'd prepared. It was turning into a major effort, fighting the urge to tell Sam that Brendan was an utter twerp and she was well rid of him.

It was like living with a crack addict. One minute Sam could be bright and optimistic, the next she could be plunged into dark despair by hearing

229

'their' song on the radio, or finding one of Brendan's socks stuffed under the bed.

Lola had to sleep with Sam's phone under her pillow to stop her sending drunken, pleading text messages, and listened patiently as she endlessly analysed their relationship. All the time she tried hard to stop her thoughts drifting back to the tour. What was everyone doing? Was Rick behaving himself? Was Tiffany back in rehab? Had Hamish finished a *Times* crossword yet?

The only person she didn't think about was Jay. She wouldn't allow herself to think about him.

Then, four days after she'd first arrived, she came home from a trip to the supermarket and heard Sam talking to a man in the living room.

Thinking it was Brendan, she stormed in ready to give him a piece of her mind—and found Sam and Jay on the sofa together.

She was so shocked to see him that at first she didn't take in the pile of hacked clothing in the armchair across the room.

'What are you doing here?' She managed to get the words out finally.

'That's a nice greeting, isn't it?' Sam said. 'Your brother comes all the way to see you and you make it sound as if he's not welcome.' She turned to Jay. 'You must excuse my friend,' she said politely. 'She has the social skills of a four-year-old.'

Lola stared at them, sitting side by side on the sofa, mugs of half-finished coffee in front of them. It was so bizarre to see Jay there, in her old home. He looked the same as ever, in his scruffy jeans, T-shirt and leather jacket, but he belonged to her other world, her other life.

'Why aren't you in the States?' she asked.

'I got bored on my own,' he shrugged. 'So I decided to come over and visit my mum. And since I was here anyway I thought I might as well take a trip up here and see the sights of Leeds, too. As you made it sound so wonderful.'

'Blimey, and I thought you said you hadn't taken any drugs?' Sam said to her.

Lola was hardly listening. She was struggling with the insane and wholly inappropriate urge to rush across the room and hug him.

'Sorry I didn't make it to dinner that night,' she said. She'd been so busy booking a flight after Sam's call, she'd barely had time to explain.

'Some other time,' Jay smiled warmly

She dragged her gaze away with an effort, and spotted the sleeve of a shirt draped over the back of the armchair like a dismembered limb.

'What have you been doing?' she asked Sam.

'Cutting up that bastard's clothes. I think I must have reached the Anger stage.' Sam smiled brightly and picked up Jay's mug. 'Another coffee?' she said.

Jay barely waited for her to leave the room. 'When I got here she was slashing through that lot like Edward Scissorhands. Is she OK?'

'She is now,' Lola said. 'There were a few dodgy moments when I thought she was going to be stuck in Denial, but I think she's on her way to Resolution. Any day now she'll be looking for another boyfriend.' She only hoped she'd find someone better than Brendan.

But it looked as if Sam had already got someone in mind when Lola went into the kitchen to help her with the coffee.

'You've been holding out on me,' Sam accused,

closing the door behind her.

'Have I?'

'Why didn't you tell me your brother was so gorgeous?'

'I can't say I noticed.'

'Then you must be mad.' Sam took a packet of HobNobs out of the cupboard and put them on the tray. 'I'm telling you, he's hot. I wouldn't mind having a crack at him myself.'

Lola was surprised by how much the thought unnerved her. 'I thought you were off men?'

'That was before I met Jay.' She gazed longingly at the door. 'Do you think I stand a chance? Does he have a girlfriend?'

'Not that I know of.'

'What type of woman does he go for?'

'How should I know?' Lola failed to keep the irritation out of her voice. 'What happened to the broken heart you were nursing when I left an hour ago?'

'It got fixed.' Sam sent her a quizzical look. 'I thought you'd be pleased.'

'I am. I just don't think it's the right time to think about getting into a new relationship—'

'Oh, shut up. You sound just like those stupid self-help books.' Sam forced down the plunger on the cafetière. Real coffee, Lola thought. She must be out to impress.

'I've got an idea,' Sam said, as they took the coffee back into the living room. 'Why don't we go out this evening? You could sample the nightlife of Leeds.'

'Sounds good.' Jay turned to Lola. 'Are you up for it?'

'I . . .' Lola caught sight of Sam's discouraging

face. 'I think I need an early night,' she said.

'What?' Jay frowned at her. 'I come halfway across the world to see you and you want to go to bed?'

'Clubs aren't really her thing,' Sam put in helpfully. 'In fact, Lola has the social life of an agoraphobic OAP.'

'Then maybe we should do something about it,' Jay said.

'I didn't think you were the sociable type,' Lola reminded him.

'Only when it comes to rock stars' parties. This is a night out in Leeds we're talking about.'

Sam looked at them both. 'You two are seriously weird,' she declared.

They made a strange threesome, heading off for a night on the town. Having gone back to his B&B to change, Jay returned looking very similar, only in a slightly smarter pair of black jeans.

'Sorry, I wasn't expecting to hit the clubs when I packed,' he'd said apologetically, when Sam looked askance at him.

Sam, by contrast, was glammed up to the eyeballs in a skimpy gold halterneck top, cream trousers, strappy high heels, and maximum make-up.

Lola was somewhere in between, in her best dark denims, black vest top and her highest-heeled boots.

It took a while to find a club with a relaxed enough dress code for them. As soon as they'd got their drinks and found a booth to sit, Sam went into full flirtation mode, laughing, teasing, chatting and generally making sure Jay's eyes never got a chance to stray further than her face or her

233

cleavage.

Lola sat quietly across the table from them, drinking her beer and wishing she wasn't there. It wasn't that she begrudged her friend the chance of being happy again. It was certainly better than seeing her curled up with a box of Coco Pops, sobbing her heart out.

They might make a good couple, she thought. Not an obvious pairing, but opposites attracted, didn't they? Sam might even end up being her sister-in-law . . .

The insistent techno beat slowed to a smoochy number, and Sam immediately put her drink down and dragged Jay on to the dance floor.

Lola watched them. She'd never seen Jay dance before. He moved pretty well, she thought. Usually men and dance floors didn't mix. Either they shuffled around in an embarrassed Dad Dance, or turned into a toe-curling John Travolta, with a lot of arm thrusts and knee bends, and a bit of Michael Jackson moonwalking thrown in for good measure.

But Jay did neither. He and Sam moved together perfectly, arms wound around each other, hips touching and grinding in time to the music. They looked so good together, she felt slightly sick.

She let her gaze wander anywhere else but on to the dance floor. She looked around the darkened club, at the sea of heads bobbing in the pulsing lights.

Finally the music changed, and Jay came back.

'Where's Sam?' Lola asked, as he slid on to the seat beside her.

'Gone to the loo.' His mouth curved. 'She's quite a girl, isn't she?'

'She certainly is.'

'A bit too full-on for me, though. Not really my type.'

Lola, who'd been bracing herself to hear him declare he'd fallen in love, was ashamed at the surge of relief she felt. 'Really? I mean, oh dear.' She lowered her voice from a squeak. 'She's not usually this hyper.' After her burst of disloyalty she now felt obliged to defend her friend. 'It's all the stress of splitting up with her boyfriend. She's a nice girl really.'

'I'm sure she is. But I saw her hacking at those shirts, remember? I wouldn't like to be on the receiving end of those scissors.'

'She'll be disappointed,' Lola said. 'But I don't think she'll take a pair of scissors to you,' she added, as Jay looked wary.

'I'm glad to hear it.'

'So what is your type?' Lola couldn't stop herself asking.

'Now there's a question,' Jay replied.

Suddenly it felt as if the atmosphere had been charged with millions of tiny sparks. Lola almost expected to get an electric shock when she picked up her glass.

Just then Sam returned, weaving her way through the crowd, and squeezed herself on to the seat beside Jay and Lola.

'Who's for another drink?' she said.

'Actually, do you mind if we call it a night?' Jay said. 'I'm a bit jet-lagged.'

'Are you sure? We could go on somewhere else . . .'

'Really, I should get back. I have to make an early start back down south tomorrow.'

Sam pulled a face. 'You're leaving tomorrow?'

'Sorry, I promised Mum I'd see her again before I headed back to the States. The tour starts in a couple of days.'

Don't I know it. Lola felt a pang of longing.

They walked back through the rain-slicked streets to the taxi rank in the city centre. Again, Sam wedged herself in between them, on the pretext of sheltering under Jay's jacket. Lola wished she'd learn to read the signals better, then perhaps she could save herself some heartache.

For once they didn't have to wait too long for a taxi.

'When are you coming back on the tour?' Jay asked, as they headed out of the city centre.

'Soon,' she promised.

'Good. I don't think we'd survive without you.'

'That's not what you said a few weeks ago.'

'A lot's changed since then.'

Tell me about it, Lola thought. She glanced at Sam, who'd gone ominously silent, staring out of the window.

They dropped Jay off at his B&B. No sooner had the taxi driven off than Sam turned on her.

'What exactly is going on?' she demanded.

Lola took a deep breath. She'd been expecting this. 'I'm sorry, Sam. I don't think he's very interested,' she said. 'It's not you,' she gabbled on. 'I just don't think he wants to get—'

'I'm not talking about me,' Sam cut her off. 'What are *you* up to?'

'Me?'

'Come on, don't play the innocent with me. I saw the way you were looking at him. And I saw the way he looked at you, too.'

236

'I . . . I don't know what you're talking about,' Lola stammered.

'Oh, please. Why do you think I've been throwing myself at him all night? I've been trying to keep the two of you apart. Although it was pretty bloody obvious I was wasting my time.' Sam shook her head. 'For God's sake, Lola, he's your *brother*. What are you playing at?'

Lola stared down at the toes of her boots, stained by the rain. There didn't seem much point in denying it any more.

'I don't know,' was all she could say miserably.

Sam sighed. 'Bloody hell, and I thought I was the one with the messy love life. You don't do things by half, do you?' She thought for a moment. 'You're not really going back on tour with him, are you?'

'They're expecting me. I can't let them down.'

'And you can't bear to be away from him a moment longer?' Sometimes Sam knew her far too well. 'Lola, I mean it. You've got to be very careful. Otherwise you could get *really* hurt.'

Lola stared out of the window. 'You think I don't know that?' she said.

CHAPTER TWENTY-SEVEN

She rejoined the Poleaxe circus just as it rolled in to Tampa, Florida. And not a moment too soon, as she discovered when Hamish briefed her in the production office.

'The lighting guys are up in arms because the promoters haven't supplied half the equipment we stipulated in the rider, Simon's left his favourite bass back in Wyoming, and the support band are making a fuss because they reckon we're not giving them enough time for their sound-check. But apart from that, everything's just fine,' he said.

She sighed. 'Is there any good news?'

Hamish thought about it for a moment. 'Not that I can remember . . . Oh, hang on. Tiffany's got an audition for a movie.'

'How do you know?'

'She told me.'

'You've been talking to Tiffany?'

Hamish rearranged his stationery on his desk. 'We may have chatted a couple of times. She's not that bad once you get to know her,' he mumbled.

Lola peered at him. There was a definite tinge of red under that floppy fringe. 'You're blushing,' she accused.

'I'm not.'

'You are. Don't tell me you've got a crush on Tiffany?'

'No, I just feel sorry for her, that's all. People don't understand what she's like.'

'You mean she's not a spoilt, selfish little brat?'

'No. I mean, yes, she is. But it's all an act. She only does it to get attention.'

'You're telling me.'

'It can't be easy for her. She's had no stability in her life, and her parents are far too wrapped up in themselves to give a damn about her.' He twisted a paperclip out of shape. 'She's got this big down on herself. Every time it looks like things are going OK for her, she presses the self-destruct button.'

Lola grinned. 'You *have* got a crush on her.'

'Don't talk tosh.'

Hamish was the only man she knew who'd use the word tosh seriously in a conversation. 'Just as well,' she said. 'Because she'd eat you alive.'

The phone rang. It was Britt.

'I need to do some shopping,' she announced. 'Send someone to pick me up from the hotel in half an hour.'

'The drivers are all busy for the rest of the afternoon.'

'Then you'll have to do it.'

Lola looked around despairingly at her cluttered desk. 'I can't really leave the office. I've just got back and Hamish has left everything in a right mess.' She stuck her tongue out at him as he looked up, outraged.

'But I have to buy your father an anniversary present.'

'Can't you get a cab?'

'I'll expect you in half an hour,' Britt said, and hung up.

'You'll wait a long time,' Lola muttered as she put the phone down.

'Who was that?' Hamish asked.

'Take a guess.' Lola glared at the phone. 'Britt wants me to drop everything and take her shopping. Well, tough. I've got better things to do than trail around after her all afternoon.'

'Are you sure?' Hamish looked worried. 'Rick's told everyone we've got to keep her happy. I think they went through a bad time while you were away.'

Lola sighed. 'You mean he's cheated on her again and now it's up to the rest of us to make it up to her?'

'Something like that.' He shrugged

239

apologetically. 'She's been in one of her "difficult" moods for days.'

'And now I have to go shopping with her,' Lola said.

It took her twenty minutes to battle her way down I-4 from the Florida State Fairground to the West Shore area. The sticky heat and leaden skies of the morning had finally given way to afternoon rain. By the time she reached the hotel, Lola's neck ached from having to peer through the blurry windscreen.

She'd barely pulled up before Britt flounced out of the hotel. She was wearing white jeans, a soft tan leather jacket, high-heeled sandals and huge sunglasses. She had an oversized Chloe bag tucked over one arm and Bjorn under the other.

'You're late,' she snapped as she dived into the back seat.

Lola pressed her lips together and counted to ten. 'Where to?' she asked.

'West Shore Plaza.'

Lola twisted round in her seat to face her. 'But that's only two blocks away.'

'So?'

'So couldn't you have walked?'

Britt stared at her. 'It's raining.'

'Yes, I know,' Lola said. 'It's been raining ever since I left work. On the other side of the city,' she added pointedly.

Britt's mobile rang. Lola listened to her yapping in Swedish as she prepared to join the tangle of traffic again.

'How's your friend?'

Lola didn't realise she was being spoken to until she checked in the rear-view mirror and those icy

240

blue eyes met hers. 'Sorry?'

'Your friend. The one you went to see in England. The one whose boyfriend cheated on her.'

'Ah. Right. Getting over it slowly, I think.'

'She's lucky. Sometimes you never get over a betrayal like that.'

Lola didn't know how to reply, but she'd just pulled into the parking lot of the West Shore shopping mall, so thankfully she didn't have to say anything

'Was she in love with him?' Britt asked, as they cruised the rows of cars, looking for a space.

'Unfortunately yes. More than he was with her, anyway.'

'Why do you say that?'

'It's obvious. If he loved her, he wouldn't cheat on her.'

Too late she realised what she'd said.

'That's not true,' Britt said flatly. 'All men cheat. It's just the way they are. Any man will do it if they get the chance. It means nothing.'

To her utter relief, Lola found a parking space. 'Here we are,' she said. 'Call me when you're ready to leave.'

'Aren't you coming with me?'

'Why would I?'

'I don't think Rick would like the idea of me being alone. Not with that madman sending those horrible threats.'

She was already out of the car, giving Lola no time to argue.

Shopping with Britt was a whole new experience. No cramped changing rooms for her; she headed straight for the VIP area, where she soon had a team of personal shoppers running here and there, gathering armfuls of clothes from the rails while she sipped champagne on the velvet sofa.

'That one,' she pointed imperiously. 'No, not the blue. The orange. And I saw a Zak Posen coat in *Vogue*. Do you have that?'

Meanwhile Lola sat on the other end of the sofa and tried to stifle a yawn.

'Don't you like shopping?' Britt asked.

'I'm more of a George at Asda kind of girl.'

'George Atazzda.' Britt looked thoughtful. 'I've never heard of him. Is he Italian?'

Finally she made her selection and headed off to the dressing room to try them on.

'What do you think?' She emerged wearing a brown and orange retro-print halterneck that would have looked like granny's curtains on anyone else, but somehow looked fabulous on her.

'Stunning,' Lola said, absently patting Bjorn's head.

'I'm not sure . . .' Britt frowned at her reflection. 'I think it makes my ankles look thick.'

And so it went on. Every time she tried on a different dress she was even more critical. Her backside was too flat, her shoulders too broad, her thighs too flabby, the colour was all wrong for her skin tone . . . her faults were endless. At first Lola thought she was doing it to win compliments. Then she saw the self-loathing on her face.

'I don't get it,' she said. 'You were a supermodel, for heaven's sake. Surely you must know how beautiful you are?'

'Exactly the opposite.' Britt twisted round to scowl at her back view in a Marc Jacobs cutaway shift. 'From the age of fourteen I've had model agencies and designers telling me I'm too fat, too tall, too short, that my feet are too big, my eyes are too wide apart. Now every time I look in the mirror all I see is another sag, another wrinkle.'

'I can't see any wrinkles.'

'That's because you don't look as closely as me.' She examined her face in the mirror. 'When you're a model, there's always someone younger, thinner and more beautiful waiting around the corner to take your place.'

'And there was me, thinking it was dead glamorous.'

'Believe me, it isn't.' Britt pulled the dress off and stepped out of it. 'I'm bored,' she announced, scooping Bjorn into her arms. 'I think we should have lunch.'

Lola glanced guiltily at the disappointed faces of the sales assistants, who'd spent the best part of an hour fetching and carrying. 'Aren't you going to buy anything?' she said.

'Of course.' She waved her hand at the clothes scattered around. 'I'll take all of them. Now where shall we eat?'

'Do I get to choose?' Lola asked.

Britt sent her a cautious look. 'Maybe.'

*   *   *

'This wasn't quite what I had in mind,' she said, as they queued up at the Chick-Fil-A counter in the food court ten minutes later. 'Isn't there somewhere else we could go?'

'You said I could choose,' Lola reminded her.

'I didn't realise you were going to pick this

243

place.' Britt frowned up at the illuminated pictures of fast food. 'I suppose it's too much to ask that they have anything low carb?'

In the end she settled for a small green salad with no dressing, while Lola tucked into a chicken sandwich and waffle fries.

'Don't give him that,' Britt said, as Lola fed Bjorn a piece of chicken. 'He's a vegan.'

'He's a dog.'

'He has a very delicate digestion.' Britt watched her bite into her sandwich. 'It must be nice not to care about what you look like,' she said.

'Thanks a lot!' Lola said.

'I mean it, I envy you. Rick would go mad if I put on a pound.'

'Surely if he loves you he wouldn't care what you looked like.'

Britt sent her a pitying look. 'Is that what you really think?' She shook her head. 'Being married to a rock star is even worse than modelling. There's always someone waiting to take your place there, too.'

She picked morosely at her salad. Then she asked, 'Was it the first time your friend's boyfriend has cheated on her?'

'As far as I know. I can't imagine Sam putting up with him otherwise.'

'You'd be surprised what you can put up with when you love someone.'

'Is that why you put up with Rick?'

She saw the warning flash in Britt's eyes and wondered if she'd overstepped the mark.

'Why else would I stay?' she said.

'I don't know . . .' Lola eyed the carrier bags around her feet. 'The lifestyle, maybe?'

Britt laughed. 'You think that's why I'm with him? Because he buys me dresses? I was a successful model, remember. I can afford my own clothes.'

'All the same, it must be quite glamorous, being a rock star's wife.'

'You've seen what it's like. Do you really think it's glamorous, travelling in a bus from city to city, every night another place, another hotel room? Do you think it makes me happy to watch all those girls fawning over him, pushing me out of the way to get to him, giving him their phone numbers right in front of me, as if I didn't exist?' She mindlessly reached for one of Lola's fries. 'It wouldn't be so bad if I thought he wasn't interested. But I know he sleeps around. Most of the time I tell myself it doesn't mean anything. But deep down I know my replacement is waiting somewhere out there.' She stuffed another fistful of waffle fries into her mouth. 'In three years I will be forty. Then my life will be over.'

'You're still a lot younger than Rick.'

'That's different. No one ever heard of anyone trading in a rock star for a younger model.'

She reached for another chip, then changed her mind and picked at her salad instead. 'I have a sister, back in Sweden,' she said. 'She's married to man who makes furniture. Sometimes he can sell it, sometimes he can't. My sister has no money, three children and she's let herself get fat. But she's happier than I will ever be, and do you know why? Because she knows her husband loves her more than anything else in the world.' She looked up at Lola, her eyes swimming with tears. 'Do you think Rick would love me if I got fat and let my hair go grey? He can't even stay faithful to me now.'

To Lola's horror, she started to cry; big, noisy sobs that shook her thin frame. Lola hesitated, then put her arms around her and hugged her.

'Why do you stay with him, if he makes you so unhappy?' she said.

'B-because I l-love him.' Britt's voice juddered as she fought not to sob. 'And I know he loves me, deep down. It's just this life . . .' She pulled out of Lola's embrace and rummaged in her bag for a tissue. 'I never get him to myself. There are always people hanging around him, wanting him to do this or that. Sound-checks, interviews, go here, go there. Maybe if he didn't always have to be somewhere, we could start to make a life together.'

She found a tissue and scrubbed at her eyes. Then she took a deep breath, mentally pulling herself together, as if it had suddenly dawned on her that she'd let her guard down. A second later her ice-queen mask was back in place.

'Come,' she said, pushing her salad away. 'I have more shopping to do.'

There was a slightly different atmosphere between them as Lola watched her browsing around Victoria's Secret. Britt's guard was back up, and she was as frosty as ever, but now Lola had seen her vulnerable side.

On the way back to the parking lot, they bumped into Tiffany coming out of Abercrombie and Fitch, laden down with carrier bags. She and Britt both stiffened like a pair of cats meeting in an alley.

Lola tried the bright and breezy approach to break the ice. 'Been shopping?'

246

'Duh. Yeah.' Tiffany rolled her eyes.

Be patient, Lola told herself. Remember what Hamish said. She's not really a spoilt, selfish brat at all. She's just misunderstood.

'We're just heading back to the hotel, if you'd like a lift?'

Tiffany eyed Britt. 'No thanks, I've got my car.'

As she went to leave, Lola said, 'Congratulations on the audition, by the way.'

Tiffany's eyes narrowed. 'How did you know about that?'

'Hamish told me. I think it's brilliant news.'

'Yeah, well, I haven't actually got the part yet.'

'What audition?' Britt asked, when Tiffany had gone.

'She's up for a part in a new movie.'

Britt tutted. 'I expect she'll screw it up, as usual.'

Lola watched Tiffany heading in the opposite direction. For all her attitude, she looked very lonely.

Maybe Hamish was right, she thought. Maybe no one did give her a chance.

CHAPTER TWENTY-EIGHT

As Britt predicted, Tiffany was making a good job of screwing things up. She lay on her bed, staring at the pages of her script. No matter how hard she tried, the words wouldn't sink in. They might as well have been written in Swahili for all the sense she could make of them.

Every time she tried to concentrate, the same thoughts went round and round in her mind: *Why are you even doing this? You know you're going to fail. You might as well just give up now, before you make a fool of yourself.*

It didn't help that she'd heard on the grapevine that her former friend, major bitch Ashley Anderson, was also up for the part. She was probably screwing the director and half the camera crew right now to make sure she got it.

Tiffany threw the script into the corner and went to check out the mini-bar instead. A miniature bottle of Absolut, two tubes of Pringles and a Snickers bar took away some of her stress, until she'd finished them and the loathing started to creep in. Not only was she a useless failure, she had no self-control, either.

She tried to remember what they'd told her in rehab, about talking through her feelings instead of keeping them all bottled up.

Her mother had flown in to catch up with the tour for a few days, so Tiffany thought she'd try her first. She was in the production office, taking a call on her mobile.

'Please, Tiff, I hope you're not going to give me any more problems?' were her first words. 'I'm already up to my neck in it trying to fix up some dates in Japan next year. I don't need any more hassle. Yes, I'm still holding,' she said into her phone.

Tiffany glanced across at Hamish, who was busy typing something on his laptop. Her mother's assistant Carlos was by her side, pretending to make a call. But Tiffany knew he was listening to every word.

'It's about this screen test,' she said.

'What about it?'

'I'm not sure if I can . . .' she started, but her mother held up her hand to silence her.

'What do you mean, they're not sure they can do Tokyo?' she barked into the phone. 'Tell them Tokyo is the deal-breaker, do you understand? Two nights at the Dome or we're not getting on that plane.'

She snapped her mobile shut. 'Now what were you saying?' she asked Tiffany.

'I'm not sure if I can do this screen test.'

She flinched as her mother's eyes narrowed to dark slits, a sure sign she was about to administer a lecture.

'Do you know what it took me to get you that test?' she said, her voice dangerously soft. 'Do you know how many favours I had to call in, how many strings I had to pull just to get that director to see you?'

'I—'

'I'll tell you, shall I? A lot. So I don't want to hear you telling me you're punking out because you've made other plans, OK? I just don't want to hear it.'

'But I wasn't—'

'Good. Because if you let me down on this, Tiffany, I swear your credit card won't be the only thing I put a stop to.'

She left the office, Carlos scuttling after her, leaving Tiffany with her mouth open, still trying to get the words out.

As the door closed behind her, Hamish looked up. 'No pressure, then,' he grinned.

Tiffany twisted her mouth wryly. 'Man, am I going to be in trouble.'

'What makes you say that?'

' 'Cos I'm going to screw this up for sure. The screen test is in less than a week and I still haven't learned my lines.'

'Why not?'

'I don't know. I'm really trying, but it's just not happening. I guess I'm just too dumb. A dumb blonde, that's me.'

'Not all blondes are dumb. What about Einstein?'

'Who?'

'Einstein? Theory of relativity? Actually, he was more white-haired than blonde, but I'm sure it counts.'

'You see?' wailed Tiffany. 'I have no idea what you're talking about. I told you I was stupid.'

'You don't have to know a load of useless facts to be smart. Also,' he lowered his voice, 'I happen to know for a fact you're not a natural blonde.'

She gasped. 'Who told you?'

'With your mum's dark hair it would practically be a genetic impossibility. Unless you were switched at birth, which is unlikely.' He tugged at one of her plaits. 'Underneath all that peroxide you have your mother's sultry dark looks and her sharp business brain.'

Tiffany brightened up. 'You think so?'

'I know you do.'

'So why can't I learn this stupid script?'

'Maybe you're going about it the wrong way. I could go through it with you, if you like?'

'Would you? I think it might help to say the lines, instead of just trying to think them.'

'I believe Lord Olivier said the same thing.'

'Who?'

'It doesn't matter.' He smiled. 'Where's the

250

script?'

She gave it to him, and he flicked through it. 'What's it about?'

'Just the usual teen movie stuff. Good-looking girl, geeky guy best friend. She really likes someone else, doesn't realise geeky guy is really the one for her.'

'Not exactly Shakespeare, then.'

'Are you going to help me, or are you going to bitch about it?'

'Sorry.' He went on flicking. 'So who am I?'

'Dexter.'

'Is he Geeky Guy or Hot Guy?'

'Geeky.'

'Story of my life,' he sighed. 'Where do we start?'

'Here.' She found the page for him. 'The scene I've got to do for my test is where he's asking her to the prom but she turns him down.'

'Why?'

'Because she's hoping Hot Guy will ask her out instead.'

'Ah. And does he?'

'Oh, yeah. But then Hot Guy turns out to be a real creep who just wants to score with her so he can brag to all his friends about it afterwards.'

'Bastard.'

'So she tries to cosy up to Geeky Guy but he's brought someone else to the prom and doesn't want to know. And he's had a makeover so now he's a hot guy, too, and the heroine's totally sick about it.'

'Let me guess. He's taken off his glasses.'

She stared at him in surprise. 'How did you know?'

'They're always hot when they take off their glasses. Haven't you noticed that? It's against the laws of nature to have a sexy guy in spectacles.'

'That's true. It *is* against the laws of nature.'

'Excuse me?'

'How many hotties do you know who wear glasses?'

He thought for a moment. 'Clark Kent?'

'Only when he takes them off and turns into Superman.'

'So it's just me, then.'

She laughed. 'Oh, sure.'

'It's true. We make a unique couple. I'm a stud muffin in glasses; you're an intelligent blonde.'

Tiffany considered him for a moment. 'What would you look like without them?'

'I have no idea. I can't see myself in the mirror when I take them off.'

'Let me have a look.' She reached out and gently unhooked them, then leaned closer to study his face. She was so close she could smell his minty breath.

'You have big, soulful brown eyes,' she said. 'Like a golden retriever.'

'Thanks a lot.'

'I like golden retrievers.'

'They're hardly the hottie of the dog world, are they? Not like a Dobermann. Now that's a really macho dog.'

'I've dated a few Dobermanns in my time and believe me, they're not worth the effort.'

'Is that so?' He took his glasses from her and hooked them back over his ears. 'Shall we get back to the script?' he said.

*   *   *

Three days later Hamish took her to the airport to catch her flight to LA. She was hoping that her mom and dad might have come to see her off, but of course they were busy doing their own stuff.

She was surprised that Lola came along for the ride.

'I just wanted to wish you luck,' she said.

'Er, thanks.'

In the airport Lola fussed over her like a mother hen, checking over and over again that she had her ticket. 'Don't forget I've ordered a car to pick you up from the airport. And I've arranged for the housekeeper to be at Doheny Drive when you arrive.'

'No wild parties, then? Just kidding,' she said, as Lola's face fell.

Strangely, she didn't feel resentful that Lola was taking over, bossing her around. If anything, it felt kind of nice to know someone cared.

They said goodbye at the security gate, and Tiffany held herself stiffly, overwhelmed by embarrassment as Lola hugged her. 'Take care of yourself,' she said, 'and call me as soon as you get home.'

'Sure,' Tiffany lied. The first thing she was going to do was call up some of her friends to catch up on the gossip.

She turned to go and slammed straight into Hamish. He towered over her, all arms and legs and angles.

For a moment they just looked at each other, neither of them sure what to do. Then awkwardly he leaned down and planted a chaste kiss on her cheek.

'Thanks for helping me,' she mumbled.

'No problem,' he smiled. 'Just remember me when you make your Oscar-winning speech, OK?'

CHAPTER TWENTY-NINE

I don't believe this, Lola thought. Any second now I'm going to wake up and find it's all been a horrible dream.

But when she rubbed her eyes she was still there, standing in the hospital emergency room. And Kyle was still there, too, sitting on a gurney nursing his bandaged hand.

'It's not as bad as it looks,' he said cheerfully. 'They've done an X-ray and at least it's not broken.'

Lola tried to smile but her face muscles weren't up to it. It was 3 a.m. Half an hour earlier she'd been happily tucked up in bed. Then she'd got the call from Kyle.

'How exactly did it happen?' she asked.

'Well, y'see, I was in this lap-dancing club and—'

She held up her hand. 'No, on second thoughts, don't tell me. I don't think I want to know.'

'It wasn't my fault,' Kyle said. 'The table landed on my hand, what could I do?' He sent her a wary look. 'You won't tell Dinah about this, will you?'

'Kyle, I think she might notice, don't you?' He blanched and she understood what was going through his mind. He would rather break a hundred fingers than have to face the wrath of his manager.

By the following morning the swelling still hadn't gone down. There was no putting it off any longer; Dinah had to know.

They caught up with her backstage at the theatre.

'That's it. We're going to have to cancel the gig,' she said, after twenty minutes of hurling abuse at cringing Kyle. He towered over her, hanging his head like a child. 'There's no way you can go on stage like that.'

'It's not so bad now. Just a bit stiff.' Lola saw him wince as he tried to waggle his fingers experimentally inside his bandage.

'Christ, this is a nightmare.' Dinah steepled her fingers over her eyes. 'I've got a whole bunch of execs from the record company flying in from New York for this gig. What the hell am I going to tell them?'

'Can't you get someone else to play instead?' Lola suggested.

'What do you suggest I do, go through Yellow Pages?' Dinah snapped, then let out a sigh. 'Sorry, I shouldn't take it out on you. I'm just feeling kind of stressed at the moment.' She paused and took a deep breath. 'You're right, we could try to get someone else. It's short notice, but it's worth a shot. And it's got to be better than cancelling the gig.'

She pulled out her mobile and hurried off to make some calls.

'I feel really bad about this,' Kyle said.

You should have thought about that before you got into a fight at a lap-dancing club, Lola was about to say. But Kyle already looked so wretched she didn't have the heart to make him feel any worse. 'Dinah will sort it out,' she said soothingly.

But for once Dinah couldn't make the problem go away. She came back half an hour later looking even more worried. 'Everyone's out of town, or booked already,' she said. 'It was a pretty long shot, anyway. I mean, we're hardly likely to have a fantastic lead guitarist ready and waiting right on our doorstep, are we?'

Lola and Kyle looked at each other.

'Actually, there is someone,' Lola said.

'Who?'

'How about Jay?'

'Jay?' Dinah frowned. 'Rick's son Jay? Can he even play the guitar?'

'Like you wouldn't believe,' Lola said.

'He's as good as me,' Kyle put in. 'Well, nearly,' he added.

Dinah looked thoughtful. 'Do you think he'd do it?'

*　　　*　　　*

'No,' Jay said when Lola tracked him down backstage. He was taking Kyle's guitars out of their cases, ready for that night. 'No way.'

Lola was taken aback. She'd been so certain he'd jump at the chance. 'But I told Dinah you'd do it.'

'Then you'll just have to tell her I won't.' He gently brushed the strings of Kyle's favourite acoustic, listening to the sound.

Lola stared at him in frustration. 'I don't understand. Why won't you do it?'

'I'm not sharing a stage with my father.'

She knew that wasn't the real reason. There was

256

something else going on behind those green eyes of his, something she couldn't fathom.

'Don't you think you're only spiting yourself?' she said. 'You could be missing your big chance here.'

'That's my problem, isn't it?'

'But there are going to be some important people from the record company there tonight. This could be your opportunity to show them what you can do.'

'And what if I can't do it?' He looked up at her and Lola suddenly realised it was fear she'd seen in his eyes. 'What if I get up on that stage and make a fool of myself?'

'Of course you can do it. I've heard you play. You're brilliant.'

He smiled cynically. 'What if I'm not brilliant enough? I don't want to fall flat on my face in front of thirty thousand people.'

'You won't.' Impulsively she reached out and squeezed his hand. He still had Kyle's guitar balanced on his knee, and even though it wasn't electric she felt as if a shock had shot straight through Jay and into her.

She looked down at her hand. Her brain was telling her to move it, but it wouldn't budge.

'There you are.' The clattering of Dinah's high heels as she approached seemed to break the spell. She nodded to Jay, all smiles. 'Have you given him the good news yet?'

'He says thanks but no thanks,' she said.

Dinah's smile vanished like the sun going behind a cloud. 'What? You're not serious? Don't you realise this could be your big—'

'Chance? Yes, I know. I've already had that

257

pointed out to me, thanks.' Jay ran his hand over the body of the guitar, then put it back in its case. 'Maybe I'm just destined to be one of the backroom boys,' he said.

Lola willed Dinah to argue, but all she did was shrug. 'Sounds like your mind's made up.' She looked at her watch. 'I'd better go and break the good news to the guys from the record company. I'm sure they'll be thrilled that they've come all this way for nothing.'

*   *   *

Dinah decided to hold off making any decision about whether to cancel the gig until closer to the time, to see if Kyle's hand improved. And it seemed as if her gamble paid off.

Lola could hardly believe it when Kyle came into the production office later on that afternoon with his bandages off.

'My hand's fine now,' he announced, wiggling his fingers to prove his point. 'Simon gave me some great painkillers, and they've really worked. I can't feel a thing.'

Lola frowned suspiciously. 'What kind of painkillers?'

'No idea,' Kyle shrugged. 'But they were terrific.'

Lola exchanged a glance with Hamish. Simon's pharmaceutical stash was legendary, and not strictly legal. He'd collected enough prescription drugs from the Internet and other dodgy suppliers to keep Boots in business for years.

Fortunately Kyle didn't keel over and die during the afternoon. But when she and Hamish went into the dressing room to check on the band shortly before they were due to go on stage, they found him swallowing a couple of tiny yellow pills.

'The others were starting to wear off, so Simon gave me some stronger ones.'

'Are you sure that's a good idea?' Lola peered at his glassy-eyed, grinning face.

'We'll soon find out,' Hamish muttered.

They both watched anxiously from the wings as he bounced on stage with the others, fist thrust skywards. The band went straight into their opening number, 'Bite Me', and Kyle joined in enthusiastically, slamming his guitar, jumping around the stage and turning in his usual energetic performance.

'I wouldn't mind some of those pills myself,' Hamish commented. 'I've never seen him so good.'

And then, three songs into their set, it all started to unravel. Kyle's riffs became ragged; he couldn't keep time. From her place in the wings, Lola could see Rick sending him anxious looks as he staggered around, knees buckling, as if his guitar was too heavy.

They limped through another two songs. Jay had to keep running on to the stage to change guitars for him because Kyle kept getting entangled in the straps.

'He's a mess,' he told Lola and Dinah when he came off stage. 'I don't know what Simon's given him, but he's dead on his feet out there. I've had to prop him against an amp to keep him upright.'

Dinah cast an anxious look towards the stage. The sounds of slow hand-clapping and stamping feet were slowly building, like a rumble of distant thunder. 'The record company guys aren't going to be too impressed with this,' she said. Lola could see her dark eyes darting, the way they always did when she was thinking fast. Then she turned to Jay. 'Right, you've got to go on.'

'What? No way.' He was already backing away, shaking his head vehemently. 'I can't. I'm not ready . . .'

'You can't be any worse than Kyle is right now. He's practically asleep. If you can just manage to stay awake it will be an improvement!'

Lola looked at Jay. All kinds of emotions were racing across his face—fear, doubt, uncertainty.

Then, without a word, he grabbed one of the guitars lined up on the rack.

Lola saw Rick's face darken as Jay walked on to the stage. Kyle was already being helped off by a couple of stagehands. Jay calmly stepped past him, his face expressionless. But Lola saw his hands shaking as he plugged the cable in to the amp.

He and Rick didn't look at each other as he went straight into the opening chords of 'Kiss of Death'. But out in the vast black auditorium, the crowd were still getting restive, almost drowning the music with their slow hand-clapping. They'd come to see Kyle perform his magic, and here was a young man in a scruffy Poleaxe T-shirt and jeans, looking like a roadie.

Lola's heart was in her mouth. If they slaughtered him, she wasn't sure his ego could take it.

But she was wrong. Once he was on stage with a guitar in his hands, Jay seemed to become a different person. There was nothing shy or diffident about the way he looked up and faced the crowd, his eyes fixed on them, daring them not to like him. He silenced them with a couple of crashing chords, then went into a riff so brilliant and complex that even Rick stopped singing for a moment and watched him, startled.

'I don't believe it,' Dinah breathed. 'Is that really the same guy?'

'That's Jay.' Lola felt herself swelling with pride. She wouldn't have believed it herself, but he'd taken to the spotlight as if he'd been born there. The crowd loved it, too. Soon their jeering had turned to cheering and they were screaming for more.

The only one not reacting to him was Rick. He and Jay didn't look at each other, and even from the wings Lola was aware of the icy tension between them.

'Someone doesn't like the competition,' Hamish remarked.

When the show was over, Dinah went off to catch up with the record company bosses. 'Don't forget to tell Jay I need him in the meet and greet area,' she said to Lola. 'These guys are going to want to talk to him.'

'I will.' She couldn't wait to tell him. Jay deserved a break, after being in the shadows for so long.

Rick came off stage, grim-faced, shouldering past her without a word. The others followed behind. Lola had never seen Jay on such a high as he bounced off stage.

'You were brilliant,' she congratulated him.

'Was I?' He looked anxious. 'I thought I was a bit off in "Turn Me On".'

'It didn't sound like it to me.'

'What do you know?' He smiled teasingly.

'True. But the crowd loved you.'

'Do you think so?'

'Didn't you hear them?'

'I was too busy thinking about not cocking it up.' A grin lit up his face and before Lola knew what was happening, he'd snatched her up and swung her round in his arms. 'God, that was fantastic! Thanks for making me do it.'

'Any time. But would you mind putting me down now? You're making me feel a bit sick.'

'Sorry.' He set her down on the ground but kept his arms around her. Lola didn't move, either. Despite the roadies bustling past, for a moment it was as if they were the only people in the world.

Then he seemed to remember and released her abruptly. 'Well, um, I'd better see about sorting out these guitars,' he mumbled.

'Dinah wants you in the meet and greet area, too.'

She watched him amble off, head down, back to the diffident, guarded Jay who was too shy to let anyone hear him play. But something had changed tonight on stage, Lola thought.

And something had changed off it, too.

One way or another, she had a feeling things were never going to be the same again. For either of them.

CHAPTER THIRTY

Rick woke the following morning to sun streaming in through the windows of his hotel suite, the smell of fresh coffee—and Britt standing at the foot of the bed, dressed only in a thong.

'Happy anniversary, baby,' she purred, leaning over to give him a lingering kiss. She tasted of minty fresh toothpaste. 'I thought we could have breakfast in bed.'

'Why don't we forget the breakfast and go straight to the bed bit?' he said, pulling her down on top of him.

'But I've ordered bagels,' she protested, seconds before his mouth claimed hers.

Half an hour later they finally surfaced. They took a long, sexy shower together, and just as Rick was going to drag her back to bed, the phone rang.

Britt answered it. Rick listened to her speaking in rapid Swedish and realised a marathon sex session was no longer an option. Once Britt got talking to her family back in Stockholm she could be on the line for hours.

He admired the outline of her slim body as she stood there, wrapped only in a bottom-skimming hotel towel. She might be fifteen years younger than him, but he still had what it took to keep her happy, he thought with satisfaction.

He passed the time by helping himself to coffee and a bagel from the breakfast tray, and browsing through the morning paper. Usually he never read newspapers; world events didn't interest him much. No one would ever catch him doing a Bono and banging on about ethical this and that and trying to save the world. He would have been hard-pressed to point to Africa on a map.

But he was a damn good rock singer and a pretty good lay, so who cared?

He was flicking through the newspaper, trying to find something that wasn't about boring old politics, when a headline caught his eye: 'rock 'n' roll revival!' Then underneath, in smaller letters, 'Poleaxe rock fans in Seattle.'

He took a bite of his bagel and read on: 'Last night veteran rockers Poleaxe performed the best gig of their current *Bleeding Heart* tour, and possibly their last ten years.' Veteran rockers? Bloody nerve, he thought. 'And their return to blazing form was all down to the talent and energy of the Wild Man.'

Rick allowed himself a quick preen. Maybe they meant the others were veteran rockers. Jonno and Simon were getting on a bit, after all. Then he read on: 'But this wasn't the Wild Man as we know him. Last night, old pretender Rick had to hand his rock 'n' roll crown over to his son and heir, Jay.'

Rick nearly choked on his bagel.

He squinted at the last couple of paragraphs, hardly daring to read the words. It got worse. Apparently Jay had 'left the rest of the band literally standing with his high-octane performance'. It also said Poleaxe hadn't played so well since 'the old glory days of the late lamented Terry MacIntyre'. In fact, it went on, 'Jay's performance bore a striking similarity to Terry Mac, with his lightning chord changes, blinding riffs and sheer energy. Last night it was almost as if the MacMeister had never gone.'

Rick let the newspaper drop and pushed his plate away. Suddenly he felt sick. He desperately needed some air.

In the living room, Britt was still yakking on to her relatives. Her voice was beginning to grate on his nerves. Rick dressed quickly, snatched up the newspaper and slipped out of the suite.

264

'Rick? Where are you going?' Britt appeared in the doorway, but he didn't reply.

He went straight down to see Dinah, who was having breakfast in the dining room, her mobile clamped to her ear.

'Have you seen this?' He threw the newspaper down on the table.

'Sorry, I'll have to call you back.' She hung up the phone. 'You mean the review? It's great, isn't it?'

'Are you serious? It's terrible. I want something done about it now.'

'Like what?'

'I don't know . . . Make them print a retraction, or something.'

Dinah gave him that wise-ass smile he'd always hated. 'You mean you want them to say they got it wrong and the band wasn't that good after all?'

'Yes . . . no . . .' He was so angry and frustrated he didn't know what he wanted any more. 'I want that journalist fired!' he decided finally.

He threw himself down in the chair opposite hers and took an angry bite out of her cold toast.

Dinah was watching him, and he knew she was trying to decide between the sympathetic approach and getting tough. He didn't know why she bothered; she was about as sympathetic as a fascist dictator.

'Look, Rick,' she reasoned. 'I know it was a bit harsh on you, but it was great for the band.'

'What are you talking about? I *am* the band! Do you really think the fans come to see Jonno or Simon? No, they come to see me. I'm the frontman. Without me there wouldn't be any Poleaxe.' He was shouting loudly enough for the

265

rest of the dining room to hear, but he was too angry to care.

'That's what they used to say about Terry Mac,' Dinah reminded him quietly.

He reeled back as if she'd slapped him. 'What are you saying? Do you want to get rid of me now? Is that it?'

'That's not what I'm saying at all, and you know it.'

'You'd better not be.' Rick did his best to sound threatening, but deep inside he was the one feeling threatened.

'But I *was* thinking of asking Jay to join the band.'

'*What*?' He sat upright. 'No way. Over my dead body. We've already got a guitarist.'

'It's not unheard of to have more than one.'

'I don't think Kyle would see it that way.'

'Actually, I've already talked to Kyle and he thinks it would be a great idea. He reckons Jay would be an asset to the band.' She put her hand over his, which was always a bad sign. 'Look, Rick, I know you and Jay have got issues—'

'I don't know what you're talking about. I don't have issues.' Apart from the fact that just having him around made him feel old and clapped-out. 'He's the one with the issues, not me.'

'Whatever. The fact is, we could use some new blood in the band. You saw the fans last night; they were going crazy. Jay's a very talented young man.'

Young man. There it was again. He was the young pretender, waiting to snatch the crown. Well, Rick wasn't ready to hand it over. They'd have to unscrew his head if they wanted it.

'It sounds as if you've already made up your

mind,' he said coldly.

'Obviously we wouldn't do anything without your approval. Like you said, you're the main man.'

But for how long? Rick thought.

He shook his head. 'He's not right for us,' he said firmly. 'OK, he might be able to cut it for one night, but he'll never be anything more than a second-rate session musician.'

'You don't know that. If you gave him a chance—'

'I don't want to give him a chance. I'm not having him bring the rest of us down.' His voice rose again. 'If Jay joins this band, then you'll have to find yourself another lead singer. Because there isn't room for us both in Poleaxe.'

'Rick—'

'I mean it, Dinah. It's him or me. Now you choose.'

He stormed out before she had a chance to answer. As he swept past the table by the door, he barely registered the solitary young man with dark curls reading the Poleaxe review in the newspaper.

And even if he had recognised his own son, he wouldn't have cared.

*   *   *

It was rare for Britt to put in an appearance at the production office. Usually she just telephoned imperiously from her suite when she needed anything, like an appointment with a *feng shui* therapist or Bjorn taken for a colonic irrigation.

So when she rushed in mid-morning, Lola realised something was wrong. She wasn't

267

glammed up, either. Another bad sign; if they'd been given the four-minute warning of an impending nuclear attack, Britt would have still found time to put on some mascara and lippy.

'Have you seen Rick?' she asked.

'Not since last night. Why?'

'I can't find him. He ran out of our suite this morning and I haven't seen him since.'

She looked so anxious that Lola did her best to reassure her. 'He'll be back. Maybe he's gone to buy you an anniversary present?' she said brightly.

To her astonishment, Britt burst into tears. 'I'm sorry,' she sniffed, as Lola rushed around trying to find her a tissue. 'It's just I've had a phone call from home. My mother's been taken ill.'

'Oh, I'm so sorry.' Lola hesitated, then put her arm around Britt's bony, heaving shoulders. 'Is it serious?'

'It's her heart. They think she'll be all right, but I want to go and see her. And someone has to look after my dad, too. I feel so useless being stuck over here when they need me.'

'Of course you must go to them,' Lola said. 'Do you want me to organise a ticket for you?'

Britt nodded, gulping back tears. 'Yes, please. But I don't know what to do about Rick. I don't like leaving him on his own.'

Lola understood immediately what was going on in her mind. Left unattended, Rick was capable of doing almost anything. With almost anyone.

'Do you want me to keep an eye on him?' she asked.

From the grateful look Britt gave her, that was exactly what she'd been thinking. 'Would you? I'll only be gone a couple of days. But I know he gets lonely if he's left on his own . . .'

'I understand.' Lola gave Britt's shoulders a comforting squeeze. The poor woman was frantic with worry over her sick mum. She shouldn't have to worry about whether her husband could keep it in his trousers for a couple of days. She wished Rick would grow up, instead of acting like a stupid, overgrown teenager.

By that night's show, Rick had turned up and Kyle's hand had recovered enough for him to take his usual place on stage. Lola came up behind Jay as he stood in the shadows, watching them.

'Do you wish you were still out there?' she said teasingly.

'That's the last place I'd want to be.'

'I thought you enjoyed it last night?'

He shook his head. 'I don't belong there.'

She laughed in disbelief. 'You're kidding. Didn't you read that review? It said you were—'

'I don't care what it said.' He turned around and she was shocked by the bleak expression in his eyes. 'I'm not good enough, and I never will be. I'm just a second-rate session musician.'

'Says who?'

He glanced back towards the stage. 'My father,' he spat out bitterly, then stalked off before she could ask him any more. Lola watched him go, then turned back to the stage, where Rick was strutting, fists thrust skywards, blasting out vocals and sending the fans wild.

Jay must have imagined it, she thought. There was no way anyone would be that cruel, not even Rick.

After the show, she hung around to make sure Rick got back to the hotel. The dressing room was already crowded with the usual backstage hangers-on and giggling girls picked from the stage door. But there was no sign of him.

'Has anyone seen Rick?' she called out, pushing past a moody-looking girl with dyed blonde hair and way too much lipgloss.

They all shook their heads.

'He's off the leash tonight, he could be anywhere,' Jonno joked, his arm clamped around a redhead with the biggest, fakest boobs Lola had ever seen.

'Maybe he's gone to hook up with Tawnee Wallis?' one of the techs suggested, and they all laughed. All except Lola, who was too scared it might be true.

She searched backstage until she was certain he wasn't there. Then she drove back to the hotel. He wasn't there, either, and the slim young man on reception confirmed he hadn't picked up the key to his suite.

'I haven't seen him tonight, and I definitely would have remembered,' he said, his eyes gleaming with unrequited lust.

Lola thought for a moment. Rick wasn't at the gig or at the hotel, so where was he? Where would a middle-aged rock star go when his wife was out of town and he wanted to have a good time . . .

She had a brainwave. Turning to the man, who was dusting down his computer monitor, she said, 'Where would I find the nearest lap-dancing bar?'

He stopped dusting and blinked at her. 'Excuse me?'

'A lap-dancing bar. You know, naked girls and stuff ?' She took one look at his appalled face and realised he probably didn't know at all.

'I really have no idea,' he replied stiffly. 'I'd have to ask someone.'

A quick consultation with the concierge, who was obviously a man of the world, and Lola had the address. It was the only lap-dancing club in town, and the one Kyle had been thrown out of the previous night.

*   *   *

The bar was hot and crowded. Lola stood for a moment, her eyes adjusting to the pulsating lights. Up on the podium that ran the length of the room, near-naked girls writhed suggestively around poles to the insistent beat of dance music, watched by rows of eager men. Others moved between tables, ready to offer a personal dance whenever a fifty-dollar bill was waved in their direction.

Lola scanned the tables looking for Rick, uncomfortably aware that she was the only woman in the club dressed in more than a thong. Some of the men were looking in her direction, some curious, most irritated by her presence.

She stopped a scantily-clad girl passing by with a drinks tray. 'I'm looking for Rick Wild. Have you seen him?'

The girl hesitated just a fraction too long. 'Who?' she said.

'Will this jog your memory?' Lola took out a twenty-dollar bill and put it on the girl's tray.

The girl looked at it and licked her lips. 'Are you the press?' she asked finally. 'Only we're not supposed to talk to the press, so it'll cost you extra.'

These girls obviously weren't picked for their

271

IQ, Lola decided. 'No, I'm not the press. I'm his . . . personal assistant,' she said.

The girl nodded towards the door. 'Upstairs,' she said. 'In the champagne lounge.'

Gus was standing at the top of the narrow flight of stairs that led to the private VIP area, which was closed off by heavy crimson velvet drapes. He stepped into Lola's path.

'Sorry, can't let you in,' he said gruffly.

'I need to talk to him.'

'He's busy.'

'I'm sure he is.' Lola shuddered to think what was going on behind those curtains. Whatever it was, she certainly didn't want to walk in on it.

Standing her ground, she called out, 'Rick!' Silence. 'Rick, get out here now!' More silence. Lola took a deep breath. 'Fire!' she screamed at the top of her voice.

A second later the curtain flew open and two girls rushed out yelping. They pushed past Lola and clattered down the stairs. Rick appeared behind them, pulling on his shirt, his fair hair tousled.

'What's going on?' He looked wildly from Gus to Lola. 'Where's the fire?'

'There isn't one,' she told him calmly.

'What the . . .' He squinted at her, as if noticing her for the first time. 'What are *you* doing here?'

'I've come to take you back to the hotel.'

He faced her like a defiant child. 'I don't want to go.'

Lola leaned forward and sniffed. 'Have you been drinking?'

'So what if I have?'

'Oh, Rick.' She shook her head reproachfully.

'Britt will be so disappointed.'

'Britt's not here, is she?'

'Is that why you decided to go on a bender?'

He looked mutinous. 'I can do what I like. I'm a grown-up.'

'You could have fooled me,' Lola muttered. She braced herself, taking charge. 'I'll take you back to the hotel. With any luck we can sneak out before anyone realises you're here.'

'Too late,' said Gus, who'd been whispering into his mobile. 'That was the front desk. There are a couple of guys with cameras sniffing around outside.'

'So what?' Rick shrugged. 'Let them take my picture if they want. I don't care.' He flung his arms wide. 'I'm a rock star,' he proclaimed drunkenly. 'This is what rock stars do.'

'Not if they're married.'

'*Especially* if they're married.'

Lola turned on him in disgust. 'You're pathetic, do you know that? It's your wedding anniversary, your wife's on the other side of the world taking care of her sick mother, and all you can think about is getting drunk and cheating on her. Don't you give a damn about how Britt might feel?'

He stared at her with glazed, uncomprehending eyes. 'But I'm a rock star.'

'You're a loser.'

'That's where you're wrong, see?' He jabbed his finger at her, narrowly missing her nose. 'I am Rick Wild. The Wild Man. And I've still got what it takes, whatever any crappy newspaper says.'

Now what was he on about? Lola shook her head, uncomprehending. She had a good mind to leave him there and walk away. Why should she

273

bother saving his skin, anyway? It would serve him right to be snapped in a drunken stupor, half-dressed and wrapped around a couple of lap-dancers.

But she wasn't doing this for him. She was doing it for Britt, to save her from even more heartache.

She handed Gus her keys. 'We'll take my car; they won't be looking for that. Bring it round to the back entrance.'

'Excuse me,' Rick said, as Gus lumbered down the stairs. 'I told you, I'm not going anywhere.'

Lola whipped out her mobile phone. 'Do I have to ring Dinah and tell her about this?'

The name was like a bucket of icy water, sobering him up instantly. Rick's eyes darted around. 'How do we get out?' he whispered.

They found the back entrance and hid in the doorway, waiting for Gus to appear with the car. As they shivered in the night air, Rick said glumly, 'Maybe this wasn't such a good idea, was it?'

'I think it was a very bad idea,' Lola agreed.

'It was that newspaper review,' Rick mumbled. 'It just made me feel so old . . .'

At that moment, a car came round the corner. Lola grabbed Rick's arm, dragging him out into the alley. But as the headlights trapped them, she suddenly realised that the man behind the wheel wasn't Gus.

'Get back!' She tried to shove Rick back in through the rear entrance, but it was too late. A flashbulb exploded in their faces. They were caught.

CHAPTER THIRTY-ONE

For the second day running, Poleaxe made it into the newspapers. But this time the news wasn't so good.

'WHAT A COVER-UP!' screamed one headline above a blurry photograph of Lola and Rick cowering under a neon-lit sign that said 'Girls, Girls, Girls'. Underneath was the line: 'While wife nurses sick mum, daughter sneaks rock star Rick into club for night of lust with lap-dancer.'

They made her sound like his pimp.

She couldn't face breakfast with the rest of the crew; she was sure they'd all have plenty of amusement at her expense, and for once she didn't feel like laughing. All she could think about was how Britt was taking it.

It was too much to hope that Britt hadn't seen the headlines, but by the middle of the morning Lola managed to convince herself that maybe the news hadn't travelled as far as Stockholm, or that Britt had been too busy to notice.

Then, just as she was beginning to breathe a sigh of relief, Britt called.

'How could you?' were her first words.

'Britt, I can explain everything—'

'There's nothing to explain. You betrayed me.'

'I didn't!'

'You conspired with my husband to humiliate me.'

'But I had nothing to do with that. I was sneaking him *out* of the club, not in.'

'And that makes it all right, does it?' Britt gave a

hollow laugh. 'I was wrong to trust you,' she said. 'I should know better than to trust anyone by now. But I thought you were different. I thought you were my friend.'

Lola caught Hamish's eye across the office. 'I *am* your friend. I was trying to protect you.'

'By lying to me?' Britt's voice rose hysterically. 'Thanks, but I don't need anyone else to do that. What I need is someone to tell me the truth for once.'

'You're right, I'm sorry. I should have been honest with you. But I was only trying to help,' she insisted. 'I didn't want you to get hurt. Ask Rick if you don't believe me.'

'I can't. He's not answering his phone. He's probably too scared, the coward.'

Lola held the phone away from her ear, as Britt launched into a tirade of abuse in Swedish, with some ripe English words thrown in for good measure.

Finally she calmed down. 'Anyway,' she said, 'I've decided. He can go to hell. I never want to see him again.'

'You don't mean that.'

'Don't I? I'm meeting my lawyers later. I've already made the appointment.'

'Wouldn't it be better if you talked to Rick first?'

'How can I, when he won't answer his calls? Anyway, I have nothing to say to him. He can kiss my backside.'

'I'll talk to him,' said Lola.

'If you can find him,' Britt said. 'And if you *do* find him, tell him I'm taking him for every lousy penny he's got.'

Britt was right; no one seemed to know where Rick was. Or if they did, they weren't telling. His suite was empty, and the gay man on reception could only tell her that he'd checked out early that morning with his minder, Gus. But no one knew where he had gone or for how long.

'He'll turn up when we get to Phoenix,' Dinah predicted confidently when Lola tracked her down in the hotel spa. She was having a massage by the poolside. 'The next gig isn't for four days. He'll be back by then.'

'Do *you* know where he is?'

Dinah shrugged. 'Somewhere he doesn't want to be found. He always goes to ground when he's done something wrong. He hid for a fortnight when he slept with Simon's ex-wife.'

Lola sat down on the lounger next to her. 'I wish I could find him. Poor Britt's really upset.'

'Britt's always upset. She has a nervous breakdown when she chips her nail polish.'

Lola was shocked by her lack of sympathy. 'This is a bit worse than a chipped nail.'

'She knew what he was like when she married him. Anyway, she didn't seem to mind him cheating when *she* was the one he was sleeping with on the side.' She craned her neck to look up at the muscular young masseur who was pummelling away at her shoulders and listening avidly. 'And if you repeat a word of this conversation, I swear you'll never work again,' she added.

The masseur went pale under his tan and said nothing.

277

'So you think it's OK for him to cheat on her?'

'Honey, he cheats on everyone. He sees a wedding ring as a challenge, not a commitment. I put up with it for a while but in the end I had too much self-respect to stay. So I bailed out. Just like the Swedish meatball should have done a long time ago.'

'Maybe she loves him?'

'And I didn't? Don't you think it hurt me to know my husband was sleeping in someone else's bed?'

'In that case, you must understand what Britt's going through.'

'Like I said, it serves her right.'

'You don't mean that.'

Dinah was silent for a moment. Lola thought she was just enjoying her massage too much to speak, but then she said, 'I know where he'll be if you want to find him.'

'You do?'

'I know everything about Rick, remember? I can read his mind, God help me.' She shuddered.

'Where is he?'

She lowered her voice to a whisper. 'On his farm in Wales. It's where he always goes to hide out.'

'I didn't know he had a farm,' Lola said.

'Why do you think it's such a good hiding place?' Dinah said.

As Lola left, she called after her, 'But don't tell that bitch Britt, will you? I don't want her to think I feel sorry for her or anything.'

Lola smiled. 'Don't worry, your hard-as-nails reputation is safe with me.'

*　　　*　　　*

It was nearly midnight when Tiffany flew in from LA. The first thing she did when the cab dropped her off at the hotel was head for Hamish's room.

She had to hammer on the door for a long time before he answered it. He was fumbling to hook on his glasses, his dark hair sticking up on end.

'Tiffany?' He squinted at her. 'Do you know what time it is?'

'Sorry, I just got back and I had to see you. Cute PJs, by the way. What do you call that stuff ?'

'Tartan.' He reached for a bathrobe and shrugged it on quickly. Tiffany giggled. As if she was going to ogle him! 'What is it you wanted?'

'I had to tell someone. I got the job!'

His face broke into a smile. 'That's great news. Congratulations.'

'Thanks. I can hardly believe it myself.' She threw herself down on his bed. The sheets were still warm and rumpled where he'd been sleeping. 'I was *so* nervous, I was sure I'd screwed it up. And it didn't help that Ashley Anderson was there, making out like she already had the part and I was wasting my time. Ha! I showed her.'

'You did indeed.'

'You bet I did. I acted the liposuctioned ass off her.'

Hamish perched on a corner of the bed. 'Have you told your mum?'

'Not yet. I wanted to tell you first.' For some reason, that was the bit she was most excited about, telling Hamish.

'I'm flattered.'

There was an awkward pause.

'And I got you a present,' Tiffany added. She

279

reached across the bed for her holdall. 'To say thank you for your help. And for not thinking I was a dumb blonde.'

'You didn't have to do that.'

'I wanted to. I would never have got through that screen test if you hadn't helped me.' She found the package and handed it to him. 'I hope you like it.'

He rattled the box. 'It's not an "I heart Hollywood" keyring, is it? Only I've got a million of those.'

'Open it and see, dumbass.'

She could hardly breathe as she watched him unwrapping the gift. She couldn't have been more excited if someone had given *her* a present.

He seemed to take for ever to unfasten all the knots and fold out the paper. Tiffany fought the urge to grab it out of his hands and rip off the wrapping.

Then, suddenly, there it was.

'It's a Patek Philippe limited edition,' she said. 'You wouldn't believe how tough they are to find. Brad Pitt's been looking for one for ages, apparently.'

Hamish looked down at the watch, dazed. 'You shouldn't have,' he said. Then he snapped the box shut and handed it back to her. 'I can't take it.'

Her excitement took a freefall into disappointment. 'Don't you like it?'

'It's just too much.'

'But I can afford it.'

He frowned. 'You don't get it, do you? I don't want expensive presents. You don't need to buy me like you do the rest of your friends.'

Tiffany jerked back as if he'd slapped her in the

face. 'Is that what you think? That I have to buy my friends?'

'That's not what I meant—'

'Let me tell you something,' she cut him off, her voice shaking with anger, 'I wouldn't try to buy you, because you're not worth the money!'

'Tiffany—'

'Go to hell.' She snatched the watch back and stormed out, slamming the door behind her.

She didn't stop running until she reached her hotel room. When she let herself in the phone was ringing. She unplugged it and hurled it at the wall.

Screw him, she thought.

CHAPTER THIRTY-TWO

Fat Cat Farm wasn't quite what Lola had been expecting. She'd imagined something grand, with smartly converted outbuildings, a gleaming 4×4 sitting on the gravelled courtyard, and maybe a couple of thoroughbred horses in a paddock so Rick could play at being the gentleman farmer.

But the dilapidated huddle of farm buildings that nestled in the green valley below her was humble, to say the least. There were even sheep grazing on the hills around it.

Lola parked her rental car in a lay-by on the narrow track and consulted the directions Dinah had given her. Maybe she'd taken a wrong turning somewhere? Then she spotted the CCTV camera hidden in the overgrown hedgerow beside the five-bar gate and knew she was in the right place.

She left the car at the top of the hill, went

through the gate and followed the twisting dirt track down to the farm. It had been raining, and the air smelt fresh.

It was almost lunchtime, and she felt as if she'd been travelling for ever to get here. She only hoped her journey would be worth it.

The yard was muddy and littered with rusting farm machinery. It was surrounded on two sides by barns and tumbledown outbuildings, and on the third by a two-storey stone farmhouse. It might have been chocolate-box pretty once, but now the paintwork was peeling and the whitewashed walls were smudged with green moss and brown rust from the dripping drainpipes. Weeds squeezed out of the cracked paving.

Rick came out of the house, stooping under the low lintel of the front door. Lola barely recognised him in his mud-spattered jeans and thick Guernsey sweater.

'You do know it's illegal to conceal a CCTV camera, don't you?' she said.

'How did you know where I was?'

'Dinah told me.'

'Treacherous bitch.'

'I had to force it out of her, if it's any consolation.'

'I bet you did,' he said grimly. They stood facing each other across the yard. 'What do you want?'

'Aren't you going to ask me in?'

'I suppose.' He grudgingly led the way in to the kitchen. It was a big room, with all the makings of a glossy magazine farmhouse kitchen—stone-flagged floors, narrow casement windows with deep sills, a shiny green Aga, dresser and big scrubbed wooden table. But there was something sad and neglected about it.

It lacked a woman's touch, Lola decided, looking at the muddy boots carelessly abandoned by the door, and the dirty dishes piled in the Belfast sink.

'Nice place,' she said.

'It suits me.' He crossed the room to the Aga and picked up the kettle. 'I suppose you want tea?'

'Yes, please.'

She sat down at the table and watched him fill the kettle. 'Are you here on your own?'

'I haven't got a woman hidden away upstairs, if that's what you mean.'

'You do surprise me.'

He set the kettle on the hotplate to boil, then pulled two odd mugs out of the sink and rinsed them carelessly under the tap. 'I brought Gus with me.'

'Where is he now?'

'He went into the village to get some ciggies.'

Lola watched him moving around the kitchen, opening and closing cupboard doors, cursing under his breath.

'Lost something?' she asked.

'I can't find the tea.'

'Try that tin on the dresser. The one with "Tea" written on it.' Lola nodded to a caddy on the shelf.

'Ah. Right.' He picked it up, unscrewed the lid and peered inside uncertainly. 'Are you sure you wouldn't rather have a beer?' he asked.

Lola smiled. 'Have you ever actually made a cup of tea?'

'Not recently.'

'Shall I do it?'

'Would you mind?' He handed her the caddy.

She couldn't find a teapot, so she dropped a teabag into each mug instead. 'Aren't you going to ask how Britt is?' she said.

'I don't think I want to know.' He paused. 'How is she?'

'Heartbroken.'

'She'll get over it.' Rick picked up the pile of post on the kitchen table and began flicking through it.

'I wouldn't bet on it. She's been talking to her lawyers.'

'She's always talking to her lawyers. She's got them on speed-dial. It doesn't mean anything.'

Lola swung round to face him. 'You really don't care, do you? You think this is all a big joke.'

'Look, it's done, it happened. I don't know what the big deal is, anyway.'

'You don't know?' Lola stared at him. 'It was your wedding anniversary,' she said. 'Your wife was looking after her sick mother. Then you went off to a lap-dancing club and picked up a cheap tart. What have you got to say about that?'

He tore open a letter, glanced through it, then threw it to one side. 'There were two. And they weren't that cheap,' he said.

Lola gripped the edge of the worktop to stop herself throwing a mug at his head. 'Do you know why I came here? I thought I might be able to help you save your marriage. But maybe I shouldn't have bothered. Maybe I should be telling Britt to go ahead and see her lawyers, because she deserves better than being married to a selfish pig like you!'

'I know,' Rick said quietly.

'This isn't funny, Rick. You stand to lose a lot

284

more than you can ever—' She stopped. 'What did you say?'

'You're right, she deserves better than me. I don't know why she hasn't realised that yet.'

Before Lola could reply, the door flew open and Gus burst in. He was red in the face, his chest heaving.

'I saw a car parked up on the road,' he panted, then he saw Lola. 'Oh, it's you.' He glanced at Rick. 'Everything OK, boss?'

'Yeah, yeah. Everything's great. Did you get the ciggies?'

Gus reached into his pocket and handed them over. Rick grabbed them and tipped one out.

Lola listened to him laughing and joking with Gus. His mask was back in place and he was as arrogant as ever. She wanted to scream with frustration.

'Why don't you show me round the farm?' she suggested.

He looked at her blankly. 'Do you know anything about farming?'

'Do you?'

'As a matter of fact, I do.'

'So why don't you teach me something?'

He eyed her narrowly. 'Only if you promise not to nag me about Britt.'

'I promise.'

They trudged across the yard, Lola struggling to keep up with Rick in her borrowed wellington boots, which were several sizes too big.

'How long have you had this place?' she asked.

'About thirty years.'

'You haven't done much to it in all that time.'

'It's a working farm, not a show home. Anyway,

it's not easy when you're on the road half the year, and in the studio the rest.' He pushed open a gate at the other side of the yard and headed purposefully up a grassy track that climbed upwards away from the farm.

Lola stopped and looked to the crest of the hill. 'We're not going all the way up there, are we?'

'Why not? The view's spectacular.'

'I'll take your word for it.'

He grinned. 'I thought cops were meant to be fit?'

He certainly was, Lola thought as she struggled up the path behind him. He covered the path quickly with his long, loping strides.

Just as she thought her heart was going to explode in her chest, they reached the top of the hill. Rick was right; the view was amazing. The fields were spread out below them, green and gold under the clear blue sky. The air felt fine and cool against her flushed skin.

Rick pointed out the boundaries of the farm, and the grazing sheep. 'They're not actually mine. I rent the land to a farmer next door.' He shaded his eyes and gazed down the hill. 'But one day I'd like my own flock.'

Lola laughed.

'What's so funny?' he demanded.

'Nothing. I just can't imagine you as a sheep farmer, that's all. All those early mornings and getting your hands dirty.'

'You'd be surprised,' Rick said. 'I've always liked being out on the land. My uncle used to have a place like this, when I was a kid. We used to go and stay with him and his family for holidays. I loved it. I never wanted to go home. I always told myself if the band made it big I'd buy my own farm.'

'Has Britt ever been here?'

His face darkened. 'She'd hate it. The only great outdoors she knows is what she passes through on her way from her taxi to the hotel.' He turned on her. 'Anyway, you promised you wouldn't talk about her.'

'I promised I wouldn't nag you. I didn't say I wouldn't talk.'

He sighed impatiently. 'Look, Britt and I are cool, OK? I'll sort it out with her. I always do.'

'By getting her an expensive gift?' Lola guessed. 'What's it going to be this time? Another Cartier watch? A Porsche?'

'I don't know. What do you suggest?'

'I suggest you go back and try talking to her. Tell her you love her. Because that's what she really wants, not some expensive trinket.'

Rick laughed. 'You don't know my wife.'

'No,' Lola said. '*You* don't know her. How do you think she feels, wearing that jewellery, when every piece reminds her of another time you cheated on her? She'd rather have a husband who loved her enough to stay faithful than another piece of junk from Van Cleef and Arpels.'

Rich scanned the hillside, the breeze ruffling his hair. 'She knew the score when I married her. Anyway, it's good to keep her on her toes, stop her getting too comfortable.'

Lola stared at him in disgust. 'Is that why you sleep with other women, to keep her on her toes? God, you're even more despicable than I thought.'

'Now just a second—'

'Just go away, Rick. I don't want to talk to you any more, OK?'

She began to stomp back down the hill, her boots skidding on the damp grass.

'Was she really upset?' Rick called after her.

'What do you think? She loves you. Although God knows why, the way you treat her.'

'You're wrong,' Rick called. 'She doesn't love me. She loves Rick Wild.'

Lola turned and squinted back up the hill towards him. 'What do you mean?'

He moved his arm in a sweeping arc over the valley. 'Look at this place. *This* is me, the real me. What do you think Britt would made of it? She'd take one look and run straight back to Beverly Hills.'

'You don't know that.'

'Don't I? Listen, when we met she was a supermodel and I was a rock star. It was like a marriage made in the stars. But it was the image she wanted, not really me. She wanted the Wild Man. So that's what I have to be.'

Seeing him standing there forlornly on the hillside was a revelation. 'So all this womanizing is just an act you put on for her sake?'

'You've seen her. She's young, she's stunning. OK, maybe I can still compete if I try hard enough, but I don't know how much longer I can go on doing it. There are so many other guys around.'

'There's always someone younger, thinner and more beautiful waiting around the corner, to take your place,' Lola murmured.

'Sorry?'

'Nothing,' she said. 'Just something someone once said to me.'

'They were right. Britt could have her pick of anyone. But me?' He turned to face her. 'Look at me, Lola. Without all the money and the flash and the rock star stuff, I'm just a middle-aged man. I know I'm going to lose her one day.'

'You'll lose her a lot sooner if you keep treating her the way you do.'

'It hasn't happened so far.'

'That's because she loves you. But there's only just so much humiliation a woman can take.'

He glanced uncertainly at her. 'You really think she loves me?'

'I think you should sit down and talk to her. Be honest for once. You might both be pleasantly surprised.'

They headed back down the path to the farm. Going downhill was even harder than climbing up. Lola had to grip Rick's arm to stop herself slipping and sliding.

'Thanks for coming,' Rick said when they got back to the yard.

'Someone's got to try to talk some sense into you.'

'I don't know if you'll ever do that.' He smiled ruefully.

'But you'll promise to talk to Britt?'

'If she'll ever speak to me again.'

'She will.' They stood in the porch and pulled off their boots. 'But no more lap-dancing clubs, OK?'

'Oh God,' he groaned. 'Thanks for trying to rescue me.'

'It didn't do much good. Everyone's blaming me as much as you.'

'Maybe we should both hide out here for a while?'

Lola shook her head. 'You've got a tour to

finish, remember?'

'If it doesn't finish me first.' Rick hesitated for a moment, then said, 'You might as well know, I had another letter this morning.'

'From your Devoted Fan?'

He pulled it out of the back pocket of his jeans and handed it to her. Lola recognised the scrawly handwriting on the blue envelope straight away. 'What does it say?'

'Read it for yourself.'

She pulled the letter out and unfolded it. It was just five words, written in bold capital letters: 'YOU'LL DIE IN LOS ANGELES.'

'Short and to the point, isn't it?' Rick joked weakly.

Lola stuffed it back in the envelope and handed it to him. 'Have you shown this to the police?'

'I haven't even shown it to Gus. I kind of hoped if I ignored it, it might go away.'

'I don't think that's going to work somehow.' Then a thought struck her. 'Can I see the letter again?'

'Take it. I don't want it.'

Lola studied the envelope. 'Who else knows you're here, apart from me and Dinah?'

'Just a few of the crew. I try to keep this place secret.' He frowned. 'Why do you want to know?'

'Just a thought.' She looked back at the envelope. All the rest of Rick's post had been redirected. This was the only letter with the farm's address on it.

Which meant whoever sent it had to know where Rick would be.

'Look on the bright side,' he laughed nervously. 'At least I know I've got a couple more weeks to

290

live!'

* * * *

Despite her objections, Rick insisted on returning to Phoenix with her the following day.

'Maybe you should cancel the rest of the tour?' she said as they drove to the airport. They'd left Gus to pack Rick's things and lock up at the farm. 'No one would blame you, under the circumstances.'

'Are you kidding? Dinah would have my balls for earrings if she had to give the promoters back their cash. Besides, my fans want me to be there.'

'One of them wants you dead,' Lola said.

He shuddered. 'Don't remind me.'

He turned up the CD player and leaned back in his seat, letting the music wash over him.

'This is pretty good,' he said. 'Who is it?'

'Do you really want to know?' Lola looked sideways at him. 'It's Jay.'

His eyes flicked open. 'Jay?'

'Do you like it?'

'It's OK, I s'pose.'

Lola smiled. Would it really kill him to admit his son had talent?

She tried to win him round with flattery. 'He takes after his father, doesn't he?' she said.

Rick stared grimly out of the window. 'Doesn't he just?' he muttered.

CHAPTER THIRTY-THREE

Tiffany clung to the toilet bowl, sweating and exhausted. She'd never thrown up this much in her life, not even when she had an eating disorder five years ago. She felt as if her stomach had been turned inside out.

She pressed her face against the cool porcelain and closed her eyes, too weak to crawl back to bed. What was the point when she'd only need to throw up again five minutes later?

She squinted over her shoulder through the open bathroom door at the clock on her bedside table. Three twenty-seven, the illuminated figures said. Another three hours and she'd be leaving for LA to start filming. Her suitcases were already packed and waiting at the foot of her bed.

Perhaps it was nerves, she told herself as she reached for a length of toilet roll to wipe her mouth. But she knew it was more than butterflies that was making her sick every five minutes.

She pulled herself up to a kneeling position and faced herself in the bathroom mirror. Her face was white and slick with perspiration. Damp strands of hair clung to her cheeks, and there were huge purplish circles like bruises under her eyes.

She looked like a movie star, all right—that kid in *The Exorcist*.

Oh God, why did this have to happen to her now? Her first big break, her first chance to show everyone that she wasn't the loser they all thought she was, and now this.

Life really sucked sometimes.

Too weak to make it back to bed, she sank down again and curled up on the bathroom floor. Thank heavens for smart hotels and their underfloor heating, she thought, as her face touched the warm tiles and sleep overcame her.

She'd hoped a couple of hours' rest might make her feel better. But by the time her alarm call came two hours later she felt far worse. Every muscle in her body ached. Even her eyeballs hurt. It was like having flu and the world's worst hangover mixed together, with a touch of dysentery thrown in.

Just the thought of dragging herself to the airport and on to the plane made her feel like giving up.

She thought about calling them to explain, but she knew there would be no point. The director had already warned her that the tight production schedule left no room for manoeuvre. If she didn't turn up to the first day's filing then that was it. She was fired.

You have to do this, she told herself as she slowly peeled off her pyjamas. The cotton fabric felt damp against her skin. Still unable to make it to her feet, she crawled into the shower and scrabbled for the controls.

She sat propped in a corner of the shower cubicle as the cool water cascaded over her skin. She tried to wash her hair, but she could barely lift her arms to massage in the shampoo.

Somehow she managed to get herself dressed in a cotton mini-skirt and T-shirt. She plastered on some concealer to hide the shadows under her eyes, threw up, brushed her teeth, then threw up again.

She was trying to brush her teeth for the second

time when there was a brisk knock at the door and a voice sang out, 'Taxi for Miss Wild.'

Tiffany rinsed her mouth out then went to answer the door.

'Take the cases, I'll be there in a—' She stopped. 'What are *you* doing here?'

'Giving you a lift to the airport. Are these all your bags?' Hamish moved past her to collect them.

Tiffany glared at him. They hadn't seen or spoken to each other since he'd so rudely turned down the watch she'd bought him. She'd been avoiding him, mainly out of embarrassment. Now her anger had died down she could see he'd been right; it *was* an over-the-top gift. After all, she barely knew the guy.

'I didn't ask for you,' she said.

'I know,' he agreed. 'But believe it or not, there weren't many runners queuing up for the chance to get up at dawn and take you to the airport. Besides, I wanted to see you before you left.'

'You did?' She felt a tiny flutter in her throat.

'I wanted to say sorry for being such a pig. You bought me a present and I was very churlish about it.'

'It *was* a bit extravagant,' Tiffany mumbled.

'It was the thought that counted. And if I'd thought about it, I could have sold it for a fortune on eBay.'

'Too late,' she said. 'I already did.'

'Great minds think alike.' His eyes twinkled behind his spectacles. 'Anyway, I've got something to give *you*.' He reached into his pocket. Despite the early hour he was dressed as immaculately as ever in a suit and tie. 'It's not much, but I'd like you to have it.'

Tiffany studied the small silver charm on a chain that he'd dropped into her hand. It was a tiny little guy with what looked like a pack—or was it another person?—on his back.

'It's a St Christopher,' Hamish explained. 'The patron saint of travellers. I thought it might help keep you safe while I'm not there to look after you.'

Tears pricked her eyes, but Tiffany warned herself not be be pathetic. 'You don't need to buy me like you do the rest of your friends,' she said.

Hamish winced. '*Touché.* But actually, I didn't buy it. It was given to me by my late grandfather. Shortly before he was run over by a bus.'

Tiffany looked at him sharply. He was smiling when he said it. It was so hard to work out when he was joking and when he wasn't. 'You're weird,' she said. And then, 'Excuse me,' as she clamped her hand over her mouth and fled to the bathroom.

This is crazy, she thought as she hung over the toilet again. I can't even be sick any more. Any time now she expected her eyeballs to fall out and plop into the water.

Hamish was waiting anxiously by the door as she staggered out. 'Are you OK?'

'Just nerves,' she lied.

'Are you sure?' He peered at her. 'You look very peaky.'

'What the hell is peaky?'

'Take a look in the mirror.'

She managed a weak smile. 'Just get me to the airport, will you? I don't want to miss that flight.'

In the car, she slumped in the back seat, eyes closed, and drifted in and out of sleep as Hamish chatted on. She couldn't get comfortable; either the sweat was making her clothes stick to her, or she was shivering with cold. Poor Hamish switched wildly between heating and air con, not knowing what to do.

And then the nausea hit her again.

'Are we nearly there?' she said through clamped lips.

' 'Fraid not. There's a traffic snarl-up ahead.' He caught her eye in the mirror. 'Don't worry, we've still got plenty of—'

'Stop the car!' she screamed.

He took one look at her face, jerked the wheel and came to a screeching halt in a lay-by. Tiffany just managed to wrench the door open before she threw up in the gutter.

'Wow, you really are nervous, aren't you?' Hamish commented.

'I think I've got a bug.' Tiffany fumbled in her bag for a tissue.

Hamish reached over and passed her his handkerchief. White cotton and perfectly laundered, of course. 'I think that's an understatement.' He pressed his hand to her face. His fingers felt deliciously cool against her cheek. She wished he'd leave it there, cooling her down. 'You're burning up. I think you should see a doctor.'

'I'll see one when I get to LA.' Tiffany slammed the car door shut and fell back against the seat.

She must have drifted off to sleep again. She awoke just as they were pulling up. At first she couldn't figure out where they were when she saw the parking attendant in his strangely familiar maroon uniform. Then it dawned on her.

They were back at the hotel.

'Why have we come back here?' She looked at her watch. Her flight left in less than an hour. 'I'll never make it to LA!'

'You're right. The way you look you'll probably die before you get to the airport.' Hamish handed the keys to the parking attendant. 'You're too sick to go anywhere. You need to rest.'

'I need to go to LA.' She watched him taking out her bags and handing them to a bellboy. 'Don't touch those!' she snapped, as he started to pile them on a trolley. She swung round to face Hamish. 'I demand you take me to the airport now.'

'No.'

'Fine. I'll get a cab.'

She tried to get out of the car but her treacherous legs buckled under her and she fell into Hamish's arms.

'Be reasonable, Tiffany. Even if you did make it as far as the airport they'd never let you get on that plane.' He propped her up against him. His arms felt strong yet gentle at the same time.

'Then you'll just have to drive me to LA. I can't miss this,' she pleaded.

He looked down at her, his brown eyes gentle. 'You don't get it, do you? You're really sick. Look at you, you can barely stand up.'

'I don't care,' she croaked. 'I don't care if I die the minute I step on to that set. I just need to get to LA now.'

And then she fainted.

*   *   *

297

The doctor diagnosed a viral infection. 'Make sure she gets lots of rest and plenty of fluids,' he told Hamish. 'And if her temperature's not down in twenty-four hours, call me straight away.'

'I will,' Hamish promised. 'Believe me, I'll make sure she doesn't move out of that bed.'

'Promises, promises,' Tiffany murmured sleepily. She didn't have the strength to put up a fight. She'd already missed her flight and besides, it felt so good to be snuggled up in a nice bed. Not to mention having someone to take care of her.

Feeling safe, warm and comfortable, she sank back against the pillows and went to sleep.

She slept on and off for the next twenty-four hours. Whenever she opened her eyes there was Hamish in the armchair beside her bed. He pressed cold flannels against her face, gave her sips of water, and generally fussed over her.

'You don't have to stay,' she murmured as she watched him work his way through a mountain of paperwork by the dim light of the bedside lamp. 'You can go back to the office if you like.'

'Are you kidding? You'll be on the next plane to LA as soon as my back's turned.' He bossily straightened her pillows for her. 'Besides, I might get some funny looks if I go in to work now. It's two in the morning.'

'Is it?' She looked towards the bedroom window. She hadn't even noticed the day drifting into night. 'In that case you should get some sleep.'

'I'd rather stay here with you.'

She smiled sleepily. 'You're sweet.'

'So are you.'

'No one's ever called me that before.'

'They obviously don't know you as well as I do.'

She went to sleep again as he stroked her face.

When she woke up, the sun was streaming in through the curtains again, and she could hear her mother's voice.

'So she didn't make it to LA. Why am I not surprised?' she was saying.

'She's sick,' Hamish said.

'Oh yeah? Another drunken bender, I suppose?'

'Actually, the doctor said it was a severe viral infection.'

'Doctors will say anything if it helps push their bills up.' Her mother sounded weary. 'I guess she knows she's blown this whole movie deal? Josh called me last night. They don't need her any more.'

'But I phoned them yesterday,' Hamish said. 'I explained the situation. They seemed OK about it.'

'That was before the press got hold of the story. Apparently a reporter from *The National* called to check if it was true Tiffany wasn't allowed to fly to LA because she was too drunk to get on the plane.'

'That's a lie!'

'Who cares? It's what gets printed in the papers that counts. That's what Josh reads. He told me he didn't need a leading lady he'd have to sober up every morning before she went on set.'

Tiffany kept her eyes closed, but hot tears spilled out and rolled down her cheeks towards her ears.

'I hope you told them Tiffany wasn't like that?' Hamish said coldly.

'Why should I? We all know what she's like. She's a liability.'

'She's also your daughter.'

'You think I don't know that? Why do you think

I wake up with a headache every morning?' Her mother's voice rose, then fell again. 'Tell her to call me when she comes to.'

'Don't you want to stay with her for a while?'

'I can't. I've got a meeting in half an hour. And you should be back in the office,' she added. 'I don't pay you to play nursemaid to my daughter.'

'No,' Hamish said. 'I do it for free. Because I happen to care about her.'

Tiffany didn't hear her mother's reply, but a moment later the door closed. Tiffany opened her eyes as Hamish came back to sit beside her bed.

'Has she gone?' she said.

Hamish looked wary. 'She, um, didn't want to disturb you.'

'Liar.' Tiffany smiled. She appreciated that he'd tried to spare her feelings. There weren't many people who did that, her own mother included. 'I heard everything.' She sighed. 'I guess this means my movie career is over?'

Hamish's eyes darkened. 'I'll sort it out,' he promised. 'I'll call them again—'

'You heard what Mom said. There's no point.' The director was probably on the phone to Ashley Anderson right now. 'I'm sorry you won't get to go to the Oscars,' she said.

'There's always next time.'

'Somehow I don't think there'll be a next time.' Her mother was right; no one would want to touch her now. Her reputation, unfair or not, preceded her.

'It was a terrible movie anyway,' Hamish said loyally.

'You didn't say that when you were helping me with my lines. You said it was a masterpiece.'

300

'I was just being nice. It was actually a piece of rubbish. Whoever heard of a gorgeous girl falling in love with a geek?' He reached for her water glass. 'I'll refill this for you.'

'You should go back to work.'

'I'd rather stay here.'

'But Mom wants you back in the office. There's no point in both of us being fired, is there? Honestly, you should go. I'm feeling loads better, anyway.'

'Are you sure?' Hamish looked troubled. 'What if you need something while I'm gone?'

'Then I can call you. Go, will you?' She gave him a little shove.

In the end she persuaded him. But he still insisted on fussing around, making sure she had everything she needed.

'Right, I've lined up water, tissues and the TV remote right there for when you need them,' he said. 'And here's the phone.' He wrapped her fingers around it. 'Call me if you need anything at all, OK?'

'Yes, Mom.'

She felt a little lump rise in her throat. Where *was* her mom, exactly? She hadn't even stayed long enough to say hello.

Hamish hesitated a moment, then leaned over and planted a gentle kiss on her forehead.

'Euw.' Tiffany grimaced. 'Don't do that, I'm all sweaty.'

'I don't mind.' He smiled down at her. 'Now, don't forget—'

'Call you if I need anything. Yes, I know. You've told me a million times.' She rolled her eyes. 'Now go, before I throw up all over your nice shiny shoes.'

As soon as he'd gone she wished she hadn't sent him away. The room felt strange and empty without him. Tiffany thought about texting him, but she knew that would be stupid.

And she felt stupid enough already. Stupid and useless.

What was it her mother had called her? A liability. Tiffany wasn't even sure what it meant, but it didn't sound good.

And she'd tried, she really had. She knew she'd messed up in the past, but this time she really wanted to make it work, to prove to everyone she could do it. She'd worked so hard to get that part. OK, so maybe Hamish was right; it *was* a pretty rubbish movie. But at least it meant she'd achieved something real, not just another headline or a stupid photo in a magazine.

And now she'd screwed it up again. Just as everyone expected her to. It felt as if, no matter what she did, the whole world was waiting for her to fail.

At least she never disappointed them.

Her mobile vibrated in her hand. Thinking it was going to be Hamish checking up on her, Tiffany answered it with a cheery, 'You'll be pleased to know I'm still in bed.'

'I'm glad to hear it,' a deep voice on the other end of the line chuckled. 'And are you naked by any chance?'

Tiffany yanked the covers up over her pyjama top and struggled to sit upright, shocked by the voice from her past. 'Tony?'

'How are you doing, babe?'

He sounded warm and friendly, as if he'd never

been away. Let alone dumped her for her ex-best friend.

'OK.' She knew she should be angry but she still felt a thrill at hearing his sexy voice again. 'I got a part in a movie.'

'Hey, that's great. Congratulations.'

'But then I got fired.'

He laughed. 'Same old Tiffany. What happened? Did you get wasted?'

She stiffened defensively. Why did everyone immediately think that? 'It wasn't my fault. Anyway, it was a lousy movie. I think they've given my part to Ashley.'

'That figures. Her career's so far down the tubes these days she'd jump at an acne cream commercial.'

Tiffany smiled and snuggled further down under the covers. There was nothing more satisfying then hearing someone bitch about a rival.

And then, just to make her feel even better, he said, 'I miss you, babe.'

'Really?' Remembering to play it cool, she added, 'It's taken you long enough to call me.'

'I know.' He sounded wretched. 'I wanted to, I really did. You don't know how often I picked up that phone. But I couldn't do it. I wasn't sure if you'd want to hear from me after all that stuff with Ashley. Which wasn't even true, by the way,' he added hastily. 'It was just a load of lies put out by her publicity guys to make her look hot.'

So that photo of you sneaking out of her apartment didn't really exist? Tiffany thought. But she was enjoying the moment too much to spoil it.

'Go on,' she said.

'Anyway, I really do miss my little Wild child,'

303

Tony said. 'Things have been way too quiet without you around. So I was thinking . . . maybe we should hook up, have some fun?'

All her instincts screamed out for her to say no. Tony Sciotta was trouble.

'I can't. I'm in Vegas,' she said.

'I know. So am I.' She could hear the smile in his voice. 'Why do you think I called you? I'm over here to meet some guys about opening a new club. I heard you were in town, so I figured I could mix business with pleasure.'

In other words, you were at a loose end so you thought you'd give me a call. Tiffany tried to push the unworthy thought from her mind.

'So what do you say?' Tony said. 'I could swing by your hotel and pick you up in about half an hour, if you like?'

'In the middle of the afternoon?'

'The casinos never close, baby. We could play some machines, hang out. Whatever you like.' His voice was deep and husky with meaning.

Tiffany hesitated, biting her lip. 'I'm pretty sick,' she said.

'I'm sure Doctor Tony could sort you out with something that'll make you feel a whole lot better.'

She knew exactly what he meant. It was Tony who'd helped get her seriously into drugs in the first place.

She felt as if she were standing at the top of a giant ski slope, teetering on the edge. She had to save herself.

'C'mon,' Tony coaxed. 'Why don't you come and have some fun?'

Tiffany searched her minds for reasons why not. But all she saw was her mother, the film director and everyone else telling her what a screw-up she was.

Surely they couldn't all be wrong about her? If she was that bad, what did she have to lose?

She took a deep breath, closed her eyes and launched herself forward, hurtling down the slope.

CHAPTER THIRTY-FOUR

'Rien ne va plus.'

The croupier gave the roulette wheel a spin. Tiffany clutched the edge of the table for support as she watched the ball clickety-clicking around. The wheel wasn't the only thing that was spinning.

It stopped. Beside her, Tony gave a snort of disgust as the croupier raked in their chips. If she realised Tiffany was completely wasted, her bored face didn't show it.

'Can we go somewhere else now?' Tiffany whined.

'In a second, babe. Just give me a chance to win my money back.' Tony's eyes gleamed as he pushed another stack on to one of the red squares.

Don't you mean *my* money? Tiffany thought sourly. She wasn't so hammered she hadn't noticed whose credit card had bought all those chips Tony was so busy throwing down the toilet.

This didn't feel like fun any more. That naughty feeling had lasted for as long as it took to sneak out of the hotel. But as soon as she saw Tony again she'd realised her mistake.

She glanced sideways at him. He hadn't changed, but somewhere along the line, she had.

305

As they sat in the bar and she listened to him talking about himself, his new club, all the great connections he'd made in Las Vegas, a strange feeling began to creep over her. At first she thought it was the drugs Tony had given her, then it came to her: she was bored.

She didn't even fancy him any more. She used to think he was a sexy Italian stallion. But now she found that tuft of hair sprouting out of the top of his open-necked shirt vaguely repulsive. And as for all that flashy gold jewellery and those improbably white capped teeth . . .

'Lost again! Aw, man!' Tony cried out in frustration. He held out his hand. 'Quick, babe, I need more chips.'

Tiffany regarded him blandly. 'What do you expect me to do about it?'

'Please, Tiff ? I'll pay you back. I can't leave my place, this is my lucky chair.'

Tiffany nearly choked on her champagne. 'If it's so lucky, why don't you have any chips left?'

'It'll be cool, I promise.' Tony lowered his voice. 'All I need is another thou and I'll win the whole lot back.'

'And then can we do something else?'

'Yeah, sure. Anything you say, hon. Just hurry up with those chips, OK?' He didn't even look at her, his eyes already fixed greedily on the spinning wheel.

Tiffany slid out of her chair and made her way unsteadily across the casino floor. It was the size of a football pitch, crammed with slot machines as far as the eye could see. The flashing lights and noise disorientated her, and she staggered into the ladies room to get her bearings.

Jesus, she looked a wreck. Her cheeks were two hectic spots of colour in her white face. Her eyes were feverishly bright. She looked like a reanimated corpse in a silver Dolce & Gabbana dress.

She didn't go back to the roulette table. She went to the bar instead and ordered herself a double vodka. Screw Tony, she thought. He could come looking for her.

But he didn't. Tiffany ordered two more doubles and sank them defiantly, her eyes scanning the bar, looking for Tony. By the time her fourth drink arived, she'd worked herself up into a state of outrage. Why hadn't he come looking for her?

Because he doesn't care, a small voice inside her head said. He doesn't give a damn about you. Do you really think he would have called you if he hadn't happened to be at a loose end in a strange town?

'Mind if I sit here?'

A shadow fell over her. Tiffany looked up and was about to tell him to get lost when she realised who it was.

'Hamish!' She stared at him in disbelief. 'What are you doing here?'

'Looking for you.' He hitched up the knees of his trousers and sat down. He was still wearing his suit. 'I came back to the hotel after work but you'd gone. I thought you were going to stay in bed,' he said reproachfully.

'Sorry. How did you find me?'

'I asked the guy on the door at the hotel. He remembered getting you a taxi to this place.' He looked around, then back at her. 'So what happened?'

'Tony—my ex—called.'

'And you came running.' He nodded, as if it all suddenly made sense. 'Where is he now?'

'Somewhere.' She waved her hand vaguely in the direction of the gaming tables. 'I don't really care,' she admitted. 'I've just realised he's really boring. And he's only after my money. Isn't that wonderful?' She squeezed Hamish's hand.

He frowned. 'You like the fact that your boyfriend's a boring gold-digger?'

'No, silly!' She slapped him playfully. She could hear her own voice rising, getting thoroughly over-excited. But thanks to the booze and drugs she couldn't control it. 'I'm over him. Isn't that great? Now I can get on with my life.'

Except she didn't really have a life. The only thing she knew was getting papped and getting wasted. The thought was sad, but it still made her giggle.

Hamish regarded her warily. 'What have you taken?'

'Oh, not much. Just some champagne—quite a lot of champagne, actually—a few of these,' she held up her near-empty glass, 'and a couple of pills Tony gave me.'

'What kind of pills?'

'How should I know? I think they were blue. Or they might have been pink.' She tried to think, then gave up. 'Anyway, they made me feel a lot better. What's the matter? Why are you looking at me like that?'

'Oh, Tiffany.' Hamish shook his head. 'Why? I thought you were doing OK.'

There was something about the disappointment in his eyes that crushed her. She'd gone through her whole life letting people down, but somehow Hamish's reaction was too much to bear.

She fought against it by going on the attack. 'Well, I'm not. I'm a mess. And do you know what? I like being that way. So you can spare me your stupid lectures, because I'm not interested.'

'Obviously,' Hamish said.

She drained her drink and slammed the glass down. 'What has it got to do with you, anyway? You're not my mother, I don't have to answer to you. You're no one.'

She saw the way his face fell, and immediately wished she could take back the words. But it was too late. He was already standing up.

Tiffany stared up at him, full of panic. 'Where are you going?'

'Back to the hotel. You're right: this has absolutely nothing to do with me. I don't even know why I got involved in the first place. No, tell a lie, I do know,' he corrected himself. 'I did it because I liked you. I actually thought that inside that self-centred little bitch there was a bright, sweet girl who could make something of her life if someone just gave her the chance. But I was wrong, wasn't I?' he said bitterly. 'Like you said, you're a mess and you want to stay that way. Who the hell am I to interfere with that?'

Tiffany made a grab for him and caught a handful of trouser fabric. 'Hamish, don't go,' she begged.

'Bye, Tiffany. Keep taking the tablets. If that's what you want.'

Just as he was walking away, Tony appeared.

'What's going on? Where are my chips?' He looked from Tiffany to Hamish, and she could see his brain working slowly, adding up the numbers and getting them wrong.

He pointed at Hamish. 'Is this guy bothering you?'

'Apparently yes,' Hamish said. 'But don't worry, I'm just leaving.'

Macho hero that he was, Tony waited until Hamish was walking away before he shouted after him, 'Go on, run away. And don't let me see you around my girl again.'

Hamish stopped. Tiffany could almost see the muscles stiffening under his suit jacket.

Slowly, he turned. *'Your* girl?' he echoed, his voice full of disgust. 'You take her money, pump her full of drugs and abandon her to drink herself stupid, then you have the nerve to tell *me* not to go near her?' He took a step towards Tony, who backed away, colliding with a chair. 'Now listen to me, you worthless lump of scum. I'm not a violent man, but right at this moment nothing would give me greater pleasure than to take that ridiculous medallion and shove it right up your—'

'Is there a problem, sir?'

Two uniformed security men loomed out of nowhere and formed a solid wall of flesh across the bar exit.

'Yes, there is a problem.' Tony was the first one to speak. He pointed at Hamish. 'This guy just pulled a knife on me.'

'No, he didn't!' Tiffany tried to protest but her voice seemed to be coming from a long way away, so far she could hardly hear herself. She felt as if she was in a car, reversing very fast.

She watched in horror as the men closed in on Hamish. She tried to launch herself at them, but

310

she caught her foot on the leg of the table and pitched forward, just as everything went black.

That was the last thing she remembered for a very long time.

*　　　*　　　*

This is getting to be a habit, she thought when she woke up the following morning with a couple of jackhammers pounding in her head and a mouth that felt as if she'd been gargling with tar.

She tried to sit up, but the bed rocked nauseatingly around her. As she flopped back down again, she vaguely registered a disturbing fact.

She had no idea where she was.

She opened one eye and risked a cautious glance around the room. A motel room, she guessed. Small, bland, with grubby beige walls and thin blue curtains that barely held out the sunlight. The air conditioner rattled and coughed, and did nothing to cool the stale heat of the room.

Tiffany focused on a cheap print of the Grand Canyon on with wall opposite and tried not to panic.

Right. OK. The main thing was, she was alive. Just.

'Hello?' she croaked. No reply. Apart from the death rattle of the air con and the sound of cars outside, there was silence.

She closed her eyes and tried to piece together the events of the previous night. She could recall odd snapshots, but nothing seemed to connect. She remembered meeting Tony, going to the casino, getting blind drunk. She remembered Hamish turning up, then a fight, and then . . .

That was when it all started to get hazy. She vaguely recollected being in a car, neon lights flashing past, lots of people. She remembered being cold, and someone putting their jacket around her bare shoulders. Elvis was there . . .

She gave up. It was all too surreal to be true.

Very slowly she pulled back the covers and got out of bed, slightly surprised by the silver Dolce & Gabbana dress she was still wearing. She inched her way to the bathroom, turned on the taps and ducked her head to sluice her face with cold water. She came up dripping, caught sight of her reflection in the cracked basin mirror—and screamed.

She had a black eye. No, scratch that. She had a purple, blue and black eye. And it hurt, too. She ran her finger experimentally along her cheekbone and winced. She hadn't noticed it before, with all the other aches and pains racking her body. But now it seemed to throb uncontrollably.

She backed out of the bathroom, just as the motel room door opened and Hamish came in, a brown paper bag in his arms.

'Ah, good. You're up. I've brought breakfast.' He dumped the bag on the chest of drawers. 'I hope you like Egg McMuffins; they didn't have anything else. Oh, and I've brought you some painkillers, too. I guessed you might need them.'

'I've got a black eye . . .' Tiffany started to say, then she stopped. Hamish had one too. Same eye, only his was even more spectacular than hers, magnified behind his glasses.

'Snap,' he said.

'How?' A horrible thought struck her. 'We

didn't . . . fight, or anything?'

'Actually, we did. But not with each other. I got smacked by a hotel security guard, and you hit yourself on a table when you fell over.' He frowned, thinking about it. 'I think that's what happened, anyway. It was all pretty quick.' He took a cardboard cup out of the bag and handed it to her. 'Don't you remember anything about last night?'

She shook her head. 'I don't even know where we are.' She looked around. 'Where is this place?'

'To be honest, I have no idea. All I know is we left Las Vegas and kept driving. We must be about a hundred miles from the city, I reckon.'

'How did we end up here?'

'It's a long story . . . Are you sure you don't remember anything about last night?'

'I told you, it all turned into a bit of a blur after you showed up.'

'You were pretty hammered,' Hamish agreed, taking another coffee cup out of the brown bag. 'Your boyfriend Tony must have slipped you something really nasty.'

'*Ex*-boyfriend.' She shuddered, remembering how readily she'd taken the pills he'd offered. She'd been so desperate to get off her head and forget her troubles that she hadn't even bothered to ask what they were. What with the virus still in her system, and all the booze she'd consumed, it was a wonder she was still alive to tell the tale.

But then Hamish had come to rescue her, like a knight in shining armour.

'Thanks for coming to look for me last night,' she said, feeling suddenly shy. 'It was really nice of you.'

'I was worried about you.'

'Why? No one else worries about me.' It bleakly occurred to her that she could have ended up dead in a gutter somewhere and no one would have cared.

'Then perhaps it's time someone did. I'll get you some water for those painkillers,' he said gently.

'So is there anything I should know about last night?' she asked, as he filled a glass from the bathroom tap.

'Well . . .'

'Oh God, there is, isn't there?' she groaned. 'Did I make a complete fool of myself? Did I do something really stupid?'

He came back with the water and handed it to her. 'Depends what you call stupid, doesn't it? Mind that water, by the way. It's a strange colour.'

Tiffany grimaced at the rusty water and put the glass down. 'Come on, tell me. What did I do?' Her mind was already reeling, imagining all kinds of terrible things.

He looked at her carefully. 'Are you *sure* you don't remember?'

'I wouldn't be asking you if I did, would I?' Tension was making her impatient. 'Tell me, Hamish. I'll find out from the papers anyway, so I might as well know the worst now.'

He paused, and she could see he was trying to work out where to begin. 'OK, we might have done something a bit drastic last night,' he admitted finally.

'Which was?'

'What do people usually do in Vegas?'

She shrugged. She was too tense and hungover for guessing games. 'I don't know, do I? Gamble away all their money? Sleep with hookers? Get married?' She noticed Hamish had suddenly gone very silent. 'Hamish, what did we do?'

He looked up at her, his eyes owlish behind his spectacles. 'Well, the good news is we didn't lose our money or sleep with any hookers.' He took a small box out of the bag and held it out to her. 'McMuffin?' he offered.

CHAPTER THIRTY-FIVE

She stared at the bright yellow carton he was holding out to her.

'We didn't,' she said.

'I'm afraid we did.' He gave up on offering her the McMuffin and opened it himself. 'If you check your left hand you'll find you have the ring to prove it.'

Tiffany stared at it. There, on her third finger, was the cheapest, ugliest ring she had ever seen in her life. Why hadn't she noticed it before?

Hamish read the disgust on her face. 'Cartier was closed,' he said defensively. 'We had to go to the twenty-four-hour pawn shop.'

'Ugh!' She yanked the ring off and flung it into the corner. It was a wonder it hadn't made her finger turn black and drop off.

'Don't blame me; it was your idea,' Hamish said through a mouthful of McMuffin. 'You were absolutely insistent.'

'Oh God.' Tiffany buried her face in her hands. She was so dead. She might as well just walk out in front of the nearest truck and spare her mother the

315

trouble of killing her. 'You'd better tell me what happened,' she moaned.

'It was just after we got thrown out of the casino,' Hamish said. 'I was trying to get you back to the car, but you wouldn't go. You kept telling me how great I was, saying I was your hero. Then you kissed me.'

'I *kissed* you?'

'Don't look so shocked; it's not *that* hideous a concept.'

'Well, no . . .' She couldn't imagine it was. 'Did you . . . kiss me back?'

'Sort of. It seemed rude not to, and you were very determined.' His cheeks turned pink. 'Anyway, then it all got a bit out of hand, and you suggested we should go to a hotel for the night—'

'Oh God.'

'So I jokingly said you'd have to marry me first, and for some reason you thought that was a great idea. The next thing I knew we were trawling up and down The Strip looking for a wedding chapel.'

The vague flashbacks she'd had all seemed to drift into some kind of order. 'Was Elvis there, by any chance?'

'You see? You *do* remember.' Hamish's face brightened. 'He was a witness. We needed two, which was a bit of a drawback, but then we found a really nice girl called Roxy just hanging around outside one of the hotels, and she very kindly stepped in. Then Elvis sang "Love Me Tender", and we had our pictures taken. I've got them here somewhere . . .' He started to reach into his pocket but Tiffany stopped him.

'Don't,' she said. 'I don't want to look at them.'

'Suit yourself. But I think we made a lovely

316

group. Apart from our black eyes, but you can hardly see them—'

'Just let me get this clear,' Tiffany interrupted. 'Last night I got totally off my head on booze and God knows what else, we both got into a fight, then we bought a ring in a pawn shop and got married with Elvis and a hooker looking on. Am I right?'

'That's about the size of it, yes.' Hamish smiled. 'Something to tell the grandchildren, isn't it?'

'And it never occurred to you at any point that it might not be a good idea?'

'It never occurred to you, either,' Hamish replied defensively.

'There's a difference. I was comatose and you were stone-cold sober.'

'True,' he admitted. 'But like I said, you were very insistent. Aggressive, even. Anyway, I quite liked the idea of getting married.'

'I bet you did,' Tiffany muttered. A depressingly familiar idea was beginning to form in her head.

Hamish frowned. 'What's that supposed to mean?'

'Oh, come on. I know I can be dumb at times, but even I'm not that stupid. You must have thought you'd won the lottery when you put that ring on my finger.'

He stared at her uncomprehending for a moment. Then, slowly, realisation dawned. 'You think I married you for money?'

'No,' said Tiffany. 'I think you're going to be divorcing me for money.' She swallowed a mouthful of the rusty water without thinking, then grimaced at the metallic taste. 'Why else would you go through with this stupid wedding? You know my parents will bail me out of it with a big cheque, the

317

way they always do when I've been dumb. You won't have to be a crappy accountant any more. You'll be set up for life.' She stared at him across the room. 'Well?' Desperation made her snap. 'What have you got to say for yourself?'

Deep down she wanted him to deny it, to tell her he'd married her because he loved her and wanted to be with her for the rest of his life. But he didn't. He'd gone ominously silent, his dark brows drawn together.

He tossed the remains of his McMuffin into the bin. Then, in a cold voice, he said, 'We'd better get back and give your folks the good news then, hadn't we?'

*   *   *

They headed back to Las Vegas in sullen silence. Tiffany knew she'd upset him, but she wasn't sure how to make it right.

As the road began to cut through desert towards the city, she said, 'Could we stop soon?'

Hamish shook his head. 'The sooner we get back, the sooner I can collect my *big cheque*.'

'But I need to use the bathroom!'

There was a truckstop on the dusty road about five miles further on. Hamish pulled in reluctantly and Tiffany got out to go to the loo. Truckers sitting in the window of the diner stopped eating to stare at the girl in the silver dress picking her way past the window in strappy stilettoes.

When she got back, Hamish was sitting on the bonnet of the car, drinking a bottle of water. He'd taken off his suit jacket and rolled up his shirtsleeves in the scorching heat of the midday

318

sun. He offered her the bottle.

'Thanks,' Tiffany said.

'No need to thank me. I'll add it to the payout your parents are going to give me.' He kept his gaze fixed on the horizon. 'How huge do you think it's going to be, exactly?'

'I don't know,' Tiffany muttered.

'Come on, you must have a figure in mind? Thousands? Millions?'

'Will you shut up about it?' A fly buzzed close to her nose and Tiffany batted it away irritably.

'You brought it up, not me.'

'I'm sorry I mentioned it, OK?' She thrust the bottle back at him. 'But we both know it's true. Why else would you marry someone like me?'

'Is that what you really think?' His frown deepened. He was going to need serious Botox if he kept that up, Tiffany thought distractedly.

'Why not? It's all anyone else has ever wanted me for.' Tiffany tried to swallow the lump of self-pity that rose in her throat. 'Everyone always wants a piece of me. Either they want to be seen with me to make themselves famous, or to sell a story about me, or because I always pick up the tab when we go out.' That was why Hamish had touched such a nerve when he said she'd had to buy her friends. 'They wouldn't want to spend time with a loser like me otherwise.'

'You're not a loser,' Hamish said gently.

'Oh, sure. Even my own parents don't want anything to do with me.'

'That's their problem, not yours.' Hamish reached out and ran his hand up the length of her bare arm, leaving a trail of hairs standing up to attention. 'They've got their own issues. And, from what I can see, they've let *you* down, not the other way round.'

Tiffany smiled. 'Thanks. But I haven't exactly been the perfect daughter.'

'They haven't been the perfect parents, either. They're both so wrapped up in their own worlds, doing their own thing, they haven't given you the time and attention you deserve.'

Tiffany batted away another fly. Maybe he was right. She'd wasted so much energy trying to get them to notice her but they probably never would.

'I'll sure get my mother's attention when I tell her we got married!' she said wryly.

Hamish didn't smile back. Tiffany had the feeling she'd said the wrong thing, but she didn't know how.

She had the same feeling as they headed on to Vegas. Hamish was just as silent as he had been for the first half of the journey, leaving Tiffany miserably alone with her thoughts.

His silence unnerved her. They'd had a moment back there at the truckstop when everything seemed all right, but now he was angry again and she couldn't work out what she'd done.

All she knew was that she didn't want him to be angry. She wanted him to be nice and kind and funny, and to make her laugh the way he always did, even when she didn't feel like laughing. She wanted to look into his face and see those warm, gentle brown eyes twinkling back at her, not the icy expression she saw now.

She wanted him to go to being lovely Hamish. The man she'd fallen in love with.

The thought caught her unawares and she stared out of the window, trying to come to terms with the unfamiliar feeling. When had that happened? She hadn't seen it coming because it was so wrong. Hamish was so not her type. It was a joke. She went for brash, confident, macho types, who crashed noisily into her life, left her shattered and then crashed out again. Not quiet, unassuming Scottish guys who quietly worked their way into her heart and stayed there for ever.

'How do you want to do this?'

It took her a moment to realise Hamish was speaking to her. 'Excuse me?'

'Breaking the news to your family. How do you want to play it? Do you want to tell them by yourself or would you rather I was there with you?'

Tiffany thought for a moment. Either way, it was going to be a grim meeting. 'I guess I'd rather not tell them at all,' she said.

'Wouldn't that defeat the whole point?' Hamish muttered. 'You're hardly going to shock them if you don't tell them, are you?'

Tiffany frowned. Who said anything about shocking them? That was the bit she was least looking forward to.

Besides, her mother would only steam in and get the whole thing annulled, and she was quite enjoying being married to Hamish. Even if it was only a make-believe marriage.

'Maybe we should leave it for a while,' she suggested.

Hamish shook his head. 'Oh no. I think we should face the music and get this over with as soon as possible, don't you?'

Tiffany stole a glance at his profile. His face was rigid as he stared at the road ahead. *Get it over with*. She wasn't surprised. He was far too nice to want to be stuck with someone like her.

But just because he wanted out of the fantasy, that didn't mean she was ready for it to be over . . .

'Turn the car around,' she said. 'I need to go back to the motel.'

'What? Are you serious? We must be halfway home by now.'

'Please? I've forgotten something.'

She thought he might argue, but with a sigh of stretched patience, he swung the car around and headed back. 'What the hell have you forgotten? It's not like you packed a trousseau, or anything. You didn't even bring a toothbrush.'

Tiffany didn't reply. She knew she was being stupid, but she couldn't help it.

It took them a while to find the motel again in the daylight. Finally, after much argument over directions, they discovered the shabby green and white sprawl of chalets a couple of miles off the main road.

'Classy,' Tiffany commented as they got out.

'It was dark,' Hamish said defensively.

The manager refused to let them back into the room unless they stumped up for another night's rental. Tiffany reached for her purse but Hamish got to his wallet first. 'Allow me,' he said.

'I hope they haven't cleaned the room yet,' Tiffany said, as Hamish fought to turn the key in the lock.

'Unlikely, I should think.' He gave up and shouldered the door open. Inside, the air conditioner was still clattering inefficiently, and the room was hot and stale. The bedcovers had been carelessly pulled up over the pillows.

'What do you know?' Hamish said. 'They *have*

cleaned it.'

But Tiffany wasn't listening. She was too busy searching the corner of the room behind the tiny portable TV.

Hamish sat on the end of the bed and watched her. 'What are you looking for, anyway? Apart from signs of possible infestation.'

'I know I dropped it here . . . ah, got it.' She spotted a dull gleam under a turned-up corner of the rug and pounced on it.

'You came back for your ring?' Hamish said. 'I thought you hated it.'

'That doesn't mean it's not special.' She slipped it back on her finger.

Hamish watched her admiring it for a moment. 'Ah, I get it,' he said. 'That will really wind her up, won't it?'

'Sorry?'

'Your mother. Her blood pressure will shoot up when she sees that on your finger.'

She frowned at him. 'This has got nothing to do with my mom.'

'Of course it hasn't.' His voice dripped sarcasm.

'Look, what is this? You've been in a funny mood ever since we hit the road. What's your problem?'

'If you must know, I don't like being used,' he said.

'Who's using you?'

'You are.' He sent her a level look. 'You can't wait to get back to Las Vegas and tell your paents about us getting married because you want to cause trouble and make yourself the centre of attention. I just think it's a bit pathetic, that's all.'

'Yeah, sure.' Tiffany folded her arms. 'That was

obviously my plan all along. That was why I drugged you and dragged you off to a wedding chapel, then made you drive out here to the middle of nowhere. How clever of you to work it out.'

The slightest smile twitched the corners of his mouth. 'OK, it might not have started out like that,' he said. 'But admit it, you're looking forward to seeing their faces when you break the news.'

'As a matter of fact, I don't care if I never tell them,' Tiffany said. 'I don't even want to go back there because—'

'Because what?' Hamish said gently.

'Because I know that when we do my mom's going to step in and break us up and spoil it all.'

'Isn't that what you want?'

'No,' she admitted in a small voice.

He smiled. 'Then it doesn't have to happen like that.'

'You don't know my mom.' There was no way in the world her mother was going to tolerate her being married to Hamish, even if he wasn't after her money. Tiffany was already beginning to cringe at the thought of what she might do.

'We don't have to go back yet,' Hamish said. 'We paid for the room for the rest of the night, remember?'

Tiffany eyed him uncertainly. 'What are you saying?'

'I'm saying we're still officially on honeymoon.'

He reached for her hands and drew her towards him into his lap. He moved to kiss her, but Tiffany pulled away.

'Don't. I haven't brushed my teeth for about four days.'

'Neither have I.'

She had never had sex while sober, Tiffany reflected, as they slowly removed each other's clothes on the bed. She'd had wild sex, dirty sex, even sex in public places. But she'd always needed a few shots of booze or a couple of lines of coke to make herself want to do it.

Now, as she watched Hamish unbuttoning his shirt, she found to her surprise that she was a quivering mass of anticipation. So much so, that it took all her self-control not to rip the shirt off his back herself.

Underneath, he was a revelation. Who would ever have imagined there would be a body like that hiding under such a sober suit? As he took her in his arms, his skin was soft and smooth and smelt faintly of cheap motel shower gel.

She was so turned on she wanted him there and then, no foreplay needed. But Hamish tantalised her, taking his time, stroking and kissing ever inch of her body, his tongue flicking over her, driving her wild. So wild that she forgot her virtuoso porn star performance and found herself enjoying it instead. She forgot to groan and sigh in all the right places, and she even forgot to fake it.

So that's what it's like, she thought as the climax shuddered through her body. That's the real thing.

Afterwards they lay in the hot, damp tangle of sheets. Tiffany stared up at a crack in the ceiling and tried not to cry. Maybe they shouldn't have done it, she thought. It was like being given a wonderful gift and then having it snatched away from her.

Hamish rolled over on to his side and looked at her. 'You've gone very quiet,' he said.

'I was just thinking.'

'Sounds ominous. What about?'

She couldn't tell him. He was so nice, he'd think he'd have to stay married to her or something, and she didn't want him to feel trapped.

So she smiled instead, and said, 'I thought married sex was supposed to be dull?'

'Ah, well, I think it can be.' His face was grave as he pretended to consider the question. 'You just have to make sure you don't get into a boring rut.'

'Have we got into a boring rut?'

He smiled, his hand snaking under the sheets. 'Let's find out, shall we?'

CHAPTER THIRTY-SIX

By the time they got to Reno, all was well with the world again. Rick had somehow managed to sweet-talk Britt into coming back from Sweden once her mother's health was improving and they were behaving more like honeymooners than a couple on the brink of divorce.

'Sickening, isn't it?' Dinah said. But Lola noticed even she was making a special effort to be nicer to Britt. Lola hoped her heart-to-heart had helped her see things from the other woman's perspective.

She might have helped sort out Rick's marital problems, but a couple of things still troubled her.

One was that Hamish had disappeared. He'd called her from his mobile to tell her he was taking a short break in Las Vegas and would catch up with them when they got to Chula Vista, California in two days' time.

'I hope you haven't done anything daft?' Lola joked.

'Like what?'

'I don't know . . . lost all your money, married a showgirl?'

He laughed. 'No, I haven't married a showgirl. I'll tell you all about it when I get back,' he'd promised.

As he rang off, Lola was convinced she'd heard a woman giggling in the background. For an insane moment she'd thought it sounded like Tiffany. But as far as she knew, she'd headed back to LA. At least, that's what everyone has assumed.

Her second, biggest worry, was knowing that Rick's Devoted Fan was waiting to strike. Now she knew it was an inside job, Lola was driving herself crazy suspecting everyone. She couldn't look at any of the riggers, sound and lighting guys, or even the bus drivers without wondering if they could be the one.

She even found herself wondering if it might be one of the band, until she realised they were all too dim or stoned to write a shopping list, let alone a poison pen letter.

You'll die in Los Angeles . . . LA was less than a week away.

She tried to put it to the back of her mind as she got on with her work. With the end of the tour fast approaching, there wasn't quite so much to do. But there were still people to be paid, press and publicity events to organise, as well as putting together the guest list for the final night's after-show party.

If there *was* a party. The thought nagged away at the back of her mind as she sat at her desk on the hot August afternoon, chewing the end of her pencil, trying to remember which journalists Dinah had told her to invite, and which were on the Shit List, as it was known in band circles.

She was still pondering when a low humming noise made her look up. There, hovering above her, was possibly the biggest, scariest-looking creature she'd ever seen in her life. Two inches long, with a metallic blue-black body and orange wings, it buzzed and batted angrily against the half-open slot window above the filing cabinets.

Stay calm, Lola told herself. It's probably completely harmless. But perspiration had broken out on her brow just looking at it. She tried to ignore it. But it was like trying to ignore an Apache attack helicopter as it hovered above her, occasionally swooping down to buzz the top of her head.

'Right, that's it.' She threw down her pen. 'You're not going to go away quietly, are you?'

She pulled her chair over to the high slot window, climbed up and opened the catch. 'Out you go, you stupid thing. Go on. Get out.'

The creature did a quick circuit of the room, checked out the window, then whizzed past her right ear and hovered near the coffee machine.

At which point, Jay walked in. 'Hi, I—' He stopped. 'What are you doing up there?'

'Trying to persuade that thing to leave.' She pointed.

Jay looked, and jumped back. 'Holy crap. What is *that*?'

'God knows. I think it's some kind of giant, evil wasp. But it's not in a good mood.'

Jay eyed it warily. 'Couldn't you just swat it?'

328

'OK, for one thing, swatting stuff is not very good for one's karma. And for another, I think it might fight back.'

'You're right,' Jay agreed. 'It looks like it has nuclear capability to me. Look out.' He ducked as the megabug swung past him and headed back towards the window. 'He's coming your way!'

'He's not getting away this time.' As the wasp drew closer, she tried to gently bat it towards the window. 'That's it, just go away, nice little— *Ow!*' She screamed with shock and pain, as the wasp swooped off out of the window.

Jay just caught her as she stumbled off the chair. 'Where did it sting you? Let me see.'

She shook her head. It felt as if she'd been stabbed by a red-hot poker, right through the back of her hand. 'I . . . I can't. It h-hurts too much . . .' she wailed.

'Let me see.' Jay was panicking; she could hear it in his voice. He reached for her hands and separated them gently. 'Come on, it can't be as bad as all— Bloody hell!'

'What is it?'

'Nothing.' But he'd turned white. Even his lips were drained of colour. 'It's just . . . big, that's all.'

'What? Let me see.' Lola took her hand away and looked at it. A three-inch aureola of reddened, angry flesh radiated out from a raised white blob in the centre. 'Oh my God. That's it. I'm going to die, aren't I?'

'Does it still hurt?'

'What do you mean, does it still hurt?' she snapped. 'Look at it, of course it still . . .' She gently touched the wound and panic overcame her. 'No, it doesn't. I can't feel a thing. It's gone completely numb.'

'That's a good sign, isn't it?'

'Not if it means it's about to drop off, you idiot!'

'Excuse me? Who's the idiot around here? I'm not the one who tried to talk it into fluttering out of the window instead of just bashing it.'

They were still arguing when a woman walked in. In her mid-fifties, she was fair-haired and pretty in a tired, harassed kind of way.

'There you are,' she said to Jay. 'I've been looking everywhere for you. You said you'd only be a couple of minutes.'

'Sorry, we had a bit of an emergency.' Jay let go of Lola's hand at the same moment as she snatched it away.

'Oh dear, what happened?' The woman turned to Lola, her face full of concern.

'I got stung by a wasp.'

'She's being heroic. She got stung by something the size of a Tornado jet.' He turned to Lola. 'Sorry, I should have introduced you. This is my mother, Annie. Mum, this is Lola.'

'Pleased to meet you. Now, let's see that hand.' Annie was briskly efficient as she examined Lola's hand. 'Oh yes, that is nasty, isn't it? You're not allergic or anything, are you?'

'Not that I know of. Although I've never met anything like that thing before.'

'I think you would know about it by now if you were.' Annie examined her hand more closely. 'It seems to be going down a bit. At least it was just a wasp. If it was a bee it would have had left its sting in there.'

'Aren't I the lucky one?' Lola said through gritted teeth.

330

'All the same, you should get some antihistamine on it as soon as possible. I think I've got some somewhere . . .'

As she rooted through her bag, Jay explained to Lola, 'Mum's a school nurse. Just in case you thought she was a weird walking medicine cabinet or something.'

'Ah.'

'Here we are.' Annie produced a white tube. 'I'll just pop some of this on, and you should be fine.' She smiled up at her as she rubbed in the cream. Laughter lines crinkled around her green eyes. 'This is a very strange way to meet, I must say.'

'Isn't it?' Lola agreed. 'But I'm glad you're here.'

'Mum's visiting for a few days,' Jay said. 'That's why I came in here. I wondered if you could organise a pass for her.'

'No problem.' She went to the drawer, opened it with her good hand and pulled out a laminate from the pile. 'There you go.' She handed it to Annie. 'Keep that with you and you can officially access all areas.'

'Ooh,' Annie laughed. 'I'm not sure I'd want to do that.'

Jay's mobile rang. He pulled it off his belt and turned away to answer it, leaving Lola and his mother to make conversation.

'When did you arrive?' Lola asked.

'This morning. Jay only just gave me time to unpack, then brought me straight here. I think he wanted me to meet you,' she confided.

'Me?'

Before Annie had time to say anything more, Jay hung up his phone. 'I've got to go,' he said.

'One of the local guys has unpatched the effects without telling anyone. I've got to sort it out.' He turned to Annie. 'Will you be OK here for a couple of minutes?'

'I'll be fine,' Annie assured him with a smile. 'You go and patch up your whatsits. Maybe Lola can show me where to get a cup of tea, since you didn't give me time to have one at the hotel.'

'Sorry.' Jay dumped his bag on the floor and headed off.

Annie turned to Lola. 'So,' she said. 'How about that cup of tea?'

They went to the catering wagon. Lola had offered to make Annie a cup of tea in the office, but she insisted on going to the van. 'I smelt frying bacon as I came past. I wouldn't mind a sarnie,' she said.

Ten minutes later, they were sitting at one of the white plastic tables outside the catering wagon, tucking into doorstep bacon sandwiches and mugs of brick-coloured tea.

'This is better,' Annie said, wiping ketchup off her chin. 'I can't stand aeroplane food. Not that I make a habit of flying, except when my son's paying,' she grinned.

'Do you get to see much of him while he's on tour?' Lola asked.

'Not as much as I'd like. He's always so busy. I don't like to be around too much when he's working.' She gazed around as a couple of burly riggers went past. 'I never liked all this backstage stuff much. I always felt in the way.'

It gave Lola a shock to remember that she must have experienced all this first-hand, when she was married to Rick. Looking at her now, middle-aged in her jeans, jumper and sensible trainers, she couldn't imagine her as a rock wife.

'I know what you mean,' she agreed. 'It took me a while to settle in.'

'Yes, but it's different for you, isn't it? You've got a job to do. I didn't have anything.' She sighed. 'That's the way it is in Rick's world. You either fit in or you're out.'

'Have you seen Rick yet?' Lola ventured.

Annie shook her head. 'I'm not going out of my way to meet him. Don't get me wrong, I don't hate him or anything. Our paths have crossed a few times, over the years. But to tell the truth, I never know what to say to him when I see him these days. It was all such a long time ago.'

'You don't miss him, then?'

'Heavens, no! I wouldn't go back to that life for anything. I'm very happy with what I'm doing now. I've got my job at the school, a nice home, lots of friends. I've even got a man I see now and then,' she confessed, blushing. 'Nothing serious, but you never know.' She tucked a lock of hair behind her ear. 'No, I'm very content. I just wish my son could be the same.'

Lola added another dollop of ketchup to her sandwich. 'He and Rick don't get on, do they?'

'They never have. Jay blames him, you see. I feel so bad about that. I just wish I'd—'

'What?'

'I wish I'd tried harder to make it right between them.' Her eyes were troubled. 'Rick tried hard to be a father to Jay, but he was away so often, they were like strangers when he came home. And it didn't help that he used to see me getting so upset . . .' She twisted her paper napkin in her hands.

'When we split up, I tried to explain that it was just as much my fault as it was his father's. But children only ever see things in black and white, don't they? As far as Jay was concerned, I was whiter than white, and his father was the vllain of the piece.'

It felt strange to be sitting there in the sunshine, chatting to a woman she'd only just met about her marriage break-up. Especially when she was guiltily aware that her own mother had been one of Rick's flings.

'Don't you feel it was all Rick's fault?' she asked.

'Not at all,' Annie said firmly. 'All right, maybe he wasn't the greatest husband or father in the world. But I was just as much to blame, in my own way. I knew Rick was ambitious when I married him. But I ignored it. I thought it would never happen, that the band would never make it. Then, when they did . . .' She took a sip of her tea, grimaced, then added a spoonful of sugar. 'Rick changed when the band took off, and I didn't change with him. I wanted everything to stay the same, just him and me and none of the fame. So I stuck my head in the sand and tried to pretend it wasn't happening. He wanted to go in one direction, and I was pulling him in another. I suppose if I'd gone with him, been more like Dinah or Britt, we might have stayed together. But I made my choice, and I can't blame him for it.'

'It's a pity Jay doesn't feel like that,' Lola said.

'I know,' Annie sighed. 'Believe me, I wish I could help him get past all this resentment and move on. He needs his father, more than he'll ever admit. He certainly looks up to him, otherwise he would never have followed him into this business.'

'It must be in his blood,' Lola said.

'Maybe.' Annie gave her a funny little smile. 'What I do know is he and Rick could really grow to like each other, if only . . .' She shook her head. 'Anyway, listen to me, rattling on. And we've only just met! Jay's right, you are an easy person to talk to.'

Lola could feel the heat rising in her face. 'Jay said that?'

Annie nodded. 'He really likes you.'

Lola hid her embarrassment with a laugh. 'He didn't like me when we first met!'

'My son puts up a lot of barriers. Sometimes people don't try too hard to get past them.' Annie looked at her consideringly. 'But you certainly did that. He couldn't stop talking about you when he came to visit me in England. Between you and me, I think he was only using me as an excuse to come over and see you.' She grinned. 'That's why I decided to visit. I wanted to meet you for myself.'

Lola didn't know what to say. Annie was talking as if she was Jay's prospective girlfriend, rather than his half-sister.

Fortunately she was saved from answering by the bleep of her mobile phone. It was a text message from one of the runners, asking her to call him about an urgent delivery.

'I'm sorry,' she said to Annie. 'I'm going to have to go back to the office and sort this out. You're welcome to come with me, if you like?'

'No, no, I'll be fine here. I expect Jay will find me soon. How's your hand, by the way?'

'What? Oh, that. It's fine.' She held it up, waggling her fingers. 'I'd forgotten all about it. It must be your miracle cream.'

335

'I'm glad it worked.' Annie smiled up at her, her eyes crinkling. 'It was lovely to meet you, Lola.'

'And you.' Even if it was a bit weird, too.

The phone was ringing when she got back to the office. It was the runner again. 'Jay's asked me to pick something up, but there's no sign of it on the gate. I don't suppose he's left it with you, has he?'

'Not that I know of . . .' She spotted his bag, lying on the floor beside her desk. She leaned over and rifled through it. 'I can't see anything . . . hang on, what's this?'

'Have you found it?' the runner asked.

But Lola couldn't answer him. She was too busy staring at the blue envelope she'd just pulled out of Jay's bag. An envelope with Rick's name scrawled on the front in that sickeningly familiar handwriting.

Then Jay walked in, and Lola quickly stuffed the letter back into his bag. 'I'll call you straight back,' she said to the runner, and hung up.

She turned to Jay, pinning a smile on her face even though she was shaking inside. 'That was Del. He wants to know about a package you wanted delivered?'

'Oh, right. I ordered some strings from the local store, but they gave me the wrong gauge so I'm sending them back. Don't worry, I'll sort it out.' He looked around. 'What happened to Mum?'

'I left her at the catering truck.'

'I'd better go and fetch her, or she'll be in there telling them all how to do their job!' He picked up his bag and swung it over his shoulder. Lola watched him walk away and willed herself to say something.

'What was that letter?' she managed to blurt

out, just as he reached the door.

He frowned over his shoulder at her. 'What letter?'

'The one in your bag. In the blue envelope?' she prompted, when he looked blank.

'Oh, *that* letter. It came yesterday, while you were taking Britt to the hairdressers. I saw who it was from and intercepted it. I meant to give it to you but I guess I just forgot.'

A tiny voice nagged at the back of her brain. 'Why did you intercept it?'

'I didn't want it to upset anyone. It's been so peaceful around here lately; I knew it would all just kick off again if anyone saw it.'

'I didn't know you cared,' Lola said.

'I don't. But I'd prefer not to live in a war zone.'

As he turned to go, Lola said, 'Can I have it?'

He frowned. 'Why?'

'I'm just curious, that's all.' She hoped her face didn't give away the truth. If Jay really did intercept the letter then it would be covered in fingerprints, including those of the Devoted Fan. But if his prints were the only ones, then it could only mean one thing . . .

Not taking his eyes from hers, Jay put down his bag and pulled out the letter. Holding her gaze, he took a lighter from his pocket. Lola watched, transfixed, as he set light to one corner of the letter. The flames were almost touching his fingers before he finally dropped the smouldering remains into the bin.

'Now it's not going to upset anyone, is it?' he smiled.

CHAPTER THIRTY-SEVEN

'You're kidding, right? Please tell me you're not serious?'

Tiffany winced. It was just as she'd suspected. Her mother wasn't taking the news well.

She took a deep breath. 'No, Mom, it's true. I'm now Mrs . . .' She glanced at Hamish. 'Sorry, what was your name again?'

He sent her a long-suffering look. 'McTavish.'

'Mrs Tiffany McTavish.' Tiffany McTavish. It had a nice ring to it, she thought. Shame she wouldn't be able to keep it.

It was a shame she wouldn't be able to keep Hamish, either.

'Oh my God.' Her mother buried her face in her hands. 'I just can't believe it. You've made some serious screw-ups in your time, but this has to be the biggest.' She planted her hands on her hips. 'Do you have any idea what you've done? Do you? I'll tell you, shall I? You've just kissed goodbye to a hell of a lot of cash. I don't suppose it occurred to you to get him to sign a prenup?'

Tiffany glanced at Hamish, who shook his head.

'I guess not,' she admitted lamely.

'Of course not. Why would it? That would be way too sensible for you.' There were tears in her mother's eyes; Tiffany decided it must be rage, and not disappointment at being denied the chance to buy a wedding hat.

She risked a glance at Hamish. He was standing there, perfectly composed as uaual. He obviously hadn't seen Dinah Abraham in full furious flight,

338

or he might have been more terrified.

Or maybe he wouldn't. Nothing seemed to faze him, she marvelled. It was just one of the amazing things she'd found out about him over the past few days.

And the more she found out, the more she loved him.

She didn't dare hope he felt the same about her. She'd probably driven him crazy, like she did with most of the guys she met.

Now he was about to be put to the test, as Dinah turned on him. 'And what what have you got to say for yourself ?' she demanded.

He considered the question for a moment. 'I suppose it wouldn't be a good time to start calling you mother?'

In spite of her terror, Tiffany couldn't help the laughter that bubbled out of her. He had some nerve, her husband.

Her husband. She savoured the phrase for a moment, wished she could say it out loud. But she didn't want to drive her mother even further over the edge.

Dinah shot her a narrow look. 'I don't know what you're laughing at. This guy's made a complete idiot of you. I'm sure your father won't find it so funny when he finds out about it.'

'He won't care,' Tiffany said. 'He never cares about anything I do.'

'That's not true.'

'Oh, come on. Since when did he take any notice of me? Or you,' she added. 'You ignore me most of the time.'

'Is that what this is about? Dinah demanded. 'Because if it is, you've picked a pretty expensive way of getting our attention.'

'This is nothing to do with getting your attention.' She surprised herself when she said it, then realised it was true. Once it would have been the ideal stunt to pull, but somewhere along the line her feelings had changed. Now she didn't even care if her parents noticed her or not. As long as she had Hamish.

Dinah turned her back on her and faced Hamish. 'OK, let's cut the crap and get down to business. How much do you want?'

'I'm sorry?'

'Don't mess with me. I'm not as dumb as my daughter. How much is it going to take to make this go away?'

Tiffany felt her stomach tighten. This was the bit she'd been dreading.

Once again, Hamish considered the question, his dark brows beetling behind his spectacles. 'Nothing,' he said finally.

Her mother took a deep breath. 'Oh, I get it. You want to play hard ball, do you? Wait for me to come up with a figure, then double it? Well, no dice, sonny. This is your game; *you* make the first move.'

'Please,' Tiffany cut in, as her mother and Hamish faced each other like adversaries, 'do you have to talk about me like I'm a piece of meat?' She knew this was going to be difficult, but she hadn't realised just how awful she would feel.

'Don't you get it? That's all you are to this guy— a piece of property to be traded for the best price. And right now he thinks he's got us over a barrel.' Her eyes gleamed with the light of battle. 'But he's wrong. I've dealt with much bigger bastards than

340

him in my time. Compared to those sharks, he's nothing but . . . a . . .'

'A minnow?' Hamish suggested helpfully. 'If you're trying to think of a comparison, then that's a pretty small fish. Although technically you couldn't really compare it to a shark, because they live in salt water, and minnows—'

'Plankton,' Dinah interrupted, jabbing a scarlet-tipped finger at him. 'You're nothing but plankton.'

Hamish made a pained face. 'Again, not a good comparison to a shark,' he mused. 'And not that great a comparison to me, either, since very few plankton have a Masters in business administration.'

Tiffany stifled another giggle. It was quite fun to see her mother being wound up. She could practically see the steam coming out of her ears.

Hamish seemed to realise he was pushing things too far, because he started to backtrack.

'Look,' he said, 'I think we got off on the wrong foot here. Shall we start again?'

Dinah eyed him warily. 'Go on.'

'Now if I'm not mistaken, you seem to be offering me money to divorce your daughter. Is that right?'

'That's about the size of it, yes.' Dinah's teeth were gritted. 'So how much do you want?'

'Nothing,' Hamish said again.

Dinah heaved a sigh. 'This really isn't getting us anywhere,' she said. 'Look, just give me a figure and—'

'You're misunderstanding me,' Hamish said patiently. 'All I want is to stay married to Tiffany.'

'Really?' Tiffany, who'd been bracing herself

341

and closing her eyes, opened them wide in disbelief.

'If you'll have me?' Hamish smiled shyly. 'I mean, I know I'm not exactly the kind you usually go for—'

'Why?' Dinah said.

He frowned. 'Well, I'm not Italian for a start. And I don't go to the gym as much as I should—'

Dinah sighed impatiently. 'I meant why do you want to stay married to my daughter?'

'I love her.'

'You do?' Tiffany said breathlessly.

'You do?' Her mother stared at Hamish as if she was trying to see into his soul. 'It's a trick,' she declared finally. 'He's up to something, I can tell.'

'Why is it so hard for you to believe someone could be in love with your daughter?' Hamish asked.

Dinah opened her mouth and closed it again. 'Well, I—'

'I know she can be crazy, selfish, attention-seeking and generally a nightmare—'

'Thanks a lot!' Tiffany snorted.

'But she's also sweet and funny, and she makes me happy.' He reached for her hand. 'And if you want me to sign a prenup, a postnup or any other kind of nup to prove how much I love her, then I will.'

'Really?' Tiffany could hardly believe what she was hearing. 'You really think I'm OK?'

'More than OK.' Hamish smiled warmly at her. 'Actually, I've been mad about you since the day you first walked into the office.'

'But I'm a disaster area,' she wailed.

'I know. That's what makes you so interesting.'

He pulled her into his arms. 'I want to spend the rest of my life looking after you.'

'I'm glad someone does,' Dinah muttered.

Hamish turned his head to look at her mother. 'Although there is one thing I'd really like.'

Dinah rolled her eyes. 'Oh yeah?'

'I want us to have a proper wedding. Last time Tiffany was too unconscious to remember it. This time I want her to mean it when she says, "I do."'

Tiffany saw her mother's ears prick up. 'Did you say she was unconscious?'

'Pretty much.'

'But that's great!' Dinah brightened. 'You realise what this means, don't you? If you weren't aware of what you were doing, the marriage contract can't be legally binding. We can get it annulled.'

'Fine,' Tiffany said defiantly. 'Then we'll go straight back to Vegas and do it again.'

Dinah stared at her. 'You're really serious, aren't you? You want to marry this guy?'

Tiffany looked up at Hamish. 'I do,' she said.

CHAPTER THIRTY-EIGHT

The Hollywood Bowl, California. It was a warm, sunny afternoon, yet Lola couldn't help shivering as she stood in the wings of the famous arched stage and watched Jay at work. He sat cross-legged on the floor at the far side of the stage, his toolbox beside him, rewiring one of the Marshall amps. He was concentrating hard, his dark head bent over his work.

343

Lola gave a little cough and he looked up. 'Oh, hi. I didn't see you there,' he said. 'Why aren't you at lunch with the others?'

'I could ask you the same question.' She crossed the stage to stand over him. 'What are you doing?'

'One of Kyle's guitars kept cutting out last night. I thought it might be a problem with this.' He tapped the amp case with his screwdriver.

'And?'

'And I've taken this whole thing apart but it's still a mystery.' He looked up at her with a quizzical smile. 'What's the sudden interest, anyway? Are you after my job, or something?'

'No. Why?'

'I just wondered. Only you've been following me around for the past three days, watching my every move. Either you can't resist my new aftershave or you've got something on your mind. So which is it?'

'It's nothing, honestly.' But she was lying. She'd had something on her mind ever since she found that letter in Jay's bag.

She wished she could forget about it, but it haunted her. Something just didn't add up. If Jay hated his father so much, why would he go to all that trouble to hide the letter from him? Surely he wouldn't care about him being upset?

She chewed her lip as she watched him screw the back of the amp case into place. She hated herself for doubting him, but what else could she do?

Jay dropped his screwdriver into his box and jumped to his feet. 'Should be quite a night tonight,' he said.

Lola stared at him. 'What do you mean?' she said sharply.

'It's the last night of the tour. There's always a really good atmosphere.' He frowned at her. 'What did you think I meant?'

She shook her head. 'It doesn't matter.' Half of her felt wretched for suspecting him, but the other half was convinced he must be Rick's Devoted Fan.

'Are you sure you haven't got something on your mind?' he asked.

'Have you?'

He looked taken aback. 'Why do you ask?'

'You would tell me, wouldn't you? If something was bothering you. I mean, we are friends, aren't we?'

He tilted his head. 'Have you been on Simon's medication?'

I wish, Lola thought. Then maybe she could get rid of all these horrible suspicions buzzing around in her head.

'So what are you planning to do when the tour finishes?' Jay asked, as they headed back to the bus.

'My washing, mainly.' Lola grimaced. 'After that, who knows? How about you?'

He shrugged. 'It's usually pretty quiet for a while, until the band goes into the studio to work on the new album. If there is one.'

'What makes you say that?'

'I've got a feeling there might not be any more Poleaxe after this tour.'

Lola looked at him, her heart in her mouth. 'Meaning?'

He sent her an enigmatic smile. 'You'll have to wait and see, won't you? But let's just say that by this time tomorrow the band could be missing one vital member.'

The sun was going down over the Hollywood hills. Below them, the city of LA was coming alive.

Out in the auditorium the crowd was restless with anticipation. But for once the atmosphere backstage was tingling even more. Even Dinah seemed on edge as they gathered in the band's dressing room.

'You don't have to do this,' Britt told Rick. 'You don't have to go on tonight.'

'She's right,' Dinah agreed.

'Are you kidding? If that crazy bastard doesn't get me, the fans will. Either way I won't get out of this place alive.' Rick tried to laugh it off, but Lola could see his face muscles were clenched with the effort of smiling.

'At least if you get out of here alive you'll never have to do this again,' Britt said. 'There are no more tours after this one.'

Jonno looked up from applying eyeliner. 'Aren't we going to Japan next year, then? I thought it was all sorted.'

There was a tense silence. Britt looked at Dinah, who looked at Rick.

'You haven't told her, have you?' she said.

Rick looked awkward. 'I was kind of waiting for the right moment.'

'Told me what?' Britt demanded, clawing at his arm. 'What haven't you told me?'

Rick opened and closed his mouth, but no sound came out.

In the end Dinah answered for him. 'The record company want the band to do another tour of

346

Japan next year. It'll only be a few weeks—'

Britt cut her off. 'No!' she said flatly. 'You can't do this to me. Not again.'

'Britt—'

'You promised, Rick. You told me this would be the last time.'

'It will,' Rick said. 'After Japan . . .'

'You don't get it, do you?' Britt shook her head. 'I'm not going to do this any more, Rick, I *can't* do it.'

'Britt, baby—' He reached for her hand but she pulled away from him, her face cold.

'I'm sorry, Rick,' she said. 'If you want to go out on that stage and get yourself shot, that's up to you. But I don't have to stay here and watch.'

'Britt—'

But she'd already gone, the door crashing behind her.

'Wow, what was that about?' Rick broke the tense silence.

'She's worried about you,' Lola said.

Rick laughed. 'The worst thing that's going to happen tonight is me forgetting my words.' But Lola noticed his hands shaking as he reached for another cigarette from his nearly empty packet.

Half an hour later, they were taking the stage. The atmosphere was electric, for all the wrong reasons, as the opening chords of 'Bite Me' crashed like a tidal wave through the auditorium. The fans went crazy.

'Look at them all,' Dinah said, chewing on her manicured nails. 'That madman could be somewhere out there.'

Or here, Lola thought. That was what really worried her. 'Have you seen Jay?' she asked.

347

'Not since this afternoon. Why?'

'No reason.' She had to stick close to him. Maybe, she thought desperately, he wasn't the Devoted Fan, but she knew she was clutching at straws.

'He'll be staying close to Kyle. That's where he usually is . . . oh shit!' Dinah swore as she snapped off an acrylic tip between her teeth. 'I can't stand this any more,' she said. 'If anyone wants me I'll be in the office making calls.'

Lola made her way around the back to stage left, where Kyle stood. Dinah was right; Jay was usually hanging around in the wings, lining up his next guitar and making sure everything was in place. But there was no sign of him.

'Has anyone seen Jay?' She pushed her way around the narrow backstage corridors, asking everyone she met. They all shook their heads.

And then she spotted him, on the other side of the stage, lingering in the shadows. She saw a flash of metal in his hands, and her legs turned to rubber.

Somehow she managed to get back around to the other side of the stage, tripping over cables and jumping over equipment cases. She came up behind him as he took a step towards the stage, his hand raised . . .

'Jay!'

He turned around, his hand to his chest.

'Christ, you frightened the life out of me. Do you have to creep up on people like that?'

'What are you doing?' she said.

'The tech's getting dropouts on Simon's bass. I came round to see if I could fix it.'

She eyed the screwdriver in his hand. 'Why isn't

Simon's tech fixing it?' she asked.

'He doesn't have my genius with amps.' He smiled at her quizzically. 'Why are you looking at me like that?'

Before she could stop herself she blurted out, 'I know, Jay.'

'Know what? What are you talking about?'

'You don't have to hide it any more. Look, I realise you're angry at your father, but this isn't the way to solve anything.'

'I'm sorry, I have no idea . . .' And then it dawned on him. 'You think it's me, don't you? You think I'm the one who's been threatening him.'

'I found that letter in your bag.'

'I told you what happened. I was hiding it.'

'Since when did you start worrying about protecting Rick?'

'I wasn't doing it for him. I was doing it for Britt. You've seen her, she's a nervous wreck.'

She wanted to believe him, more than anything in the world. 'You told me there was going to be one less member of the band after tonight.'

'Because Kyle's thinking of leaving! He's been asked to join Maneater on their European tour next year.' He looked dazed. 'You really thought I could do something like that?'

'I know how much you hate your father,' she said quietly.

'I don't hate him enough to kill him.'

She saw his desolate face and realised just how utterly, utterly wrong and stupid she'd been.

'How could you?' His voice was drowned out by the sound from the stage but she could still make out every word. 'How could you even think I'd do something like that?'

'I'm so sorry,' she whispered.

'It's too late for that now.'

'Jay, please.' Lola reached out to touch his arm, but he shook her off.

'Don't touch me,' he snapped. His eyes were cold. 'Christ, what kind of monster do you think I—'

A shot rang out.

The crowd's roar changed to screams of terror. Jay sprinted on to the stage. Lola started to run after him. The rest of the band had hit the ground apart from Rick, who stood there, still frozen in the spotlight, dazed with terror.

'Dad!' Jay took a dive at Rick, pinning him to the ground just as another shot exploded out of nowhere.

Suddenly the stage was swarming with stagehands and security. Lola tried to push her way past them, but strong arms held her back.

'Call an ambulance,' one of the guards shouted gruffly.

Through the solid wall of shoulders and bodies, Lola glimpsed two figures lying motionless on the stage, covered in blood.

CHAPTER THIRTY-NINE

The family room did its best to disguise itself as a normal, friendly place, with soft furnishings and vases of flowers. But the smell of antiseptic and air of nervous tension gave away the fact that it was still a hospital waiting room, albeit one with expensive drapes and an Adams fireplace.

350

Rick prowled from the door to the bay window over and over again like a caged animal. Every so often he tried to sit down and flick through one of the glossy magazines thoughtfully laid out on the maple coffee table. But sitting still just made the thoughts in his brain whiz even faster, taking him down dark paths where he didn't want to go. At least pacing made him think he was doing something, even if it was only wearing a furrow in the expensive Persian rug.

Across the room Annie sat patiently, staring into space, her hands folded in her lap. She seemed composed, although Rick knew from the way her eyes moved to the clock every thirty seconds that she was as stressed out as he was. But that was Annie, always so good and long-suffering, no matter what was going on inside her head.

And then there was Lola. Rick wasn't sure what she was doing there, apart from chewing her cuticles and trying not to cry.

He wished Britt was there, too. But she'd disappeared God knew where, and no one seemed to be able to find her.

He sat down and tried to pick up a magazine again, but his hands were shaking like a man in detox.

'Why did he do it?' he said. 'Why did he try to save my life?'

'He loves you,' Annie said. She looked so tired, with threads of grey in her hair and lines around her eyes. They were like inhabitants of two different worlds, he was still in his leather and velvet stage clothes and eyeliner; she wore jeans and no make-up. What had happened to the girl he'd married? It was as if she'd grown up while

351

he'd stayed some bizarre middle-aged teenager.

'I thought he hated me.'

'Love and hate are two sides of the same coin. Sometimes they're so close you can't tell them apart.'

Rick looked at Annie, the woman he'd once loved. He desperately wanted to talk to her, to say all those things that had sat like a heavy weight on his chest for so many years.

'Annie . . .'

She glanced up, her face kind but distracted. 'Yes?'

He took a deep breath, then bottled it. 'I'm going outside to get some fresh air. Call me if there's any news.'

Out in the balmy Californian night he sat on the hospital steps and tried to light a cigarette, but somehow his trembling hands wouldn't co-operate.

Then, just as he was about to give up, a hand came out of nowhere and held his lighter steady for him. He turned and saw Lola's face illuminated briefly in the flickering flame.

At once his heart started to pound unsteadily against his ribs. 'Is he—'

Lola shook her head. 'No news.'

'They should be able to tell us something by now. How long's he been in theatre?' He started to get to his feet, ready to take someone to task, then realised he didn't know where to go or who to ask. He was totally and utterly helpless, just like he'd been most of his life.

But this time Dinah wasn't there to sort out the problem and make it go away for him.

'These things take time,' Lola said patiently. 'He's got a bullet lodged in his shoulder. That's not a five-minute job.'

Rick shuddered, reliving that moment, feeling sick when he thought of himself lying there, Jay's dead weight pinning him down, feeling the stickiness of his blood seeping out on to him.

For the first time in his entire useless life, he actually felt pain for another person. Real, physical pain.

'All those years,' he murmured, 'all that time I thought there was no bond between me and Jay, and now I'd give everything I have to be in that operating theatre instead of him.'

'That's because you're his father,' Lola said. 'Even though you might not have got on over the years.'

Rick blew a smoke-ring up into the starry night sky. He had to say something; he couldn't keep it in any longer.

'That's just it,' he said. 'I'm not his father.'

There. He'd said it. After more than thirty years, he could feel the weight floating free from his chest, allowing him to breathe again.

He sensed Lola staring at him in the darkness. 'What do you mean? Of course he's your son.'

'I'm telling you, I'm not Jay's father.' Now he'd said it out loud it wasn't so bad after all. There was no claps of thunder overhead, no bolts of lightning raining out of the sky at him.

Lola was still uncomprehending. 'But how can that be? You and Annie were married . . .'

He sent her a wry look. 'I was married when you were conceived. That didn't stop it happening, did it?'

'Yes, but—'

'What's the matter? Don't you think it's possible

353

that my saintly wife could have cheated on me, too?'

Lola didn't reply. For once she looked lost for words.

'I didn't blame her for it,' Rick said. 'If anything, I probably drove her to it.' Poor Annie, she'd tried hard to keep their marriage together. It wasn't her fault they'd grown so far apart.

Lola found her voice again. 'So how did you know the baby wasn't yours?' she asked.

'I know I might seem stupid, but even I can do basic maths,' he said. 'Jay was conceived while Annie and I were on a break. She tried to tell me there was a mix-up over her dates, but I knew she was lying.'

'Why didn't you say anything to her?'

'Because I didn't want it to be true.' He blew another smoke-ring at the sky. 'I had my pride. I didn't want to admit my wife had got pregnant by another man. Especially . . .' He stopped. 'It wouldn't have looked good for me, would it?' Rick Wild, the great womaniser, playing dad to another man's child. Anyway, Annie didn't seem to want to bring it out in the open, either, so what was the point?'

'So you never talked about it?' Lola marvelled.

'What good would it have done?'

But now he knew it had done no good to keep it quiet, either. The buried resentment was partly what had broken up their marriage. And it was the reason he couldn't bear to look at Jay.

Lola seemed to read his mind. 'What about Jay's father?'

'What about him?'

'Do you know who he was?'

354

Rick hesitated. He didn't want to say it out loud, but he knew he couldn't tell her half the story.

'Oh, I knew all right.' He looked at her through the haze of his cigarette smoke. 'Why do you think I had to stay away from Jay? Every time I looked at him I saw . . .'

'Who?' Lola urged.

He took a deep breath. 'My best friend,' he said.

It took a moment for it to sink in. Then Lola said, 'Terry Mac?'

Rick nodded. He felt sick thinking about it. He'd said he didn't blame Annie, but deep down he did. He could have tolerated it being any other man, but not Terry.

'The three of us knew each other at school,' he said. 'Annie was Terry's girlfriend before we got together.'

The coolest boy and the prettiest girl. Rick could still remember them at the school gates, sharing a cigarette.

'But Terry was heading out of control even then, experimenting with drugs, getting high all the time. Annie couldn't be bothered with all that, so she dumped him. That's when I came along.' He tapped the ash off the end of his cigarette. 'Somehow we all managed to stay friends, and Terry and I got the band together. Maybe it was because, deep down, he always knew I was second best.'

Second best to Terry Mac. The story of his life.

'And they had an affair?' Lola said.

'I don't know if you'd call it that. Like I said, we were having problems. Annie needed a shoulder to cry on, and she turned to Terry. Next thing I know, she's pregnant.'

'Did Terry know Jay was his son?'

'Terry didn't know what planet he was on most of the time. I guess that's why Annie chose to stay with me, because she realised what a lousy father he'd make. Not that I was much better,' he added grimly.

'I'm not surprised,' Lola said. 'It must have been really hard for you, knowing he was someone else's son. No wonder you've tried to keep him at arm's length all these years.'

Rick looked at her, surprised. It was such a relief to know someone understood at last, that not everyone thought he was just a selfish bastard who didn't care about his own flesh and blood.

'I don't think Jay understood why I couldn't love him.' Suddenly it was all too much for him. He dropped his cigarette and buried his face in his hands. 'Now it's too late to tell him. He'll never know how proud I was of him, how many times I wished he really was my son . . .'

'He *was*. Is. In every way that counts.'

They turned around. Annie was standing there, silhouetted against the brightly lit hospital doorway.

'How long have you been there?' Rick asked.

'Long enough.'

They faced each other in silence.

Lola tactfully excused herself, saying she was going to check on Jay. And then they were alone.

'You never said anything,' Annie said quietly.

'Neither did you.'

'I wanted to, so many times,' she said. 'I hated myself for lying to you and Jay. I think that was what split us up in the end. I couldn't live with the guilt.'

'And there was me, thinking it was my cheating.' Rick couldn't help joking.

Annie smiled ruefully. 'That didn't help. But I couldn't live with all those secrets. I wanted to make a fresh start. I wish now I'd told Jay, though. Then maybe he wouldn't have been so confused.'

'He would probably have been delighted,' Rick said. 'He always hated me.'

'He wanted to hate you,' Annie corrected him. 'He felt he should, because of the way he saw our marriage fall apart. But deep down he adored you, wanted to be like you. That was why he ended up so mixed up about everything.' She smiled wanly. 'I think tonight's proved how much he cares for you, deep down.'

Rick flinched. 'Are you going to tell him now?' he asked.

'I think it's time he knew the truth, don't you?' Annie said. 'That's why I came here. I wanted to talk to you and him.' She paused. 'You know he's fallen in love with Lola, don't you?'

'What?' Rick was blank. 'When did that happen?'

'I have no idea. But I do know he's besotted by her. And she is with him, I think. But they're both fighting it. That's why I decided it was time he knew the truth.'

'And are you going to tell him about Terry?'

'What about Terry?' She frowned, then realisation dawned. 'Hang on a minute . . . you think Terry was Jay's father?'

'Isn't he?'

'Absolutely not! Terry was your best mate. Neither of us would ever have done that to you. Anyway, do you really think I would have turned to someone like him when I was going through a crisis? He was a bigger mess than I was.'

'So who did you turn to?'

Annie stared at her hands. 'It was Brian.'

'Brian? I don't know any . . .' It took Rick a moment to register. 'Brian Reed? Our manager?' He stared at her, shocked. 'But he was so *old*.'

'He wasn't that old,' Annie defended. 'And he was kind—and caring. And he was there when you weren't,' she added defensively.

'Yeah, but Brian . . .' Rick still couldn't get his head around it. Brian Reed, with his polyester suits, cheap aftershave, gelled hair and shirt buttons straining across his paunch. 'You've got to admit, he wasn't exactly God's gift.'

'Which was exactly why I liked him,' Annie said. 'I was already married to God's gift, if you recall. And look where that got me.'

Rick didn't know whether to laugh or cry. All this time he'd felt as if Terry was mocking him from beyond the grave. Every time he looked at Jay he could almost see his friend staring back at him.

And now he was free. The curse of Terry Mac was finally lifted.

He was still thinking about it when Lola came out of the double doors.

'The operation's over.' She sounded weak with relief. 'They're taking Jay into recovery now.'

CHAPTER FORTY

Lola headed back to the hotel in the early hours of the morning, exhausted but relieved. The rain-washed, neon-lit streets of downtown LA were still alive, with people drifting between the bars, clubs and all-night delis, cars blasting their horns, police sirens wailing in the distance.

She'd left Jay groggily awake and talking to Rick and Annie. His first question, when he found out about the gunshot to his shoulder, was whether he'd play the guitar again.

She guessed he'd have a lot more questions by the time they'd finished talking to him. Lola wondered if she should have stayed with them. She knew better than anyone what it was like to get hit by that kind of bombshell.

She only hoped Jay could handle it.

'Looks like we've got company,' Gus said as they approached the hotel. Lola could see the photographers banked around the entrance, cameras poised.

'Drop me off and I'll walk,' she said.

Gus shook his head.

'I've been told not to let you out of my sight.'

'The press will be looking for Rick, not me.'

'I'm not worried about the press.'

She saw his grim expression and it dawned on her. The Devoted Fan was still out there somewhere, maybe waiting to take another shot. She'd forgotten all about him.

'Shouldn't you be at the hospital with Rick in that case?' she asked.

'I've got it covered.'

She realised what he meant when she sneaked in through the back entrance of the hotel. Black-coated security guards prowled the corridors, whispering into walkie-talkies.

Seeing them made Lola feel more nervous. 'Surely he wouldn't try anything in here?' she asked as they stepped into the lift.

'If someone can take a potshot in the middle of twenty thousand people, I reckon they're crazy enough to do anything.' His finger poised over the buttons. 'Twelfth floor, right?'

'Peninsula Suite first. Rick's asked me to check on Britt.'

They glided up to the nineteenth floor and the lift doors opened. Gus nodded to the two men standing guard on either side of the door and handed Lola what looked like a mobile phone. 'Panic alarm,' he said. 'Press that red button and everyone in the building will come running.'

At first she thought the suite was empty when she walked into the spacious living area. Then she heard Britt's voice on the phone coming from the bedroom.

'And you're sure you don't have anything sooner than that? What about non-direct flights?'

Lola crept closer. Britt was standing in the bathroom doorway, her arms full of toiletries, her mobile phone wedged between her cheek and shoulder. She was dressed in jeans, sweater and sneakers, her hair dragged back in a careless pony-tail. Without make-up, her face was gaunt and angular.

'OK, I suppose I'll have to take that one. Book me one ticket. And make it first class.'

She hung up the phone.

'Going somewhere?' Lola asked.

Britt let out a scream and dropped the toiletries all over the floor. 'Jesus, you scared me.' She put her hand to her heart. 'How's Jay? Is there any more news?'

'He's come round from the operation. The doctors think he'll be OK.'

'Thank God. I've been praying for him.' She fingered the crucifix around her neck. 'Is Rick all right?'

'He'd be better if you were there with him.'

She crouched down and began gathering up the toiletries. 'He doesn't need me.'

'That's where you're wrong. He needs you very much.'

Britt's head was bent so Lola couldn't see her face. But she could see by her shaking shoulders that she was crying.

'What's the matter, Britt? Where are you going?'

'Home. I can't stand this any more.'

'You're going back to Sweden?'

She nodded. 'I can't stay here; it's making me too crazy.'

Britt stood up and tipped the toiletries into her bag. She must be in a state, Lola thought. She was usually so meticulous about her packing.

'I can understand you're scared,' she said gently. 'But don't worry, the police will catch this guy soon—'

'You don't get it, do you?' Britt interrupted. 'I'm leaving. And I'm never coming back.'

Lola stared at her dumbly. 'What about Rick?'

'I'll call my lawyers when I get home. They can

sort out the divorce. You can tell him not to worry; I don't want anything.'

She went to the wardrobe, dragged out an armful of clothes and stuffed them in the bag.

'Why don't you tell him yourself?' Lola asked.

'I can't.'

'How do you think he's going to feel when he finds out you've gone?'

'I don't care how he feels!' Britt shouted back. 'He never cared how I felt when he was sleeping with all those whores. He never cared when he left me for months on end. Why should I care about him now?'

'I thought you'd sorted all that out?'

'So did I. Rick promised me he wasn't going to go back on the road. This was the last time, he said. Then I find out he's planning another tour. He lied, just like he always lies to me. I can't take it any more.'

She yanked at the zip on the bulging bag, then screamed with frustration when it got stuck.

'Here, let me.' Lola nudged her aside. Close to, she could smell alcohol on her breath. Britt never drank anything stronger than mineral water. She took out a dress and began folding it carefully. 'Don't you love him?' she asked.

Britt burst into tears. 'Of course I love him! I just hate what he's made me do. He's turned me into a crazy person. I look at myself in the mirror and I feel sick with myself.' She ripped the dress out of Lola's hands and flung it into the corner. 'Forget about the stupid packing. I just want to get out of here.'

She pulled the bag off the bed and headed for the door.

Lola blocked her way. 'Can't you just wait and talk to Rick about this?' she pleaded.

Britt shook her head. 'I can't face him. Not now.'

'But he needs you. Someone nearly killed him tonight.'

'That bullet was never meant for him.'

Cogs began to whirr in Lola's brain. 'How do you know?'

Britt's mouth opened then closed again. 'Work it out yourself,' she said finally. 'If someone had really wanted to kill him, they could have done it easily enough.'

'You think they just meant to scare him?'

Britt shrugged. 'Maybe. How should I know?'

She went to move towards the door, but Lola stepped back into her path. 'You said something earlier on, before you left the gig. Something about not wanting to wait around to see your husband get shot.'

'So?'

'So how did you know it was going to happen?'

'It said so in the letters, didn't it?'

'They never mentioned a gun.'

A hunted look flashed across Britt's face.

'You did it, didn't you?' Lola said. 'You took that shot at Rick.'

There was a long silence. Then, slowly, Britt seemed to crumple before Lola's eyes, as if every bone in her body had melted.

'I didn't mean to do it,' she whispered. 'I just wanted to fire it, to see what he'd do. But then it all happened so fast. Everyone was screaming and pushing around me. I couldn't see what was happening. I panicked and the gun just went off

363

again.' Her face was bleached with fear. 'Then I saw Jay lying there. I thought I'd killed him . . .'

Lola shuddered. She couldn't get that picture out of her head, either. 'You sent those letters, too?'

Britt nodded. 'I thought it would scare him, make him cancel the tour. I was never going to hurt him. But when he told me he was going on the road again, I cracked . . .'

'So you shot him?'

'I told you, I didn't mean to do it. I've never even fired a gun before.'

'Where is it now?'

Britt delved into the bottom of her bag, pulled out a small bundle wrapped in a silk Hermes scarf and handed it to Lola. 'I was going to dump it on my way to the airport,' she said.

Lola looked down at it. It felt cool and heavy in her hand. 'Where did you get it?'

'Everyone in LA has them for protection.' Britt hugged herself, as if she'd suddenly gone cold. 'Now do you see why I have to get away? I'm a sick, crazy person. I would never have done anything like this before I met Rick. Being married to him has made me mad.'

She started to cry. Lola put down the gun and held her. She could feel her bones under her thin sweater.

'Come on, it's not that bad,' she said. Then it struck her: *What am I saying? This woman has just shot someone and I'm telling her it's not that bad?* It wasn't just Britt who was crazy.

'You've got to talk to Rick,' she said.

Britt shook her head, her face still buried in Lola's shoulder. 'I couldn't face him. Not after I

364

did such a terrible thing.'

'He's done some pretty terrible things, too.'

'But I nearly killed his son. How do you think he'd ever forgive me for that?'

Lola was silent for a moment. What she was thinking went against all her instincts as a police officer, everything she'd been trained to do.

And yet . . .

'He doesn't have to know,' she said.

Britt pulled away from her. 'You're not going to tell him?'

'Not if you promise to get help. Both of you. You've got to sort out your problems before anyone else gets hurt.'

'That's impossible. Rick would never go to counselling.'

'He might if he wants to save his marriage.'

'Why would he want to do that?'

'Because, in spite of how it might look, he really does love you.'

'You think so?' Britt brightened for a second, then her eyes turned dull with defeat. 'But how could I keep a secret like this from him? It would destroy us in the end.'

'That's up to you,' Lola said. 'Maybe once you've got your relationship sorted out you'll be able to tell him. But he won't hear it from me.'

'You'd really do that? For me?'

'If you promise to get yourselves sorted out.'

Britt looked at the gun with utter revulsion. 'What shall I do about that?'

'Leave it to me. I'll deal with it.'

*　　　*　　　*

The following day a Glock handgun was found on the steps of the central LAPD precinct. There were no prints, nothing to identify it except a crumpled note from the Devoted Fan, saying he couldn't go on living with the guilt of what he'd done.

No body was ever found, but he was never heard from again.

CHAPTER FORTY-ONE

'Forget it. There's no way, man. I'm telling you, if I have to wear a skirt then I'm on the first plane out of here, wedding or no wedding.'

Lola smiled as she adjusted Rick's tie. 'You can't do that. You're father of the bride, remember?'

His eyes lit up briefly, until he remembered to frown again. 'Screw that. I'm not old enough.'

'If you say so.' Lola finished with his tie and stepped back to admire her handiwork. 'So it's a definite no to the kilt, then?'

'No chance.' He glared at her. 'I already feel like I'm in a remake of sodding *Brigadoon*.'

It was a bit over the top, Lola had to admit. The beautiful old Scottish castle was like something out of a fairytale anyway. But Dinah and her team of interior decorators had really gone to town on the Highland theme. Every chair and table was festooned with swathes of tartan, and the battlements had been ringing with the sound of pipers since the crack of dawn. Lola was fairly certain there was haggis on the wedding breakfast menu.

But it was only the best for Dinah's daughter. After her initial fury at Tiffany's surprise Las Vegas wedding, she'd embraced the whole mother-of-the-bride concept with an enthusiasm usually reserved for screwing concert promoters and record company executives into the ground. From being a strictly hands-off parent, she'd suddenly discovered a maternal streak. She and Tiffany had even been out on a girlie shopping trip together to buy wedding outfits.

'Although I still say it won't last,' she confided to Lola in private.

But Dinah had still put all her energy and organisational skills into planning her daughter's dream wedding, three months after the first. And as an added bonus, Poleaxe had come out of their brief retirement to do a very special one-off gig. As she helped Rick put on his suit, Lola tactfully decided not to mention that Tiffany had said they would have preferred Metallica.

'Look at me, playing at a wedding in a monkey suit,' Rick complained as he studied himself in the mirror. 'Not very rock and roll, is it? We'll be doing bloody bar mitzvahs next.'

'No you won't,' Lola said as she picked a stray hair off his shoulder. 'Britt won't let you.'

Britt had been keeping a very tight rein on her husband since their last fateful gig in LA. And strangely, Rick didn't seem to mind at all.

'Actually, she's lost a lot of her insecurity issues since we've been seeing that counsellor guy,' he informed her.

'Enough to let you tour Japan next year?' Lola asked teasingly.

'I wouldn't want to. There's too much

happening on the farm at the moment. Did I tell you, we bought a flock of sheep last week?'

'Nice to see Britt hasn't lost her shopping habit,' Lola grinned.

'Don't knock it,' said Rick. 'It's a hell of a lot cheaper than Harrods . . . oh, shit!' he swore, as he pulled a loose thread on his shirt and a button fell off.

'Don't worry; I've got a sewing kit in my bag.'

As he watched her rummaging, Rick said, 'Were you a Girl Guide or something?'

'No, but I spent three months babysitting an utterly useless bunch of middle-aged rock stars. That teaches you to be prepared for anything.'

Rick frowned. 'Who are you calling middle-aged?'

Unable to find the sewing kit in the depths of her bag, Lola upended the whole lot on to the dressing table and sifted through all the keys, chewing gum wrappers, pens, old shopping lists until she found what she was looking for.

'What's this?' Rick reached past her and picked a small black and white photo out of the pile. His face broke into a broad grin. 'Hey, it's me.'

'And Mum.'

He looked harder at the photo of himself with her mother and Auntie Sarah. 'Which one?' he said without thinking.

Lola looked at him. 'You really don't remember her, do you?' she said.

He shook his head apologetically. 'I'm sorry, kid.'

'It doesn't matter.' She'd long since given up hoping that one day he'd have a blinding flashback and remember that her mother was actually the love of his life, but that he'd subconsciously blanked out all memory of her because the heartache of losing her was too much for him. It would have been nice, but real life wasn't like that.

Rick handed her back the photo. 'She must have been a great lady, though,' he said. 'Because you turned out OK.'

Lola put the photo back into her bag. 'Yes,' she said. 'She was.'

The wedding ceremony began in the Great Hall. Lola watched Tiffany sweeping down the aisle in her gorgeous Vera Wang gown on the arm of her father to where Hamish waited beside the huge baronial fireplace. Then, as the guests shuffled to sit down, she crept out of the hall.

She made her way outside to the tartan-swathed marquee, where the band was due to play after the wedding breakfast. Jay sat on the stage in front of a bank of Marshall amps, tuning up his guitar. Kyle was rehearsing with Maneater for their European tour, so he'd agreed to step in.

It gave Lola a jolt to see him again. She was so overcome she could only stand and watch him for a moment.

Finally, she said, 'Don't you have a guitar tech to do that for you?'

He looked up, smiling. 'Old habits die hard.'

He carefully laid down his guitar. He still moved a little stiffly, even three months after coming out of hospital.

'Has it started?' he asked, nodding towards the castle.

'Just. Didn't you want to be there?'

'I'm not really into playing happy families. Especially as they aren't even my family any more,' he smiled ruefully.

'How do you feel about that?' Lola asked cautiously. They hadn't really talked about it after Rick and Annie had told Jay the truth. She'd thought they might have had more time but as soon as he was discharged from hospital Jay had flown back to England with his mother, and Lola hadn't seen him since.

He considered it for a moment. 'Relieved,' he answered frankly. 'Because it means I can finally stop hating everyone.'

'Including Rick?'

'Especially Rick.' He brushed an invisible speck of dust off his jeans. Ever the rebel, he hadn't given in to Dinah's demands that they dress smartly. 'I can see how hard it must have been for him now. I blamed him for leaving us, but I'm surprised he stayed around us long as he did.'

'What about your mum?'

He shrugged. 'She feels really bad about hiding the truth from me, but I understand why she did it. She was only trying to protect me. But sometimes it's just easier to face the truth in the long run.'

It would have been easier for her if she had known, Lola thought. Then maybe she could have allowed herself to give in to her feelings and fall in love with him. And maybe, just maybe, he could have fallen in love with her, too, instead of disappearing out of her life for ever.

Now any feelings he might have had for her seemed to have gone. Those three months he'd spent getting his head together had obviously been enough for him to get over her.

Unfortunately they'd had the opposite effect on her. Every day she just seemed to miss him more

370

and more. Even now, her heart was jumping at being near him again.

'How's life in Leeds?' he asked.

'Terrific.'

Terrible, she thought. She hadn't been able to settle back to her old life at all.

'I expect Sam's glad to have you around again?'

'Sam's engaged.'

His face fell. 'Not the dreaded Brendan?'

'No, this one's called Mark. And he actually seems quite nice for once.'

'So she's not pining for me?' Jay grinned.

'I'm afraid not.'

'How about you?'

'What?' She looked up at him sharply.

'Have you got a new man? Or are you still giving that guy Will the runaround?'

'Will also has a new girlfriend. Her name's Julie and she's a secretary.'

The whole world seemed to have moved on in the past few months. She was the only one left behind.

'I'm looking for a new job,' she told him.

His brows rose. 'With a band?'

'You never know.'

'I didn't manage to put you off, then?'

'Never.' Except it wasn't what she wanted any more. What she wanted was to be able to see Jay every day, preferably as soon as she opened her eyes in the morning. But that wasn't going to happen, was it?

'How about you?' she said brightly. 'How's it going with your new band?'

'Good. We've got the record deal sorted out and we're just writing some songs for our first album.'

'It sounds as if things are moving really quickly.'

'That's what happens when you've got Dinah as a manager. Now Poleaxe are no more, she's got plenty of time to devote to her new bands.'

They were talking like strangers, strained but polite. Lola knew there was something left unspoken between them. And she knew she was going to have to be the one to say it if they were ever going to break down the barriers.

'I'm sorry,' she blurted out.

He frowned, genuinely puzzled. 'What for?'

'For what I said. About you . . . and Rick.'

'Ah. You mean when you accused me of plotting to kill my own father?' He sounded stern, but she caught the hint of amusement in his green eyes. 'It's OK, I don't hold it against you. I probably would have suspected me, too, the way I carried on.' Then, just as she was breathing a sigh of relief, he added, 'It was Britt, wasn't it?'

She stared at him, shocked. 'How did you know?'

'I guessed. That letter you found in my bag . . . I got it from their hotel room. I figured she was going to post it, so I took it.'

'That's why you set fire to it,' Lola said slowly. 'You were covering for her.'

'I didn't want you to find her fingerprints on it.'

And so he'd put himself in the frame instead. That only made her love him more, if that was possible.

'Does Rick know?' Jay asked.

'I'm not sure. Britt might have told him during their counselling sessions.'

'Or maybe he's just guessed and decided not to say anything. Sometimes that's the best way, to let

372

things die quietly.'

Like us, Lola thought. The message couldn't have been more clear if he'd yelled it from the battlements.

The stirring sound of a massed band of pipers playing 'The Wedding March' filled the still February air.

'Sounds like it's all over,' Jay commented.

'Yes,' Lola said sadly. 'It is, isn't it?'

'I've got to say, they make a pretty strange couple.'

'You can't really choose who you fall in love with, can you?'

'It might be a lot easier if you could.' Jay dragged his gaze away from her towards the house. 'What's the betting there'll be a cat fight before the evening's over? My money's on Dinah and Britt in the fountain.'

'Unless Tiffany's invited one of Rick's groupies again.'

'He's over all that now. Didn't you know, he's a changed man?' Jay said solemnly. They looked at each other and laughed.

'I've missed you,' Jay said suddenly.

A lump rose in her throat, almost choking her. 'I've missed you, too.'

'But life goes on, doesn't it? We're not the same people we were three months ago.'

No, she wanted shout. Because three months ago I couldn't fall in love with you and now I can.

But her pride wouldn't let her say it. All she said was, 'I guess you're right.'

He nodded. 'That's what I thought. You've got your old life back, and I've got my new band. It's time to move on.'

'If you say so.'

*   *   *

The guests were beginning to drift into the marquee. Rick and the rest of the band took to the stage. Lola watched him consulting with Jay about their first number. She felt forgotten already.

She took one long, last look at them and then headed out into the cold, fresh night air.

She was halfway across the grounds, heading mindlessly towards the moonlit loch, when she suddenly stopped herself.

What the hell are you doing? she thought. If you walk away now, you'll never see him again. Is that really what you want?

Yes, but it's not about what you want, is it? another voice chimed in. You heard what Jay said. He's got a new life now. And he doesn't need you in it. You might as well just go back to Leeds, find a new career and forget about him. Who needs a man, anyway?

But that was the old Lola talking. The one who'd never risked letting anyone into her heart. But now she had, and it was too late.

She turned around. Hitching up her skirt, her shoes in her hand, she pelted back to the marquee. Halfway there, she suddenly realised the music had stopped. Then she saw Jay running out of the marquee and realised why.

He stood for a moment, looking wildly around—and then he saw her.

They stopped a few yards away from each other. Now they were face to face again, embarrassment made her clam up.

It looked as if Jay felt the same. She could almost see his face flaming in the moonlight.

He cleared his throat. 'You know what I said about us not being the same people we were three months ago?'

'Yes?'

'Well, it's not exactly true.' He stared out across the moonlit ground, bathed in silvery light, not able to meet her eye. 'The thing is, I can't forget about you.'

He must have registered the shock on her face because the next minute he was mumbling. 'Look, scratch that. I didn't say anything, OK?'

'But—'

'I promised myself I wouldn't do this. It's not fair on you. You've got your own life back and the last thing you need is someone like me hanging around.'

'Jay—'

'Just forget it. I'm being totally dumb and pathetic. I shouldn't have even come out here looking for you.'

'I was coming back to find you.'

Hope flickered in his eyes. 'You were?'

She nodded. 'I was going to ask if you knew of a band who needed a good tour manager?'

His lips curved teasingly. 'Why? Do you know one?'

'I might.'

'It's funny you should say that.' He reached out and took her hand, pulling her towards him. 'It just so happens we might be touring the UK soon. Do you think you could do three months on the road with me again?'

She smiled and pressed herself against him. 'I

reckon I might be able to tolerate it. If you make it worth my while . . .'